Last of the Summer Vines

Once upon a time, there was a little girl who dreamed big dreams. Let's call her Romy. Romy dreamed of one day living inside one of the fairy tales in her head. But she grew up in Durban, South Africa – not exactly the sort of place where fairy tale princesses grow up. It took the help of a great many fairy godmothers, the slaying of a few dragons, and not nearly enough pretty glass shoes, for Romy to eventually became the princess she'd always dreamed of being.

As a 2016 finalist for the Romance Writers of America® RITA Award for her novel *Not a Fairy Tale*, and Chairperson of ROSA (Romance writers Organisation of South Africa), all of Romy's dreams have come true. She is not only a multi-published author, but as a writing coach and teacher, she now helps make other writers' dreams come true too.

Though Romy's heart lies in Europe, she doesn't cope well with the col[illegible] the City of Gold, Johannesburg, where she is mom to two little princesses and a pet dragon (okay, he's a bearded dragon, but that counts!)

Romy writes contemporary fairy tale romances and short 1920s historical romances. She loves Hallmark movies, Country music, travel, and losing herself in stories.

@romy_s
www.facebook.com/RomySommerAuthor
www.romysommer.com

Last of the Summer Vines

Romy Sommer

A division of HarperCollins Publishers
www.harpercollins.co.uk

Harper*Impulse* an imprint of
HarperCollins*Publishers*
The News Building
1 London Bridge Street
London SE1 9GF

www.harpercollins.co.uk

This paperback edition 2018

First published in Great Britain in ebook format by
HarperCollins*Publishers* 2018

A catalogue record for this book
is available from the British Library

ISBN: 9780008301149

This novel is entirely a work of fiction.
The names, characters and incidents portrayed in it are
the work of the author's imagination. Any resemblance to
actual persons, living or dead, events or localities is
entirely coincidental.

Typeset in Birka by Palimpsest Book Production Ltd,
Falkirk, Stirlingshire

Printed by CPI Group (UK) Ltd, Croydon CR0 4YY

This book is dedicated to my mother, who contributed hugely to this novel by keeping the household fed and clean, and who helped me research by sharing with me many bottles (and boxes) of wine.

Also to my daughters, for giving me time and space to write, and for understanding when I am grumpy from lack of sleep – and for telling me that I should 'volow my hart'.

Finally, I dedicate this book to all those people who devote their lives to making wine: you often make life worth living.

Chapter 1

Chi lascia la via vecchia per la nuova sa quel che lascia ma non sa quel che trova

(Those who leave the old ways behind know what they're leaving, but not what they'll find)

I closed my eyes and breathed in deeply. Heavy, warm air filled my lungs, tasting of full-blown summer though back in England spring had barely sprung. After the crisp chill of London, the rich scents carried on the breeze were strangely soporific.

'You don't want air con?' the taxi driver asked, his deeply offended tone suggesting he'd prefer air con to fresh farm air.

Reluctantly, I opened my eyes again. But I didn't close the car window. Since I was paying premium price for this trip halfway across Tuscany, I'd darn well keep the window open if I wanted. I breathed in deeply again, this time not to smell the figurative roses but to calm myself. Breathe in. Count to three. Relax.

It was unbelievable that I was only now learning to

recognise the signs of stress in my body and how to deal with it. Too many years driving myself to achieve. Too many years of not taking the time to listen to my own body. All those years focused on a single target, and where did it get me? Exile.

If only I'd gone a little easier on myself. If only I'd taken a holiday once a year like everyone else, instead of clapping myself on the back for my dedication. If only I'd made a priority of a few more hours' sleep each night, maybe now I wouldn't be forced to cool my heels here in the middle of nowhere.

Already bored of 'if onlys', I slid my mobile out my handbag and glanced at the screen. No missed calls. Not even a text message. Surely *someone* at the office would have tried to reach me by now. They'd had the big meeting with the CFO of the Delta Corporation this morning. Wouldn't Cleo at least have let me know how it went?

Breathe in. Count to three. Relax.

On the plus side, I was really lucky I hadn't been fired. I'd made such a stupid mistake. A stupid, expensive mistake, the kind that required a great deal of grovelling to fix. I'd done all the grovelling I could, but the rest of my team were still having to pick up the slack.

I pinched the bridge of my nose. I was lucky to still have a job, a house, a life waiting back in England for me, but enforced 'holiday leave' didn't feel lucky. It felt like a punishment.

Once the legalities of John's estate were wrapped up, and I'd put his property on the market, what was I supposed to do with myself for another four whole months?

'It's not a punishment,' Kevin had said. 'It's every bit of holiday leave you've never taken.'

And then he'd given me *that* look, the one that said, '*and maybe if you'd taken some of that leave earlier, we'd still be together*.' As if I might actually miss him and want him back. Huh!

I only realised I'd snorted out loud when I spotted the taxi driver's raised eyebrows in the rear-view mirror.

I turned to look out the car window. We were circling Montalcino now. The medieval hilltop town caught the afternoon sun like a golden jewel, then the wide, provincial road wound away south, carrying us away from the town between undulating hills covered in the verdant green of early summer.

The Delta meeting had to be over by now. No longer able to control my fingers, I dialled Cleo's number.

'Did Delta's CFO yank their business, or has he agreed to let you re-structure the loan?' I asked, the moment my BFF answered.

Cleo sighed. 'You're on leave, Sarah. You're not supposed to be thinking about work. Doctor's orders, remember?'

I huffed out an exasperated breath. 'An actuarial doctorate does not give Kevin the right to tell me what to do.'

'No. But his being your boss gives him the right.' Cleo's voice softened. 'He cares about you, Sar. We all do. You've been working yourself into an early grave. You really need to rest.'

'I *am* resting. But do I really need to rest for the entire summer? One week is enough. Two tops.'

Cleo sighed. 'You're burned out. *You* may not appreciate

how dangerous that is, but those of us who love you do. You need to find yourself a healthy work–life balance, and you're not going to rediscover that in a week. Go read a book, or be a tourist, or get a hobby. Better yet, get back on the dating horse.' She barked a laugh. 'Not that you ever *were* on that horse! The only reason you dated Kevin was because you didn't have to leave work to meet him.'

'I don't need a man to have a healthy work–life balance. I'll sign up for yoga classes. Hell, I'll even take up meditation if it means I can come back to work sooner.'

Cleo laughed again. She had a fun laugh, easy and bubbly. I wondered what my own laugh sounded like. It'd been so long since I'd laughed at anything.

'You know what works quicker than meditation? Getting laid! Find yourself a sexy Italian stud and have your way with him. You'll feel so much better!'

Not. Going. To. Happen.

The taxi driver's gaze met mine in the rear-view mirror, his one heavy brow rising in a lewd grin. Oh God, he hadn't heard that, had he?

Not in your dreams, dude. I frowned fiercely at the mirror, and he looked quickly away.

'I'm burned out, not braindead.' I dropped my voice so the driver couldn't eavesdrop. 'Holiday romances are more trouble than they're worth.'

'Oh, I don't know. That guy I hooked up with in Spain was definitely worth it.' Cleo's voice turned heavy with suggestion.

'Yeah, so worth it you can't even remember his name!'

She giggled. 'It wasn't his name that made the impression.'

I shook my head, though I knew she couldn't see. No one knew better than I where wild and thoughtless holiday romances could lead – to relationships that didn't last, to unexpected and unwanted pregnancies, to a mother who flitted around the world trying to recapture her lost youth, and a father I'd barely known. Nope. Growing up the product of a holiday fling, no way would I ever be stupid enough to indulge in one.

One-night stands, brief flings, passionate affairs ... they just weren't my thing.

But the sudden and unwanted memory of serious grey eyes made my stomach contract in a way I'd almost forgotten. I pushed the memory aside. 'Not. Going. To. Happen.'

'I know how you feel about holiday romances, but you're not some impetuous teenager,' Cleo continued. 'You're a sensible woman, and you know all about birth control. You can't keep letting what your mother did—'

'Geraldine,' I corrected automatically. My 'mother' didn't deserve that title.

Cleo sighed. 'Okay, so no holiday romance, then. But when you get back you could—'

'If you suggest online dating again, I will have to kill you. Those three days I spent on that app were just too depressing.'

'We could try speed dating?' Cleo asked hopefully. She really was a sucker for punishment.

'Absolutely not! Dating of any kind when you're over 35 is the most demoralising experience any woman can have. All the decent single guys our age are either taken or gay. No thanks! If I can't meet someone organically, I'd rather be alone.'

Cleo sighed. 'You are not *over* 35. You *are* 35. And that is far too young to give up on sex.'

I glanced at the taxi driver, but this time his eyes stayed on the road. 'So did Delta's CFO agree to the compromise deal?'

'He did. He's allocating one of his most senior finance people to work with us to re-analyse their financials and re-structure the loan. Kevin's put me on it. Everything will be fine.'

I let out a breath I hadn't even realised I'd been holding. 'I can't thank you enough. I know my mistake has put everyone else under terrible pressure.' Guilt burned a bitter taste in my mouth. How could I not have factored in something as obvious as the client's cash flow situation? My incorrect calculations had put one of our most valued clients at risk of bankruptcy. If one of my own underlings had made a mistake like that, I'd have fired them on the spot, none of this 'shame, you've been working too hard' molly-coddling everyone was doing with me. I really was luckier than I deserved to be.

Cleo's voice softened. 'We don't mind. We care about you, and we understand that mistakes happen, especially when someone's as sleep deprived as you've been. Just promise me you'll catch up on some sleep while you're there. Enjoy the sun and breathe a little. Work will still be here when you get back.'

I sighed. 'Okay, I promise.'

'So have you met your father's lawyer yet? What's the castle like?'

I glanced out the window again. After an hour of the same view, of vineyards giving way to patches of dark forest, and then yet more vineyards, the beauty had started to pall. But now the taxi swung off the main provincial road, onto a bumpy, dusty farm road that had once been tarred. It was so rutted the sedan had to slow to navigate the bumps. 'Not yet, but we're nearly there.'

'I'm sorry I can't be there with you. You sure you're going to be okay sorting through your father's things on your own?'

'Of course I'll be fine.' It would be hypocritical to get choked up over someone I hadn't seen in years, someone I hardly spoke to. After all, it wasn't as if I'd lost a father. Aside from a handful of summers in my childhood, I'd never really *had* a father. He hadn't been involved in my life in any meaningful way; he hadn't attended any of my school concerts, or netball games, or even my graduation. All his love had been reserved for his vines, with nothing left to spare for people.

Yet when I thought of him, I could still smell red wine, lemons and sunshine. He'd taught me how to drink wine – though he'd hardly approve of the way Cleo and I sloshed down the cheap stuff.

I said goodbye to Cleo and hung up, stuck my mobile back into my bag, and turned to the view again.

The road climbed now between the rolling hills, and I recognised the landmarks – a tiny stone chapel in the fold of a valley to the left, the long low wall of a neighbour's property, then the shrine at the crossroads with its faded painting of an angel. Just around that next bend, the *castello*'s gates would appear. I leaned forward excitedly in my seat.

There had been a time, another lifetime ago, when I'd loved this place. Back in those innocent days when the vineyard hadn't seemed like a rival, but an adventure. And now I was the proud owner of sixty hectares of Tuscan vineyard, and my very own castle – the only thing John had ever given me, aside from unwittingly donating the sperm that gave me life.

My memories of this place had faded with the years, but I remembered the *castello* as a magical building, complete with turrets and frescoes, and rooms filled with treasure. It was always cool, even on the hottest summer's day, and the gardens were a paradise too, with banks of lavender and sweet roses surrounded by neatly trimmed boxwood hedges.

The driver turned the car between a pair of high, ornate iron gates, overhung by a sign that read *Castel Sant'Angelo*. Castle of the Holy Angel. The gates looked rusted, and the sign creaked ominously, but the grand entrance remained just as impressive as the first time my mother had driven me through these gates when I was five.

The long drive was even bumpier and more rutted than the farm road, and the car sent up a billowing cloud of white dust behind us. Tall cypresses lined the road, casting long, dark blue stripes across our path and blocking the view of the house.

Then at last, the trees fell away to reveal the front approach to the *castello*, and the building rose up before us, its familiar façade warm in the slanting afternoon light. The umbrella pines that dotted the slope above the *castello* had been kept at bay from the front of the house, allowing the building to bask in sunshine. For a moment, the building seemed bright with colour: from the red-tiled roof, to the mellow apricot-coloured walls, to the powder-blue shutters.

At the end of the drive the road split, the left fork circling behind the house to the back yard then continuing on to the winery, and the right forming a square forecourt in front of the house's main entrance. A fancy, low-slung silver sports car stood in the forecourt. John's lawyer was already here.

This side of the house faced west towards Montalcino, and the late afternoon sun washed the walls in golden light. But when the taxi pulled up in front of the entrance and I opened the car door, I realised the sunlight was deceptive. The house looked faded and tired.

Nothing a coat of paint can't fix.

A man waited on the front steps of the house, beneath the porticoed entrance. He stepped forward into the light, and my heart caught suddenly in my throat. Not in that panic attack way I'd started to feel lately, but in a good way.

He was the kind of man who gave Italian men their reputation for studliness. Not any older than mid-thirties, with a face that was all golden planes and sharp angles. He wore a casual polo shirt and jeans, which fit his lean figure well enough that I could appreciate the toned muscle beneath the fabric.

Oh my word. *This* was my father's lawyer?

He descended the low flight of stairs, approaching with a welcoming smile, and my heart picked up its pace in a silly pitter-patter I hadn't felt in years. Kevin certainly never made my heart go pitter-patter like that.

The lawyer's eyes were dark and smiling, the colour of chocolate, warm and rich, and just as tempting. I couldn't help myself. I sighed.

'Signor Fioravanti?' My voice sounded breathless. *Oh please. Get a hold of yourself, Sarah.*

'*Benvenuta in Toscana, signora Wells*. Please, call me Luca.' His voice matched the face, deep, golden, and deliciously accented. Then he smiled, and dimples appeared in his cheeks. Dimples! As far back as I could remember, I'd never experienced actual weak knees over a man. Until now. Maybe Kevin and Cleo were right: I must be *seriously* burned out.

I reached out a tentative hand, and Luca wrapped both his around it. 'I am so sorry for your loss.'

'Thank you. And thank you for arranging the cremation and everything.'

'Of course. John Langdon was well respected here in our little community. He was a good man.'

I blinked away an unexpected blur in my eyes and focused on the man still holding my hand. A man this hot had to be married. I sneaked a look at his left hand. No wedding ring. Okay, so probably gay then.

I retrieved my hand and turned away to pay the driver, then while Luca carried my cases from the car, I wandered around the corner of the building to look at the long front side of the house that faced south over the valley.

It was more than just peeling paint that made the house seem tired. The stucco plaster was coming loose in great chunks, revealing streaky grey travertine blocks beneath. Some of the shutters hung skew on their rusty hinges.

Rapidly, I revised my hopeful estimate of the asking price down by half a million euros. The buyer would need to do a great deal of cosmetic work.

The house also seemed smaller and less impressive than I remembered. There were still towers on either side, topped with the crenelated turrets of my childhood memory, but now I could see they were mere decorations, pretentious additions to make an ordinary villa look more like a castle.

With a sigh, I turned away. The taxi was already halfway down the drive, taking all my childhood illusions away with it, and leaving me stranded in cold, hard reality. At least I had the really hot lawyer to soothe the transition.

I rejoined Luca on the front steps. He held a large ring of ancient-looking keys, and with a flourish, he slid the largest key into the lock, turned it, and gave the big brass handle a twist. The door stuck. I had to lean on it beside him to get it to finally open, and when it swung suddenly open, squealing on its old hinges, we both fell inside.

Oh, great. Trust me to be clumsy and ungraceful in front of the most gorgeous man I'd ever stood within breathing distance of.

'The wood has swollen a little,' Luca observed, sounding inordinately cheerful considering the grim welcome.

The hall inside was dark and gloomy, the effect no doubt of all the house's shutters being closed. Luca set down my cases on the bottommost step of the stone staircase, then followed as I wandered through the downstairs rooms.

Dust sheets covered the furniture, which loomed up out of the shadows, filling almost all the floor space. As a child, I used to play hide and seek in these rooms, and searched for treasure, but viewed though adult eyes it was simply cluttered, as if several hundred years' worth of inhabitants had collected furniture as a hobby – and never threw out a single item.

'The house is about a thousand square metres in size,' Luca said as he trailed me through the rooms. When I turned a bewildered expression on him, he laughed. 'That's over ten thousand English square feet.' He wrinkled his nose. 'Feet! Not a very attractive language, your English. But the real jewel, of course, is the land. More than two thirds of the property is arable. There's a fruit orchard, olive trees, and at least half the land is covered in vines. Mostly Sangiovese, but some Malvasia and Vernaccia grapes too.'

'Do you know a lot about wine?'

'Everyone in this region knows at least a little about wine.' He smiled, and his dark eyes lit up. 'And you?'

'I know absolutely nothing about wine – except how to drink it.'

'That is a good place to start.'

I didn't plan to get started. I had zero interest in learning anything about wine farming, and was just as happy drinking wine out of a box as out of a bottle with a real cork. I suspected if I admitted that out loud here in Tuscany, I might be deported immediately, inheritance or not.

In the drawing room, the long room which faced down over the valley, I threw open the windows and shutters. The afternoon light streaming in did nothing to dispel the gloom, because now I could see the layer of dust and grime on everything, the threadbare carpet, the peeling burgundy wall-paper, and the dust motes stirred up and set dancing by the inflow of fresh, warm air.

'How long ago did my father die?'

'A little over two weeks ago.'

This kind of neglect had taken a great deal longer than two weeks to accumulate.

'Was he sick for a long time?' I didn't really want to know the answer. I felt guilty enough already. I should have known. I should have called. I should have made more of an effort to keep in touch with my own father, even though he made very little attempt to keep in touch with me.

'No, he died very suddenly. He was in the winery when he had the heart attack. Tommaso found him there.'

He spoke the name as if it should mean something to me, but I only shrugged and turned away. I hadn't been here in nearly two decades – I could hardly be expected to remember the names and faces of my father's employees.

The only person I remembered was Elisa, John's housekeeper. *Nonna*, I used to call her. *Grandmother*, though she was no blood relation. But Elisa died a few years ago. That much my father had told me in one of our rare phone calls.

'He didn't have any help in the house?' I asked.

Luca shrugged. 'After Elisa died, your father never replaced her. He was an old man who didn't like too much change, and he didn't like strangers. He only lived in a handful of rooms these last few years.'

That would explain the dirt and general shabbiness. Thank heavens the property still had all those acres of vines to attract potential buyers, or I'd be screwed.

'I'd like to put this place on the market as soon as possible. Can you handle that for me?'

'*Sì*.' He drew the word out, as if doubtful.

'What price do you think I can get?'

He studied the bubbling wallpaper as if fascinated. Now, I most certainly was not imagining his hesitance. 'It is a little complicated,' he said. 'Your father having been a resident here for so long, naturally he chose to have his will drawn up under Italian law, so the rule of *legittima* applies. It will take some time to resolve.'

What needed to be resolved? I was John's only living relative. 'How long?'

'That will depend on the circumstances of the *successione necessaria*, the statutory shares.'

I'd had enough experience with corporate speak to recognise when someone was deliberately hedging.

'I need a cup of tea.' I turned away from the scene of neglect and headed down the terracotta-tiled passage to the kitchen.

Luca's soft chuckle followed me. 'So like your father. The one part of his English heritage he clung to was his tea.'

The high-vaulted kitchen was at the back of the house, opening onto the back yard which almost seemed cut out of the hillside. The kitchen featured the same terracotta floor tiles as the rest of the ground floor rooms, and the same deep windows. Dusty Delft plates decorated one wall. At least this room looked cleaner and more lived in than the other rooms, though it still felt more like a museum than a home. In the two decades since I'd last been here, the only new appliance to find its way into this kitchen was an electric kettle. And thank God for that.

Dismayed, I eyed the antique wood stove, with its blackened top and grimy porcelain façade. It had been my lifelong dream to own a home with a great big old-fashioned Aga. This vintage stove was nothing like that Aga of my dreams. Surely this couldn't be the same stove Nonna taught me to bake in?

Beside the kettle, I found a tin of loose leaf tea that still smelled fresh, and a china teapot decorated with delicate pink roses. Setting the kettle to boil, I rinsed out the teapot at the enormous sink, noting the deep crack in the side of the marble, then brewed a strong pot of tea. The comforting, familiar smell in this alien place calmed me. Though I'd been fully prepared to drink the tea black, I discovered fresh milk in the fridge. Someone had anticipated my arrival. Luca?

I poured out two steaming cups, then sat across from Luca at the big wooden kitchen table. 'Okay. I'm ready to hear it. What haven't you told me?'

He looked distinctly uncomfortable. 'Under English law anyone making a will has the "testamentary freedom" to choose whoever they would like to inherit their estate.'

I nodded. That was easy enough to follow.

'However, here in Italy we have the rule of *legittima*, of forced heirship. This means that in Italy, the person making the will cannot freely determine who gets what. Italian law is set up to protect the inheritance of family members who might have been ... overlooked.' He smiled wryly. 'Here in Italy we cannot threaten to disinherit a family member who has displeased us, since everyone knows the law will decide who inherits and who will not, to ensure that all heirs receive a fair share.'

I sipped my tea. Could he just get to the point, already? I didn't see how any of this was relevant, since I was John's only child.

Luca's expression turned serious. 'You see, under Italian law it is obligatory for certain immediate family members to inherit a proportion of the estate, regardless of what it says in the will.'

It finally occurred to me where this conversation was headed. 'You're saying there's another heir? Someone else with a claim who might want to contest the will?'

He nodded, relieved I'd got there ahead of him. '*You* are that someone.'

It took a moment for his words to sink in. And an even longer moment for me to shut my mouth again.

Slowly, I drained the last of the tea from my cup and poured another, careful to keep my hand from shaking. Only when I'd added milk and stirred, did I risk looking back at Luca, my emotions once again under firm control.

'You are telling me that my father did not leave me any part of his estate. He left it to someone else. And it is only because of this law of *legittima* that I have any claim at all?'

'*Sì.*'

'Who did he leave it to?' My voice sounded astonishingly steady, considering my entire world had suddenly shifted beneath my feet.

Sure, we were never close, but whose fault was it that my father and I were as good as strangers? I was the only child he'd ever had, and *this* was how little he'd cared for me?

'He left it to Tommaso.'

That name again.

At my blank expression, Luca added: 'John's business partner.'

I didn't even know my father had a business partner. The last time we'd spoken, at Christmas on one of our semi-annual phone calls, we hadn't talked about anything consequential. I'd asked after the vineyard, and John told me one of his wines had won some award. He'd asked about my work, and I told him everything was fine, as I always did.

I cleared my throat. 'So what are my chances of inheriting anything?'

'The chances are good that you will receive at least half the value of the property. The courts are very fair that way, but Italian court cases can drag on for years, so we should try to settle. Tommaso is a reasonable man and we will talk to him. If we can persuade him to buy you out of your share straight away, then everything can be resolved amicably. Alternatively, the property could be sold, and you and Tommaso can split the profits equally between you once the debts are paid.'

Of course there were debts. There always were. And no one knew better than I how to finance them, re-structure them, and turn them to good use. 'How much debt?'

'Several loans, and your father re-mortgaged a few years ago to finance new equipment for the farm. The balance still owing stands at nearly three million euros.'

My breath whistled out. According to my research, properties this size sold for anywhere between three and five million. But they had fully renovated villas. So not only would I have to share the proceeds of John's estate, I'd be lucky if there *were* any proceeds.

I sipped my tea. It tasted bitter. Or maybe that was just the bad taste in my mouth. For so many years I'd resented this land because it was the only thing John ever loved. That it had so little value only made it worse. I'd been worth less to him than a crumbling building with grand pretensions and a heavily mortgaged farm.

'I guess I need to call the taxi back then. If this property doesn't belong to me, I can hardly stay here.'

'Tommaso is happy for you to treat the *castello* as your own until this is settled.'

How magnanimous. 'So what do we do now?'

'You sound like your father. Always so practical.'

What else could I be under the circumstances but practical?

Luca pushed away his cup of only partially-drunk tea. 'We will need to complete the paperwork to prove who you are, and to confirm that you will contest the will. But since it is now nearly five o'clock on a Friday afternoon, there is not much more we can do today. Tomorrow morning at ten, you and Tommaso will meet at my office, and we will discuss how to proceed.'

I walked Luca to the front door, where he handed me the massive set of keys. I took them, feeling like a fraud. This wasn't my house. My father had chosen to leave everything to someone else, someone he valued more highly than his own daughter.

Luca had to help shut the front door, him pulling and me pushing. It was not the most dignified of farewells, and with the door shut between us I couldn't even say a proper goodbye. Instead, as his little sports car revved to life and roared off down the drive, I sank back against the big warped wooden door, energy spent.

Perhaps I was more tired than I realised. I was glad I'd only have to face my father's mysterious business partner tomorrow, because right now all I wanted was to curl up in a ball, with a duvet pulled over my head, and hide from the world.

Chapter 2

Chi cerca, trova, e talor quel che non vorrebbe

(He who seeks, finds, and sometimes finds what he would rather not)

I wrestled my cases upstairs. The stairs, made of stone, seemed solid enough, but the wrought iron hand railing wobbled at my touch. The house needed a lot of work. Maybe this Tommaso guy would be just as happy as I to be shot of the place?

I couldn't remember how many bedrooms the house had. Lots, it had seemed to my kid self. But considering how impressed I'd been by a few decorative crenellations, maybe not as many as I'd thought. I started with my father's room, peeking inside, then shutting the door quickly. I wasn't yet ready to face the tumbled emotions evoked by his personal space.

Instead, I chose the guest room at the opposite end of the long corridor, the same one I'd used as a child. Both the shutters and the curtains were closed. I set my smallest bag down on the bench at the foot of the wooden four-poster bed, dropped the big wheelie bag in the middle of the floor, and hurried to open the windows. Dust motes danced in the light when I gingerly opened the drapes, but the room appeared reasonably clean, and the bed was freshly made, with new bedding; grey and masculine-looking pillows and duvet.

Kicking off my shoes, I climbed under the duvet, pulled it up over my head, and let sleep take me away – away from the strangeness of Italy, this silent house and its memories, back to the only place I'd ever felt truly at home: that sixth floor corner office in Cheapside from which I'd been banned for four interminable months.

When I woke, disoriented, and with my empty stomach complaining, reminding me I hadn't eaten anything since the quickie pain au chocolat and coffee in the airport that morning, the room was in pitch darkness. Silence reverberated in my ears. No distant hum of traffic, no muted sounds of the neighbours' telly, none of the small, comforting sounds of my housemates moving in the house. I couldn't remember when last I'd felt so utterly alone. Probably not since the last time I was in this house.

Somewhere in the house something creaked, and I shot up off the bed.

The *castello* felt very big and very empty. How far away were the nearest neighbours? Was there anyone else on the property at night, any workers, or a night watchman? Would anyone hear if I screamed for help? I hadn't thought to ask Luca.

Barefoot, I tiptoed to the bedroom door and pressed my

ear against it, but there were no other sounds. The door squeaked as I opened it, making me jump.

This is stupid. You're a grown woman. You're a competent, successful, twenty-first-century woman who can take care of herself. And I was hungry.

The kitchen hadn't seemed so far away when I was a kid. I made my way down through the darkened house, not switching on any lights. Even if I could remember where the switches were, I didn't want to turn myself into a target on the off-chance there was an intruder.

The vast kitchen with its high-beamed ceiling was eerily full of looming shadows, and the yellow lamplight spilling from the single overhead lamp did nothing to dispel the gloom. I filled the electric kettle, then rinsed out the teapot to brew a fresh pot. But tea wasn't going to be enough to silence my grumbling stomach. Had the considerate person who'd left milk and made up my bed also left food?

There was nothing in the kitchen itself, but John always loved biscuits with his tea. That would be better than nothing. So I headed into the pantry, and was still groping for the light switch when I heard a sound that turned my veins to ice. I froze. The outer kitchen door creaked open.

The wind blowing open an unlatched door? Ghosts?

But it was worse than ghosts. The high-pitched creak turned into an ominously final bang as the door shut again, and then there were heavy, booted footsteps across the kitchen floor.

My heart leapt into my throat. It was beating so hard, I was sure I was at serious risk of a coronary. Forget the stress of a corporate job. This was a million times worse.

With my heart thudding loudly enough against my ribs that the intruder could probably hear it on the other side of the pantry door, I clung to the door handle, steadying myself, relieved to be hidden here in the pitch dark. With my free hand, I groped behind me, and my fingers hit cold iron, rounding on a solid, heavy handle.

The door handle twisted unexpectedly beneath my fingers and I squealed, louder even than the handle had, giving myself away.

The pantry door swung open, and all my blood drained to my toes.

'Sarah?' He was a big man, tall, broad-shouldered, and built like a bouncer.

He reached past me, and I flinched back, swinging with all my might just as the tiny pantry flooded with cold white light.

In the moment before my weapon connected with solid flesh, I glimpsed the intruder. He was dark-haired, bearded, and terrifying. He grunted and staggered back, clutching his head.

'What the hell?!' His accent was thick, not immediately traceable, but he spoke in English without even thinking, I noted, as I gripped the heavy metal object close to my chest.

And he knew my name. Oh heavens.

Probably not a burglar after all.

The man glowered at me, still holding his head. 'Why are you hiding in here?'

'I wasn't hiding. I was looking for biscuits.'

'In the dark?' He removed his hand from his forehead and

there was a streak of blood on his fingers, and even more on his brow where a long gash oozed.

'You're bleeding!'

He scowled. 'Of course I am. You're lucky I'm not bloody unconscious, or worse.'

I glanced at the weapon in my hand. I held an old-fashioned iron for pressing clothes, one of those solid antique cast-iron types that opened up to place hot coals inside. A formidable weapon indeed. 'I am so sorry! I thought you were a burglar.'

He moved to lean against the scarred Formica kitchen counter, as if unable to stand without help, and I hurried to his side to offer support, even though I still felt as shaky as a budding spring leaf.

He brushed me away, irritable. 'How can I be a burglar when I live here?'

'You live here?' Oops. Luca hadn't mentioned anyone living here. I took a wild guess. 'You're Tommaso?'

'Of course. Who else would I be?' he snapped. I could hardly blame him for his surliness. The blood was trickling now down his temple, and his face was paler than it had been when he'd loomed over me in the pantry door.

I felt a tad pale too. The bedding upstairs was masculine. Had I pulled a Goldilocks and slept in Baby Bear's bed? Not that this man could be remotely confused with a baby bear. More like a great big, angry Papa Grizzly.

Until he swayed on his feet.

'You need to sit.' I set down the old iron and pulled out a chair from the kitchen table. Casting me another annoyed glance, he slid into it. Satisfied that at least he wasn't likely to collapse on the floor, I hurried to the cracked sink and wet a tea towel, which I used to dab at his forehead until the blood stopped trickling and the wound looked relatively clean. Thankfully it was a shallow cut and shouldn't need stitches. I just hoped the iron wasn't rusty enough to cause an infection. 'You'll need antiseptic and a band aid, to keep the cut clean. Where will I find them?'

'Under the kitchen sink.'

I found a first aid box under the sink and set it on the kitchen table, rooting through its jumbled contents for band aids and antiseptic. He flinched when I dabbed iodine on the cut but didn't make a sound. Done at last, I moved back to the kettle and set it going again. I needed tea more than ever. In fact, I could do with a shot of brandy, but I wasn't brave – or stupid – enough to ask my host where to find his liquor cabinet.

'Tea?' I offered, bringing the filled teapot and two mismatched cups to the table.

'Yes, please.'

While I poured, I sneaked a surreptitious look. He wasn't as old as the beard had at first made him appear, nor quite as rough and threatening as he'd first seemed. His thick hair was long, almost to his shoulders, though not as shaggy as I'd first thought.

But even if he wasn't a terrifying burglar, he still wasn't Baby Bear. He was the rightful owner of this *castello*, I was his guest, and probably a very unwelcome one at that – now more than ever.

'Shall we start over?' I infused as much good cheer into

my voice as my still jittery nerves could manage. 'I'm Sarah Wells, John's daughter, and I'm very grateful you're letting me stay in the house.'

He said nothing, just eyed me with a cool, grey gaze that was more than a little hostile. Okay, so I wasn't going to get the red carpet rolled out for me any time soon.

I cleared my throat and tried again. 'Luca didn't tell me you were living in the house.'

He gave me an odd look. 'I don't. I live in the cottage.'

The cottage was across the back yard. It had been converted from the old stable block back in the Fifties and was where the housekeeper Elisa had lived.

'Okay. So what are you doing here in the kitchen?'

'I saw the light on and came over to say hello. I thought you might want dinner.' He waved, and I turned to look behind me at the tray he must have set down on top of the old wood stove before coming to find me in the pantry. Only now did I become aware of the aromatic smell filling the kitchen. My stomach pulled tight, and not just from hunger.

He'd been nothing more than neighbourly, and I'd bashed him over the head with the nearest weapon I could find. Not a great way to open negotiations.

I forced a polite smile I didn't feel. 'Thank you. That's very kind.'

His eyes narrowed. An uncomfortable silence filled the room but I refused to show any weakness to this intimidating man, so I ignored it and returned his hard gaze.

There was something oddly familiar about his light eyes, blue-grey, with an emphasis on the grey.

Then realisation struck. 'Tommy?!'

The discovery that this tall, broad-shouldered, bearded man was my old childhood friend rocked me even more than the fear that a complete stranger was breaking into the *castello*. '*You* were my father's business partner?'

His eyes narrowed further. I didn't even think that was possible. 'No one's called me that since my mother died. You didn't know?'

The mental adjustment took me a long moment. I couldn't help myself – I stared openly at him now. If I looked hard enough, past the long hair and scraggly beard, I could just about see a glimmer of Elisa's grandson, the boy I used to play with when he'd come to visit during those never-ending summers so long ago.

I only ever knew him as Tommy, the English-speaking kid from Edinburgh, not as Tommaso, but of course he was half-Italian from his father's side. His accent, always a convoluted mash-up of Scottish and Italian, certainly leaned more heavily now toward his Italian side. How long had he been living here?

'I'm sorry about your mother. And Nonna.'

He shrugged, a simple gesture that managed to convey a great deal, a uniquely Italian ability. I've never met an English person able to say so much with nothing but body language.

'My grandmother was old, and it wasn't unexpected, but my mother ... it was nearly nine years ago now. She had cancer, and in the end her death was a mercy.'

I'd never met his parents, but still felt a pang for his loss. Like me, Tommy was sent to Italy alone as a child. In my case, Geraldine had been eager to get rid of me, but for Tommy it had been out of necessity. His parents had both worked, and they hadn't had time to entertain an energetic youth all summer. And his grandmother had been delighted to have him. He'd been wanted.

His visits to his Nonna Elisa had been the highlight of my summers. Even at the age when most boys would have been horrified to have a younger girl tagging along wherever they went, we'd been friends. We'd explored this big house together, run wild on the farm, gone fishing and truffle hunting and blackberry picking together. And then there'd been that last summer...

Involuntarily, my gaze dropped to his mouth. Tommy always had the most sensuous mouth for a boy, with full lips that tasted of ... I blushed, and averted my gaze, but not before he noticed.

His eyes narrowed again as he studied me. 'Your hair has grown since I last saw you.'

'Well, it has been twenty years.' I touched the end of my long braid. I'd been growing it out for years, mostly because I hadn't had time for anything but hurried trims.

'*Nearly* twenty. I like your hair long.'

'Well, I liked your hair shorter.'

The amused gleam in his eyes was very much the young man I remembered from that last summer. Always full of mischief, needling me, pushing my boundaries.

'The last I heard, you were still living in Edinburgh,' I said to fill the sudden, awkward silence.

'That was a long time ago. I moved here soon after my

mother died. Nonna was getting old, and I didn't want her to be alone.'

Nearly nine years. 'My father never told me.' I bit my lip, a habit I thought I'd grown out of. There were so many things John and I never discussed, and now we never would.

'We have a meeting tomorrow with Luca at ten.' Tommaso lifted the teapot, offering to re-fill my cup, but I shook my head. 'We'll drive together. We should leave at about nine-thirty.'

I nodded, though the thought of spending even half an hour in a car with this man I once knew so well, who was now a stranger, only made me more anxious. I rose to clear away the teapot and cups. 'In that case, I'm going to bed. It's been a long day.' A shattering day. Half an hour ago, I'd dreaded being alone, now I craved it.

Tommaso rose. 'You can leave the iron when you go to bed. This is a very safe district. You can sleep peacefully.' The wicked glint was back in his eyes.

'Thank you for the food,' I said, as he stepped out into the back yard. He merely nodded. I didn't wait to watch him cross the yard to the cottage. I shut the door, flicked the latch, and heaved a sigh. Then, grabbing the tray, I bolted back upstairs, not pausing to see what was under the cloth covering, not even pausing to catch my breath, until I was safely in my room with the door shut and my wheelie case pushed up under the door handle, creating a barrier between me and the rest of the empty, echoing house.

Chapter 3

Non tutto il male vien per nuocere

(Not everything bad that happens is wasted)

I slept in later than I had in ... well, at least since my uni days.

I'd been wary the night before of closing the curtains, in case they released another tornado of dust, but even with bright light creeping into the room, I only woke when it reached the bed. I must have been more exhausted than I realised. Not that I'd admit it. I didn't want to give Cleo the chance to say, 'I told you so'.

Broad daylight only marginally brightened the house's gloom as I tramped downstairs to the kitchen. In daylight, the pantry appeared bigger – and barer. There were indeed biscuits, a packet of factory-made shortbread biscuits, but no bread or cereal or anything else remotely breakfasty. And only instant coffee. I groaned. I didn't fancy facing Tommaso again on an empty stomach.

Though to give the devil his due, that beef stew he'd brought over last night had been really good. As good as Nonna's stews used to be.

Once I'd fortified myself with coffee and biscuits, the next thing on my agenda was to phone home. Sure, it was Saturday morning so Cleo wouldn't have anything new to tell me about work, but I needed to hear her ever-optimistic voice telling me things weren't as bad as they seemed.

But the mobile signal was so weak I couldn't dial out. I wandered from room to room, waving my phone in the air. Nothing. Not even on the terrace or in the deserted back yard, or along the drive, though I walked all the way to the gate. *Shit*. As I reached the wrought iron gates a small canary-yellow Fiat, brimming over with young men, sped past. The whistles trailing behind the little car made me suddenly and excruciatingly aware that I was still dressed in nothing more than sleep shorts and a camisole top.

So I trudged back up the drive, hesitating for a long moment at the door of Tommaso's cottage, which nestled into the slope behind the *castello*. Thankfully, the place appeared empty, and when I knocked, almost afraid he would answer, there was no response.

John must have had access to the outside world. I'd phoned him a few times here at the villa, so there had to be a landline at least. The *castello* may not yet have joined the twenty-first century, but it was certainly part of the twentieth.

There'd been a library, hadn't there? One of those rooms that was shrouded in dust cloths even in my distant youth. Opening doors on rooms that clearly hadn't seen daylight in years – a billiard room that was only used for storage these days, and a morning room with faded tapestries on its walls – I ripped off dust cloths to reveal rickety chairs, rotting upholstery, paintings caked in grime. I finally reached a room lined with books and smelling as if it has died and gone to a watery grave. The library. It had damp patches in the ceiling and the patterned parquet floor was warped from water damage. Someone should have dumped the entire contents of this room in a skip a long time ago.

There, at last, was a phone jack in the wall, and a cable clinging to flaking plaster, up through the driest part of the ceiling, up to ... where?

With a groan, I headed back upstairs, counting out my paces, not entirely surprised when I realised the rooms above the library were my father's. I pushed open the door and peered into the murky darkness.

Throwing open the shutters, I raised a sash window to let in a little light and fresh air. The bed loomed large, a massive four-poster covered with the same crocheted blanket John used even when I was young. It came with the house, he'd told me once.

How was it that the guest room had new bedding, but this one, the one that was lived in, remained frozen in time?

The phone I'd been searching for sat on the bedside table, a black thing with a rotary dial that belonged in a museum. Did those things even work in this day and age?

I lifted the receiver and heard the familiar sound of a dial tone. Hallelujah!

Cleo answered on the second ring, sounding sleepy.

'You must have had a really good date last night,' I said brightly.

She moaned. 'I wish!' Down the phone, I heard her stretch. 'I think I'm officially ready to give up dating.'

Wow, that was a first. In the dictionary, under 'eternal optimist' you'd find Cleo's name. She was a glass half-full person, especially when it came to men. Or maybe that was *even* when it came to men. 'It couldn't have been that bad...'

'Worst. Date. Ever.' Cleo's dating history could fill an encyclopaedia. She'd been on more first dates than anyone I've ever met. I quit dating after Kevin (though as Cleo so kindly pointed out, I wasn't exactly dating much *before* Kevin), but even though some of the guys she dated made Kevin look like a real keeper, she refused to give up hope that her One was out there.

She moaned again. 'He was bald. And not in that sexy Vin Diesel way. More like a 40-year-old accountant who's losing all his hair kind of way. His ear hairs were longer than the hairs on his head. The picture on his dating profile must have been at least ten years out of date. But that wasn't even the worst of it. I could overlook the fact that he lied about his looks. But he spent the entire meal talking about his ex.'

I winced. Dating really did get harder with every passing year. 'I told you online dating was soul destroying. Perhaps you should come to Italy. The men here are definitely better looking.' And charming, with one grumpy, bearded exception.

'I wish. But I haven't accrued several years' worth of leave like you have. Hang on a moment – are you referring to someone in particular? Have you met someone?'

'My lawyer looks like he stepped out of *GQ*.' I perched on the edge of the bed. 'All slick, sexy and metrosexual. It's just as well there's eye candy, since the news isn't good.'

'What happened?' Cleo was wide awake now. She listened as I filled her in, groaning in all the right places, laughing when I told her about hitting Tommaso over the head.

'Don't laugh, it wasn't funny. I might have killed him!'

'On the plus side, if you'd killed him, you would inherit everything, wouldn't you?'

'Yeah, but I might also have been calling you from jail this morning.'

'That's okay. You have your sexy lawyer to get you free. And then you and he could live happily ever after in your castle and make *GQ*-worthy babies.'

I glanced around my father's shabby bedroom. There was the door to the en-suite. How many times had the bathroom flooded to cause all that damage downstairs in the library? 'It's not much of a castle, and this inheritance may be more trouble than it's worth.'

'Nonsense. Half a vineyard is better than nothing.' And there was that injection of optimism I'd been looking for.

Cleo yawned. 'Besides, I've never known you to back down from a challenge. You're the most level-headed analyst I've ever met. If there's an advantage to be found in this situation, you'll find it.'

Yes, but that was before I'd over-estimated the repayment capabilities of one of the firm's most valuable clients and risked their biggest investment to date. I rubbed my face, glad Cleo couldn't see me now. When it came to work, I never showed weakness, not even to my BFF.

'You are not going to get back on a plane without a big fat

cheque in your back pocket. You hear me?' she said, on another yawn.

'I hear you.' I sighed. 'Besides, it's not like I have anything better to do with my time. Of course, I can do this. Piece of cake.' Though if the metaphor was going to fit my life right now, it would have to be a very heavy fruitcake. The kind where you couldn't quite identify all the bits baked into it.

'I am not selling.' Tommaso leaned across the little boardroom table in Luca's office, his arms crossed over his chest, his face set in a scowl. 'Your father left this vineyard to me because he wanted me to run it, not so it could be sold to strangers.'

I bristled. He was being unnecessarily stubborn, since Luca had already explained that it was inevitable the courts would split the inheritance 50/50 between us – eventually. 'There are other farms you could buy once we sell and split the proceeds. Why does it have to be this one?'

Tommaso's eyes turned flinty. 'How can you even ask me that?'

I shrugged. What did he expect of me? I had no ties to this land. Even my father had no ties here. He was just another foreigner who'd decided to buy a farm in Tuscany, like a less glamorous Sting. 'Then buy me out if you want to keep it so badly.'

Tommaso's scowl deepened. What had happened to that light-hearted boy I remembered, to turn him into this sullen, surly man who'd barely said a word to me the entire drive here? His pig-headedness hadn't abated any but what had been mildly irritating in a playmate was downright annoying in a man I needed to reach a compromise with.

'I can't afford to buy you out right now. All my capital is tied up in the business.'

'Then you don't have a choice. If this goes to court, you're still going to have to sell to pay me out my share.' Not that I wanted to drag this out in court any more than he did, but Tommaso didn't need to know that.

We glared at each other across the boardroom table.

'You need to be reasonable,' Luca pleaded, spreading his hands wide to encompass us both. He turned to Tommaso. 'She's right. If you can't afford to buy her out, the courts will inevitably force a sale.'

'It'll take months, if not years, for the court to hear this case, and that's all the time I need. Once the next bottling goes to market, I'll be in a better position to buy Ms Wells out.'

I leaned forward, arms on the table. 'Great. When's the next bottling?'

'After the harvest.'

I might not know much about wine farming, but I knew enough. 'But that's months away!'

'You can sell whatever is of value in the *castello*. Consider it a down payment against your share of the property.' Tommaso shrugged, as if to say, '*take it or leave it*'.

I glared at him, and he glared right back, unflinching, his cold gaze challenging. 'That's my final offer. If you don't like it, we let the courts decide.'

He'd clearly forgotten that I never backed down from a challenge. I wasn't going to start now. 'You could raise a loan to buy me out.'

Tommaso's eyes narrowed. 'Before you make any more suggestions, perhaps you should actually learn something about this business you so badly want to dispose of. The property is mortgaged to the hilt. It's coming around, but these things don't happen overnight. The next bottling was supposed to make a substantial dent in our debts, but with John's death…' He shrugged. 'Once our next bottling goes on sale, we'll be in a much better financial position, but you can't hurry wine.'

My hackles rose, but I refused to rise to the bait. I was known for being cool and level-headed. Not that I felt particularly cool right now. Really – whose fault was it that I knew nothing of the wine business? And it certainly wasn't *my* fault that John chose to make his housekeeper's grandson his partner and heir instead of me. If John had ever asked me to join him in the business … would I have accepted? I nibbled my lower lip. Who knew what my younger self would have done? There'd been a time I'd have done anything for John's love and approval. But he was gone. Whatever I'd hoped to get from him, those dreams were ashes now.

'You could split the property?' Luca suggested. 'Tommaso could keep the winery, and Sarah could sell the *castello*.'

Tommaso smiled, leaning back in his chair, arms still crossed over his chest. It wasn't a pleasant smile. 'That works for me.'

Of course it would work for him. He probably couldn't wait to unload that millstone from around his neck. And what was I going to do with a building in desperate need of repair? It didn't take a genius to work out that the value of the property was in the land and the crop, not a ramshackle farmhouse with noble pretensions. Who would pay decent money for a rundown *castello* with no land? And what little I'd make would no doubt be swallowed up by my inherited share of the debt.

I shook my head slowly, and Tommaso threw his hands in the air in an angry, despairing gesture that was entirely Italian. 'Then we are at an impasse. I will not sell the vineyard that meant everything to your father, even if you would, and I cannot buy you out until after the harvest. Go back home, and we can talk again when the harvest is in. Or we go to court.'

Go back home. I thought of my pride and joy, that terrace house in a crescent lined with cherry trees in Wanstead, thought of sitting there alone all day while my housemates went off to work. I thought of the four months that stretched out before me like a life sentence.

The thought occurred so blindingly quickly, and with such force, it almost took my breath away. I rested my elbows on the table. 'When is the harvest?'

Tommaso's eyes narrowed suspiciously. 'Usually September, weather dependent. Why?'

Four months away, and about the time I would be able to return to work.

Take up a hobby, Cleo had suggested. Renovating a broken-down house in Tuscany was a hobby, right? And she'd said I shouldn't come home until I had a big fat cheque in my pocket. But that didn't have to be today.

'I'll stay.'

'You'll what?' Tommaso leaned forward, his expression

incredulous. Luca, on the other hand, looked pleased. I was glad someone was.

'You told Luca I could treat the *castello* as my own until this is settled. So I'll stay until the harvest, and I'll fix up the *castello*. If I can sell the house at a decent price before your next bottling, we'll call it even. And if I don't—' I gave a shrug that was nowhere near as expressive as Tommaso's. 'Then you buy me out after the bottling.'

Either way, he'd get to keep his precious vines, and we wouldn't have to drag this out in court. And the cherry on top: I'd have something to keep me occupied during my enforced exile from the office.

But Tommaso didn't look happy. 'Don't you have a job to get back to?'

Breathe in. Count to three. Relax. 'I have a lot of holiday leave due.'

He huffed out a sigh. 'Go or stay, it makes no difference to me. The *castello* is unoccupied, and as long as I get to work the vineyard, you can do what you like.'

Luca beamed. 'That's settled then. I will draw up papers in which you agree to be equal partners until such time as either the *castello* sells, or Tommaso can buy you out.'

Tommaso still didn't look much happier, but he nodded.

Luca walked us to the door, shook hands with Tommaso, and leaned in to kiss me on both cheeks, his hands resting lightly on my upper arms. '*Ogni cosa ha la sua ragione.* Everything has a reason. I am glad you are not going so soon.'

His hands caressed my arms, a touch that could have been casual and meant nothing, or not casual at all. My skin tingled all the way down to my toes at the unaccustomed touch.

Tommaso, halfway down the narrow corridor, paused to look back at us, his face set in that perpetual scowl again. 'I have errands to run. I'll meet you at the car in a couple of hours.'

Without waiting for my response, he turned and walked away.

'I have errands too!' I called after him. He waved a hand in the air, without even looking back.

I frowned after him, until a light touch on my arm brought me back to the much more pleasant present. 'Your father's death was a big shock to Tommaso. He'll come around.'

My frown turned to a smile. 'That's sweet of you, but you don't need to make excuses for him.'

Luca's dimple flashed. 'That is more like it. You have a beautiful smile.' He brushed my cheek with his fingers, tucking a stray wisp of hair back behind my ear, and I shivered. There was no mistaking *that* touch for casual – not when it was accompanied by such a burning look in his eyes. *Definitely not gay then. Just too good to be true.*

No man had looked at me like that in years, and that included Kevin. My ex had many good qualities, but passion was not among them. Luca's expression made me feel oddly floaty and dizzy. Cleo would have a field day if she could see me now.

'Since you have time now, perhaps I could show you around our little town?' Luca offered me his arm, and I looped mine through it, smiling up at him.

'If your tour includes something to eat, I'm in!'

Chapter 4

Mangia bene, ridi spesso, ama molto

(Eat well, laugh often, love much)

Luca's office was in the wide road that circled around the old part of town, but behind it lay a maze of twisting, narrow streets that rose to the town centre on the crown of the hill. As we climbed uphill, Luca's hand lingered against my lower back to guide me, infusing my body with unaccustomed warmth. *Hello, Dorothy. We're not in Kansas anymore.*

My gaze was everywhere, absorbing the myriad details that reminded me that I was indeed in a foreign land – the ornate door knockers, the flower boxes at the windows, the Madonnina shrines high up on the walls of the old houses.

'I doubt Montalcino has changed much since you were last here,' Luca observed.

Since the town hadn't changed much in five hundred years, that was pretty much guaranteed, but still I shook my head. 'I don't remember much of the town. I was only a girl last time I was here, and John didn't leave the farm very often. I remember Elisa bringing me to the market, though.'

Luca showed me the Palazzo Pieri, the civic museum, the Chiesa di Sant'Agostino with its high rose window, and then we circled around to the Piazza Garibaldi, which was not much wider than a street, and nothing at all like the big piazzas of Rome I remembered from a long ago trip, back in the days when I'd still taken holidays. At one end of the piazza lay the austere, smaller church of Sant'Egidio, and on the other the tall, slender clock tower of the palazzo.

The subtle touch of Luca's hand on my back, neither intrusive nor casual, sent waves of warmth through me as we wandered the narrow, cobbled streets. It had been a very long time since a man had touched me like this, with such care and attention. So long, I couldn't even remember. Kevin hadn't been touchy-feely, and even in those rare moments when we'd been intimate, his touch had never thrilled me as Luca's now did.

The piazza was busy with tourists and shoppers, with laughing, talking people, and with music.

'But watch,' Luca whispered. 'Here more than anywhere in the town you can see that there are two Montalcinos. There's the tourist hotspot that outsiders see, and then there's our little village, where everyone knows everyone else.'

He was right. While the tourists and locals walked side by side in the same streets, it was as if they existed in two separate worlds, brushing against each other, but not merging. Neither local nor tourist, where did I belong?

He led me to a restaurant on the square, where he was welcomed effusively by the staff who clearly knew him well, and we were seated at a prime table on the pavement, sheltered by a white awning and a hedge of potted shrubs. Luca ordered a bottle of local wine, the Brunello di Montalcino, for me to try, and we both ordered the house specials.

'You are sure you don't want to keep the vineyard?' Luca asked, as the restaurant's owner himself poured our wine. 'Even when you go back to London you could be a partner in the winery, if you wanted.'

I shook my head. 'Absolutely sure. What would I do with half a vineyard?'

'You do not want to be a part of your father's vineyard?'

There was that old pain, making me feel like a wounded child again. 'There was a time I'd have done anything for John's approval, but it's too late for that now.'

Luca's eyes filled with sympathy, as if he understood the feeling. 'Then as purely a business proposition? If Tommaso is right, the vineyard will be profitable soon. Half those profits could be yours.'

I shook my head even more emphatically and reached for my wine glass. It was a deep-flavoured red, heavier and less sweet than what I usually drank.

'If you are quite sure, I can arrange a real estate agent to give you a valuation on the *castello*,' Luca offered. 'I have a friend who is with one of the best agencies in the province.'

'Thank you. I'd appreciate that.' Then, because it was too beautiful a day to waste thinking about the *castello*, I changed the subject. 'Tell me about this wine.'

Luca's face lit up with boyish enthusiasm, as if I'd asked him to show off his favourite toy. *Oh, please don't let him be one of those bores who can't shut up once they start talking about their favourite sport.* 'The Brunello is made from the local clone of the Sangiovese grapes, the same that grow in your own vineyard.'

My chest did an excited flutter at the words 'your vineyard', and I quickly squashed it. I wanted no part of this vineyard, remember?

'The Brunello grape has a higher alcohol level than the average Sangiovese, so our wines have ripe, full-bodied, concentrated flavours, and a rich lingering after-taste.'

He swirled his glass delicately and breathed in the aroma deeply before taking a sip. 'The Brunello di Montalcino is a mature wine, well-aged, which makes it expensive, both to make and to buy, but it is worth every cent.'

I took another sip, more slowly this time, breathing it in as he had done, then savouring the wine on my tongue before swallowing.

He grinned. 'Can you taste the Montalcino air in the wine? The hazelnuts, the dried fig, the anise? Younger vintages are much fruitier, but this wine is not so bold.'

Long ago, my father taught me to taste wine, explaining the flavours and encouraging me to name them. But those memories were as fleeting as the time we'd spent together. I took another sip, rolling the wine around on my tongue before swallowing, surprised when I identified the flavours Luca described. 'Wow!'

He laughed, throwing his head back, an open and infectious laugh. 'We will send you home a wine connoisseur. Do you have a man waiting for you back in England?'

Wow, he certainly wasn't shy! 'Only if you count my boss.'

'And your job – what is it you do?'

'I'm a financial analyst with an investment banking firm in the City of London.'

'They don't need you back?'

I looked down at the tablecloth, tracing the silver threaded pattern in the white cloth with my finger. 'They tell me I've been working so hard that I need to take a really long holiday.' I rolled my eyes. 'Apparently I need to find a healthy work–life balance.'

Luca took my hand in his. '*È perfetto*. Italy is the place for that. We work hard, but we also play hard.'

His thumb stroked my palm suggestively, and I pulled my hand free, fighting a blush. Geez. I was too old for a schoolgirl crush, and too young for hot flashes, so what was going on with me? I covered my awkwardness with a flirtatious smile. 'I'd much rather talk about you. Tell me about Luciano Fioravanti.'

Like any man, once given the opportunity to talk about himself, he did. But I needn't have worried he'd turn into a bore. Luca had the legendary Italian charm, and our conversation flowed almost as easily as the wine. Too easily. I felt none of the usual constraint I felt when out on a date. But this wasn't a date. Just a lawyer taking out his client for a business lunch, right?

We nibbled at the platter of bruschetta and *fiori di zucca*, fried zucchini flowers, which the owner himself brought to our table, and I soon felt lighter than I had in months. I had the undivided attention of a gorgeous man, the heady taste of a rich wine, the divine flavours of Italy, and sultry June air on my skin.

See, I can relax. I know how to have fun.

After the antipasti, came an asparagus risotto. I'd clearly had too much wine already, because the flavours hit my tongue like an explosion, and I closed my eyes, sighing, making Luca laugh again. I liked his laugh, so open and uninhibited.

'Everything tastes better in Italy,' he said, a teasing spark in his eyes.

Oh no. There was that hot flash thing again. Thirty-five was too young for menopause, wasn't it?

I basked in the golden glow of the envious glances sent my way by the other women in the restaurant, including our Polish waitress. Or maybe it was the golden glow of the wine. I didn't care which it was. I was more relaxed than I'd been in forever. Cleo would be so proud of me.

After lunch, Luca walked me to the co-op and pushed my trolley as I shopped for groceries. He even waited patiently as I scoured the shelves for baking ingredients. Since I had all this time on my hands, it wouldn't hurt to use some of it making something sweet and decadent ... something to sate my suddenly rampant hormones.

When we finally strolled back to Luca's office, Tommaso was already leaning up against his car, a compact vintage Alfa Romeo Giulietta Sprint that didn't suit the big bear-like man at all. At our approach, his perpetual scowl deepened. Like Papa Bear finding his porridge bowl empty.

'I take it your errands didn't go well?' I asked brightly. 'Or is that scowl permanent?'

He huffed out his breath as he pushed away from the car. 'I was waiting. I feel like some part of me will always be waiting for you. Like if I'm old and blue-haired, and I turn a corner in Istanbul, and there you are, I won't be surprised.'

Luca's confusion was comical, but that wasn't the reason I laughed. The laughter bubbled up, a sudden and unfamiliar sensation, and Luca's confusion turned to concern.

'You're quoting *Buffy* at me?' I managed.

Though Tommaso's expression didn't change at all, I caught the flash of amusement in his eyes, gone so quickly I'd have missed it if I blinked. 'Strictly speaking, I'm quoting Willow. I'm glad to see you haven't forgotten.'

Luca looked even more lost, and I smiled reassuringly. 'It's from a TV show we used to watch, about vampires.'

Luca pulled a face, as if he couldn't imagine anything worse than vampires. Tommaso took the shopping bags and placed them in the tiny boot of his car.

'Thank you for showing me around,' I said politely to Luca, burningly aware of Tommaso listening to every word.

'It was my pleasure.' Luca raised my hand to his lips and pressed a kiss to my knuckles in an old-fashioned gesture that made my legs go weak again. I really should channel Buffy and behave more like a kickass vampire slayer than a silly schoolgirl.

Tommaso held the car door open for me, and I had to resist behaving even more childishly and sticking my tongue out at him. Really, could he be any more obvious trying to hurry me away from Luca? What was the man so afraid of?

But Luca took no notice of Tommaso's rudeness. With a

cheerful wave, he headed into his office building, and Tommaso climbed into the car beside me. The interior suddenly felt three times smaller with him in it.

As he eased out into the street and down the hill, taking the winding corners a little too fast for my comfort, I faced him. If there'd been any space in the small car, I would have set my arms on my hips. 'You don't have to act like a dog with a bone. It was just lunch, not a conspiracy to steal away your precious vineyard.'

'It's not the vineyard I'm worried about.' Tommaso's voice was almost a growl. 'Don't put too much faith in Luciano Fioravanti.'

'John must have trusted him since he chose Luca as his executor. Or are you suggesting my father wasn't a particularly good judge of character?'

Tommaso pressed his lips together. 'Luca might have to abide by a code of ethics as a lawyer, but he's still a lawyer, and he's still a Fioravanti.'

What did that mean? I crossed my arms over my chest and turned away to look out the window. Tommaso was just jealous because Luca was everything he wasn't: personable, charming, easy-going.

The roar of the 1960s engine was hardly conducive to conversation, or at least that was my excuse for maintaining radio silence the rest of the way back to the *castello*. That and Tommaso's grim expression.

He parked in the back yard, carried my bags of groceries into the kitchen, then took off along the dusty drive that circled behind the house.

'And goodbye to you too,' I shouted after the little blue car as it shot off towards the wine cellar in a cloud of dust.

With a sigh, I returned to the kitchen and looked around. If I was going to be staying here a while longer, I needed a usable kitchen – a *clean* kitchen, with uncluttered surfaces and clean utensils – so I set to work, starting with the walls, the windows, the floor. It was well into the afternoon before I moved onto the pots and pans hanging from racks on the walls.

I left the ancient wood stove for last. On hands and knees, I scrubbed away years of accumulated grime, unable to suppress a pang for the beautiful, modern cooker in the house I shared with Cleo and Moira, another of our uni friends.

It took a couple of hours of elbow grease to get the stove clean, but beneath the layers of dirt, it was a thing of beauty, its green and ivory porcelain undamaged. It would make some antique dealer very happy.

The hard labour, while not as therapeutic as yoga or meditation, or whatever other faddy hobby Cleo had in mind for me, at least kept my thoughts occupied, and by the time the shadows through the tall windows started lengthening, the kitchen looked almost cheerful.

In the overgrown patch behind the house that had once been Elisa's herb garden, I rescued some terracotta pots, re-planted into them a few of the smaller rosemary, basil and arugula plants which hadn't yet grown woody, and set them on the kitchen window so their aroma could fill the room. I found a bright blue and yellow cloth that might once have been a rug, and once I'd beaten the dust from it, and washed it, it made the perfect tablecloth to brighten up the room.

The kitchen might not pass a food hygiene inspection, but it was liveable. And I'd hardly thought about work all day. Well, okay, two or three times, but considering my Saturdays were usually spent at the office, that was an achievement worth celebrating.

Not that there was anyone to celebrate with. I sat alone at the kitchen table to eat a simple dinner of grilled cheese sandwiches and tea, and wondered where Cleo and Moira were right now. Down at the pub? Out at the movies? On dates?

The *castello* was deathly quiet once again, and I hadn't heard the car return. Tommaso couldn't still be working at the cellar, could he?

I was tempted to knock on the cottage door to see if he was in, just to have company, but then I remembered his forbidding expression. An empty and echoing *castello* was infinitely preferable to re-opening hostilities.

It was only as I lazed in the big, ugly avocado-coloured plastic bath tub, up to my chin in water which had gurgled so slowly out of the pipes I'd managed to make another cup of tea while waiting for the tub to fill, that I allowed myself to remember the Tommy I'd known and played with so long ago.

Like me, he'd been a serious child, shy, and too much on his own, yet he'd smiled a lot too. He'd had a dry sense of humour, and we'd laughed a lot together. Not only had he been a *Buffy* fan, but he'd collected trivia, which probably made him a nerd back in school, just like me. He'd been Xander to my Willow. These days, though, he was more like the brooding vampire Angel. Did that make me Buffy? I didn't feel particularly kickass right now.

Somehow the two pictures, the one of the laughing boy and the other of the grim man, would not fit together. What had happened to replace his laughter with that furrowed brow and brooding expression? And was my old friend still buried beneath all those layers, or was he gone forever?

Chapter 5

Siccome la casa brucia, riscaldiamoci

(Since the house is on fire, let us warm ourselves)

I woke with the soft pink light of dawn filtering into the room, rolled over in bed, and reached for my watch on the nightstand. It was early still, the usual time I'd be waking to check my emails. There weren't any. Damn signal.

Rubbing my eyes, I rose and moved to open the French doors, letting in a warm rush of air. The doors opened onto a narrow, wrought iron balcony. Leaning on the railing, I looked out over the valley, at the cross-hatched patterns of the fields of vines.

The morning air was still cool, and without the sun's heat to draw out the usual heavy fragrance of the garden, the air smelled clean and fresh. The dawn sky was streaked with lilac and pink, and to the south, where the blue hills met the paler blue of the sky, I could just make out the russet and ochre rooftops of a village, catching the early morning light as a thin mist burned away. Across the valley, the nearest hills were furred with the dark green of forest, dipping down into the brighter green of rows and rows of vines in full leaf. The public road that served the farms snaked through this valley and away into the next, striped by the early morning light falling between the double row of dark cypresses marking its path.

Closer, among the rows of vines washed green and gold by the early morning sun, a red tractor chugged, kicking up white dust. I shaded my eyes against the sun. It might have been Tommaso, but I couldn't tell from this distance.

I breathed in another lungful of warm, heavy air, enjoying this strange sensation of being in a foreign place. After a childhood of constant movement and change, I wasn't a frequent traveller, preferring to enjoy my own back yard, but looking out at this view I could almost understand the allure travel held for Geraldine. There was something about being in a new place, in strange surroundings, that gave the illusion of sweeping away one's troubles. I turned my back to the view. The one thing Geraldine hadn't learnt was that you couldn't run away from your troubles. They would still be waiting at home when you returned.

Having learnt from my experience the day before, I pulled on a lightweight silk dressing gown over my sleep shorts and camisole, and headed downstairs for coffee and breakfast. The gown was one of the last gifts Kevin gave me. Jade to match your eyes, he'd said, unexpectedly poetic for a statistician. Then he'd stripped it off me to kiss his way down my body. Barely a week later he'd been kissing down someone's else's body ... I shut down that thought so quickly my head spun.

To keep both my hands and my thoughts occupied, I

catalogued the contents of the restocked pantry. Flour, sugar, eggs, milk, olive oil, and the oranges I'd bought on a whim at the co-op because they looked so fresh and appealing. Out of practice as I was, I hadn't thought to buy yeast or baking powder, but there was baking soda and I'd seen lemons on the tree in the back yard...

It might be rather pleasant to try my hand at baking again. Like riding a bike, right?

Squeezing out a couple of lemons, I made a paste with the baking soda, then mixed in the flour, sugar and oil, grated in the orange zest and juice, and finally beat in the eggs. There was something so satisfying, so deliciously primal, about being elbow deep in a bowl, with dough squelching between my fingers. It was every bit as satisfying as I remembered.

Once I'd beaten the mix into a smooth consistency, I spooned it into a rectangular baking dish, then covered it with a checkered tea towel.

Now what? I had the perfect batter for *schiacciata alla Fiorentina*, the traditional Florentine orange flat-cake Nonna had taught me to bake, but no way to bake it except in the terrifying wood oven. It might be clean and gleaming now, but I didn't have the faintest clue how to even get the wretched thing started.

How hard could it be to start a fire and get it warm enough to bake the cake? What was the worst that could happen – that the oven would either heat too fast or not enough? I might end up with a cake that was either burnt or under-cooked, but so what? Who would know but me that for once in my life I'd created something less than perfect?

There was a wood pile in the back yard. I hefted a few of

the smaller logs into the kitchen and piled them inside the stove's firebox, then set them alight with the gas lighter I found in the pantry. Instead of bursting into the kind of merry blaze Nonna used to make, the wood began to smoke. Perhaps there was too much air?

I hurriedly shut the firebox door, but that only made the smoke billow thicker. It oozed around the edges of the door, slowly filling the room with an eye-burning fog.

So I opened the door again. Oh no. That was even worse. Now, clouds of smoke pumped back into the kitchen. I choked on the smoke, covering my nose and mouth with the crook of my arm. My eyes watered from the burn as I ran for the half-full electric kettle, grabbed it off its heating pad, and returned to the oven. Hastily pouring the water from the kettle over the meagre flames, I stood back, throat burning, eyes burning. The logs sizzled, belching out even more acrid smoke, and the fire inside the stove died.

That didn't stop the smoke, though. It poured down still from the chimney. Oh heavens – had I somehow set the chimney on fire? I had no clue how chimneys worked.

Half-blinded and coughing, I was doubled up, and struggling for breath. The kitchen, vast as it had seemed before, was now so filled with smoke I could barely see a foot around me. Only the brighter patch of the door was visible, so I stumbled towards it, and straight into a wall of human. Hard, male human.

Strong arms gathered me up, sweeping me off my feet, and I was carried out into blinding sunlight. While my eyes still streamed, he sat, cradling me in his lap, one large hand rubbing soothing circles on my back while with the other he wiped away the stinging tears from my eyes.

'There's no point burning the house down,' Tommaso said. 'It's way under-insured.'

His voice was hard and unsympathetic, completely at odds with the gentle hand stroking circles on my back.

'I wasn't trying to burn the house down!' The protest was weak, my voice scratchy and still choked from the smoke.

Now that my eyes had stopped streaming, I could see we sat on the low stone wall edging Nonna's herb garden, and he'd used the hem of his T-shirt to mop my eyes. Where the shirt lifted, tanned hard muscle was visible. A six-pack. An honest-to-goodness six-pack. I'd never been within groping distance of one of those before.

I swallowed. The arms that had held me and carried me were well muscled too, and the chest I leaned against...

I should get out of his lap. I really should.

Yet somehow my body refused to obey.

'I wanted to bake,' I said weakly, ending on a hiccoughing cough.

'The stove hasn't been used in years. It needs a good cleaning.' His face wasn't any more sympathetic than before, but his voice was a little gentler.

'I cleaned it out yesterday.'

'The chimney too?'

That was a real thing?

'If there's a build-up of creosote inside the chimney, you could have started a serious chimney fire. What wood did you use?'

I glanced towards the sheltered wood pile stacked up against the yard wall.

'That figures! That's the wood I'm seasoning for winter. It's still very green, which means it creates more smoke than fire. And if the flue is blocked, you'd just make it worse.'

And I was just as green. Mortification swept through me, swift and furious. I hated being at a disadvantage, never let anyone suspect I was anything less than competent and in control, and yet I'd given Tommaso ringside seats to my ignorance.

That made twice in less than a week. First, the Delta Corporation, and now this. My eyes burned, and it wasn't just the after effects of the smoke, but anger at myself for failing. I never failed at anything I set my mind to. I didn't know how to cope with failure.

Tommaso pushed back the hair falling loose from the chignon I'd tied it up into. 'You're welcome to use my oven until we can check out the chimney.'

At the sound of an engine, we both turned to look as a familiar silver sports car appeared around the corner of the house and pulled up in the yard. Luca Fioravanti.

And though I was a little more dressed than yesterday, I most certainly wasn't dressed for visitors. If I hadn't been aware before of how the silk gown only reached mid-thigh, or the proximity of Tommaso's body, I certainly was now. A furious blush burned my face and I wriggled to get out of his lap. But he held me fast.

This was turning into one of those scenes in a really bad farce.

'Making house calls on a Sunday?' Tommaso called out as Luca stepped from the car.

With an extra hard shove at his chest, I scrambled out of his lap, burningly aware that not only was I scantily clad and dishevelled, but I no doubt also reeked of smoke. While Luca looked impeccably, impossibly perfect. Not a hair mussed, shoes polished, trousers crisply pressed, as if he had indeed just stepped from the pages of *GQ*. Exactly the kind of man I would choose if ever I were in the market for one.

He held a bouquet of pink roses. My stomach did a strange somersault thing.

'I brought the partnership agreement for you to sign.' Luca smiled his usual smooth, charming grin. 'I hope I'm not interrupting anything?'

My blush deepened. 'No, of course not.' Sure, I always entertained sexy men at home on a Sunday morning in my pyjamas. Not. 'Would you like to come inside?'

Luca looked at Tommaso, and though his polite expression held steady, it no longer seemed amused or friendly. 'I think perhaps not. I have a pen, and you can sign right here.'

He whipped out a pen from his lightweight summer jacket and held it out to Tommaso. It almost seemed like a challenge. We signed the agreement on the hood of the car, first Tommaso then me, then Luca turned his smile up a notch for me. 'I also came to invite you to lunch.'

This was no business invitation. It was definitely a date.

No holiday romance, no holiday romance.

But as much as I chanted the mantra, my body was shouting 'yes, please!'

As I opened my mouth to accept, Tommaso spoke for me.

'That's very kind of you, but we already have plans today. We're going to lunch with the Rossis.'

I opened my mouth again, this time to protest, but Tommaso continued without pause. 'Alberto Rossi was one of your father's oldest friends. He'd be offended if you turned down his invitation.'

I pressed my lips tight, to stop myself from doing yet another fish impression, shot Tommaso a glance that threatened all sorts of retribution, then turned to Luca with a smile. 'Thank you for the invitation. Another day, perhaps?'

'*Sì, bella*. Another day.' He reached for my hand and gave it a gentle squeeze. I half-hoped he'd do that courtly knuckle kiss thing again. Though he didn't need to for me to shiver at his touch. His dimpling smile flashed as he let go of my hand. 'I will call you next time.'

He handed me the flowers and I cradled them to my chest, breathing in their sweet fragrance.

Luca was already backing out of the yard when my brain finally kicked in, and I remembered he couldn't call because my mobile didn't get signal here. Hand on my hip, I rounded on Tommaso. 'What is it with you? I'm not a kid, and I don't need you to play big brother watching over me.'

He merely shrugged. 'Aren't you pleased I came to tell you about the lunch invitation? If it weren't for that, I wouldn't have been here to rescue you.'

'I don't need rescuing. I am perfectly capable of rescuing myself.' The fact that he had indeed rescued me only made me more irritable. I was no damsel in distress, and I didn't ever plan to be. That was Geraldine's game.

I stomped back into the house, with Tommaso's amused voice trailing after. 'It was my pleasure!'

There were vases in the pantry. I filled a crystal vase at the tap and set the roses into it. They were as perfect as Luca himself; pale pink, duskier at the tips of the petals, and so breathtakingly sweet.

The kitchen was less smoky now, reassuring me that the fire was indeed out, and I hadn't set the house alight after all. Though burning the place to the ground might not be a bad place to start, even if it was under-insured.

I threw open all the windows, and the smoke began to dissipate. No harm done, except to my bruised ego.

But I was going to need Tommaso's oven. If we were invited to lunch, I didn't plan to go empty-handed. And I needed more clothes on. Especially if I was having lunch with some old friend of John's rather than a sexy lawyer who was the first man to show an interest in me in way too long.

No holiday romance, I reminded myself. But I was smiling.

Chapter 6

Una cena senza vino è come un giorno senza sole

(A meal without wine is a day without sunshine)

Our destination wasn't a house, as I'd expected, but a *trattoria* up on a hill, reached along a winding dirt road edged by trees. As Tommaso parked in the lot behind the restaurant, I cast a mortified glance down at the plastic container in my lap, containing the *schiacciata* cake I'd finally managed to bake in his far more modern oven. 'I thought we were having lunch at their home?'

'We are. This is the Rossi family farm. The land all the way down to the river has been in the family for over four hundred years. Alberto's father still owns the land, but these days it's Alberto who runs the farm, together with his sons. His daughter, Beatrice, runs the *trattoria*. It's sort of an extension of the farmhouse.'

I had to squint to see the river, a distant gleam across the wide valley. Four hundred years? The eight years I'd lived in Wanstead were the longest I'd ever stayed in one postcode.

Tommaso guided me towards the *trattoria*'s entrance, his hand hovering in the curve of my back, not touching, but close enough to feel the heat of his proximity through the thin fabric of my lightweight crepe blouse.

We rounded the low redbrick building onto a terrace. The restaurant was rustic, with simple pine tables and benches, plain tablecloths, a bougainvillea-covered trellis over the terrace, and an amazing view. My breath caught.

The *trattoria* overlooked rolling fields, broken by patches of dark green woodland. In the sloping field beneath the terrace, sheep grazed, their soft bleating drifting up on the breeze and mingling with the sounds of human voices closer by.

From here, the river cut a silver swathe across the valley, marking the border between the fields of tawny wheat dotted with red poppies, and the wilder meadows beyond. Across the valley, nestled in a fold of hill, I could see the earthen sand-coloured walls of an abbey, its bell tower standing proud over the low-sloping russet roofs.

A tall, round man with dark hair greying at his temples hurried to greet us, a welcoming smile on his weather-beaten face. 'John's daughter!' he exclaimed, wrapping me in an embrace. 'It is such a pleasure to meet you. I have heard so much of you!'

Unused to being hugged by complete strangers, I had to force myself to relax and not flinch away.

'Sarah, this is Alberto Rossi.' Tommaso made the introductions, his habitually grim expression warming as he clapped Alberto on the back.

'It's a pleasure to meet you too.' My voice sounded as formal as if I were meeting a new client, but I couldn't help myself. Where I came from, this kind of exuberance was reserved for people who'd known each other for years.

Awkwardly, I handed Alberto the plastic cake container. 'I brought dessert.'

He passed it to someone else, who passed it to someone else, so he could take both my hands in his large, rough ones. 'I am so sorry for your loss.'

I heard that over and over again as I was introduced to Alberto's wife, his parents, his sons, his daughter Beatrice, and then an extended family of brothers and sisters and cousins. I tried to look like a grief-stricken daughter should, but I wasn't really sure what that felt like.

'Is this a party?' I whispered to Tommaso, as we squeezed in on one of the long benches lining the main table. The *schiacciata* I'd made was large, but hardly enough to feed this crowd.

Tommaso's chuckle was low and almost inaudible. 'No, just a regular Rossi Sunday family lunch.'

Beatrice set out platters of antipasti and thick slices of bread – mass-produced and store-bought bread, I suspected – and one of Alberto's sons poured the wine, a Brunello from one of the neighbouring vineyards.

The chatter and noise around the big table was overwhelming, and the Italian so quick I had no hope of keeping up. But in true Italian style, they all spoke with their bodies, keeping me hugely entertained trying to discern the topics of conversation from the body language.

I also didn't need to understand the words to see that this was a warm and affectionate family, despite the teasing between the cousins. They were a good-looking family too. Perhaps it was in the genes. Or the local water. I should bottle some and take it home with me in case I ever did decide to start dating again.

Tommaso moved away to sit beside Daniele, Alberto's younger son. From the gestures that accompanied the animated conversation, I decided they were discussing wine.

I wasn't alone for long. Beatrice slipped onto the bench beside me. She was a pretty woman, perhaps only just thirty, with warm, smiling eyes and thick, dark hair that she wore tied back in a long and intricate braid. Though she'd just stepped from the kitchen, she looked fresh as a daisy, and effortlessly classy in her simple but stylish linen dress.

My insecurities had faded along with my twenties, but beside Beatrice's bold colouring and curves, I couldn't help but feel plain. My pale skin, with its tendency to freckle, and fine, straight hair, weren't exactly head-turners. The one thing I had going for me was the colour of my hair, a rich chestnut that was still completely natural.

Beatrice dipped a wedge of the bread into a bowl of herb-scented olive oil. 'Are the men still talking wine? Daniele wants so badly for us to plant grapes so he can make his own.'

'Why doesn't he?' I dipped a slice of the bread too, though with less enthusiasm. The ciabatta's crust was too thin, and the ratio of air holes to bread not on the favourable side. I'd been looking forward to eating the real deal here in Tuscany, but honestly I'd baked better ciabatta bread. Once upon a time, at least two promotions back, baking had been my Sunday morning ritual. Other people slept in, or went to church, or played golf. I baked.

'Like most farms in Tuscany, this is a family farm,' Beatrice explained. 'The traditions are passed down from generation to generation, and our family have always farmed wheat and dairy. Not as glamorous as wine, sadly.'

'Not as glamorous, but definitely more essential.'

Beatrice giggled. 'Sh! Don't let Tommaso hear you say that!' A shout of laughter rang out from the far end of the table. At my unintentional flinch, Beatrice pulled a wry face. 'We're a noisy lot, but you get used to it after a while.'

'I live in London. I'm used to crowds.' Or I should be. But I didn't like crowds. It was why I loved Wanstead so much, with its quiet, village-y feel. And it was part of the reason I worked such long hours. I caught the tube to work before the morning rush hour and left the office long after the evening rush hour.

'You have a big family?' Beatrice asked.

'No. It was always just me and my mother.' Belatedly, I realised I'd had a father too, but Beatrice didn't appear to notice my blunder.

She shook her head as she looked down the long table crowded with people. 'I envy you. Here, there is always someone around, always someone getting up in your business.' She frowned. 'I think that is the right way to say it?'

I laughed. 'Yes, that's the right way to say it. But it must be wonderful to have so many people care about you.'

'You wouldn't say that if you had two brothers.' She threw

her hands up in the air. 'Italian brothers! Even if they are younger than me, they treat me like a child.' Beatrice cast a dark glance at Daniele then leaned closer, dropping her voice. 'They think if a woman isn't married and doesn't yet have children of her own, they can tell her what to do. But if I try to find myself a man, they think no one is good enough. It drives me *pazzo!* You have it easier, I think?'

I cast a glance across the table towards Tommaso. At the ripe old age of thirty-five I was only just discovering what it was like to have a big brother hovering protectively. Beatrice had all my sympathy. I leaned closer too. 'I'll let you in on a secret: it's even more difficult to find a man in London, because there aren't any decent, single, straight men left. I've seen more attractive men in the two days I've been here than in the entire last year in London.'

My thoughts flashed to Luca, and heat spread through me. Fortunately, Beatrice didn't seem to find it odd that I had a sudden need to fan myself.

'I spent a few years in London when I was in my early twenties.' Beatrice looked down at the bread she was picking apart with her fingers. 'I remember some very attractive men.' Her blush was unmistakable. Interesting. But before I could probe, she asked, 'your mother – she never re-married?'

I filled my mouth with the pimento-stuffed olives from the bowl between us, so I wouldn't have to answer. Didn't they know that Geraldine and John had never married? How did I explain to someone so clearly rooted in her big, solid family and traditional heritage, that I was born out of wedlock? Or that my mother had spent her entire adult life flitting from man to man almost as frequently as she'd flitted from place to place? Somehow, I didn't think that would go down well in the present company.

Thank heavens Beatrice was called back to the kitchen, saving me from answering. Instead, a cousin slid into her place. But my relief was short-lived. The cousin subjected me to another round of grilling about my mother, my job, my life in London – and my single status.

The antipasti was followed by a hearty bean and vegetable soup, the *ribollita,* and then a dish of *pappardelle* pasta, a broad, flat pasta, in a simple but flavourful sauce of tomato and garlic. With each course, and in the long spaces between, the seating arrangements shifted with the fluidity of flowing water. Only I kept my place through this game of musical chairs, as a succession of cousins and aunts and uncles moved to sit beside me and engage me in conversation, in their careful, heavily-accented English.

Eventually, my initial discomfort at the repeated questions faded as I realised there was no judgement in the questions, simply an interest in getting to know me, and my mother, who they all seemed to regard as John's estranged wife, rather than the young tourist he knocked up. Had John been the one to spread that illusion, or was it just an assumption by a family that couldn't conceive of anything else?

The only person who didn't try to talk to me was Tommaso. He as good as ignored me as he moved about the table, chatting to different members of the family in voluble Italian. He seemed very much at home with the family, more 'Italian' than I ever remembered him being, though of course he'd spoken the language fluently as a child. He seemed lighter and more relaxed too. Maybe it was just me who brought out the worst in him?

There was more wine with each course. 'I don't suppose there's ever an Italian meal without wine?' I joked with Daniele, as he moved to top up my glass once more.

He placed a friendly hand on my shoulder as he leaned over to reach my glass. 'Of course not! We have a saying here: *una cena senza vino* è *come un giorno senza sole.* A meal without wine is like a day without sunshine. And we don't get too many days without sunshine.'

As abstemious as I tried to be, sipping carefully, the wine had its effect. A relaxed laziness flowed through my veins, dulling the edges of my awkwardness. The family might be loud and intimidating, but they were also friendly and welcoming. There'd been a time long ago I'd dreamed of being part of a big family like this, of having brothers and sisters, and parents close by who would get 'all up in my business'. But that was a long time ago, and I'd outgrown it.

We lingered over each course, an unhurried meal accompanied by a steady flow of wine and lively banter, taking time to savour the food. In the periphery, I was aware of other diners coming and going on the terrace, and the wait staff moving to attend to them. Mostly tourists travelling from vineyard to vineyard, I guessed, but also a few locals who stopped by to greet Alberto or stay for a glass of wine before moving on.

The pièce-de-résistance of the meal was cutlets of fried wild hare, seasoned with fennel.

'I can't possibly eat any more!' I protested, as Alberto's wife Franca ladled yet more food onto my plate, but Franca only shook her head and tutted. 'If you don't eat enough, we are very poor hosts.'

By the time the meal was done, Tommaso had made his way back to the seat beside me, though he immediately – and rudely – launched into a conversation in Italian with Alberto who sat on his other side.

With the meal served, Beatrice also returned, sliding into the empty space to my left, forcing me to edge up against Tommaso on my right. Our thighs pressed against each other, but he seemed not to notice, and I didn't want to call attention to my discomfort by moving away. So instead I had to contend with a very unexpected and searing awareness shooting through me. *It's just the summer heat, and the unaccustomed crowd. Nothing more.*

'That was a wonderful meal,' I thanked Beatrice. 'I've never tasted such amazing flavours. I'd love to know your secret.'

'The trick is to use only fresh, local ingredients. I never shop at the supermarket, and we don't use processed foods. If I can't get it fresh from our own farm, or from the local markets, then I don't cook with it.'

'I remember a market Nonna used to take us to…'

'That would be the market in Montalcino. Market day is Friday, so you just missed it, but there's also a market in Torrenieri on Tuesdays.' Beatrice waved her arm, proudly taking in the land stretched around them. 'Here, we make our own olive oil, my mother makes all the preserves, and we make cheeses with milk from our own goats and cows. We even make our own honey. If you ever need milk or butter or cream or eggs, you come to us, okay?'

'Thank you. It would be wonderful to bake with farm-fresh ingredients.'

'Of course, I remember now – your father told us you were a baker.'

Odd that he'd remembered that. I shook my head. 'Not really. I baked for fun, but that was ages ago.' When last had I done anything for fun? But work was fun, right? 'There's something so satisfying about making desserts and pastries, the joy they bring to people. It's like Christmas every day.'

Beatrice laughed. 'While I have grown up on a wheat farm, and this ciabatta is the only kind of bread I can make. And I know it's not even that good.'

'As long as you serve food like this, you hardly need anything else.'

When Beatrice turned to answer a comment from her grandfather, who sat on her other side, I looked down the long table, at the smiles, the laughter, the easy comfort the family shared with one another. The feeling it gave me, all warm and fuzzy, was an alien sensation. I'd never experienced anything like it before, even visiting Cleo's family. It was rather nice.

Behind me, Tommaso and Alberto were engrossed in an increasingly heated discussion. I was about to give up even trying to understand the conversation, when my attention was snagged by the name Fioravanti.

My nice warm bubble burst. Could Tommaso have the audacity to sit right beside me and discuss our legal issues with someone else, in a language I was so rusty in that I couldn't follow?

'Are you talking about Luca?' I asked, leaning forward to butt into their conversation.

Tommaso scowled at the intrusion, but Alberto shook his head. 'His father. His is the farm next to yours. He has released a new blend.'

All this heated conversation was about a wine? I turned away, but the warm-and-fuzzies had been replaced by a niggling feeling. Luca hadn't mentioned we were neighbours. I frowned. Perhaps it wasn't important to him.

The sun began to dip across the western hills when wooden boards of cheeses and more of the plain, store-bought sliced bread were carried out, and Franca brought out my orange-flavoured *schiacciata* cake. I'd decorated the cake with a thin spread of lemon curd and a dusting of icing sugar, and it glistened temptingly. Slices were handed around on plain white plates, with generous dollops of fresh farm cream. There was only just enough for everyone to have a small piece, and for a moment the noise levels around the table dipped as they all tucked in. Just like I'd told Beatrice: it was that Christmas feeling.

'Aah,' Alberto sighed, his voice a satisfied rumble. He turned to Tommaso. 'This is just like the cake your Nonna used to bake.'

'She's the one who taught me to make it,' I said.

Tommaso shifted to look at me, as if he'd forgotten I was there, and the pressure of his leg suddenly disappeared. Not that the absence of his touch brought any relief, because now

I found myself pinned by his grey, inscrutable gaze. Feeling oddly flustered, I was grateful when Beatrice pushed her empty plate aside and touched my arm to catch my attention. 'This is so good! How did you get the texture so light and moist at the same time? I tried making this cake once, and it didn't rise. It was solid as cement.'

I smiled. 'After the meal you've just served, that's the highest compliment I could receive.'

'Food yes, pastries no.' Beatrice shrugged. 'Other than bread, baking isn't a big thing in Tuscany. Here, cheese and fruit are all we need for dessert, but the tourists, they want more. We have reviews on TripAdvisor complaining about our lack of desserts.' She rolled her eyes. 'But my cousin Matteo is the cook, and he's so good at everything else I could never replace him – even for a cook who can make pastries.'

'You could hire a pastry chef.'

'That would mean a full-time salary I can't afford.'

'And there isn't someone in the neighbourhood who bakes that you could buy from? Surely that would still count as being locally sourced?'

Beatrice's eyes glittered. 'There is now! Would you consider it?'

'Me?' Though my first impulse was to say no, I paused. There'd been a time when baking had been a joy, almost a therapy, but it would be a challenge. I hadn't really baked in so long. My mouth kicked up at the corners. I did love a challenge.

'Please?' Beatrice begged, her eyes big and round and pleading. 'Everyone I know who can bake even halfway decently already has their own commitments. I would really appreciate it!'

My heart picked up its pace, not in that anxious way that had grown so familiar I hardly noticed it anymore, but with a thrill of excitement. The thrill I used to feel when I delivered on a really big deal at work. 'What sort of quantities would you need, and what type of desserts?'

Beatrice shrugged. 'Whatever you want, and however much you can provide. For us, anything will be better than nothing, and our menu changes every day, depending on what is in season, so you can make whatever you like.'

I really shouldn't say yes. I was supposed to be resting, and Cleo would have a fit if she found out I'd taken a job, even a job baking. But what Cleo didn't know, wouldn't hurt her... 'Okay, but on three conditions.'

Beatrice waited for me to continue, her dark eyes alight.

'First, I want to use my own kitchen.' That way I could still oversee house renovations and keep up a semblance of being on holiday.

Beatrice nodded.

'Second, I don't have a car, so you'll need to send someone to collect from me each day.'

She nodded again.

'And third, it'll only be for the summer. I have a job in London I must get back to at the end of September.'

'You have a deal!'

We shook hands on it, and I laughed, Beatrice's delight infusing me with sudden warmth. As we lingered over the cheese board and frothy cups of cappuccino, we chatted about breads and cakes and quantities, and I'd never been happier – and it wasn't entirely the effect of the mellowing wine.

This enforced holiday no longer seemed as bleak and terrifying as it had a couple of days ago. Now I wouldn't have to sit idly and count down the days of my exile. All I needed was a stove that didn't have it in for me.

Chapter 7

L'uomo giusto arriva al momento giusto

(The right man comes at the right time)

The next morning I was in the pantry, purging the shelves of expired tinned foods, spider webs and grime, when I heard the familiar throaty roar of Tommaso's vintage car pull up in the yard behind the house, then a few minutes later a quick knock at the open back door.

'You can come in,' I called. 'I'm in the pantry, but I'm unarmed.'

He was dressed for work, in jeans and a plain grey T-shirt, with heavy work boots on his feet. He loomed so large in the low entryway that he blocked out most of the light. 'If you're going to be baking for the *trattoria*, we should get that chimney cleaned.'

'I was kind of hoping I could carry on using your oven.'

His mouth ticked up at the corner. 'Coward! You used to be more kickass than that. But seriously, bread baked in a wood oven tastes better than that baked in an electric one.'

He was right, much as it galled me to admit it. I followed

him back into the kitchen and eyed the old stove with trepidation. My initial wariness of it had morphed into full-on distrust since what I referred to as The Smoke Incident. 'What do you suggest I do?'

'I don't suggest *you* do anything. I suggest *we* check the chimney first.'

How chivalrous that he was offering to help, but it still didn't answer my question.

Tommaso held out his mobile phone. 'Old-fashioned trick passed down through the generations.' He unhooked a wooden pizza paddle from the wall beside the stove and laid his mobile face-up on it. Then he slid open the hatch in the side of the stove. I bent forward, curious, as he switched on the phone's camera, set it on video mode, and slid the board into the hatch. When he slid the phone back out, I leaned even closer, my head almost touching his, to watch in fascination as he replayed the shaky video. On the screen, a full moon shaped ball of light was visible at the end of the flue.

'No nests or any other obstructions blocking the flue, so it's probably just old residue lining the chimney walls that needs to be cleaned out.' He shut the hatch, then looked up, and my breath stuck in my throat. Our eyes were nearly level, our faces so close that if either one of us moved an inch, our mouths would meet ... I jumped back.

'Old family trick, huh? Where did you really learn to do that?'

'From television.'

When my eyebrows arched in incredulity, he laughed. 'Yes, I still have a dark side.'

I clearly watched the wrong kinds of TV shows. *The Great*

British Bake-off hadn't taught me how to light a fire or check a chimney for obstructions.

'I suppose that means I'll need to get a chimney sweep in.' Was there even such a thing these days? Probably just an expensive contractor who'd charge me the equivalent of a limb for ten minutes' work.

'Or we can do it ourselves,' Tommaso offered. 'If you don't mind getting a little dirty?'

He'd already seen me in my pyjamas, choking on smoke. How much worse could a bit of dirt be? 'I don't mind.'

'Lay a few dust cloths around the stove. I'm going up on the roof.'

Dust cloths were the one thing there was no shortage of in the house, with the exception of spider webs, so I hurried off to collect an armful. When I returned to the kitchen, the reverberation of Tommaso's footsteps sounded extra-loud on the tiled roof above. I laid the cloths over the floor, table and counters, then hurried outside, anxious to check on his safety. Standing far back in the yard so I could see up on the roof, I shielded my eyes against the morning light to watch as Tommaso bent over the square, redbrick chimney. He had already removed the chimney cap and was now screwing a square-shaped chimney brush onto the end of what looked like a very long, stiff hose. Had he learned to clean chimneys from television too?

He twisted the brush down the chimney, pumping hard to extend the brush all the way down the chimney. As he brought the brush back up, he coughed on the cloud of sooty black dust that billowed up.

Just as well it was him up on that roof and not me. I'd

already swallowed enough smoke and ash for one week.

Partially silhouetted against the rising sun, his body was clearly outlined. Tommaso might be built bigger than Luca, but there was no spare fat on him. He was all lean muscle and sinewy strength. As he worked the long brush up and down the chimney, his arm muscles bulged beneath the taut fabric of his shirt. I'd always liked a man with strong arms. I swallowed a very inappropriate sigh and looked away.

When he'd removed the brush and its hose attachments, and replaced the chimney cap, I moved to the base of the ladder leaning up against the wall to hold it steady. Tommaso came down the ladder rung by rung, his boots coming first into my line of view, then his denim-clad calves and thighs. The soft denim was worn into the shape of his body, hugging the lean thighs and firm backside that drew level with my gaze.

I coughed and averted my gaze. This was Tommy, the boy I'd played with as a kid. I didn't want to think of him in any other way. Especially in any way that would make me go weak-kneed or lose my head.

Until the *castello* sold, or he bought me out, we were rivals for this property. Luca's contract might call us partners, but we still had to negotiate the terms for divvying up my father's inheritance between us. I couldn't afford to forget that or go soft on him – which was most likely the only reason he was being so helpful, anyway. Either that or to make sure I wasn't in his space any more than necessary. I wasn't sure which of those reasons was most offensive.

'Thank you,' I said gruffly when he'd jumped from the bottom rung to stand back on solid ground.

'Shall we get a fire going, and see if it's working now? I brought some well-seasoned wood.'

As much as I wanted to say 'thanks, I can take it from here', and as much as I didn't want to owe him any more than I already did, I couldn't refuse the offer. Reluctantly, I led him back into the kitchen.

The dust cloths had done their job, though there wasn't as much soot in the kitchen as I'd expected. The oven was thankfully well-insulated and would need little more than a wipe down, but the firebox inside needed a good brush out. I used the brushes from the big copper pot beside the oven to clean out the soot, while Tommaso carried in armfuls of piney-smelling wood from his car.

He showed me how to build and start the fire, using kindling and air for an effective blaze, rather than simply piling in the wood. Then, once he was satisfied, he stood back, wiping his hands on the back of his jeans. 'No smoke! That should sort you out now.'

The scent of the burning wood smoke definitely added a homelier feel to the kitchen. A way homelier scent than clouds of acrid smoke.

'Thank you,' I said again, meaning it, but clearly my tone didn't carry as much gratitude as I intended, because Tommaso frowned.

'Are you always this grumpy about accepting help?'

Pots and kettles. I turned away to collect the armful of dust cloths. 'Just out of practice. I don't usually need anyone's help.' And two times in as many days was about as much as I could handle.

Tommaso shrugged, his expression back to its usual surly look. 'Well, that's okay then, because I didn't do it for you. I did it for Beatrice. True Tuscan breads and desserts should be baked in a wood oven for authentic flavour.'

For Beatrice. Of course. The sudden spike of jealousy was completely irrational. I knew that, but it didn't stop me from feeling it. I dumped the dust cloths beside the big sink and washed my hands. 'I hope I haven't kept you from your work for too long.'

And why on earth was he still hanging around, when his expression so clearly showed he didn't want to be here? Instead, he hovered just a few feet away, his presence so dominating he might just as well have been standing right beside me. I dried my hands on a tea towel and turned back to him, eyebrow arched enquiringly.

He didn't look at me as he ran a hand through his thick hair. 'You should come up to the cellar. Take a look at the improvements we've made. Your father cared very deeply about the winery.'

If my back hadn't already been up, now it was. I didn't want to see the winery, and I didn't need to be reminded that my father loved the winery more than he'd loved anything else. And if Tommaso thought for even one moment that mentioning the winery or John was going to make me soft and sentimental so I'd cut him a good deal, then he clearly didn't know me. I was practical and efficient, and never let sentiment get in the way of the numbers. 'Thanks for the invitation, but I have a busy day planned.'

'Suit yourself.' He slammed the kitchen door as he left, and the shutter outside the kitchen window fell to the ground with a heavy clunk.

I rolled my eyes heavenwards. Now what had gotten into him?

I didn't watch as he strode back to his car. I had bread to make, and bread wasn't complicated like people. Bread didn't have a hidden agenda, didn't have an attitude, and didn't get grumpy just because a woman didn't fall for emotional manipulation.

'So what exciting adventures did you get up to today? I could do with some light entertainment,' Cleo asked. There'd been a tube strike, it had taken her hours to get home, and she sounded exasperated.

I had to rack my brain for something to say. '*I checked out my old playmate's butt, and he's actually kind of hot*' didn't sound appropriate, much though it would cheer Cleo up.

'Tommaso cleaned out the chimney, and I unblocked a bathroom drain. It was riveting stuff. Want to hear about it?'

'God no! Not until I've had at least two glasses of wine. Have you heard from that sexy lawyer of yours?'

'Nothing. Not even a text.' Though to be fair, since the *castello* didn't have signal maybe he had tried. I hoped. And then hated myself for hoping. 'What's been happening at the office?'

'This and that.'

Uh-oh. Cleo was hedging. 'That bad?'

'I met the guy from the Delta Corporation today. The one I'll be working with for the next few months.'

'Please don't tell me he's twelve and still has acne.'

'Worse.'

'Balding, paunchy and single, and already asked you out on a date?'

'Nope. He has a full head of hair.'

'So married or gay then. Oh well, that's just typical.'

'No...' Cleo was definitely hedging now.

'So...?' I prompted.

'He's the most arrogant, annoying...' She sucked in a breath, as if she'd said too much.

I bit my lip. 'I am so, so sorry. It's my fault you're in this position and having to work with the man.'

'Bullshit. It's not your fault he's an arse.'

'What did he do? Try to feel you up in the break room?'

'Worse. He asked me to make his coffee. As if I'm some twenty-year-old Girl Friday!'

'And did you?'

'Well, yes, but that's beside the point. Even if I survive the week working with this man, I think I might need to join you on "garden leave".'

'Great idea. You can help unblock the drains.'

'On second thoughts, maybe I'll hang in here a little longer. But if I get arrested for murdering him, would you put up bail for me?'

'Of course. And I promise I'll find you a very sexy lawyer.'

At last Cleo laughed. Job done.

Chapter 8

Chi ha la sua casa, poco gli manca

(He who owns his own house, lacks for nothing)

I was up early the next morning, though not as early as Tommaso. His car was already gone from the yard when I wandered into the kitchen and switched on the kettle for tea.

The driver who'd collected the bread loaves and desserts yesterday had brought a box of goodies from Beatrice, including a glass bottle of milk with a layer of cream floating on top. I surveyed the ingredients I'd spread across the kitchen table, feeling like a contestant in a cooking show. A jar of raspberry jam with the Rossi farm logo, which would take care of the 'locally sourced' requirement, almonds, creamed cheese, and precious, blessed yeast...

I heaved out a breath. Baking in a big old kitchen a half hour drive from the nearest store required a whole lot more creativity than baking in my high-tech kitchen in Wanstead with a Tesco's in walking distance.

What could I make with what I had?

Et voilà! Okay, wrong language, but right sentiment – I would make mini raspberry bakewell tarts, with a sweetened cream cheese filling. *Mary Berry, eat your heart out!*

With a smile worthy of any on-air contestant about to annihilate the competition, I washed my hands, and set about creating the tart dough, sifting flour, sugar and salt together, digging my fingers in to rub in the butter until the mix formed a pastry of fine crumbs. Then I added eggs and milk to create a firm but soft dough, careful to ensure the dough became neither too warm nor too sticky. Wrapping the dough in cling film, I set it aside in the pantry to chill, and took a fresh cup of tea and a plate of toast out to the terrace.

The sun had risen to its zenith, filling the valley with warm, bright light. The trellis that covered the paved terrace sagged beneath the weight of a massive wisteria, its vivid purple blossoms turning towards the sun. It was the largest wisteria I'd ever seen, easily triple the size it had been when I was last here.

I sat on the wooden bench, which was set at the optimum angle to take in the view, and propped my feet up on the sun-warmed balustrade, breathing in the fresh air. A tractor hummed in the distance, birds sang, and cicadas buzzed loudly in the still, heavy air.

For the first time since I'd woken, I thought of the office, wondering how Cleo was coping with The Arse. It was probably raining in London. I lifted my face to the sun. A little sunshine could fix almost anything. Maybe Cleo *should* come out for a few days before the summer was over.

I breathed in deeply, tasted the rosemary, lavender, and dark earth.

How long had it been since I'd done nothing but sit idly in a patch of sun? When last had a day stretched out before me, with no To Do list, a day where I didn't have to be responsible to anyone? Not since I was a teen, for sure. Maybe I really did need this holiday.

My eyes fluttered closed, and I let out a long sigh. The sun's glare battered against my eyelids.

The distant tractor sound choked and cut off, and I frowned at the rude interruption of my reverie, reminding me this wasn't a holiday, and that I was still here, in a decrepit *castello* in need of some serious TLC. But at least I had dough rising in the kitchen. As long as there is dough, there is hope, Nonna used to say.

Back in the warm kitchen, the dough had risen faster than it would have in the cooler English climate. I rolled it out, lined Nonna's sturdy muffin pan with it, then added baking paper and baking beans, before setting the pan in the oven to bake.

While the pastry cases baked, I whisked up the creamed cheese, adding butter and caster sugar, and beat the mix until it was light and fluffy. Then I added yet more eggs (I'd need to buy a whole lot more of those soon), ground the almonds and folded them into the mix, and finally added a touch of lemon zest – also locally sourced, right off the lemon tree in the back yard. I'd never baked with ingredients I'd actually picked myself before.

The kitchen filled with the warm, satisfying aroma of baking pastry, and I hummed as I worked. When the pastry cases were done, I removed the beans and paper from the tart pans, spread a thick layer of raspberry jam over the pastry crusts, spooned in the sweet filling, then slid the tarts back into the oven.

I was raiding the overflowing patch in the herb garden for fresh strawberries to use as garnish, when a car turned into the *castello*'s long drive. I shielded my eyes against the sun, and my heart did a silly little skip as I recognised the silver sports car.

Luca wasn't alone, though. He'd brought the real estate agent to value the house.

The realtor was a woman – a curvy woman with lustrous dark hair swept up in a loose tumble of curls, and wearing a figure-hugging dress in fire engine red, and heels I wouldn't be able to walk in.

Beside the realtor, with floury hands stained pink with sticky strawberry juice, and dressed in the ridiculous floral apron I'd found in an upstairs closet, I felt woefully plain.

The estate agent wandered from room to room, tut-tutting, and making copious notes on her clipboard. I trailed after them but, since they spoke mostly in Italian, I was only able to understand every other word. And Luca was no fun today. He was all business – no sidelong smiles, no casual touches, no flirting. I was pleased when the mobile in my apron pocket buzzed to warn me the tarts were done, giving me an excuse to escape back to the kitchen.

Alone, I admitted my disappointment. *What the hell are you thinking? No holiday romances, remember? This is for the best.*

Except it didn't feel like it was for the best. This was why I hated dating. That up and down, 'Does he like me? Doesn't he like me?' nonsense. My friends might have thought Kevin was dull, but at least I'd never had any doubt about his interest in me. Right up until I realised I wasn't the *only* one he'd been interested in.

Half an hour later, when the tarts were cooling on the kitchen table, Luca and the statuesque estate agent traipsed back into the kitchen. She handed me a list that was several pages long. 'You fix these, then we take pictures and put the house on our website. But the way the *castello* is now, *no di certo*! No chance! There are already too many rundown farmhouses on the market.'

I glanced at the list, and my mouth fell open. Some seemed easy enough: fix the front door, re-paint the interiors, clear the clutter, but the rest...! Plumbing, wiring, plastering, the access road to be re-tarred – I might as well re-build the *castello* from the ground up to make it sellable. Maybe a fire would have been a blessing. I would certainly need a contractor to tick off at least half the items on this list.

I walked them out to the car, the list still clutched in my floury, sticky hand. For one brief moment as we said goodbye, with the estate agent already seated in the car, I caught a glimpse of the Luca who'd taken me to lunch and charmed me with his attention.

'You need help hiring a contractor?' he asked. The mischievous spark was back in his eyes, but it didn't have its intended effect. What was it with all these men treating me like a delicate flower? I needed Luca's help even less than I'd needed Tommaso's.

'I'll be fine.' Making a few phone calls and getting quotes

was hardly up there with brain surgery. Or with structuring private equity deals.

A day later, I no longer felt quite so confident. I cradled the old rotary phone in my lap and resisted the urge to smack it violently against the bedpost. How was it possible there wasn't a single building contractor in the whole of Siena province willing to look at the house before Christmas?

I was in the kitchen, pounding out my stress on a fresh ball of bread dough, this time for my own consumption, when Daniele arrived in the farm's battered pick-up truck to fetch the daily delivery for the *trattoria*. He carried in a basket of brown eggs and set them on the counter beside the kitchen sink. 'What's got into you?'

'Nothing.'

He chuckled. 'When a woman says "nothing" it definitely means "something".' He leaned against the doorjamb. He wore work-stained cargo pants, scuffed boots, and a checked shirt, and looked as if he'd just stepped off a tractor. I'd never before thought a farmer could be sexy, but I was rapidly changing my mind. If I were ten years younger, I'd be salivating about now. Instead, I simply felt old beyond my years beside his youth and vitality.

I eased up on the pummelling I was giving the dough and wiped my hands on the apron. 'This place needs urgent work done, and I can't do it on my own. But I'm struggling to find a single contractor who will even meet with me to give me a quote.'

Daniele shrugged. 'Most contractors in Tuscany book up

years in advance. But I'll ask around. My father knows everyone in the area – maybe he can find someone who can at least give you a price?'

I smiled for the first time in over an hour. 'Thank you. I'd really appreciate that.'

'That's what neighbours do.' He leaned over the box of fresh ciabatta loaves and small dinner rolls I'd packed ready for him to take away. 'Mmm. Something smells good in here.' He reached inside and, knowing exactly what he was going for, I playfully swatted his hand away. 'Those are for the *trattoria*, not for you!'

He pulled a face, looking like a big kid. 'But *zeppole* are my favourite! Did you make them with cream or custard?'

'Neither. I made them with ricotta.' I laughed at his expression. 'No don't tell me – ricotta *zeppole* are your favourite?'

'But of course!'

'There's another batch in the fridge. You can have a few if you promise to ask your father about the contractors.'

'I promise.' He was already headed across the kitchen to the old fridge, and I laughed again. He returned a moment later with a handful of the deep-fried doughnut balls. 'You are a goddess! How is it possible some man hasn't married you yet?'

I made a face. 'Probably because I don't need a husband.'

Daniele grinned. 'No woman *needs* a husband. But wanting one is a different matter entirely.'

I had a pretty good idea now how Beatrice felt when she was badgered by her brothers. 'What about you – you plan on marrying any time soon?'

Daniele laughed, his grin deepening. 'I want a *lot* of women. Until I find one who makes me stop wanting all the others, I don't plan to marry.'

Typical man. They all wanted to have their cake and eat it too. 'Shouldn't you be getting back to the *trattoria*? Your sister will want this stuff before the lunch rush starts.'

Taking the hint, Daniele loaded up the box and headed out to his truck, whistling jauntily. I didn't watch him leave. I contemplated the egg basket, my mind already moving on to fresh possibilities. Would John's private cellar contain any sweet wine? I'd never made *zabaglione* before, but if I could find a nice Moscato ... I barely even heard the truck pull out the yard.

The next day Alberto arrived with a contractor friend of his – a small, round, balding man with a moustache that overcompensated for the lack of hair on his head. I was so pleased to see them both, I could have hugged them. Instead, I settled for a polite handshake, and handed over the realtor's list.

The contractor muttered to himself as we traipsed after him through the *castello*.

'It's bad. Very bad,' he said at last, when we returned to the kitchen.

Of course it was bad. I could see that much for myself. 'But what will it take to make the place at least *look* habitable?'

The little man shrugged, making the Italian palms-up gesture for 'who knows?' I slid a bowl of fresh *zeppole* in front of him, this time sweetened with strawberries from my own garden. I wasn't above a little bribery.

The contractor popped two of the doughnut balls in his mouth while he thought about it. When he'd finally swallowed, and named a staggering number, I should have been sitting down. The point of this exercise was to sell the *castello*, not sink my life's savings into it.

'I don't need a miracle – just a coat of paint and some carpentry. Maybe even just half the items on the list?' I asked hopefully. After all, the realtor surely couldn't expect the house to be in mint condition to sell?

The man shrugged ruefully and explained something in Italian to Alberto who then passed on the translation. 'This is a heritage building. Not important enough to get historic conservancy funding, but all the renovations have to fit the tight regulations that govern older buildings. It can be very expensive.'

The little man nodded fervently. 'If you wait to the new year, I will give fifteen per cent discount,' he offered in his slow English, as he eyed the remaining *zeppole* hopefully.

'But I can't wait until after Christmas!'

Alberto spread his hands. 'What's the hurry? Fifteen per cent is a lot of money.'

They didn't understand. It wasn't about the money. I had a job to get back to, a life to get back to. It was one thing to use my enforced summer holiday to get the house fixed and sold, but I didn't want to be tied to this place any longer than necessary. And I had no faith that a single bottling going to market would earn enough to enable Tommaso to buy me out. How much could a few barrels of wine really make?

No, the best Christmas present anyone could give me would

be to be shot of Castel Sant'Angelo, and everything it represented.

If I couldn't get a contractor in, then I'd simply have to do the work myself. I was a competent modern woman, not afraid of hard work, and I knew how to use YouTube. How hard could it be to do a little painting and plastering?

Chapter 9

Chi trova un amico, trova un tesoro

(He who finds a friend, finds a treasure)

I woke to a puddle seeping out of John's room and into the hallway. A pipe in his bathroom had burst and not for the first time, I was sure, considering the damage in the rooms below. By the time I'd found where to switch off the water supply to that bathroom, I was sopping wet, filthy, and in desperate need of a shower and tea. I was also way behind schedule with my morning's baking. Thank heavens I'd already prepared the bread dough the night before, but there wasn't time for the elaborate and delicately layered *sfogliatelle* pastries I'd hoped to make for the *trattoria*'s daily dessert. Instead, I fell back on an English favourite: bread and butter pudding.

In the absence of sultanas and currants, I substituted the dark chocolate chips intended for the *sfogliatelle*.

I was only halfway through mixing the warmed milk and eggs, using Nonna's Fifties' aqua-coloured Sunbeam mixer, when a car entered the yard. It wasn't the unmistakable sound of Tommaso's vintage car, the familiar rattle of the Rossi farm van, or the purr of Luca's sports car. Curious, I switched off the mixer and headed to the door, wiping my hands on the big floral apron.

The car that parked beside the house was a cherry red Fiat hatchback, and from it Beatrice emerged, looking as effortlessly elegant as she had before, though today's dress was a simple halter neck in primrose yellow that set off her gorgeous olive skin.

'*Buongiorno*!' she called, waving. She shut the car door and crossed the yard, gliding in her low heels as if the gravel yard was smooth as tar.

There definitely had to be something in the local water. Hopefully some of that effortless style would rub off on me if I stayed long enough.

'*Buongiorno.* I'm afraid I'm not yet ready with today's delivery,' I apologised, welcoming her into the kitchen.

'*Scialla*. No worries. Today I take you to the market.'

An outing! I'd been dying to get out of the house all week, and was desperately low on provisions, but... 'That's kind of you, but I still need to finish today's dessert.'

'I will wait until you're finished, then we drop the pastries at the *trattoria* on the way to town.'

I poured the milky mix over the oversized baking pan layered with buttered bread slices and chocolate chips, then sprinkled cinnamon across the top. Once the pan was safely stowed in the oven, I settled the old kettle on the hob. Aside from saving electricity by using the already-heated wood stove, there was something rather satisfying about the whistle of an old-fashioned kettle. In less than a week I'd become a convert.

As we sipped our tea, Beatrice peeked into the box destined for the *trattoria*, just as her brother had done, humming her appreciation as she breathed in the aroma of fresh baked bread and sighed. 'You have a magic touch!'

She pulled up a chair across the table from me and sat, resting the steaming cup of tea between her hands. 'Your ricotta *zeppole* were such a hit. We've even had a review on TripAdvisor praising them.'

I glanced at the porcelain wood stove, and the vintage mixer still propped over the equally vintage Tupperware mixing bowl. 'I wish what I was offering you was more professional. This kitchen may not look like much, but at least it shouldn't violate any health codes.'

Beatrice waved that expressive hand in the air again, dismissing my concerns. 'It looks just like our old farmhouse kitchen. It looks like home. And that is what we promise our customers: good, home-style food.'

This wasn't my idea of the ideal home, but looking around, I could see what Beatrice meant. Perhaps not the sort of slick, modern interior design I'd choose for myself, but the sort of home where people would pile around the table for noisy meals. It had to have been at least three decades since this kitchen had been the heart of any lively family meal. John and I had usually eaten our meals alone in the dining room, or when he was working, I had eaten in the cottage with Nonna and Tommaso.

Beatrice looked around too. 'I've always wanted to see inside this *castello*. *Papà* used to come here to play *briscola*, the card game, and sometimes your father would come to our house, but I've never been inside.'

'I'll give you a guided tour, but don't expect much. The house is in a very bad state.'

And yet, as I led Beatrice from room to room, the house no longer seemed as depressing as it had a week before. With the dust cloths removed, and the vacuuming, dusting and de-cluttering I'd managed, and with the shutters open to the gorgeous summer sunshine, the rooms looked a great deal more cheerful than when I'd arrived. I could even overlook the cracks in the plaster, or the peeling wallpaper. I avoided the library though, and when we'd passed through the dining room with its faded frescoes, Beatrice had a first-hand glimpse of the small mountain of assorted chairs, spindle-legged tables and other odds and ends which I'd dumped beneath the staircase.

'There is a furniture shop in town that does repairs,' Beatrice offered. 'We will ask Bernardo if he can fix and sell some of this for you, if you want?'

I nodded vigorously. There were only so many side tables one house could hold. Some rooms in the house looked like they belonged in an episode of *Hoarders*.

When the bread and butter pudding was done, I rid myself of the apron, and we loaded the box into Beatrice's little car, where it filled the back seat.

First, we drove to the *trattoria*, where Beatrice's cousin Matteo took possession of the box, cooing over its contents in incomprehensible dialectic Italian. Then, with the car's air con turned up high, we headed towards Montalcino, chatting loudly over the voice of Taylor Swift on the car's sound system. The rolling countryside of the Val d'Orcia spread out around us, farm houses sprinkled across the landscape, between seas of vines and patches of dark woods, the same classic views that decorated guidebooks, tourism posters and calendars the world over.

The road twisted and turned, circling westward around the old town perched on its hill. At last, in the middle of a hairpin bend that had me clinging to my seat, a gate opened up a view through the walls into the village. Barely slowing, Beatrice continued past it, across a roundabout with a statue of Bacchus, god of wine, at its centre, then along the wall of the *fortezza*, the ancient medieval fortress which dominated the town. She drove straight past the large paid parking lot too, to an unpaved area beyond.

'This is where the locals park,' she said, tapping her nose. 'It's our little secret. I always find a spot here, even when the town is full with visitors, like today.'

It was gone half ten when we arrived at the market set up in the Piazza del Popolo, where the market stalls and wagons were already thronged with people. The atmosphere was lively, the piazza filled with colour, music, voices, and enough scents to make even the most die-hard non-foodie's mouth water.

There'd been a time I'd considered myself something of a foodie, when most of my shopping had been done at Borough Market, or on Berwick Street, rather than at Tesco's, back in the days before long working hours and the relentless urge to stay ahead of the game had kicked in. Now, standing in the heart of the bustling market, buffeted by the scents and sounds, I felt oddly as if I'd come home.

'Next week, we come earlier,' Beatrice said. 'Montalcino is

at its best in the early mornings and late afternoons, when it's not so hot, and the tourists are not so many.'

I'd thought the co-op was well stocked with fresh produce, but it was nothing on the goods on display here: flowers, fruits, vegetables, preserves, and even fresh meat – and none of the cheap mass-produced tat that I remembered from the markets in Rome. 'I've died and gone to heaven.'

Beatrice laughed. 'Of course, we don't import from all corners of the globe, like in London, so you won't find the same range of choice. Here, the produce is all seasonal.'

While she focused on her shopping list for the *trattoria*, I lost myself among the food stalls. The bargain-priced produce on display was nothing like the hard, early-picked, never-going-to-ripen-but-perfectly-shaped produce more likely to be found these days in supermarkets, but they were the luscious kind of fruits I remembered from childhood, blemished, less than perfect, and dripping with juice.

My mouth watered as I wandered through the stalls, admiring the salamis and zucchini, olives, fat pears and tomatoes – not the watery, pale, over-sized tomatoes mass-produced for the big chains, but misshapen tomatoes full of colour that still smelled of earth and sun. I pointed to the wooden crate. 'Two dozen, *per favore*.'

The stall holder began to select tomatoes and pack them into a brown paper bag for me, but then Beatrice materialised at my shoulder.

'*È questo il tuo amico?*' he asked, glancing between us.

'*Sì*, this is my friend Sarah. She is baking now for the *trattoria*,' Beatrice replied.

With an apologetic shrug, the man emptied the brown bag back into the crate and bent down to dig under the stall's counter, to re-pack the paper bag from an unseen stash.

'The stall holders keep the best produce aside for regulars,' Beatrice explained in a whisper.

'You try?' the man asked, holding out one of the smaller tomatoes. 'I grow everything myself.'

With a smile, I bit into it, and the succulent, sweet flavour exploded on my tongue.

I wiped my chin. 'That's so good! Do you have celery too? Then I can make tomato-and-herb bread.'

The stall holder grinned, and handed me the brown paper bag, now filled with the reddest, lushest tomatoes I'd ever seen and several giant sticks of celery.

I'd never had so much fun shopping before. We wandered from stall to stall, with Beatrice introducing me to more people than I could hope to remember, and by the time the stall holders began packing up their wares at noon, we'd filled the wheeled basket Beatrice had brought. We packed our purchases into the little red car, then I insisted on treating my new friend to lunch at one of the town's sidewalk cafés.

We ate *crostini* with a summer vegetable stew and washed it down with creamy pistachio gelatos which we ate in the Piazza Cavour, a neat and colourful little garden at the bottom of one of the main roads, where there were benches and a fountain.

'This is my favourite place in the town.' Beatrice sighed happily, watching people idling by and stopping for a gossip. 'The tourists seldom make it this far from the main part of town. They come in their big tour busses, visit the *fortezza*, taste a few wines at the *enotecchi*, then they leave. They miss all the best parts of the town! Over there—' she pointed across the garden '—there are displays of art in the municipal buildings.'

'I can't imagine why you wanted to live in London, when you have all this.' I waved my arm to take in the town and the landscape beyond. I mean, I liked London, but if it wasn't the centre of the finance world, I probably wouldn't have chosen to live there.

Beatrice blushed, not looking at me. 'I left for the usual reason. I went there because of a man.' She shrugged, a uniquely Italian gesture that said *I care, but I want everyone to think I don't.* 'It didn't work out.'

The usual story, then. And since I'd hate anyone poking around in the ashes of my own love life, I didn't press her for more. Instead, I licked the last of the sticky ice cream from my fingers. 'Everything in Italy tastes so much better!'

'We're not still talking about men, I hope?' Beatrice winked. 'But whether you're talking men or food, I think you're right – everything here tastes better.' She raised her eyebrows hopefully. 'Maybe if we find you a nice Italian man, you'll stay longer than the summer?'

'No chance! I have a really good job to get back to.'

'I thought you worked in a bank?' Beatrice wrinkled her nose.

'Not just any bank. An investment bank. We specialise in corporate finance.'

Beatrice didn't look any more convinced, but she smiled. 'You can't blame me for trying! I like having happy customers. And I like having someone to shop with.'

I smiled. 'I like having someone to shop with too.' The one

time I'd dragged Kevin around Borough Market, he'd been so bored I'd had to leave him in a pub while I browsed the stalls.

Beatrice wiped her fingers clean on a paper napkin. 'How is Tommaso?'

Her gaze was steady, and I couldn't detect any blush that suggested my new friend harboured an ulterior motive for asking. Instead, it was I who looked away. 'Fine, I guess. He's so gruff and moody all the time, it's hard to tell.'

'Now there's a man who would benefit from a woman in his life.'

'You and he never...?'

Beatrice laughed. '*Oddio*! Never! Tommaso and I are just friends.' She shrugged, imbuing the gesture with regret. 'Sadly, we have no chemistry, because he is exactly the kind of man my brothers would approve of – he has wine in his veins. But no, he's not my type, and I'm definitely not his.'

'He has a type?' I resisted the urge to clap a hand over my mouth. I didn't want to know, and I didn't care. Well, maybe I cared just a little ... we had been friends once upon a time.

'Tommaso's type is any woman who doesn't stay long enough for things to get complicated.' Beatrice dropped her voice to a stage whisper. 'Daniele says he's a hot favourite with the female tourists.'

I rolled my eyes. Clearly Tommaso had even more in common with my father than I realised.

Beatrice waggled her eyebrows suggestively. 'But since you're not staying, maybe you and he...'

My look of horror made Beatrice laugh. 'Okay, so he's not your type either.'

I shrugged. 'He's not at all like the kid I remember from my visits to my father.'

Though Tommy hadn't exactly been a kid that last summer we'd both spent here. He'd filled out those broad shoulders, and his face had been all golden angles and planes. If I could have guessed then what he would look like when he was older, I'd have guessed he'd turn out more like Luca.

At the thought of Luca, I dug my mobile out of my bag. There was signal! I switched on my mobile data, and my inboxes were immediately flooded with Facebook messages, emails, texts, including one from Luca. I didn't pause to read any of the messages – that would be rude – but I smiled. It was good to know I was missed and that people cared – and that Luca was still interested.

I stashed my mobile back in my bag, but not before Beatrice raised an eyebrow in curiosity. 'And that look? *Is* there a man in your life?'

'I'm only excited because I finally have mobile reception.' I patted my handbag. 'The signal at the *castello* is non-existent.'

'But the cellar must have Wi-Fi? It is a business, after all.'

I should have thought of that. And since I didn't want to admit that in the week I'd been in Tuscany, I hadn't yet visited the winery, I changed the subject. 'Why did Luca Fioravanti not tell me his father and mine were neighbours?'

Beatrice leaned back, her arm looped over the back of the bench, as if settling in for a good story. 'There has been rivalry between the two farms for as long as anyone can remember, long before your father even came to live at the *castello*. Luca's grandfather offered to buy the vineyard from the old *marchese* who was the last of the Sant'Angelo line. The old man had no heirs, and though he was too old to run the place on his own, he refused to sell even one hectare to the Fioravantis. By the time your father arrived, and made a much lower offer, the vineyard had fallen into terrible disrepair. Since the *marchese* would do anything to spite Luca's grandfather, even sell to an outsider, he accepted your father's offer.' She broke off, looking embarrassed. '*Scusa*! I do not mean that we did not grow very fond of your father, but—'

'But my father wasn't Italian. I understand. But surely there can't still be a grudge between the two families? My father lived here in Tuscany for more than forty years. That was all so long ago.'

'People have long memories here. Over the years, Luca's father made offers over and over again to buy the vineyard, but your father always refused. And then when your father died, Tommaso refused too. Perhaps Luca thought it best not to let you think there was a conflict of interest. He *is* a good lawyer, you know.'

He hadn't pressured me to sell to his father, and hadn't appeared partisan in any way, but what if Luca had invited me here to deliberately upset Tommaso's plans, as a punishment for refusing his father's offer?

I shook my head. No, I couldn't believe Luca would be so underhanded. He seemed too open and straightforward for that kind of spite.

'You said something about visiting a furniture store?' I prompted, rising and dusting off the seat of my tailored trousers.

Beatrice rose too. 'Yes, we should go. The shop will be closed now for the afternoon, but Bernardo will be excited to meet you.'

We walked back up through the streets of the town, quieter now, with many of the stores closed against the afternoon heat.

'Early evening is the best time of day here,' Beatrice said. 'When the air cools, it is *passeggiata*, the time when everyone comes out for an evening walk.'

We knocked on the shuttered door of the furniture store, and Beatrice introduced me to Bernardo, a trim, middle-aged man whose face did indeed brighten at the invitation to visit the *castello* to look at the furniture.

Then Beatrice drove me home, Taylor Swift once again providing the soundtrack to the lush scenery rolling past the car's windows.

'It has been wonderful getting away from the *trattoria* for a few hours, and having a girls' day out,' Beatrice said. 'Can we do this again next week?'

'I would love to. It's a date!'

Beatrice helped me unload the bags of fresh fruit and vegetables, then I waved her goodbye before heading back into the kitchen with its delightful aroma of cinnamon and baked bread. Alone at last, I clicked open Luca's text and warmth blossomed in my chest.

I wasn't some gullible tourist to be seduced into a holiday romance, but that didn't mean I'd say no to letting a handsome man take me out to lunch. In the interest of restoring neighbourly relations, of course.

Chapter 10

A tavola non si invecchia

(At the table, one does not grow old)

My second week in Tuscany flowed past surprisingly quickly. Maybe I pushed myself a little harder than I needed to, and certainly harder than Cleo would approve of, but staying busy kept at bay thoughts of work, and everything I was missing back home in London.

In the mornings, I baked bread loaves, scones, fruity *crostata* pies, ricotta cheesecakes, and *semelle* rolls, experimenting with recipes I found in a cookbook of Nonna's that looked as if it had never been opened. After the Rossi farm driver collected the day's contribution for the *trattoria*, I ate an early lunch on the terrace, soaking in the view and the sunshine, before getting stuck into cleaning. Room by room, I worked through the downstairs, sweeping, washing, vacuuming, dusting.

Within a week, with the exception of the mouldy library, I'd completed the ground floor. All the excess furniture I piled in an ever-growing mountain beneath the stairs, crowning the tottering heap with moth-eaten drapes, threadbare rugs, broken lamps and chipped ornaments, all destined for the skip I needed to arrange. The activity tired me out in a way that fourteen-hour days at the office had never done, but the results were deeply satisfying.

I hadn't seen Tommaso in days, though I sometimes heard his car leave at dawn and return late at night. He worked even longer hours than I had at the bank.

I was balanced on the rickety stepladder, polishing the drawing room chandelier until it sparkled, when next I saw him. He announced himself by calling through from the kitchen.

'In the drawing room,' I called back, instantly regretting it as I glanced down at myself. I'd spent the afternoon on my hands and knees polishing floors, and my jeans were dusty, with spots on the knees where I'd knelt. My T-shirt was even worse, and since my hair kept escaping from its bun, I'd wrapped a scarf around my head. I quickly pulled it off and tried to tuck away the wisps which had come loose.

I needn't have bothered. Reassuringly, Tommaso looked even more unkempt than I did. Clearly he wasn't the sort of boss who sat around in an office all day.

He paused in the wide doorway, filling up the space with his presence. '*Ciao*.'

'Hi.'

He held out a hand to help me down from the ladder. 'The place looks good.'

'It's just a few rooms so far.'

'It's a start. The house will sell better if it is cleaner and less cluttered. And maybe if you find a buyer, you can leave.'

My thoughts exactly.

'Have you had dinner yet?' he asked.

I hadn't thought of food in hours, but now that he mentioned it, I was starving.

'I have a beef stew I can warm up,' he offered.

My stomach rumbled loudly, and Tommaso laughed. His laugh was nothing like Luca's. Not open and unrestrained, but low and warm, as if it came from deep inside. 'I'll take that as a yes.'

I climbed down from the ladder and moved to the door. He stood aside, and even as wide as the door was, I brushed past him, the unexpected contact stirring a nervous flutter in my stomach. Or maybe that was just the hunger speaking.

Increasingly self-conscious, I wiped my hair back from her cheek, and his gaze followed the movement. Oh great. Had I smeared dirt across my cheek?

I ducked my head, but Tommaso only smiled, reaching up to brush the smudge away. It was nothing more than a small half-smile yet it transformed his face.

I was surprised to find that it was already dark outside. 'How late is it?'

'Past seven o'clock.'

No wonder I was hungry. I'd worked solidly for hours, stopping for nothing more than a sandwich and cup of tea for lunch.

'You're home early this evening,' I observed as we crossed the yard to the cottage. 'You're usually home much later than this.'

Then I realised it might sound as if I'd been stalking him, but Tommaso wasn't the least perturbed. He held the cottage door open. 'Why come home when there's still work I could be doing? It's not as if there's anything to hurry home for.'

His words stung, leaving me oddly breathless, and it was a moment before I realised why. My father had said the same thing many years ago. '*Why hurry home when there's still work to do?*' I'd only been ten, and I'd wanted to cry and say, '*But* I'm *here, Dad.*' I'd wanted to, but I hadn't. Not then or since. Maybe that was when he'd stopped being 'Dad' and become 'John' to me.

Tommaso's cottage looked exactly as it had in Elisa's time. The downstairs area was open-plan, with a terracotta-tiled floor and low, beamed ceilings. The kitchen with its familiar pine table opened into a living room where a large flat screen TV was the only new addition. Upstairs, I remembered, were two small bedrooms, tucked in under the eaves, and a compact bathroom squashed between them.

We washed our hands at the big kitchen sink, then Tommaso moved to the stove to warm up the pot of stew, and I set the table. We worked silently, not needing words, as if from long practice, though it had been nearly twenty years since we'd shared a meal in this kitchen.

I'd grabbed a crusty bread loaf on our way through the *castello* kitchen, and now I sliced it while Tommaso poured us each a glass of wine, then we sat on either side of the pine table to wait for the stew to heat.

'This is one of our own,' he said, nodding to the wine bottle.

'A Brunello?'

He shook his head. 'We make the Brunello, of course, but this wine is a blend your father and I worked on together, the Angelica. It's good, but not quite where we want it yet.' He took a sip, rolling the flavours around his tongue before swallowing. 'The tannins on this vintage were still too overpowering. This year's bottling will be more subtle.'

I breathed in the bouquet, then took a tentative sip, closing my eyes to concentrate on the taste. I had no idea what a tannin was, but he was right that there was a little too much of something. Not in the initial mouthful, but a slight bitterness in the lingering aftertaste.

He slathered the thick slices of bread in creamy butter, which looked very much like the farm butter Beatrice sent me, and took a large bite.

'Hmmm. This *is* good. You bake really well for a banker.'

Financial analyst, not just a banker. But I didn't correct him. I was too busy willing away the heat spreading under my skin at the compliment. I looked away, busied myself with buttering my own slice. 'I'm sorry. I didn't think to check if you're gluten intolerant, or on a no-carb diet.'

Tommaso laughed his deep barrel laugh again. 'I eat anything. And even if I had time to worry about a diet, I wouldn't need one. I'm not a desk jockey. I work on a farm all day.'

I cast a surreptitious glance his way. He wore a dark grey button-down shirt in a tough fabric that was clearly designed to withstand the rigours of manual work rather than to show off the body beneath it, completely unlike the crisp designer shirts Kevin favoured, but Tommaso had rolled up the sleeves just enough to reveal tanned and muscled forearms. I wondered what the rest of him would look like, and quickly stopped that thought before it could take root and grow.

When the stew was heated, Tommaso spooned it into bowls, and we ate in silence, both too absorbed in the food for conversation.

'This stew is good,' I said at last. 'Really good. And I'm not just saying that because I was hungry or because you complimented my bread.'

Another laugh. 'Like with you, Nonna taught me to make it. My mother wasn't much of a cook. She could just about handle macaroni cheese, and bacon and eggs, but cooking was just a chore to her. When she was sick, I used to cook for her. She loved that.'

'My mother's attempts at cooking aren't much better. Baked beans on toast is her speciality. I took over the cooking as soon as I was able.'

He leaned back in his chair. 'Where is she now?'

'Teaching English at some beach resort on the island of Koh Lanta in the Andaman Sea.' Where she'd hooked up with a Swedish dive instructor, according to her last exuberant postcard.

Tommaso's eyes crinkled in amusement. 'Still jaunting around the world?'

'As always.' I glanced away, looking around the homely little kitchen. Crocheted curtains hung at the windows, and Elisa's religious paintings still hung on the wall – pictures of Saint John the Baptist and Saint Lorenzo, the patron saint of cooks, and there was a faded picture of a former pope in a gold paste frame on top of the heavy wooden dresser.

Tommaso's gaze followed mine. 'I haven't had much time for decorating. The winery takes up too much of my time.'

Exactly what my father would have said. But John had Nonna to look after his home. Why didn't Tommaso have a girlfriend? Why the penchant for women who wouldn't get serious? Beneath the scruffy beard, he wasn't a bad-looking man. In fact, he might be rather attractive without the facial hair. He had the most unusual eyes, when they weren't frowning at me, and he still had those beautiful, full lips.

To cover the blush rapidly firing my cheeks again, I mopped up the last of the stew with another slice of the fresh bread.

I needed to think of something serious, the mental equivalent of a cold shower. Ah, that would do: if I had my way and sold the *castello*, this annexe would no doubt be sold with it.

For a wild moment I wondered if I was doing the right thing. John hadn't left any of this property to me, so why was I even contesting the will? Forcing Tommaso to buy me out would either prevent the winery from clearing its debts or leave Tommaso homeless.

'We can make it a condition of the house sale that you can stay on here at the cottage,' I offered.

His cool gaze met mine and he shrugged. 'It's just a place to stay. I can always live in the rooms above the cellar.'

No sentimental attachment here, then. Losing his Nonna's home was nothing compared to losing the vineyard. He didn't need to say it out loud for the thought to hang in the air between us, growing like an invisible monster. My heart hardened.

I had every right to contest the will and to expect a share of my own father's inheritance. It wasn't as if I'd asked John for much. He'd had no brothers or sisters, and his parents had died long before I was even born, making me his only blood relative. His only child.

I pushed away from the table, collected together our bowls, and carried them to the sink. 'I should go.'

Tommaso's elbows rested on the scratched pine table-top, his chin on his hands as he studied me. As if he was looking past all the layers of the years to the angry, hormonal teen I'd once been. Emotions I hadn't felt in years bubbled dangerously beneath the surface, that familiar heat growing in my cheeks. Familiar and yet somehow alien, as I hadn't blushed this furiously or this much since I last stood in this cottage kitchen.

'There's still half a bottle of wine to finish,' he said, reaching forward to re-fill my glass. 'Do you remember how to play Rummikub?'

I was tired, and more emotional than I had any right to be. I should probably go to sleep. But that big empty house held no appeal. 'It's been ages since I played, but it can't be too hard to pick it up again.' And it wouldn't hurt to make friends with the enemy. Negotiating my share of this property would be much easier if I had him on my side.

But while I understood my own reasons for wanting to linger, why did Tommaso? We were foes, on opposite sides of an inheritance. Or was he so lonely that even my company was better than none?

He moved to fetch a battered box from a cupboard, as I slid back into my seat. Together we laid out the numbered wooden tiles, turned them face down and mixed them up, then each took fourteen tiles and placed them on their racks. As I studied my pieces, I sipped my wine.

I was burningly aware of Tommaso's gaze on me, and when I sneaked a look at him, his brow was furrowed, as if he were troubled. Then his expression smoothed out, and I shrugged off the rather odd feeling his look had caused in the pit of my stomach.

In the heat of the game, amid the gentle ribbing, the shouts of triumph, the calculation of the pieces, my wayward emotions eased, and I let go of the little knot of stress I'd been carrying inside me since he'd invited me to dinner. Out of practice as I was, I even managed to win a fair share of the games.

We played for nearly an hour, until the bottle of wine was empty. Waving goodnight to Tommaso, I crossed the yard and let myself into the *castello* kitchen, which looked infinitely more inviting than it had a few days before. But beyond the kitchen, the dark and utterly silent house was another matter entirely. My footsteps echoed as I ascended the stone staircase and headed down the parquet-floored corridor to my room.

The startling ring of the phone, overloud in the silent house, made me jump. Heart still racing, I changed direction to John's room, flicked on the switch to flood the room with yellow light, and dove for the phone.

'I'm here!' I panted breathlessly.

Cleo laughed. 'I was about to hang up. I thought maybe you were out on a hot date.'

'Hardly.' Though dinner with Tommaso was the closest I'd come to a date since I gave Kevin his marching orders. 'I was...' I paused, not wanting to lie to my friend, but strangely not wanting to tell Cleo I'd spent the evening with Tommaso either.

I rubbed my eyes. 'I was downstairs and had to run to get the phone.'

'Pity! I hoped your breathlessness was caused by something far more gossip-worthy. So have you heard from your sexy lawyer again?'

'He's not mine, and he hasn't called since he brought the estate agent around. Just one rather vague text. Maybe he's changed his mind about taking me out after seeing me next to her. She's really stunning. Like Monica Bellucci stunning.'

'So what? You don't have to be perfect to win a guy. You just have to be perfect for *him*.'

Unseen, I felt safe to roll my eyes up to the ceiling. Then wished I hadn't. A great big spider web hung directly overhead. I wasn't afraid of creepy crawlies, but even Cleo's annoying optimism was better than spiders.

Cleo huffed out an impatient breath. 'Anyway, this is the twenty-first century. You don't have to wait for him to ask you out. You can ask him.'

That was exactly the sort of advice Geraldine would give. Geraldine never hesitated to call up a guy she liked. I wrinkled my nose. 'Tell me about your love life instead. Are you still serious about this "no more dating" thing?'

Cleo groaned. '*What* love life? Even if I hadn't sworn off men, I don't think I'll be getting the chance to date again any time soon. We're working all hours at the moment.'

Guilt tightened my chest, but then I paused. Cleo didn't sound as if she was complaining. She sounded ... animated.

'How is The Arse?' I ventured.

She was quiet for a long moment. 'Do you remember the rowing guys at uni?'

'Arrogant, entitled, terribly fit. As I recall, you were all over them like a bad rash. Thank heavens you grew out of it.'

Silence.

Uh-oh. This was bad.

'Just how hot is he?' I asked, dreading her answer. 'On a scale of one to ten, with one being a married sleazebag and ten being single, straight, good-looking and able to support himself?'

'Thirteen.'

'You are so screwed.'

'I know.' Cleo heaved a lovelorn sigh. 'What am I going to do?'

'Don't ask me. I'm even more clueless than you when it comes to men. I'm the one who dated my boss, remember? Look at how well that turned out.'

'Kevin did propose to you...'

I hated the hopefulness in my friend's voice. 'He also slept with Geraldine,' I reminded her. 'The Arse is not going to propose to you. He'll sleep with you, and he'll move on.' Just like every other man. 'Promise me you won't sleep with him.'

More silence.

'Promise me, Cleo.'

She huffed out a breath. 'Okay, I promise. No sleeping with the sexy client. Got it.'

'Good.'

When I slid under the bed covers a short while later, teeth brushed and hair freshly braided to keep it from tangling in the night, the lightness I'd felt earlier with Tommaso was gone, wiped away by concern. Cleo had a tendency to fall for good-looking narcissists. And every single time she got her heart broken.

In spite of my exhaustion, I couldn't sleep. The utter stillness of the nights still unnerved me. Even though the house in Wanstead had double-glazed windows, I was used to noise at night. Traffic rumbling past, drunken voices, TV sets and distant sirens; all those sounds of the city which formed a background to my life and which I'd long ago ceased to hear – and which I noticed now because of their complete absence.

Instead, there were new sounds, alien sounds – the rustle of wind in leaves, the hum of cicadas, a lone dog barking in the distance, and the scratchings of something up in the roof. I hoped it was an owl, because mice terrified me. Even more than spiders.

Then outside the window an owl hooted, and its mate answered from a distance away. Reassured, I closed my eyes. The owls would deal with any mice. The sound was comforting, almost companionable, as I finally drifted off to sleep.

Chapter 11

La vita è un viaggio. Chi viaggia vive due volte.

(Life is a voyage. Those who travel live twice.)

Time flowed over and around me like the slow-moving waters of a river, in that magical way that only ever seems possible in Italy, as if time were as flexible as a ball of dough, able to change its shape to fit my needs. Though I was busier than ever, I seemed able to cram so much more into my days than I'd ever managed to do in England.

Without the constant push and shove of London life, without the sense of urgency that always seemed to chase me there, I found time to sit beneath the wisteria with a cup of tea and a jam-filled *cornetto*, or to get lost in a pile of old magazines, or to idle away an hour beside the sickly green swimming pool watching butterflies dance through the overgrown flower beds, or a lizard dart up a warmed stone wall.

Cleo was very proud. 'That's exactly what you need!' she said. But I still hadn't told her I'd taken a job baking for the *trattoria*. What she didn't know couldn't hurt her, right?

Though it didn't feel like a job, but rather like a chance to explore a creative side I hadn't even known I possessed. I experimented, changing ingredients to add my own spin to old favourites, inspired by the seasonal produce in ways that supermarket-bought goods had never inspired me.

Each day, Beatrice's driver brought something fresh from the farm – goat's cheese, plums, butter, or fresh milk. I picked my own lemons, strawberries and blackberries, and even wild zucchini where it grew up between the flowers in the front garden.

Sometimes I worked in Nonna's herb garden, clearing weeds, and drastically cutting back the herbs that had gone to seed, until the little walled garden was a neat patchwork of fennel, tarragon, thyme, lemon balm, and rampant mints.

With day after day of dry weather, the front garden, facing south and basking all day in the sun, began to wilt, so on the next market day I bought an irrigation system, and using Google, and YouTube, I fitted it myself, winding the hose through tangled beds of feathery dusky pink irises, Tuscan Blue rosemary, fragile, fragrant jasmine and banks of wild roses in yellow and white. I'd never felt more capable and proudly independent than the moment when the automatic sprinklers switched on, showering the garden with a fine spray.

Bernardo from the furniture store dropped by to view the broken furniture I'd set aside, the rickety chairs and legless side tables, even an old card table that had seen better days. He wandered through the house, obviously delighted by the treasures he found. I was glad someone thought they were treasures. To me they looked like junk.

He pointed out which pieces of furniture were valuable antiques, and advised I contact an antique dealer in one of the bigger towns. Then he drove off with his little van packed full. Even better, he left me with the phone number for a reliable company that could deliver a skip for all the things that couldn't be salvaged.

By the time the sun set each day, I was exhausted – happy, but exhausted. I lay chin-deep in the hideous plastic bathtub in the guest bathroom, with the tap drip-dripping into the cooling water as I soaked away the day's accumulated dust and grime.

After several days of trial and error with the pool chemicals I'd bought at the co-op, I managed to turn the pool from green to a murky blue, clear enough that I was no longer afraid to venture into the water. At the end of a long day, there was nothing more restorative than floating in the pool as the stars came out against the darkening sky.

Then I would sit on the terrace beneath the fragrant wisteria to enjoy the sultry nights and the fresh breeze which carried with it the scents of lavender and earth from the tangled and overgrown garden. With my feet propped on the low stone wall of the terrace, I sipped wine and gazed up at the stars, trying to recognise the patterns.

I overcame my initial guilt at helping myself to the contents of the dusty wine cellar beneath the house by rationalising that at least half the wine was mine.

In the cellar I also found my father's journal, full of detailed notes on each of the bottles stored in the cellar – their ages, origins, how they'd been made, even their flavours. Armed with this notebook, I sampled the wines, and learnt a great deal more about the process of winemaking than I could have imagined.

I could even hear the echo of John's voice in my head as I read his notes, remembered evenings when he'd encouraged me to sample different flavours. My school friends had been awed that my father let me drink wine, in the same way I'd been awed that their fathers took them camping or fishing, or even someplace as simple as the movies – or remembered their birthdays.

As the sultry evening air wrapped itself around me, I learned to identify the different flavours in each wine. Not just sweet or dry, but the subtler hints of oak, cherry, pear and chocolate. I definitely liked the chocolate flavoured wine!

It was only late at night, alone with the chirp of crickets and the distant hoot of a hunting owl, that I sometimes felt lonely. Since that evening we'd dined together and played Rummikub, I hadn't seen Tommaso. I heard his car come and go, but he didn't come knocking on the door, and no way was I going to be the needy, desperate kind of woman who'd go knocking at his.

Several days went by before I even remembered Luca's text, and realised I hadn't yet replied. Since the *castello*'s phone signal was still as elusive as a decent, single, straight man in London, I sat cross-legged on the crocheted blanket spread across John's bed, and dialled his number.

'Fioravanti.' Though his answer was curt and distracted, the gorgeous tenor was enough to make my insides turn liquid. When he heard my tentative voice and gave me his undivided attention, that was even sexier.

'Tomorrow, I take you for lunch,' he said. It wasn't a question.

'If you're not too busy?'

'For you, I can never be too busy.' There was a seductive smile in his voice, and my breath fluttered in my chest.

'I also need to find a hardware store.' Nothing like killing two birds with one stone.

'No problem. I pick you up at ten.'

I woke extra early the next morning and had all the day's baking done early enough that I still had time to style my hair. Luca drove into the yard as the Rossi's farm van drove out.

I wore the one and only dress I'd packed for this trip, a shift dress in sage-green that was guaranteed to bring out the green in my eyes. The admiration in Luca's gaze made all the effort worthwhile. I might not want to indulge in a holiday romance, but he was so good for my self-esteem!

He didn't take me to Montalcino though, but rather eastwards through the Val di Chiana, through vineyards and forests and fields of sunflowers to the medieval hilltop town of Montepulciano which straddled a massive limestone ridge. It was at least twice the size of Montalcino, making the little town that had so enchanted me seem like a rustic village in comparison.

We parked in a small and cramped metered parking lot, then strolled through the public gardens, around a monstrously-sized war horse sculpture, and through the *Porta al Prato*, the original thirteenth-century gate into the town, to the *Corso*, the main thoroughfare.

'I prefer Pienza for its beauty,' Luca said as we made our way up the busy street. 'But if it's shopping you want, this is the place.'

He took me first to a coffee bar for *macchiatos*, which we drank standing at the bar. This coffee did not have the slightly burned, bitter espresso taste I was used to getting at Costa, but a rich, full-bodied brew that lingered on my tongue. As we sipped, we pored over my shopping list. There was boring, everyday stuff like nails, plaster-filler, and tools, but also more exciting things like lampshades and curtains.

Most men's eyes would have glazed over at the list, but Luca took it all in his stride. Once we'd finished our coffees, he led me to first one shop then another, even getting involved in picking out fabrics and giving advice without any dampening of his enthusiasm. He paid for the new curtains, too, insisting they were a housewarming gift and waving away my objections. Really, could this man be any more perfect, without being gay?

As we walked, I caught glimpses between the buildings of views out across the landscape. 'We must be really high!'

He nodded. 'Montepulciano is the highest hill town in Tuscany.'

My thighs agreed. No one in Tuscany needed a StairMaster, that was for sure.

Once we'd ticked off everything on my list, we returned to the parking lot to stow the shopping bags in the back seat of Luca's sports car.

'Now, we act like tourists.' Luca held out his hand, and I took it without thinking. His hand was warm and strong, not too soft, not too rough.

He took me for lunch at a *caffè*, where we were seated on a shaded terrace hemmed in by wrought iron railings, with breathtaking views of the surrounding countryside falling away beneath us. Luca ordered a local wine for me to try, the Vino Nobile di Montepulciano, an intense wine with plummy, fruity flavours, an easier-drinking wine than the Montalcino wines I'd sampled, but more complex than the Chiantis Cleo and I often drank down at the pub.

'Like our own Brunellos, this is made mostly with Sangiovese grapes, another local variant, but it is not so pure as our Brunellos.' There was affection and pride in his tone.

'You're not having any?' I asked, gesturing to his empty wine glass.

He pulled a face. 'I have to drive. It wouldn't be good for an *avvocato* – advocate – to be caught breaking the law.'

'So it's not that you're trying to get me drunk?'

He grinned, eyes flashing with mischief, and didn't answer.

The waiter took our orders, and Luca insisted, 'You must try the *ragu*. It is made with a pasta that is a local speciality, *pici*.'

When it came, the pasta was like fat, hand-rolled spaghetti, dripping in a rich duck sauce. Luca watched as I tasted the *pici*, smiling widely at my obvious enjoyment. His passion for food and wine was such a stark contrast to Kevin, who'd been more impressed by the trend factor of a restaurant than its actual food. I'd just bet Luca would love Borough Market.

'This sauce is so good!' I moaned. 'I could practically take a bath in it.'

Another dangerous twinkle lit up Luca's eyes.

'Uh-uh!' I waved my fork at him 'Don't get any ideas!'

'I make my own *pici*, but I make mine *all'aglione*, in a tomato and garlic sauce. Or in season, with truffles. You will come for dinner, and I will make it for you.'

Again, not a question, and now the dangerous twinkle was accompanied by a grin that brought out his dimple. 'But I promise it will be so good you won't want to waste it on bathing.'

I choked on my mouthful and had to dive for the water glass. *No holiday romance!* I needed a passion killer, and quick.

'You live in Montalcino? Do you live with your parents?'

Could I be any less subtle? He was a grown man in his thirties. Of course he didn't live with his parents.

Luca's espresso-dark gaze stayed steady, direct and guileless. 'I have an apartment in Montalcino, not far from my office, but my parents own the farm next to yours. It has been in our family for hundreds of years.'

Well, no one could say he wasn't being completely honest. I swallowed a long sip of the wine before I answered. 'I heard. I also heard your father wants to buy Castel Sant'Angelo.'

'It's more a point of honour with him. There is a matter of fifteen hectares that have been in dispute between our two farms for centuries.' He shrugged, expression rueful. 'Of course, we could use the extra land, but I don't think he even cares about that. He sees it more as settling an old score – winning a rivalry with a family that died out a generation or more ago. He inherited a vendetta from his father, and his father before that.'

I toyed with my pasta, twirling it around the fork. 'And you haven't inherited it?'

There was that Latinate shrug again. 'If Tommaso could be encouraged to sell, I would be happier if the vineyard sold to us, rather than to outsiders, but if he doesn't ... I'm a lover, not a fighter.' Luca spread his hands wide in a gesture of surrender and smiled. The dimple flashed in his cheek, making it hard for me to think. 'And I would rather not be saddled with that wreck of a house!'

Definitely, no one could say he wasn't being honest. Brutally honest. But I felt oddly defensive. 'It's not that bad. It has lots of potential.'

'It is a money pit! *Toscana* is littered with abandoned farmhouses and villas from more prosperous times. There are plenty of foreigners and city people with too much money and a romantic view of our region who are willing to throw their money at a building that will give them nothing in return. They think we are all fields of sunflowers and rolling hills covered in vines. They don't see the *work*.' He leaned forward to whisper. 'Don't tell anyone, but I hate to work. Life is to be savoured, not sweated.' And with that, he topped up my wine glass.

Had Luca ever had to work for anything? The car he drove, his fancy watch, the easy assurance with which he carried himself, were the marks of someone raised with wealth. And with his good looks, whatever money couldn't buy, I was sure he could buy with nothing more than charm.

I, on the other hand, had had to work hard for everything I had. My terrace house in Wanstead, the healthy bank balance, security ... I worked my ass off to afford those things.

After lunch, we wandered through the city, and Luca pointed out the sights – the palazzos and churches, of which there were many. We stood in the monumental Piazza Grande, at the highest point of the city, possibly the only flat expanse in this city of sloping streets, and I wasn't sure if my breathlessness was due to the imposing sights, the climb to get there, or the man standing half a pace behind me, not quite touching, but close enough that I was aware of his every breath in a way I really didn't want to be.

He set a hand on my waist, turning me in a slow circle as he pointed out one building after the next, and I had to force myself to concentrate on his words. The Renaissance palaces enclosing the piazza were impressive, but they also seemed austere after the homelier buildings of Montalcino. The town hall with its decorative crenellations may not have been built for defence, but it certainly had been built for intimidation. And when we turned another half circle to look at the *duomo*, the Romanesque cathedral with its forbidding, unfinished redbrick facade, I shivered.

The *duomo*'s Baroque interior, decorated in exquisite detail, was a revelation, as different to the outside as I could have imagined. The glorious, airy church was quiet, the space dominated by a magnificent triptych above the main altar, a three-panelled painting of the *Assumption of the Virgin*, set into an ornate frame of gold leaf. The painting's colours took my breath away; coral pinks, dusky blues and eye-catching reds, still vibrant after hundreds of years.

Painted by Taddeo di Bartolo in 1401, was all I managed to read in the printed brochure before Luca whisked me away. I wanted to linger, but 'churches are boring,' he said, taking my arm. 'Now I take you wine tasting instead.'

I rolled my eyes. What was it with Tuscan men and wine?

We entered the cellar by passing through an unassuming door from the street, then descended a flight of dimly-lit, never-ending stone stairs into the bowels of the ridge on which the town was built. In places, the roof dipped so low Luca had to bow his head to pass through, and the steps were uneven enough that I clung to the hand railing. The temperature dropped the deeper we descended, and Luca offered me his jacket. It was a lightweight jacket, but warm from his body, and still smelling of his subtle, masculine cologne.

I laughed softly as I imagined myself as Buffy descending into the Hellmouth, my laugh bouncing eerily off the rock walls. Tommaso would get a kick out of that. The echoes of my laughter died. Why was I even thinking of a certain grumpy Scot when I had my own personal *GQ*-worthy tour guide?

'This town is built over a honeycomb of wine cellars,' Luca said, placing his hand against my lower back. 'We are going down into one of the old Etruscan caves. These caves were used to store wine in the time before Christ, and they're still used today, though this winery has only been around a few hundred years.'

Only a few hundred years. For Luca, at the end of a long line of vintners who had worked the same land for generations, maybe that didn't seem so mind-blowing, but I couldn't quite wrap my head around the concept. My own father hadn't wanted to hand his land down even one generation.

At last we entered a warren of caves, lined with wine barrels of differing sizes, and separated by high vaulted arches of red brick which disappeared into even higher ceilings of rough-hewn stone. Then we entered one cave with a ceiling so high it looked more like a cathedral nave than a cellar. The cave held the most enormous wine barrels I'd ever seen. My awed whistle bounced off the walls. 'Wow, these things are huge!'

'At least ten thousand bottles in one barrel.'

'That's a lot of ... bottles of wine.' I'd very nearly said *boxes* of wine, and only just caught myself. 'Must be scary for the winemaker if something happened to one of those barrels. Is that why they're stored all the way down here?'

He shook his head. 'These caves keep the wine at the perfect temperature. No need for fancy air cooling when the limestone does it for free. First, the wine is stored here, then it is moved into the smaller barrels you saw before, which are used to get the tannins just right.'

We emerged into a vaulted tasting room, where we sampled a selection of local wines, Luca stepping back to allow the knowledgeable server to guide me through sampling the different varieties of *Vino Nobile* on offer, including a local Vin Santo.

I breathed in the rich golden-red liquid as Luca and the server had done. 'Sweet, like port,' I offered.

The server nodded. 'It is a dessert wine made from dried grapes. The name means holy wine, as it was often served at mass.'

I took a sip and closed my eyes as I let it linger on my tongue. Caramel, honey, hazelnut. I could imagine drinking this on a cold winter's night, with snow falling outside the windows, and a log fire roaring in the grate.

'The wine is made with the Trebbiano and Malvasia grapes that grow in your vineyard,' Luca added.

My eyes rounded. 'Do we make a Vin Santo?'

He nodded, and I didn't miss his odd look, as if he expected me to know what wines our vineyard produced. Perhaps I should.

When we emerged into daylight once again, through another entrance on the lower levels of the town, the sun was already angling down, casting golden light over the mellow stone buildings. We wandered along the medieval city walls to admire the views as we slowly made our way back towards the parking lot.

When we arrived back at the *castello*, and Luca pulled up before the portico sheltering the front door, I waved him on, towards the yard at the back. 'Until I can get a carpenter to sand it down, I'm avoiding the front door.'.

He carried my purchases into the kitchen, but before I had a chance to invite him to stay for coffee, he said, 'I need to get back to my office. I must catch up on the work I missed today.'

'Thank you. It's been a fantastic day.'

He smiled a sexy smile that made his dimple flash and my knees turn to jelly. '*Sì*. We should do it again sometime.'

'Even the shopping?'

His smile deepened. 'For you, even the shopping.'

Then he slid an arm around my waist and pulled me against him, his lips capturing mine. He tasted of Vin Santo, sweet and intoxicating, and his lips were firm and demanding. My hands slid around his waist, as I gave myself over to his kiss.

Then he let me go and I stepped back, dazed.

No holiday romance. No holiday romance. Maybe if I repeated it often enough, my sex-starved hormones would get the message.

'If Tommaso ever changes his mind about selling the vineyard, you'll let me know? Even just those fifteen hectares. My father will make a very generous offer.' His smile flashed again. '*Arrivederci*.'

I stood on the drive to watch until the silver sports car disappeared from sight. I was still wearing Luca's jacket, I realised. I hugged it tighter, breathing in his lingering scent.

No holiday romance. Absolutely not. Don't even think about it.

Chapter 12

A saper aspettare c'è tutto da guadagnare

(Everything comes to those who wait)

The craving for Wi-Fi finally drove me to brave the hike to the winery. After one of Beatrice's farm workers had driven off in the little van loaded with lemon meringue pie and big round loaves of *pane all'olio* made with marinated olives I'd bought at the market, I changed into clean jeans and a blouse, and headed out.

Today's driver had brought a container filled with thin slices of freshly smoked prosciutto, so I armed myself with a platter of juicy melon slices wrapped in the dry-cured ham. Even at his grumpiest, Tommaso couldn't say no to prosciutto, and as I said before, I'm not above bribery!

The road was dusty and longer than I remembered, following the curve of the hill through a plantation of olive trees, then through the cool depths of a forest of pine and chestnut. Wild white lilies grew at the side of the road, along with tangles of sweet blackberries which I picked and added to the platter. Patches of pink cyclamen lifted their heads above the rough, dry grass.

Then I emerged back into bright heat, the road twisting uphill through regimented rows of vines sleeping in the sun. By the time I arrived at the complex of traditional stone buildings which housed the nerve centre of the winery, I was pink-faced, dusty, sweaty, and irritable. My arms ached from carrying the platter, and my mood wasn't improved much finding the cellar as deserted as the rows of vines had been. There were no sounds of workers' voices or machinery, and no vehicles in the gravel forecourt, not even Tommaso's vintage Alfa.

Was this the thriving business he was so desperate to hang onto?

'Hello?' I called, pushing open the heavy double doors and peering into the darkened tasting room. My voice echoed off the walls, and I slipped inside. It was cooler here, and my footsteps across the stone floor sounded overloud in the unexpected silence.

I had only vague memories of the winery. John had said it wasn't a place for children, and sent us packing if we intruded too far. The public tasting room was the only place we'd been allowed, and that had changed dramatically from what I remembered.

It was still dark and cool, but there the resemblance ended. The back wall behind the bar counter had been completely removed and replaced with a glass wall that offered a floor to ceiling view into the winery itself – and that too had changed beyond belief. The mountains of small barrels I remembered had been replaced with massive stainless-steel vats. Everything looked high-tech, new and expensive.

The tasting room had been brought very firmly into the twenty-first century too. The modern stainless-steel light fittings, sleek leather sofas and bleached oak bar wouldn't have looked out of place in a trendy London wine bar.

I set the napkin-covered platter on the bar and tiptoed across the long room to the door which led into John's office.

Two large windows flooded the office with sunlight. Outside was the linden tree Tommaso and I had loved to climb, twice the size I remembered, its lowest branches surely too high now for any kid to reach.

The same two battered wooden desks stood where they had always stood, though now they sported modern desktop computers. One wall was covered in shelves of books. Looking closer, I realised they were ledgers, one for each year, starting at the turn of the century – the nineteenth century – and ending eight years ago.

Was that when Tommaso had started to work here? Because the computers were certainly his doing. My father had had the pre-computer generation's mistrust of technology.

I turned away from the ledgers and a computer screen caught my eye. No screensaver, just a spreadsheet. My gaze slid across the data, and I leaned in closer, intrigued. This was Tommaso's plan for the vineyard's future, laid out in numbers.

'What the hell are you doing here?' The office door banged explosively against the wall, and I started. Tommaso stood in the doorway, arms crossed over his chest, face glowering. His angry stance wiped away my momentary guilt at being caught snooping.

'This was my father's office. I have every right to be here,' I shot back.

'Well, it's my office now. And I'm busy. I don't have time to indulge you in a trip down memory lane.'

Too busy for you. His words set off that distant echo that stirred my indignation even further. My chin jutted out. 'You don't look busy. The entire cellar is deserted.'

'That's because everyone is out working in the fields. We're thinning the Brunello vines today.'

Breathe in. Count to three. Relax.

I'd intended this visit to be conciliatory, not to make things worse. 'You did say I should come look at the cellar.' I was pleased my voice didn't sound defensive. Not so pleased when it came out breathy. Because Tommaso had begun to peel off his soil-stained T-shirt and was reaching for the crisp white collared shirt hanging on a hook behind the door.

Oh good Lord. How long had it been since I'd seen a man's bare torso that I was practically salivating over Tommaso? Yes, sure, he was rather fit for a man approaching forty. Okay, exceptionally fit. And tanned.

And he had those sculpted V-shaped lower abs that I'd only ever seen on American TV shows or *Outlander*.

I swallowed and averted my gaze. First Luca, and now Tommaso. I seriously needed to watch a Thor marathon. A few hours of seeing Chris Hemsworth's torso should sort me out and stop me from acting as if I were twenty years younger. Pity John hadn't owned a television.

I only risked glancing up again when I was sure I had my blush under control – and Tommaso had finished buttoning up his clean shirt.

'I have a tour group due any minute,' he said impatiently. 'They've booked a tour of the cellar as well as a tasting.'

'Well, that's perfect then. I'll just tag along, and it'll save you having to show me around another time.'

He scowled but didn't disagree. Turning on his heel, he headed back into the tasting room just as the unmistakable sound of a bus engine struggling up the hill penetrated the cellar. I skipped after him. 'Though you might want to try smiling before they arrive. You'll scare off the customers with that face.'

He shot me another withering glance and strode to the front door to meet the guests. By the time I caught him up, he looked at least less forbidding, if still unsmiling.

The group consisted of more than a dozen American tourists, lively, enthusiastic, and already relaxed into their week-long Tuscan wine tour.

'This is Sarah Wells, and she'll be joining your tour this afternoon,' Tommaso announced, ending any hope I had of following quietly and unobtrusively.

'Do you know anything about wine, hun?' one motherly woman asked, herding me along with her.

'Almost nothing,' I whispered back confidentially.

She patted my arm. 'Then you stick with me. My Gordon is a huge wine buff, but for twenty years I've managed to fool him into thinking I am too. My name's Lila.'

The group gathered around Tommaso.

'Here at Castel Sant'Angelo we produce over 100,000 bottles per year, from a selection of grapes,' he began. 'We grow two whites, the Malvasia and Trebbiano grapes, though these make up less than ten per cent of our vines, and several reds, including the Sangiovese from which we make our prize-winning Super Tuscan blend, and the world-famous Brunello, a clone of the Sangiovese family.'

His audience nodded knowingly. They'd no doubt heard similar spiels from other vintners on their tour.

'Brunello means "little dark one" in the local dialect. It is grown in higher elevation vineyards, with shallower soils, and a mix of rocky lime and clay, which is nature's own fertiliser, producing fruitier wines.'

As he shepherded us through a set of double wooden doors into a long, thin room, one of the younger women in the group sidled up beside him. 'You're not from here, are you? That is such a sexy accent!'

'Half-Italian and half-Scottish,' he replied, smiling at last, and I rolled my eyes.

Was this woman Tommaso's 'type'? If so, I didn't think much of his taste in women. She had to be nearly half his age. Geraldine had been nearly half John's age when they met too.

The room we now found ourselves in had clinical white walls, and one long side contained roller doors which opened out onto the gravel drive. 'This is the processing room, where the grapes are brought as soon as they're harvested,' Tommaso said.

He walked us through the state-of-the-art equipment currently sitting silent and unused: a vibrating sorting table, the crusher which was used to de-stem the grapes, and finally the pneumatic press which separated the grape must from the skins. 'Our white grapes are pressed straight after harvest, but the red grapes are de-stemmed then crushed to break open the berries. Keeping the red grapes in contact with their skins during primary fermentation gives the wine its gorgeous deep colour.'

'Where do you do the wine stomping?' a voice called from the back of the group.

Tommaso smiled, not the warm, slightly flirty smile he'd given the young woman, but a fleeting, sardonic smile that flashed me back to old times. The Tommy I'd known might have been shy and awkward with strangers, but beneath the serious demeanour he'd had a wicked sense of humour.

'Hollywood might want you to believe different, but wine-makers haven't pressed their grapes by foot for thousands of years.' A disappointed sigh whispered through the group. 'Apart from being *poco igenico*, terribly unhygienic, and illegal in any wine sold for human consumption, it's time-consuming and inefficient. Some wineries market wine stomping as a tourist attraction, but personally, I'd rather drink our grapes than stomp on them.'

'Me too,' Lila whispered, nudging me.

The next set of doors were also wide double doors, but these were made of industrial-looking stainless steel. They led into the big room full of massive steel tanks that was visible from the tasting room. A light electric hum accompanied our footsteps and the shuffling sounds as the group fanned out around Tommaso.

'This is the fermentation room. From the crusher, the must is stored in these tanks so that the malic acid of the grapes can be converted into lactic acid, which is what turns the wine's taste from raw to creamy. In red wines, you may not taste that creaminess, but it's what gives reds their smooth, satiny mouthfeel.'

At the more technical talk, I expected at least a few of the tourists to start glazing over, but the group hung on his every word. They were clearly big wine fans. I too edged closer, mesmerised as much by Tommaso's deep voice as by his unexpected passion when he spoke of the wine.

Beyond the fermentation room were a series of small cellars. The winery was a great deal larger than I'd realised, extending deep into the hillside. The temperature here was lower than outside, and I shivered. Here at last were the rows and rows of smaller wooden barrels I remembered, stacked three high in places. The barrels ranged in size from hip-height to large enough that I could probably stand inside one without stooping.

The floor was wet. 'To keep the air in here cool and humid,' Lila explained knowingly.

We gathered around Tommaso again. 'Only after the primary fermentation phase do we press our red grapes, and then the wine is transferred into these oak barrels for ageing. The oak contains tannins, so oak ageing adds further flavours and aromas to the wine, as well as colour and complexity, and we vintners get very passionate about the type of oak we use to age our wine.' Tommaso's mouth twisted in another wry smile. 'Here at Castel Sant'Angelo, we use the larger and more traditional barrels made of Slavonian oak. Because it's simply the best. But I won't bore you with the details.'

From the relieved sigh that passed through his audience, I imagined some other vintner on their tour had already bored them to tears about his choice of barrel wood.

'Once the malolactic fermentation is complete, we add small amounts of sulphur to stabilise the wine and remove the excess tannins that may cause unwanted flavours. And this is where the fun begins ... tasting.'

There was a collective murmur of anticipation.

'Winemaking is not an exact science, so we're constantly tasting the wines during ageing to evaluate them. There are so many elements that make up a good wine – terroir, climate, tradition, blending, and ageing. Even the direction a particular slope faces, or how much moisture is available, can have a huge influence on the flavours. The opportunities for wine-makers to explore different flavours are endless.' Tommaso laid his hand against a medium-sized barrel labelled simply with the number 15, in a gesture that was almost a caress. 'Today, you are going to taste our signature blend, the Angelica, a Super Tuscan wine which blends the Sangiovese and Brunello grapes.'

'Shouldn't it be called Angelico, since the vineyard is named for Saint Angelo?' Lila asked. 'Angelico is the male version of the name, isn't it?'

Tommaso nodded. 'Sant'Angelo means "holy angel" and local tradition says this vineyard was founded when an angel answered the prayers of the first vintner and gave to him the first vine that was planted here. But this wine was named by its creator, the former owner of this vineyard, John Langdon, and since the wine has a considerable reputation, I'm not about to mess with it.'

The young woman who'd stayed glued to his side tittered, but Tommaso ignored her. I smiled.

'Who would like the first taste?' Tommaso held up a long, thin glass tube that looked as if it belonged in a laboratory and slid it into a wine-stained hole at the top of the barrel, extricating some of the wine, then pouring small amounts into a tray of waiting wine glasses.

The tourists pressed closer, and he held out the first glass. To me.

With all eyes on me, I tasted the wine as I'd seen Luca do, first breathing in the aroma, then taking a delicate sip and rolling the flavours around on my tongue for a moment before swallowing. It felt terribly pretentious, and Tommaso's eyes narrowed as if he suspected me of delaying deliberately.

Just to irk him, I took another sip before giving my verdict. 'It tastes sort of dense, and there's a smooth, buttery texture.' I wrinkled my nose. 'But there's also a slight earthy taste that isn't so pleasant. It's not yet ready for bottling.'

Tommaso's eyebrows shot upwards, then he turned to his audience. 'Sarah's right. We'll only bottle this wine in a few months, once that earthy taste has softened.'

He turned his back on me, playing the part of the genial host as he filled more of the small tasting glasses and offered them around. 'The flavour profiles emerge slowly, sometimes taking up to a year to emerge. This isn't a job for the impatient.' Another wave of laughter passed through the room.

'How long do you age your wines?' asked a tall man with a shock of white hair. He made me think of a senior government official – very upright.

By the time Tommaso had answered, listing the ageing times for each of the vineyard's wines, most of the group had finished their samples, and I collected up the dirty glasses.

'I thought you didn't know much about wine?' he asked in an undertone as I passed by with the tray.

I shrugged. 'I am my father's daughter.' It took all my effort to sound cool, and to hide how inordinately pleased I was at having surprised him. Thank heavens for John's journal!

'Any more questions?' Tommaso asked the tour group. The tension in his shoulders had eased. With such a receptive audience, who clearly weren't bored by the details of winemaking, he'd settled more comfortably into his role as tour guide.

'How many bottles are in that thing?' the Government Official asked, waving his hand at the barrel Tommaso had drawn the wine from.

'These are *botti* barrels, and they each hold about three and half thousand litres of wine. To save you doing the calculations, that's about five thousand bottles of wine, which is roughly the yield from one hectare of land.'

The man whistled in appreciation, and I agreed with the sentiment. I glanced back at the previous cellar we'd passed through, where the *botti* were at least twice the size, like the ones I'd seen in the caves at Montepulciano. Ten thousand bottles in each of those, I remembered. I hoped they were insured. Perhaps I should offer to do a risk analysis for Tommaso and check his policies.

I did a few quick mental calculations. Ten thousand bottles at current retail price was ... a staggering amount of money. But were there enough barrels ready for bottling to clear the vineyard's debt? Or would Tommaso still be in the red once he'd bought me out?

The last stop on the tour was the bottling plant, housed in a new building across a small courtyard, but built of the same stone to match the older buildings. 'When ready, the wine is racked, filtered to remove sediment, then it comes here for bottling. We only started bottling our own wines a few years ago. It has made our vineyard completely self-sufficient.'

Another of Tommaso's innovations, I was sure. Now I understood why the vineyard was encumbered with so much debt. At a hundred thousand bottles a year, bottling our own wines made sense. No doubt we were making a massive cost saving – though calling it self-sufficiency made for better PR spin.

Since the weather was good, the wine tasting took place in the sunny courtyard, the air scented with the lavender planted in a low border around the yard. The tourists sat at wrought iron tables as Tommaso introduced each of the vineyard's wines, and I helped him pour and distribute the samplers to the visitors.

The last wine he presented was the *vino rosato* which, Tommaso explained, was the winery's most popular export; a dry but refreshing wine, drunk chilled. He held up a glass of the rose-pink wine, and the sunlight caught the colour and added depth and sparkle to the glass. 'Our Tuscan reds are complex and profound, perfect for long winter nights and as an accompaniment for the rich local dishes, but they tend to overwhelm summer foods. This *vino rosato* is made from

Brunello grapes, but we remove the skins early in the process to achieve the softer colours, and the lighter, more refreshing flavours. It's best served with the classic combination of prosciutto and melon.'

Cutting short an amused laugh, I slipped away into the tasting room, returning moments later with the platter I'd brought. I would have given double my annual performance bonus to capture the look on Tommaso's face when I removed the napkin to reveal the platter.

I moved between the visitors, offering the appetiser, and giving Tommaso a moment to regroup. He blinked, and cleared his throat, before again addressing his audience. 'Finally, as I'm sure you've already learned on your tour, wine is a living, ongoing chemical process. The wine continues to change in the bottle, so even after you've taken your wine home, its correct storage and handling is critical.'

Done with the appetisers, I distributed order forms while Tommaso answered questions on shipping arrangements.

'Do you make the Rosso di Montalcino wine as well?' one of the men in the group asked, his accent a pronounced Southern drawl. 'That's also a local specialty, isn't it?'

Tommaso gave the questioner a dirty look, as if he'd suggested we make vinegar. 'We don't make the Rosso here. It's the poor man's Brunello, made by the impatient vintner in a hurry to turn a profit.'

I shot him an arch look, and looking suitably penitent, he continued, his voice less astringent, 'In Italy we say "*ogni cosa ha il suo tempo*". Everything needs time to be accomplished. That could be our motto here at Castel Sant'Angelo.'

Turning away so Tommaso couldn't see, I rolled my eyes. In my world, if you didn't act right now, you were swept under the bus.

Half an hour later, the happy and chattering tourists were once again boarding their bus. Lila and her husband Gordon hugged me farewell. Italy was clearly rubbing off on me, because I no longer felt the urge to flinch at the touch.

We waved as the bus pulled down the drive, and as soon as it disappeared from sight, Tommaso sighed, letting out a long breath as if he'd just survived an ordeal.

'That was a great idea to bring the prosciutto and melon. How did you know?'

'I didn't. It was just serendipity.' Or pure, dumb luck.

He looked thoughtful. 'It's a good idea. We should do that for all our tastings. We could do other pairings too.'

It was on the tip of my tongue to correct him. There was no '*we*' in this. But I bit back the words. There was no point arguing with him, not when he was finally softening towards me. Assuming the lack of a scowl meant he was softening.

'I need to get back to work.' He shielded his eyes to look out over the patchwork fields. 'You can come with if you'd like.'

'Is that an invitation? Because you know it would be much more inviting if you didn't sound as if it was killing you to make it.'

He smirked. 'Please?'

I punched him playfully in the shoulder. 'Wow, you do know how to use that word! And thank you – I would love to see more of the vineyard.'

Chapter 13

Buon vino fa buon sangue

(Good wine makes good cheer)

I had to jog to keep up with Tommaso's long strides as we set off through the rows of vines. The bushes were gnarled, and not as tall as I remembered. The sun dipped over its zenith, and light shone golden through the vine leaves. It might even have been beautiful if I'd had a chance to stop and look.

It was another long hike to reach the corner of the farm where the workers were busy on the vines, and by the time we arrived I was flushed in a seriously unattractive way, and my hair had begun to escape from the neat chignon I'd pinned it in. And I probably had the start of a serious sunburn on my neck and nose.

'Geez, is the weather always this hot? Doesn't it ever rain here?'

Tommaso's mouth curled up in a half-smile. 'Yeah, it's always bright, sunny and beautiful. However do we endure this torment?'

I giggled, then had to run to catch up with him again.

'We get rain in autumn and spring,' he said, without even slowing his stride. 'And a little snow in the winter. But we're protected from the worst weather by Monte Amiata.' He waved towards the deep blue smudge of distant mountains on the horizon. 'But mostly it's just perfect grape weather: sunny, dry and hot.' He cast a glance back at me. 'Did you know that Monte Amiata is the highest extinct volcano in Italy?'

It was the game we used to play as kids. I smiled back, ready to play along. 'Did you know that cypress trees were originally planted around houses, churches and graveyards so their scent would guard against demons?'

His half-smile was back. It was definitely a better look on him than his usual scowl. 'Did you know that the cypresses help prevent erosion of the top soil?'

I took a moment to think, then: 'Okay, I don't have anything more. You win.' And I was running out of breath.

'You're out of practice.'

'Clearly. I haven't met anyone else who collects trivia the way you do.'

'I thought you worked in Geektown?'

'Bankers aren't geeks.' I tried to sound offended but it didn't work. I pictured Kevin, always immaculately dressed, only dining in the best restaurants, reading the *Financial Times* for fun ... no, no one would ever mistake Kevin for a geek.

The fields we'd reached sloped down to a hollow where a narrow stream bubbled playfully over rocks. There were farm workers busy at the vines, pruning back leaves from the grapes. As we made our way between the rows, Tommaso stopped here and there to inspect the work being done, and to exchange comments with the workers. I trailed after him, still trying to catch my breath. Running from the tube station to the office was about as much exercise as I was used to.

At the edge of the field, Tommaso took over a pair of pruning shears from one of the workers, replacing the man at the vine with nothing more than a curt nod so the worker could take a break.

He'd told me he wasn't a desk jockey, but watching him work, I gained a whole new respect for him. His movements were quick and deft as he snipped at the leaves surrounding the bunches of grapes.

'I thought this farm grew mostly red wines?' I asked. 'But all the grapes I've seen are green or pink.'

Tommaso laughed. 'All grapes start out green, because of the presence of chlorophyll. In the beginning they're small, hard and highly acidic. They need sun to ripen. Now at midsummer, we have *veraison*, that's the moment when the grapes start to change colour. Green grapes turn golden, and "red" grapes, depending on the varietal, turn pink then red or purple or even blue or black. From now until harvest they'll grow darker and larger as they accumulate sugars.' He resumed his work with the pruning shears. 'Which is why we cut away the leaves, so the grapes get maximum exposure to the sun.'

He moved to the next vine bush splayed horizontally along a wire frame. When I glanced back, I saw the sturdy woman working on the next vine over cut off an entire cluster of grapes. The grapes dropped to the ground. I gasped, and Tommaso looked up, concerned.

'She's cutting off the grapes!' I hissed.

His concern turned to amusement. 'Of course she is. Too much fruit on the vine, and none of it will ripen well. So we cut away the clusters that aren't developing properly, to let the vines concentrate their nutrients on the best clusters. That way we get a better yield of higher quality fruit, and we also get more even ripening.'

I watched the wasted grapes fall to the ground. It was almost as if I were watching dollar signs flash before my eyes. *Ker-ching*. And another cluster of winery profit fell to the ground.

Tommaso glanced up from what he was doing. 'It's not all wastage. Some of the unripe grapes we collect to make verjus for cooking, and the rest turns to mulch and goes back into the ground. It's all just part of the cycle of life on a farm.'

I felt better, but only marginally.

Tommaso frowned. 'We used to come down here sometimes and watch the workers thinning the vines when we were kids. Don't you remember?'

I shrugged and turned away. That was all so long ago. And I'd blanked out a lot of those years. 'So how do you know which bunches to cut and which ones to leave?'

'I don't. That's why I leave the grape pruning to Carlotta. She has a lifetime of skill, while I'm still learning.' He paused to wipe his brow with his sleeve, and to watch Carlotta as she worked, her movements precise and quick, her neat hands completely at odds with her solid build.

Then he moved further down the row, and I followed after him. Since his frown was back in place, maybe now wasn't the time to ask, but who knew when I'd get another opportunity like this. 'There's something I've been wondering...'

He nodded for me to continue, but his hands didn't stop working.

'That last summer we were here together, you were studying for a business degree in hospitality management. And then a few years later Elisa told me you were working for a major hotel chain in Edinburgh and doing really well. How did you land here?'

He straightened and turned to look at me. 'I didn't "land" here. I *chose* to come here. You might have stopped visiting as soon you were old enough, but I still visited Nonna every summer. Your father taught me a bit about the wine business, and I was hooked. After my mother died, when Nonna's health was deteriorating, I chose to move here full time to learn the trade from your father.'

Or had he seen an opportunity, and thought that inheriting a wine farm held more appeal than managing someone else's hotel?

But then I remembered the way his eyes had lit up as he led the tour group around the winery, and his passion for the winemaking process. Maybe I was doing him an injustice, suspecting him of duplicity just because I couldn't wrap my head around the idea of giving up a successful career for this life.

Tommaso moved on to the next stretch of vine. 'You ready to give it a try?' He held out his shears, and I backed away, hands held up in front of me as if to ward him off.

He clucked like a chicken, and I pulled a face. 'Okay, fine!'

I grabbed the shears, and strode past him to the vine he'd been pruning.

'Like this.' He moved behind me, placing his arms around my waist, and his hands closed over mine. Against my back, the heat and pressure of his hard, male body sent an electric current through me. What was happening here? I was too old to behave like a besotted teen. Especially since I wasn't at all besotted. No way.

Maybe this heat flashing through me was nothing more than a memory of my teen self. That last summer I'd have died and gone to heaven to have Tommy pressed up against me like this.

Together, we snipped at the vine, as he showed me just how much of the leaves to prune back.

'There. Now you do it on your own.' He stood back, and I had to catch my breath, wanting that annoying, teasing, exhilarating sensation back.

Tommaso hovered to watch my progress, and I felt as self-conscious as I had at seventeen. When I reached the end of the row, and he was satisfied, he disappeared, returning moments later with another pair of shears. We moved on to the next row, working side-by-side, a few feet apart. The sun dipped behind the tall trees edging this section of the vineyard, but the air didn't get much cooler, as a warm breeze floated up from the valley.

'Everyone keeps talking about tannins,' I said, hesitant and hating to expose yet more ignorance, or open myself up to another jibe about not knowing anything about my father's business – but I bit the bullet anyway. 'What are they?'

'Tannins are plant-derived polyphenols.'

He might as well have spoken in Greek, for how much of that I understood. 'And now in English?'

He laughed. 'They're biomolecules that bind to proteins and kick-start a chemical reaction. Tannins are the structural element which gives a wine its form and grip.'

He picked a grape from the vine and held it up to the light. For such strong, calloused fingers, there was a great deal of gentleness in the way he rolled the grape between his fingers. 'Tannins are present in the grapes' skins, stems and seeds. White wines generally have no tannins, or at least very little, since they're fermented without their skins, but red wines are fermented on the skin. Tannin ripeness is essential for a good mouthfeel, as unripe tannins give a green, stalky taste to the wine. Like that earthy taste you identified earlier. They soften with age, which is why ageing a wine for the proper length of time is so important.'

He held the grape out, and I leaned closer, hand outstretched. But he didn't hand me the grape. He raised it to my lips, and I bit into it and swallowed. 'Ugh! It's sour!'

'That's the unripened malic acid you're tasting. When they're ripe, these grapes will have a much higher sugar content and should be ready to harvest.'

'When will that be?'

'How long is a piece of string? We'll harvest when the grapes taste right.' Tommaso shrugged. 'While there's some science involved in winemaking, it takes gut instinct to make a really good wine. Everything we do here is governed by gut instinct.'

I shook my head. 'That doesn't sound scientific at all.' It sounded downright unreliable. I preferred to make decisions with my head, decisions based on facts and numbers. I trusted my head. My gut hadn't been particularly effective in the past. My gut hadn't warned me that Kevin couldn't be trusted, and it hadn't protected me from getting hurt.

I was glad Tommaso wasn't looking my way as I pushed those feelings back into the past where they belonged.

'Perhaps,' he answered. 'But that's also where the magic lies. With so many variables, there are an infinite variety of options available for the oenologist to play and experiment with. It's what your father loved most about winemaking: experimenting. Not just the act of creating something out of nothing, but the art of discovering something new and wonderful.'

The way I felt about baking. With nothing but flour and sugar, milk and eggs, an endless combination of wonderful things could be created. It was rather startling to realise maybe I had something in common with my father after all. Pity it was too late to share that connection with him now.

At the approach of cheerful voices, Tommaso looked over his shoulder. Most of the workers were packing up and heading our way, and one of the older workers gathered up our tools in a big wicker basket.

'Tomorrow is another day,' he said to Tommaso in Italian.

Tommaso clapped him on the back. '*A domani*.'

We strolled back through the lengthening shadows towards the *castello*, hot, dusty, sweaty, and in better accord with one another than we'd been all week long.

'I owe you a dinner,' I said when we reached the yard

between our houses. 'If you like, I can throw together a pasta? I'll supply the meal, if you supply the Rummikub.'

Though his face was in shadow, I was sure he was smiling another of those half-smiles, the kind that kicked up the corner of his mouth and lit his eyes. 'I'll have to check my calendar. Because, you know, my social diary is so full these days.'

I fought to keep a straight face. 'I'll take that as a yes, then.'

Chapter 14

A goccia a goccia, si scava la roccia

(Drop by drop, water carves through rock)

As June passed into July, I made good use of the new détente between me and Tommaso. A few times each week I carried my laptop to the winery to use the Wi-Fi to research the rules and regulations governing the renovation of heritage buildings, until I became a pro in what I could and couldn't do. Though without skilled labour, I didn't make much progress.

On Fridays, Beatrice and I dawdled through the market until I knew all the stall holders by name. And twice more, I let Luca take me out to lunch. He was more than eager to play tour guide, driving me to little towns that barely featured on any tourist map, and introducing me to new wines.

Often now, Tommaso joined me on the terrace for a glass of wine in the evenings. Occasionally we ate together, but more often we simply sat in companionable silence, listening to the night birds, and the owls calling to each other through the dark, as we sipped our wine. When the sky grew dark, we searched for satellites against the velvet sky. The nights no longer seemed quiet, but a rich tapestry of sound, and the dark house was no longer terrifying in its emptiness. It was as if the house had been sleeping and was slowly coming awake.

One evening I showed Tommaso John's journal, and together we pored over the cramped handwriting. From then on, with each bottle of wine we shared, we added our own notes to the journal. I learned to detect the tannins in the wines, and identify which wines were young and which were well matured. Sometimes Tommaso brought a wine from which he'd removed the labels, and he made me guess the grape varietal from the taste alone.

'With time, you'll be able to taste the vintage too. You can taste the yearly floods and heat and rains and frosts that are in each wine,' he said.

I raised a sceptical eyebrow. Sure, sometimes I imagined I could taste the sun in a wine, but the rain...?

Tommaso nodded. 'In 2010, this region was drier than the rest of Tuscany. That year we had a long, slow ripening which resulted in a truly exceptional vintage which still has excellent ageing potential. I will bring you a bottle, and you'll taste the difference.'

'I'll have to take your word for that.' I didn't share his confidence in my palate.

One sweltering summer's day, Luca drove me to the small town of Bagni San Filippo on the eastern edge of Monte Amiata, where we hiked through shady forest to reach the white-blue thermal pools set amid impossibly white calcium rocks. The stink of sulphur hung in the air, but the heated springs were surprisingly pleasant to swim in. The pools were all the more stunning for being set outdoors in the heart of the Tuscan Forest, though the best view wasn't the landscape. Without a doubt, the best view was the sight of Luca in nothing but swimming trunks and wet skin.

A hand offered to help me into a pool, a brush of thighs, an arm around my waist, a gentle caress of my shoulder as he pushed back my braid ... Luca found every excuse to touch me, each touch inflaming me, robbing me of breath.

Today there was no doubt in my mind about whether his touch was merely casual or meant something more. It meant *everything*.

The heat in his eyes made me feel like a goddess. Not like a boring banker in her mid-thirties, still single, but a woman who was wanted. So who could blame me if I let him kiss me when he drove me home? A few passionate kisses pressed up against the front door didn't count as a holiday romance, right?

Besides, men like Luca should come with a health warning: *liable to cause sex-starved women to lose their heads*.

After Luca's car disappeared down the long drive, I walked around to the back yard. Tommaso's vintage car was parked there, so, feeling charitable with the world, I knocked on his door. There was no answer. Odd. If his car was here, so should he be.

Frowning, I headed into the kitchen to put the kettle on, and that was when I heard it – a muffled voice shouting my name. When I reached the drawing room, Tommaso's voice was louder, distinct enough that I could hear his exasperation.

I turned to the French doors that led out to the terrace, and my jaw dropped. The room no longer had a view across the valley. Now it had a view straight into the wisteria. The trellis hung at a precarious angle, sloping down across the French doors, the big purple blossoms and thick foliage obscuring the view. No way would I be able to open the doors with all that weight pressed up against them.

'Tommaso?'

'About bloody time! The ladder's fallen. Bring it here!'

A please would have been nice. My golden glow fading, I circled the house to reach the terrace. Only when I got there did I understand why he'd been so rude.

Tommaso hung by his fingertips from a gutter pipe more than a storey up. His legs flailed in mid-air, and the pipe creaked ominously. I gasped.

I had to crawl on my hands and knees beneath the trellis to reach the old wooden ladder that was only just visible. The dense branches snagged at my hair and clothes.

'Hurry!' he called.

'I *am* hurrying!' I slid the ladder out from beneath the tangled wisteria, crawling out again after it, and set it hastily beneath where Tommaso's feet hung. The ladder was rickety, and I had to hold it firm while he swung his legs to reach the top rung. When his feet connected, he let go of the gutter and my heart stopped until he'd gained his balance at the top of the ladder. Then he collapsed onto the top rung and sat rubbing his arms.

'What were you doing up there?'

'I heard a sound and came to investigate. One of the beams

of the trellis seemed to be hanging at an odd angle, so I got the ladder and some tools to fix it. Then, when I was up there, the whole damned thing came down, knocking the ladder out from underneath me.'

I giggled.

Tommaso glared back. 'It's not funny. I can't feel my arms.'

I straightened my face. 'How long have you been up there?'

'Five minutes. Ten minutes. Eternity.'

'And do you plan on coming down any time soon or will I be propping up this ladder all night?'

Another glare. Slowly, painfully, he climbed down, the ladder wobbling treacherously. I gripped it harder, bracing my whole body against it. Though that was in part to hide the fact that my shoulders were shaking with laughter. Yes, I knew it wasn't funny, but still ... all that testosterone dangling from a gutter pipe. Next time he got all scowl-y with me I was going to enjoy this memory.

Then Tommaso was on the ground, wisteria leaves tangled in his thick hair, and an expression like a thundercloud. His nose wrinkled. 'What is that awful smell?' He sniffed harder, leaning towards me. 'Have you been rolling in a dung heap?'

'It's sulphur. I went to the thermal spa at Bagni San Filippo today.'

He took a comical step backwards. 'That'll be it then.' He glanced towards the collapsed trellis. 'The wood's rotted through. It couldn't hold the weight of the wisteria any longer.'

I glanced up at the house's façade. The creeper had pulled away from the wall, bringing with it great big chunks of stucco. I guess I should have added 'remove wisteria' to my list of things to do. They were famous for getting between bricks and causing havoc. The rotted trellis had probably done me a favour, collapsing before the wisteria brought the whole house down. 'I need a drink.'

'You and me both.' His surly expression had eased a little now he was back on solid ground, though he still rubbed his arms vigorously to get the blood circulating again. 'But it's going to have to wait. I came home early to invite you to movie night. The Rossis have invited us to join them for a picnic before the film starts.'

'Movie night?'

A ghost of a grin flitted across his dark features. 'An outdoor cinema is set up inside the old fort, and everyone brings picnics. It's a major event in the town's social calendar.' He brushed the leaves from his hair, suddenly looking awkward. 'Of course, the film will be in Italian. I'll understand if you don't want to go—'

'No, I'd love to go.' What better way to improve my language skills? 'I just need to get changed.'

His nose wrinkled again. 'You might want to shower first too – and you'll probably need to burn your swimsuit.'

I giggled. 'And you're definitely going to need to brush out your hair, or everyone's going to wonder what you've been up to.'

'You too.' He brushed a leaf from my hair. There was an unexpected twinkle in his eyes. 'Or we could go as we are and have everyone wonder what we've *both* been up to.'

I laughed.

*

The car park was packed, and the entire town seemed to be headed in the direction of the *fortezza*. Within its high medieval walls, we wandered through the crowds, stopping to chat with people Tommaso knew.

'John Langdon's daughter,' they all said, as if I were some sort of local celebrity. I'd never felt more like a phony in my life.

We joined the Rossis, who were camped out in the very centre of the wide open space, with a prime view of the enormous screen that no one seemed to be watching. Tommaso opened up several bottles of chilled *vino rosato* from our own vineyard and shared them around.

Darkness fell, and lamps were lit. Children darted between the picnic blankets and the assorted chairs that had been sent out. Adults wandered from group to group, sipping wine and visiting.

I must have met every single inhabitant of the town tonight. All except the man who'd kissed me senseless just a few short hours earlier.

Maybe Luca was working late to catch up on everything he hadn't got done at the office today while playing tour guide. Though I rather suspected he wasn't so dedicated to his job that he'd forego a night out on the town. So where was he?

Later, when the crowd grew mellow, we stretched out on the picnic blankets to watch an Italian comedy on the big screen. With Beatrice and Tommaso on either side, each giving me a running commentary of the movie, I didn't need to understand a word of the language to enjoy the film. I wouldn't have heard a word of it anyway.

It was well after midnight when we drove home. Tommaso walked me to the *castello*'s back door, and we paused on the doorstep, in the patch of yellow light spilling out from the kitchen.

I smiled up at him. 'Thank you for a wonderful evening.'

He nodded. 'If you need to get into town on your own, we have a truck at the winery you can use. We keep the keys behind the bar in the tasting room. If I'm not in, just leave a note to let me know you've taken the truck.'

Had he figured out that Luca had been driving me around? Was this his way of trying to keep us apart? Sheesh. I might as well be back in fourteenth-century Verona. 'Thank you, but I'm fine. I can manage on my own.'

'Don't be stupid. You need to be able to get around.' He shrugged, as if it made no difference to him, but his eyes told a different story. It was as if shutters had suddenly slammed down over them. He took a step back.

Now what was that all about?

'Let me get this straight – you spent the whole day half-naked with a Latin god—'

'Demi-god. He's not immortal.'

'Fine, demi-god then,' Cleo huffed. 'But then you went out to movies with the man you hit over the head with an iron?'

'His name is Tommaso, and he's my business partner.' I had no idea why I felt so prickly. It had been the perfect day, right up until that moment on the kitchen doorstep.

'Stop interrupting! I'm having a hard time here processing that Little Miss "I don't believe in holiday romances" is now dating *two* men on her Tuscan holiday – and I'd like to point out that you met both of them *organically*.'

I shrugged defensively, though I knew Cleo couldn't see. 'Going to the movies wasn't a date. The whole town was there.'

Though to be fair, there'd been more people packed into the Royal Albert Hall when Kevin had taken me to the Proms, and that had most definitely been a date.

But dates ended with goodnight kisses, didn't they? Not with Tommaso stalking across the back yard as if he couldn't get away from me fast enough. Or with my chest tightening with anxiety, feeling as if I'd disappointed him, and having no idea why.

Chapter 15

Chi bene vive, bene dorme

(He who lives well, sleeps well)

The first time I ventured out alone, driving the winery's battered pick-up truck, I went to Pienza, the pretty Renaissance town Luca had praised. There was a delicious freedom in wandering the streets on my own, not needing to keep pace with a companion. From one of the town's outlook posts, I paused to watch sheep grazing in the fields below, and later discovered that the town was famed for its pecorino, the hard, salty sheep's milk cheese. I browsed in the stores, bought new patio furniture to replace the old bench that had been crushed by the wisteria, stopped for chocolate mint gelato, and took my time looking at the Flemish tapestries and illuminated manuscripts in the Palazzo Borgia.

Growing braver, I ventured further, all the way to Arezzo to attend the huge monthly antiques market. This sprawling city, more than an hour's drive north of Montalcino, was in the Val di Chiana, with apartments and shops spreading out far beyond the town's medieval walls. I wandered through the market, browsing through the stalls that spilled through piazzas and side alleys. I chatted to the stall holders, showing them pictures on my mobile, and by the time I headed home I'd secured promises from an art dealer, a book antiquarian, and an antique furniture dealer that they would visit the *castello*.

A few days later, Carmelo the antique appraiser made his house call. He spent an age working his way through the house, stroking the furniture and making purring noises.

'Are you sure you want to sell these?' he asked with a frown, once we'd agreed a price for the furniture he would cart away.

'Absolutely sure.'

Several days later, it was the art appraiser's turn. 'Are you sure you want to sell these? Some of these paintings are very old and valuable. Surely they must have been in your family for many generations?'

'Not my family.' I thought of the old *marchese*. He was probably rolling in his grave about now. John's passion had always been the vines, but he too would probably not have approved of me selling off the *castello*'s contents.

But I wasn't selling off the house's contents to make myself rich. I was selling them to make the house liveable. I thought of the cost of contractors, of the front door that was impossible for one person alone to open, of the water damage in the library, and the rotted wood trellis I'd only just started to clear, of all the good the cash could do. And then I thought of the winery's debts, and the way Tommaso's eyes lit up when he spoke of his wines, and I knew I was doing the right thing.

I had no doubt both John and the old *marchese* would vote to save the winery rather than a bunch of old paintings.

The book antiquarian spent half a day sorting through the least damaged books in the library, and though he wasn't exactly purring, he seemed happy enough to be there. I was glad to leave him to it. I was far happier in the open air, hacking away at the downed wisteria, than stuck in there with that smell of decay.

When the art dealer called to tell me the amount the *castello's* artworks had raised at auction, I sagged back against the headboard of John's bed. Closing my eyes, I imagined all the wonderful things I could do with the cash: new wallpaper for the drawing room, new drapes for the bedrooms. Maybe even a new stove for the kitchen. Or maybe not. That old wood stove really did bake the most amazing breads.

'The money's half yours,' I said to Tommaso when he joined me on the terrace that evening. It was the first time we'd been able to sit out there since the Great Trellis Debacle, as I'd taken to calling it. Sawing off branches and rotted poles, and carting both to the skip, had been harder labour than I'd done in my life, and though it was far from done, at least we had a spot to sit again. But I ached all over. My strained muscles could do with another trip to the hot springs.

'With your share, you could pay off some of the winery's debt,' I offered.

For a moment he looked tempted to accept my offer, but then he pressed his lips together, shrugged, and settled into one of the new deep-backed Morris chairs I'd bought for the terrace. 'Keep it. Consider it a down payment on the winery so you can go back to England.'

Usually, I'd have bristled at the offhanded reminder that he wanted me gone. But I didn't. I was too exhausted to take offence, and Tommaso looked just as tired. I was even stupidly grateful he'd made the effort to join me this evening, tired as he was. In that, at least, he was unlike my father.

I studied the wine in my glass. 'Actually, I'd like to re-invest the money in the *castello*. It's looking more presentable, but before I put it on the market, I need to do some basic repairs, and pretty the place up. If that's okay with you?'

'Are you asking if I mind that you're fixing up the house, or if I mind that you still want to sell it?'

I huffed out a dramatic sigh. 'I'm pretty sure you don't mind me fixing up the house. Have you eaten dinner yet?'

'No. I was with the accountant until late, and then I sat looking at the books on my own for a while after that.' He stretched cramped muscles. He looked as stiff and sore as I felt. Clearly sitting at a desk all afternoon was as hard on him as manual labour was on me.

'I've already eaten, but I can make you something if you'd like – how about cheese on toast?'

'Sounds great.'

When I returned to the terrace a short while later, with grilled cheese sandwiches made with the pecorino cheese from Arezzo, and fresh rosa tomatoes and basil from the herb garden, I had to wake him to eat.

'And scones!' His eyes lit up at the sight of the second plate I set beside him. 'I can't even remember when last I ate scones.'

I'd slathered them in Beatrice's blackberry jam, and Tommaso wolfed them down. 'The only two things I miss from back home are scones and cream buns. My grandmother – my Scottish grandmother – used to make the best cream buns. I'd come home from school and she'd have them still warm on the kitchen counter.'

I remembered the year his grandmother died. Tommy was twelve, and I was nine, and he arrived later than usual to visit Nonna that summer, because his Gran had been so ill. He'd only flown to Italy after the funeral, and I'd been so excited to see him. I'd been bored out of my mind the three weeks I'd been on my own at the *castello*. Those were the weeks I first started baking with Nonna, just to fill the loneliness.

'You don't miss anything else about Edinburgh – the buzz of city life, the noise, the traffic, the constant rain? Not even warm beer down at the pub, or late-night kebabs?'

'Those are all the reasons I *left* Edinburgh.' Tommaso laughed, but there was a bitter sound to it, and for a moment I wondered if there was some other reason he'd left.

Since he hadn't shut me down yet, and since that shuttered look hadn't descended, I probed deeper. 'There's no one there who misses you?'

'My father still lives there. He's more Scottish than I am these days. He still works and is very involved in the local golf club. I don't think he misses me much. And he has a girlfriend.'

'I'm ... sorry?' I suggested tentatively.

This time Tommaso's laugh was more genuine. 'No need to be sorry. I'm happy for him. Mary's a nice woman, and it's been years since my mother died. Besides, that's what normal people do, don't they? They move on.'

There was that bitter undertone again. Had someone moved on and left him behind?

I looked away, out into the darkness. I had no clue what normal people did. Neither of my parents had ever had a relationship that even remotely resembled normal. John was a virtual recluse, obsessed with making wine to the exclusion of all else. In all my life I'd never once known him to go on a date, let alone have a girlfriend.

Geraldine had more than made up for that, though. She'd moved on, and on ... and on.

Tommaso pinched the bridge of his nose. 'I'm sorry I'm such bad company tonight. It's been a long day, and numbers give me a headache.'

'You're not bad company. And you do know I've worked in finance for over a decade? Is there anything I can do to help?'

He leaned forward in his chair, cradling his half-empty wine glass in his hands. 'Maybe you can. I need to calculate how much profit we can turn with the next bottling, and I'm also trying to calculate the net worth of the vineyard so we can arrange an equitable division of your father's assets.'

So that he could buy me out. So I could leave. It hadn't hurt earlier, but it hurt now. I swallowed the lump in my throat. 'I'd love to help.'

The next day, I cycled around the hill to the cellar, on the squeaky, blue bicycle I found in the garden shed. The ride was pleasant, gold-green light shining prettily through the vine leaves.

'Cream buns?' Tommaso's eyes widened when I walked into the office with the box I'd stowed in the bicycle's basket.

'I won't hope they're anywhere near as good as the ones your grandmother made, but they're still warm.'

He sat and ate the cream buns, licking the whipped cream from his fingers while I tried to concentrate on the spreadsheet he showed me. It was a simple cash flow projection for the vineyard, but it wasn't the one I'd glimpsed before. This one was far bleaker. And Tommaso had bigger worries than just buying me out. If the accountant's projections were right, the vineyard was running on a very tight operating margin, and Tommaso was going to have a tough time keeping up with his loan repayments. Why hadn't he accepted my offer of the cash last night? It might not be much in the grand scheme of things, but desperate times called for desperate measures.

The first hurdle was the easiest to deal with. 'You have too many loans. You need to consolidate your debts.'

'That's what the accountant said. But it's beyond his level of expertise, so we'd need to hire in a financial consultant – which I can't afford.'

I eyed him levelly. 'You have one sitting across the desk from you. If I can consolidate your debts into one loan at the best possible interest rate, will you let me do it?'

'Sure. Go ahead.' Tommaso shrugged. This shrug said *I'm weary and I don't really want to think about it*.

'Next: why have you estimated your yields so low for the coming year? You've cut your predicted yield by twenty per cent from last year.'

'Climate change. Experts are predicting that this year Italy will have its smallest wine harvest in over half a century, what with water shortages and uneven ripening. We had to adjust our expectations accordingly.' He smiled, but it wasn't a convincing smile. 'But it's not all doom and gloom. The good thing about fewer wines reaching the market is that scarcity will drive prices up.'

My forehead furrowed as I looked back at the spreadsheet. So much of the winery's success relied on factors that were completely beyond Tommaso's control: weather, climate, trends. I didn't know how he managed to sleep at night.

There had to be other ways, more stable and dependable ways, for the vineyard to boost income, which didn't depend on weather or water. I remembered the spreadsheet he'd had open on his screen before and swung my chair to face him. 'What is *agriturismo*?'

'It's farm stay accommodation. A lot of vineyards are doing it these days to bring in additional income. Why do you ask?'

'You had a plan for the vineyard that involved *agriturismo*.'

Tommaso paced to the window, turning his back on me. 'Not anymore. It was a stupid idea anyway.'

'But your background is in hotel management, and the *castello* would make a lovely farm stay destination if it were fixed up. It'd be a perfect fit.' Then ... oh heavens, I was such a fool! 'You and John already had plans to convert the *castello* into accommodation, didn't you?'

'Not John, and it doesn't matter now.' He stared out at the linden tree, as if engrossed in its foliage. 'I had a partner who was going to work with me to set it all up, but it didn't pan out. That was a long time ago.'

He'd planned to invest a great deal in that new venture. Surely he wouldn't have done that if he hadn't believed it would succeed? I frowned at his intractable back. 'But it's still possible. It shouldn't be hard to find locals to cook and clean.'

Tommaso shifted to look at me.

'And *pici* making lessons seem popular at other guest houses.' Okay, now I was babbling, but his hard gaze unnerved me.

His shutters were down again, putting the frown lines back on his forehead. 'It can't have escaped your notice that I can't afford to buy out your half of the property and still invest in making this a going concern.'

'But what if you could? What if you could sell just one piece of the vineyard in return for enough cash to buy me out?'

'What piece of the vineyard?' His voice was low and steady, but the narrowing of his eyes didn't bode well.

I took a deep breath. I'd given this a great deal of thought since Luca had made the suggestion over lunch in Montepulciano. 'Fifteen hectares. Luca's father has offered to pay a substantial amount for the fifteen hectares that adjoin his land.' I said it quickly, to get it over and done with.

Tommaso's eyes turned hard as steel. 'I know the land he wants. He's been after it for years.' Now his voice was a growl. 'But even if it that land was utterly barren, I wouldn't sell it to Giovanni Fioravanti. He believes his money can buy him anything he wants. But it can't buy talent or taste, and it can't buy me. My answer is no.'

'You can't just say no. We're equal partners. We should discuss this.'

'We have discussed it, and my answer is still no. And as you so rightly point out, we're *equal* partners, so you cannot sell any part of this *castello* or vineyard without my consent.'

I rose to face him. 'Why do you have to be so stubborn? I thought you'd be more realistic. This offer makes sense. You can clear the vineyard's debts and get rid of me. Isn't that what you want?'

He glared, not saying anything. The silence stretched between us, taut as an elastic band about to snap. Then he heaved out a breath. 'I will never let Giovanni Fioravanti turn our years of hard work into vinegar.'

'You've turned into a snob, Tommaso di Biasi. A wine snob.' Hands on my hips, I glared back at him. 'What does it matter what kind of wine he makes? What does it matter if he chooses quantity over quality? This is business, and in business you sometimes have to make compromises. This compromise could save the vineyard.'

With a careless shrug, and his hands in his pockets, he strode across the room. The door banged shut behind him.

I sank back down into the chair and stared at the spreadsheet on the screen without seeing it. John's premature death had wrecked Tommaso's plans. *I* had wrecked his plans. No wonder he was grumpy so much of the time.

Not that he'd been grumpy these last few weeks. Ever since I'd shown an interest in the winery, it had been almost like having my old friend back.

But now I wasn't so sure I even knew him anymore. My childhood friend had been stubborn, but he hadn't been stupid. This offer was his chance to save the vineyard, to clear his debts so he could grow the business, and he'd rejected it. All because he didn't like their wine? I didn't get it.

That night Tommaso didn't join me for our usual glass of wine on the terrace, and it was only in the early hours that I heard his car on the drive. He hadn't come from the direction of the cellar, but along the main road from town.

He had gone into town. And for some reason, all I could think of was Beatrice's words: '*he picks up women in bars*'. I didn't know why that thought bothered me so much, but it was a long time before I fell asleep.

Chapter 16

A caval donato non si guarda in bocca

(Don't look a gift horse in the mouth)

'You are phoning to finally accept my invitation for *pici*?' It had been nearly two weeks since I'd last seen Luca, and absence hadn't lessened the impact of his voice any.

I grinned. 'No, I'm shamelessly using you.'

'Lucky for you I like to be shamelessly used.' His teasing tone gave way to a dramatic sigh. 'What shopping do you need to do this time?'

'Not shopping. I just want someone to keep me company on the drive to Grosseto.'

'Why on earth would you want to go there? There are other, far prettier, places to visit. Let me take you to Cortona or Volterra or Monteriggioni instead.'

'Yes, but do they have vintage sinks at bargain prices?' I'd spent half a day at my father's desk in the winery searching for the identical sink to the cracked one in the kitchen. If there'd been another that would fit the kitchen unit anywhere else north of Rome, I'd have driven there too. With or without the comfort of an air-conditioned sports car.

He laughed. 'Okay, *that* I cannot help you with. And if I drive you to Grosseto for a sink, you will let me take you to dinner?'

'I think that can be arranged.' I suppressed a delighted smile. So far I'd resisted all his invitations to dinner. Maybe it was silly, but somehow dinner seemed like a much bigger deal than lunch. I didn't fancy having my willpower tested if – when – he inevitably asked me to stay the night. But ... vintage sink.

'You look happy,' Tommaso observed as he strode into the office a short while later.

'I *am* happy. Tomorrow I'm going to fetch a new old sink for the kitchen.'

He shook his head.

In the end, we drove to Grosseto in the winery's pick-up, Luca's car being too small to fit a sink carved from Carrara marble. He looked just as effortlessly elegant and at ease in the passenger seat of a battered pick-up truck as he did in a stylish sports car. I tried to imagine Kevin lounging in this old truck and giggled.

On the outskirts of the city we found the salvage yard, and Luca and a man with a prolific moustache wrestled the sink into the bed of the truck, covered it over with a tarpaulin, and strapped it down.

Luca held out his hand for the truck keys. 'I drive the rest of the way, and you can enjoy the scenery.'

'The rest of the way? I thought we were going back to Montalcino for dinner?'

He shook his head. 'We have hours yet before dinner, so I'm taking you to the beach.'

I had visions of beaches swarming with regimented rows of sun loungers, and the over-tanned, over-manicured bodies of tourists in lycra, but I needn't have worried. The coastline of southern Tuscany proved to be an undiscovered gem. Low-slung hills grazed by long-horned cattle gave way to the kind of landscape that inspired tourism posters: a road that twisted high above an azure sea, craggy cliffs dropping down to secret coves, and stretches of sandy beach, all guarded over by ancient stone watchtowers.

Luca turned off the coastal road onto a narrow spit of land that ran through a lagoon of crystalline blue waters. I breathed in the scent of the rosemary-scented scrub edging the road and eyed the mountainous island looming out of the sea.

'Monte Argentario,' Luca said. To our right, lay a small port town. 'That's the main town of Porto Santo Stefano.' He swung the car left. 'But we go to Porto Ercole.'

This little village, a cluster of pink and orange houses in the shadow of a fortress, overlooked a port crammed with ferries, fishing boats and yachts. 'The island was heavily bombed in the war and re-built in the Fifties,' Luca said, in his best tour guide voice. I'd realised long ago he enjoyed playing tour guide. He liked knowing stuff I didn't, and not in that teasing 'Did you know?' way Tommaso had.

We parked and wandered through the town, a pretty little seaside resort made all the prettier by the scorching sun, which picked out the vibrant colours of the buildings, abundant bougainvillea, and the lush vegetation of the sloping hillsides.

At the edge of the harbour, we paused to listen to the breeze singing a song through the rigging of the yachts, and the gentle waves slapping up against the jetty. Luca took my hand.

I steadied my breathing. His thumb stroked my palm, sending a tingling sensation up my arm.

'So where are we eating dinner?' I asked, looking across the harbour to the row of restaurants, full and busy though it was mid-afternoon.

'Are you hungry?'

'No, but isn't that what we came here for?'

'Are you always in such a hurry to move on to the next thing?' Luca smiled, amused.

'I'm a Londoner. I have only two speeds: full tilt and dead.'

He grinned. 'You are in Italy now. Here, the journey is more important than the destination.'

I shook my head. Growing up with Geraldine, my childhood had been one long journey without a destination. Her life was a whirlwind of new boyfriends, new homes, new jobs, new countries. I liked destinations.

In spite of Geraldine, or maybe because of her, I'd mapped out my life before I even finished high school. First class degree? Check. Great job? Check. Professional respect? Check. My name on a mortgage of my very own? Check.

Other people might think me dull and predictable, but I didn't care. Dull and predictable was safe. Or at least it had seemed safe, until even dull and predictable Kevin hadn't proven reliable. I shrugged off that old sense of betrayal. Kevin made a great boss, even if he'd been a lousy boyfriend. And he'd taught me a valuable lesson in never mixing business and pleasure.

As if to prove that journeys could be fun, Luca hired a small motorboat, and we set off around the headland into the fresh breeze. Many of the coves we motored past were accessible only by water. A few were unspoiled, half-moon-shaped wedges of sand, but most were occupied, with zodiac inflatables and motor boats and families playing on the beaches.

Watching the summer tourists, my heart tugged with an unfamiliar emotion, a sense of yearning. Not for their vacation time, but for the shrieks of children's laughter, for melting ice creams and suntan lotion and cheap plastic beach toys. There'd been a time when I'd wanted that for myself, when I'd dreamed of having a family as well as a career, a partner and children to fill my home, rather than housemates.

But I was a practical person. As the years rolled past without meeting that special someone to build a family with, I'd stopped yearning for what I didn't have and got on with the business of pursuing what was achievable. Then Kevin had asked me to marry him, and for three glorious months I'd thought maybe my dream of having it all wasn't so impossible after all.

I shielded my eyes from the glare of the sun against the water, as if it was the light burning my eyes.

As the sun angled low over the sea, glossing the azure with gold, Luca drove me further along the island's coast, along a panoramic, cliff-hugging drive to a posh hotel.

He was right. This was much better than one of the port-side cafés. The hotel nestled in a fold of mountainside dropping down to the sea, its terracotta-coloured buildings framed by umbrella pines. We drank negroni cocktails on a terrace overlooking the hotel's private beach and talked and laughed as the sun set over the ocean.

When it was dark, and the mosquitoes came out, we moved inside to the hotel's sophisticated, Michelin-starred restaurant. The setting was elegant but not flashy, and though I was woefully underdressed in the teal sundress I'd bought at the market, the glamour of bygone eras so permeated the air that I felt like a Twenties' movie star.

Luca ordered the wine, a local Maremma Syrah. My eyes rounded at its price on the menu, but Luca didn't even blink. The sommelier filled our glasses with an intense ruby-red wine. 'This wine is produced by the Frescobaldi family, who have been making wine since 1308,' the sommelier said, assuming my accent made me a tourist in need of educating. I resisted rolling my eyes. John's cellar contained more than a few Frescobaldi wines, and only a few nights earlier Tommaso and I had shared one of their Cabernets. Beside the entry in John's journal, in his neat handwriting, had been the note '*the Frescobaldis traded wine with Michelangelo*'.

I sipped the Syrah. Plush and juicy, full-bodied, tasting of dried cherries and plum. Not as good as any of the Castel Sant'Angelo wines, but maybe I was just being partial.

When the sommelier stepped away, Luca raised his glass. 'To love.'

I raised my glass to his. 'To friendship.'

He took my free hand. 'We could be so much more than friends, *bella*. You cannot deny the chemistry between us.'

'Chemistry is seriously overrated.'

He lifted my hand to his lips, brushing the back of my

hand with a feathery touch. 'I am descended from generations of winemakers. I believe in chemistry. You should try it, *bella*.'

Gently, I extricated my hand from his grasp. Sure, this chemistry felt great. For now. But when I was living nearly 800 miles away, that chemistry wouldn't warm my bed at night, or wake beside me in the morning, or make plans for a life together.

We dined on seasonal vegetables and seafood fresh from the sea, so beautifully presented that it looked too good to eat. Throughout the meal, Luca kept my glass topped up while drinking very little from his own. Between the wine, and the admiration in his dark eyes, his seduction was tempting. But I kept thinking of those kids playing on the beach.

The waiter cleared away our dinner plates and brought the dessert cart, decorated with a dazzling array of sweet treats. I looked longingly at the tempting desserts, but... 'I never thought I'd say this, but I can't.' I wasn't entirely sure if I was regretting the desserts or Luca.

Waving the cart away, we ordered coffees instead. They arrived with a cheese board which included the pale, tangy-sweet *caciotta* cheese, another Tuscan speciality. The restaurant had begun to empty when Luca unwrapped my fingers from the stem of my empty wine glass and enveloped them in his. 'I have a proposition for you, *bella*.'

Here it was – the moment we'd been building to from that first kiss on the day he took me to Montepulciano. The moment when I had to say 'no, thank you. I don't want to sleep with you' and risk losing his friendship. Or rather: 'I do want to sleep with you, but I won't'. My stomach knotted.

'Did you speak to Tommaso about selling those fifteen hectares of land?'

Wow. Okay. Well, that wasn't what I'd expected.

I nodded. 'I did, and he refuses to sell.'

Luca didn't seem surprised. 'My friend works at the bank in Montalcino. He tells me you have been asking about consolidating the vineyard's loans.'

I removed my hand from his and waited for him to continue, one eyebrow raised, my stomach unclenching in relief. Chemistry might scare the daylights out of me, but business I could handle.

'I might be able to assist you. I have a client with some cash to spare who would be willing to take on your debt at a very reasonable interest rate.'

Luca named a percentage, and only long years of experience at negotiating deals kept my expression neutral. That was a *more* than reasonable rate. 'Why would your client offer such generous terms?'

'Castel Sant'Angelo has a solid liquidity ratio and assets that can be leveraged. My client would be willing to accept a portion of your property as collateral against the loan.'

I wasn't so intoxicated that I didn't notice the slight emphasis on *your property*. Clever, but I wasn't falling for that emotional manipulation, no matter how subtle. 'How big a piece?'

'Fifteen hectares.'

Coincidentally the same amount of land his father wanted to buy. And there were just two things I didn't believe in: coincidence and leprechauns. 'Does your generous benefactor have a name?'

Luca's expression seemed guileless. 'My father.'

I emptied the last, cold dregs of my coffee while I considered the proposition.

Fifteen hectares. A quarter of *castello* land as collateral for an interest rate that was far lower than we'd get anywhere else. It would certainly ease the pressure on Tommaso's cash flow situation. But would Tommaso go for it? It wasn't as if he'd lose the land. Just tie it up until the loan was repaid.

If it sounds too good to be true, my father once said, *it probably is.* He'd been speaking about some bright idea Geraldine had been determined to follow, running a ski chalet in Bulgaria. It *had* been too good to be true, and Geraldine returned to London with her tail between her legs, and considerably lighter in the purse.

'What's the catch? Why would your father do this, after all the years of bad blood between the two vineyards?'

Luca twirled his wine glass between his long, slender fingers. 'No catch. My father wants to put an end to the feud, and to make interest back on his investment while doing it. So what do you think?'

'I think there's more you're not telling me.'

Luca's dimples flashed as he smiled. 'I told you that my father is a sentimental man. For him it is not about the money. That land was lost by my great, great grandfather to the *marchese* of that time. My ancestor was a bad gambler.' He shrugged. 'My father knows that Tommaso will never sell him the land. But as collateral, in the event that Castel Sant'Angelo defaults ... that is the only chance we have to restore the loss.'

Though Luca didn't emphasise the *we* this time, I didn't

miss it. He might be a lawyer by profession, but he still saw himself as a Fioravanti first. Of course he did. Winemaking in Italy was a family business.

He leaned forward, conspiratorially. 'My father, too, is a bad gambler. I have told him it is unlikely he will ever get that land, and that he will make a better return if he charges higher interest, but it is a gamble he is willing to take.'

I'd seen Tommaso's figures. Luca's father was indeed a bad gambler. Short of an unforeseen act of God, there was no chance Tommaso would default and lose those fifteen hectares.

'I've had too much wine tonight to make a decision now. I will come to your office tomorrow, and we can discuss it then.'

'You do not need to discuss it with Tommaso?'

I thought of Tommaso rubbing his forehead, of the tiredness in his eyes. *Go ahead*, he'd said. 'That won't be necessary. I have his authorisation to re-finance this debt as I see fit. Shouldn't we start heading back? It's a long drive home.'

Luca reached for my hand again, his thumb stroked my palm. 'Or we can stay? I can get us a room...'

With considerable effort, I detached my hand from his. Out of the frying pan, and back into the fire. 'I'm very flattered, but no.'

He shrugged, and his dimple flashed again, and relief swamped me that he hadn't taken offence at my rejection. I wouldn't have to lose his friendship just yet...

Chapter 17

Non c'è rosa senza spine

(Every rose has its thorn)

It took a few days of to-ing and fro-ing to iron out the details of the new loan agreement. Since Tommaso was away meeting distributers in Rome, I had to fill him in on the details over the phone – which made it easier for me to omit the name of our new creditor. Yes, it was cowardly of me. But, I rationalised, Tommaso didn't like Luca, and he was just stubborn enough to turn down this incredible offer because Luca had brokered the deal.

I was in the kitchen, trying my hand at a Tuscan pork and bean stew, when Tommaso's car pulled into the yard. Unexpectedly, he didn't go to his own cottage first, but came to knock on my door. It was still light outside, and I'd left the door standing open to let in the light evening breeze.

'You've started removing the shutters on your own?' he asked, not bothering with a greeting.

I stirred the contents of the pot and brushed my hair off

my face with the back of the oven mitt. 'Hello to you too. Of course I did it on my own. Every contractor I called was busy until the new year, and those shutters aren't just an eyesore, they're dangerous.' I lifted my chin, defiant. 'Besides, I'm not some feeble little girl who can't unscrew a hinge.'

Though in all honesty, it was turning out to be a tougher job than I'd expected. Some of the hinges were caked in place by layers and layers of paint, and others had rusted so badly they flaked to splinters at a touch. I'd broken the skin on my palms trying to remove them. And a nail too. I wasn't vain about my hands, but it had broken right down to the quick, and had hurt even more than the shutter that fell on my foot when I dropped it.

I was trying very hard not to think about how I was going to re-hang those shutters on my own after I re-stuccoed the house's exterior. Both tasks seemed monumental.

'You don't need a contractor, just a handyman.' Tommaso pushed away from the door. 'Why is it so difficult for you to ask for help?' He sounded exasperated.

'Just place an ad in the local paper and welcome in whichever stranger turns up?' I didn't intend to sound sarcastic, but his question nettled. Yes, I hated asking for help. I was a modern, independent and capable woman who had functioned perfectly well on my own for nearly two decades. And I certainly didn't need a man's help. I'd spent my entire career proving that.

'I'll ask around,' Tommaso offered, not in the least perturbed by my rudeness. 'One of the farm workers must have a relative looking for work. And if you need help, I'm around too.'

I shrugged, trying not to look as relieved as I felt. Someone to do the heavy lifting would be a huge help, though I wasn't going to admit it out loud. Then I smiled. 'We have something to celebrate! As of today, because of the agreement I signed, the strain of the interest payments on your cash flow will ease up.'

'If there's enough food in that pot to feed a hungry man too, I'll provide the champagne. Better yet, we can make it a real party: dinner, followed by a big night at home in front of the telly.'

I closed my eyes, as if in prayer. Television! I hadn't even seen one of those in months. I was so desperate I'd even watch *Real Housewives of Cheshire* (dubbed into Italian). 'What did you have in mind?'

'How about a *Buffy* marathon? I have box sets.'

'Deal!'

He slipped away, his footsteps receding across the back yard. When he returned, freshly showered and smelling faintly of lemongrass, I had the big speckled enamel stew pot simmering on a low heat and had set the table on the terrace. The air was cooler out there, and the sky was shot through with every shade of pink and lilac imaginable, casting a rosy light across the terrace.

Tommaso wore his damp dark hair slicked back, and had changed into jeans and a clean, collared white shirt. I wished I'd thought to do more than remove my apron. I still wore the dirty cargo pants and T-shirt I'd worn all day. Tommaso's eyebrow arched as he took in the shirt: the Sunnydale High School Slayers.

He smiled. Not one of his little half-smiles, but a full-on smile which lightened his face, crinkled his eyes and eased the lines of tension on his forehead.

I raised both eyebrows in mock shock. 'What is that thing on your face?'

'What thing?' He wiped at his face, and I bit back a grin.

'That thing with your mouth? If you were anyone else, I'd swear you were smiling.'

His smile turned into a laugh that lit up his eyes.

I felt a strange sensation in the pit of my stomach, a mix of anticipation and longing, and quickly dipped my head to hide my blush. 'The stew needs to simmer a little longer. Should we start on the champagne while we wait?'

Tommaso shook his head. 'Wine tasting first.'

I rolled my eyes but didn't complain. On the solid wooden dining table which now had pride of place on the wisteria-free terrace, he set down two bottles of red wine from which he'd removed the labels.

'Don't you ever eat in the dining room?' he asked.

'It feels too formal. Anyway, as long as the weather is so lovely, it's a pleasure to eat outdoors. I won't be able to enjoy all of this when I'm back in London.' I waved my arm to take in the view, the sky, the garden.

'Pity. That big dining table is just begging to be used. It was made to host a big family, and dinner parties, not to stand around as decoration.'

I thought of Sunday lunch at the Rossis' *trattoria*. How long had it been since the *castello* had hosted a party? And how long since anyone but my father had dined at that table?

Tommaso poured a small sample of the first wine into a glass and held it out to me.

'You're not having any?' I asked, eyeing his empty glass.

He shook his head, and after a moment's hesitation I took the glass and sipped. Now that I'd grown used to the denser, richer Brunello, this red wine tasted inferior – though it probably wasn't much different from the box wines Cleo and I used to share.

'It's a very young wine,' I ventured. 'The tannins are still high. It's a little too bold.' And because of the acidity of the tannins, it ended on a tart, astringent note. The wine made me think of a woman in a too-tight, too-short red dress, all bust and curves but not much class. 'What is this?'

'A Rosso.' He pulled a face. 'From our neighbours at the Fioravanti vineyard.'

I took another sip, really hoping a second taste would be better than the first. There was nothing wrong with it, exactly, but now I'd learned a little about wines, and tasted some of the best Italy had to offer, I'd grown spoiled. 'I can see now why you're not a fan of the Rosso.'

'Not all Rossos.' Tommaso sprawled back in his seat. 'Some are very high standard. But the Fioravantis don't care about making quality wine. They only care about quantity and making easy money.'

They certainly knew how to do that. I thought of Luca's flashy car, of his tailored clothes, how little work he seemed to do, and of his father's generous agreement to finance our debt. But I kept the observation to myself. Drawing attention to their success was not going to endear them any more to Tommaso, I suspected.

'It tastes a little like box wine,' I suggested after another sip.

'It *is* box wine. That's where the Fioravantis' money comes from. Cheap mass market wines sold to the international market.'

When I'd finished sampling the Rosso, Tommaso filled both our glasses from the second bottle.

'What do you think this one is?' He leaned back and watched me as I sampled it. A small smile played around his mouth.

I let the wine sit on my tongue before swallowing, then waited a moment for the aftertaste to settle. 'A blackberry and black plum taste. Predominantly Sangiovese?'

'Correct!' He sounded like a teacher pleased with the progress of his pupil. 'And?'

There was an '*and*'? I took another taste. 'It has a slight chocolatey finish, and the tannins are more mellowed.' This wine made me think of an elegant, long-legged woman in a classic Chanel LBD, with a string of pearls around her throat.

He nodded. 'Want to venture a guess where this wine is made?'

'Here.' Without a doubt. His smug little smile gave him away.

'This is the 2012 Angelica. It was the first blend your father let me make on my own.' He leaned forward, dropping his voice to a furtive whisper. 'The secret to the Angelica's success is the Malvasia Nera. The grapes aren't as popular as they were a few decades ago, and most vintners now blend their Sangiovese with Cabernet Sauvignon instead, but it's what adds the chocolate notes.'

'Mmm. You had me at chocolate.' After the Fioravanti wine, the Angelica was smooth and satisfying on the palate, not so cloying. I was never going to be able to go back to drinking cheap wines now, was I?

'How is the house decorating coming along?' Tommaso asked.

'Would you like to take a look?'

He smiled again. 'I'd like that.'

I led him through the kitchen, so I could give the stew another stir, then gave him the same grand tour I'd given Beatrice. Now that the house had been cleaned, top to bottom, it looked more cheerful. With the heavy wisteria gone, the south-facing rooms caught the evening sunlight, making the cracked and peeling paint appear rustic rather than depressing.

'Wow! I'd say there's been a *lot* of improvement!' he said.

I tried to see the rooms as he did. Not as a project with a hundred things still undone, and not as a To Do list, but as rooms that could be lived in. And I had to agree, there had been a vast improvement.

In the living rooms, I'd chosen to keep only the bare minimum of the existing furniture, buying instead a couple of modern, and far more comfortable, sofas to replace the antiques. The new sofas had cost a fifth of what I'd made on the high-backed Baroque couches – and they didn't require polishing.

I'd replaced the moth-eaten drapes with lightweight white cotton curtains which stirred in an unseen breeze, and the fussy, fringed and faded lampshades had been replaced with simple ones in matching ivory shades. The result was rooms that were lighter, brighter, and more modern. Even the library looked – and smelled – less unpleasant with the rotting books removed. Though now the shelves looked very bare, as if waiting for a new family to stamp the space with their mark.

'You've done an amazing job,' Tommaso said, admiring the guest bedrooms upstairs. 'A lick of paint to match and you'll be ready to start advertising the place.'

I shook my head. The house wasn't yet ready. And not just because there were still so many items to tick off on the realtor's list, but because *I* wasn't yet ready. For someone who'd been in such a hurry to leave two months earlier, my determination to get the house not just to saleable condition, but to its full potential, seemed to grow with each passing day.

I left my own room and my father's off the guided tour. John's room was the only one I hadn't had the heart yet to clear out.

Back in the kitchen, I ladled stew into two large bowls, which we carried out to the terrace. Shadows had gathered in the valley below, and the sky was no longer pink but a soft violet.

After dinner, I dug my precious tub of chocolate chip gelato (reserved for special occasions) out of the freezer, and we headed to Tommaso's cottage.

Champagne, gelato, and *Buffy*. I'd died and gone to heaven.

'The only thing missing from this scene is a dog.'

'A golden Labrador?' Tommaso asked, with one of his half-smiles.

'Of course.' As a child, I'd desperately wanted a golden Labrador, but it had never been possible. We'd moved too many times, often living in flats that didn't allow pets. And then after uni, I'd been too busy to look after a pet.

'Why don't *you* have a dog?' I asked.

He shrugged. 'I did. She died of old age about a year ago and I haven't replaced her yet.' He stretched, and his shirt lifted, revealing taut stomach. I swallowed and focused intently on the television screen where Buffy and Angel were now meeting for the first time. Oh, be still, my beating heart!

'Still Team Angel, I'm guessing?' Tommaso smirked.

'Of course. Spike was never good enough for the Sunnydale Slayer.'

Tommaso covered us with Nonna's old patchwork quilt, a glorious handmade work of art, and I cuddled down beneath it. It was a pity that removing shutters had worn me out. With each successive episode I slunk further down the sofa, and deeper under the quilt. It was so warm and cosy, and I was so tired...

I woke with a start. In my dream, someone was hammering and shouting, setting me into a panic. I opened my eyes to a darkened room lit only by the flicker of the DVD's home screen, and the muted tones of the *Buffy* theme tune playing on an endless loop.

The noise wasn't only in my dream. Someone was banging on the door, shouting for Tommaso. Only when he stirred, did I realise that the warm, comfortable cushion beneath my cheek was his chest.

I shot to the other end of the sofa, scrambling to fix my

hair which had come loose from the chignon I'd had it tied up in. I prayed I hadn't drooled on his chest.

'Tommaso! *Sbrigare*! Be quick!' A man's deep voice called.

Tommaso was on his feet, hurrying to open the cottage door.

I heard excited voices in rapid Italian and moved to join them. It was black as pitch outside, and cool. The night air, hitting my face, brought me fully awake. 'What's wrong? What time is it?'

Behind the two men, who both stood in shadow, the winery's pick-up truck was parked at an awkward angle on the drive, as if it had pulled to a stop in mid-flight. Tommaso's face was pale in the dim light, tense with anxiety, as he turned to me. 'Vandals!'

We piled into the truck, Tommaso driving, and me squashed between the two men. As we bumped along the road to the winery, travelling way too fast considering nothing was visible beyond the headlights, Tommaso filled me in. 'Marco was on night duty tonight. He heard a noise, went to investigate, and found taps open on two of the *botti*.'

My stomach clenched in the same panic I'd felt in the dream, and not just from Tommaso's hair-raising driving. One tap open might be an accident, but two was definitely deliberate.

'You didn't see anyone?' I asked Marco.

He shook his head. 'I did my rounds at eleven o'clock, and everything was fine. Then I heard the sound of a voice, and went to look, but they must have heard me coming. All I saw was two people running away. I didn't go after them, because I had to turn off the taps.'

Tommaso nodded approvingly, though his eyes never wavered from the road.

'Does this sort of thing happen often?' I asked, clinging to the seat, and thinking of how often I left the kitchen door unlocked at night.

'I've heard of an incident or two, but no, not often.' Then, his thoughts no doubt matching mine, he added: 'We'll need to review our security.'

The truck skidded into the gravel forecourt in front of the cellar, and Tommaso slammed on brakes. He barely paused to turn off the engine before hurrying inside, Marco and I close on his heels.

The cellar where the wine had spilled was deep inside the hill. When we reached the arched entrance to the chamber all three of us stood, speechless and hearts thumping. It was the chamber with the biggest *botti*, and the wine was nearly ankle deep. It had spilled like a pool of blood into every corner. And it was blood: blood, sweat and tears.

I blinked against the tears prickling my eyes. How much wine had we lost? This had to be at least several thousand litres.

Marco fetched mops and buckets, and in sombre silence we set about cleaning up. Only once the worst of the spill had been cleared, did Tommaso turn on the hose to wash out the rest.

'Which wine is this?' I asked, squeezing scarlet water out of my mop and into a bucket.

'The Angelico.' Tommaso's voice was terse, his face strained.

'This is the wine that was due to be bottled after the harvest,' Marco added in a hushed voice.

The next bottling. The one Tommaso had such high hopes for. The one that was supposed to pay off the winery's debts. No wonder he looked so grim.

By the time we were done, and the cellar looked just as it had before the drama, though with the pungent smell of wine thick in the air, pink streaks were already lighting the horizon.

Tommaso and I drove home in silence. He parked beside the cottage. The dawn light had turned the yard grey and ghostly. For a moment we sat inside the stationary truck. Tommaso looked so devastated, I wanted to offer some comfort, to reach out and touch him, but I didn't know what to say.

I cleared my throat. 'What happens now?'

He rubbed his dirt-streaked face tiredly. 'I'll need to calculate how much wine spilled before Marco managed to get the taps closed. And I guess we'll need to get the police in, so we can process an insurance claim.'

Then he smiled. His face no longer looked bleak, though the smile didn't reach his eyes. 'Thank heavens you re-negotiated our interest payments. If it weren't for that, I'd be really worried about how this would affect our cash flow. As it is, the next year is going to be really tight for us now, but at least we shouldn't have to default on the loan.'

With a nod of farewell, he climbed out of the truck and headed into the cottage. I needed a shower too, and to get started on the day's baking, but I couldn't move. I sat in the truck's cab, alone with my thoughts.

Giovanni Fioravanti was just a bad gambler, right? He couldn't have deliberately vandalised our barrels to force us to default on our loan repayments. I shook my head. It was just lack of sleep and heightened emotions making me imagine such intrigue. There was no way Luca would be involved in anything so devious and underhanded. But one thing was certain: I wasn't going to be able to mention the Fioravantis' involvement in the loan to Tommaso now, because I doubted he'd agree.

Chapter 18

Non si serra mai una porta che non se n'apra un'altra

(A door doesn't close without another opening)

Later that morning, Tommaso was back at the *castello*. This time when he pulled into the back yard, a small white Vespa followed him in. I'd just seen off the Rossi farm van, so I headed outdoors to greet them.

'I found a handyman for you,' Tommaso said. He looked tired, and his eyes and mouth showed strain.

I glanced at the scooter, where a mountain of a man was dismounting. My chest tightened, and I swallowed, my mouth suddenly dry. The handyman wasn't just intimidatingly large. He had a shaved head, and tattoos spiralling his bare arms, heavy ink drawings of swords and scorpions and barbed roses. I was no expert in prison tats, but if I'd ever imagined what they looked like, it would be like this.

He strode towards us, with that rolling gait of someone so musclebound he could barely straighten his arms.

As grateful as I was that Tommaso had remembered his

offer in the middle of his own crisis, did he really have to invite someone quite so terrifying into my home? I hoped the man was a fast worker, so he could be gone as soon as possible. I hoped I was still alive when he left.

Tommaso waved towards the mountain. 'This is Carlotta's cousin, Ettore. Ettore, this is Sarah Wells.'

Screwing up my courage, I held my hand out to Ettore. His grip was strong, his hand big, rough and calloused, making me feel weak and vulnerable.

'*Piacere di conoscerti*,' he said. *Nice to meet you*.

'Ettore doesn't speak much English,' Tommaso explained.

Well, this just got better and better.

'But he's worked on old houses before, and he knows the renovation restrictions.'

Once Tommaso left us alone, Ettore untied a toolbox from the back of the Vespa and dropped it beside the back door, then I walked him through the house, pointing out tasks that needed to be done. I was forced to exercise my rusty Italian, and thankfully, with quite a bit of miming, we were able to communicate.

I suggested that the first job, the most important one – and coincidentally the one I'd dreaded most – was to finish removing the shutters from the front façade of the house, and re-stucco the exterior, covering over the gaps where the trellis had been.

He nodded but said nothing.

Back in the kitchen, I made tea, and we sat awkwardly across the table from one other. His arms crossed in front of him on the table, and heavens, but they were enormous! I tried not to look, but it was impossible to resist. The scorpion's tail seemed to ripple with movement as he lifted the fragile porcelain teacup. I bet he could wrestle an ox with arms like those. Or kill someone with a single blow. I swallowed, and offered him a plate of *sfogliatelle*, seashell-shaped flaky pastries stuffed with sweetened mascarpone.

He grinned, delighted, and took three.

'So tell me about yourself,' I invited, more to fill the silence than from a desire to get to know him.

Through a mouthful of *sfogliatelle*, Ettore launched into a voluble answer, from which I was only able to get a gist. I caught the words *prigione* and *primo giorno di lavoro*, and my breath caught. I'd been half-joking when I thought they might be prison tattoos, but it seemed that not only was he an ex-con, but this was his first job since getting out. I swallowed anxiously. Should I hide the silver?

As soon as he'd emptied his cup, and the entire plate of *sfogliatelle*, Ettore rose to loom over me. 'First I fix the front door,' he said, as if he hadn't heard a word I'd said.

So I showed him the garden shed where I'd stashed all the assorted tools I'd found about the house, as well as the new bags of stucco mix, and left him to it. Then, not wanting to seem as if I was keeping an eye on him, I fetched the gardening tools from that same shed, and began weeding and pruning the little patch of garden within the circle of the driveway, close enough that I could keep an eye on him without being too obvious.

Ettore removed the front door, set it up on trestles he'd magicked from heaven only knew where, and not only sanded the door down to size but had even given it a fresh coat of paint by the time I felt the sting of sunburn on my neck and realised the sun was already well past its zenith. I hurried to make ciabatta sandwiches of salami and tomato, and brought a plate out to Ettore, with a tall glass of homemade lemonade.

'*Grazie*.' He downed the entire glass in one long, thirsty gulp, then sat in the shade to eat. He didn't try to make conversation, which was a relief, but I had the uncomfortable feeling he was watching me as much as I was watching him.

When he got stuck into removing the remaining shutters – finally – I returned to the kitchen to bottle the cherries I'd collected a couple of days earlier, following a recipe for *Amarena* I'd found on the internet to preserve them in alcohol for winter use. When Ettore popped his head in, ostensibly to fill a bucket of water – which he could just as easily have done at the garden tap – I was *sure* he was watching me too.

And that was when the penny dropped.

Tommaso hadn't just hired Ettore to do handiwork. He'd hired Ettore to keep an eye on me.

Did he suspect that there was something more sinister behind the vandalism than bored teens taking advantage of our minimal security? Did he think I was in danger? Or worse, that I might be involved?

I sat down hard in the chair beside the kitchen table. Surely not. Not after we fell asleep together on the sofa, watching Buffy kicking ass.

And he couldn't possibly know that the Fioravantis were our creditors.

But when he'd introduced Ettore, he hadn't looked me in

the eye, and the warmth and friendliness I'd felt from him last night were absent. Was that due to the strain, or because he'd found out my secret?

I moved around the kitchen, banging cupboard doors and pots, my thoughts circling. He didn't know ... I was imagining it ... of course he wasn't so friendly today; he was stressed.

I was driving myself crazy. I needed to stop these thoughts, and there was only one way I knew how to do that. I pulled out the dough board and began to make the most complicated recipe in my repertoire: chocolate soufflé.

It worked. The concentration required to get the soufflé exactly the right delicate consistency took all my attention, and it was late afternoon when I pulled the fluffy, light soufflés from the oven. Four perfect little rounds of heaven.

I made espressos, set a tray, and carried the tray out to Ettore, who was now atop a ladder, unbolting a shutter from the wall with a confidence and speed I certainly hadn't had when I'd done the job.

'Would you like coffee before you finish for the day?' I asked.

He scuttled down the ladder at surprising speed, moving with a lightness I hadn't believed possible for so big and heavy a man, and his dark eyes lit up when he saw the soufflés. We sat together on the terrace, and the ecstasy in Ettore's expression when he reached the molten chocolate heart of the soufflé made me giggle. This was why I loved baking: the enjoyment it brought to others. Selling to the *trattoria* was all well and fine, but I missed seeing the pleasure in someone's eyes as they savoured something I'd created.

When we were done, Ettore moved to pack up his tools.

'How long until the exterior will be finished?' I asked. I'd been practising the question in my head all the while he'd been eating.

'Shutters.' Ettore held up two fingers. 'Stucco – ten days. Maybe more.'

'Two weeks?' I supposed I should be glad of the help. And he'd been nothing but polite. But I hoped my nerves survived two weeks.

Ettore shrugged. '*Roma non fu fatta in un giorno*.' Even I understood that one: Rome wasn't built in a day.

He strapped his tool box onto the back of the little Vespa and hopped on. '*A domani*!' And with a cheerful wave he was gone, putting away down the drive towards the main road.

With a sigh, I headed back into the house. I needed wine.

The next day, Ettore brought a boombox on the back of his Vespa, and while he worked, he played opera. And he didn't just listen. Sneaking out of the kitchen mid-morning, my hands still full of flour, I tiptoed around the house to eaves-drop. Balanced on an upstairs wrought iron balcony to remove the upper storey shutters, Ettore was singing along with the music, in a rich, golden baritone that soared above the recorded aria. The sight of the muscle-bound, bald man singing opera brought on a fit of giggles, and I had to hurry back to the kitchen before he heard me.

By the third day, I was no longer scared of him. Beneath the intimidating exterior, I suspected he might be a teddy bear – or at least I hoped so. Though I still wouldn't want to meet him alone in a dark alley late at night.

When he offered to show me how to lay stucco, I accepted. Working side-by-side, accompanied by Puccini, we stripped off the old stucco from the walls, and laid a fresh layer. We made good progress – if a strip several feet wide could be considered good progress for a half day's work. It was hard work, with the sun beating down on us, and soon I'd built up both a sweat and a sunburn. If only Cleo and Kevin could see me now.

Since Ettore worked faster without my 'help', I decided I was more useful in the kitchen, keeping his prodigious appetite fed.

With someone as easily pleased as Ettore to cook for, I experimented not only with new pastries and cakes, but also with traditional Tuscan foods. Cooking Tuscan-style was good for the soul. There was no need for clever ingredient combinations, or complex preparations or artistic presentation. Tuscan food was just simple food cooked well. It was all about the flavour, rather than fancy combinations and elaborate displays.

Not the sort of food I'd have eaten back home in London, where my diet consisted of instant microwave dinners, or meals out in the kind of restaurants where presentation was considered more important than sustenance.

Wow. I hadn't thought of London in days. I looked around the *castello* kitchen, with the afternoon sun edging in through the windows and the terracotta tiles cool beneath my bare feet, and tried to conjure up a picture of my chrome and white kitchen back in Wanstead, with all its sleek, modern appliances. The memory took an effort.

London seemed a world away and a lifetime ago. This, with

Ettore's voice rolling rich and lovingly through the unknown words of an aria, and the scents of basil and rosemary and lemons heavy on the warm, still air, felt more solid and real than my life in England.

Chapter 19

Non sono tutte rose e fiori

(It's not all sunshine and roses)

A strong wind rose, blowing up suddenly from the coast and sweeping inland. Before I went to bed, I checked all the windows and doors to ensure they were tightly fastened, but still I couldn't sleep. The wind howled beneath the eaves, thrashed at the umbrella pines on the slope above the house, and battered at the windows. The frames rattled, and the loose tiles on the roof above lifted and clattered. I hoped the owls had found someplace safe to shelter.

The shutters on the west side of the house had not yet been removed, and one blew loose, banging against the wall with frightening force. I lay in bed, the duvet pulled up under my chin, and listened to the creaks and groans of the old house, as it protested the abuse.

The loose shutter banged again, hitting the wall in a furious volley as the wind picked up. The sound came from below my bedroom, perhaps from the "salon", as John had called it, though

I preferred to think of it as the den. If I got myself a television, it would be the perfect place for watching *Buffy* marathons.

Geez, I was losing it. I didn't need to buy a television. I already owned one. In Wanstead.

Now there was rain too, hammering against the windows. What if the shutter broke the window? What if I woke to shattered glass *and* a soaked carpet? The Persian carpet in the salon was one of the few valuable items I'd kept.

Reluctantly, I left the comfort of the warm bed, and made my way downstairs through the darkness. Lightning illuminated the salon for a split second before I fumbled for the light switch, and soft, comforting electric light flooded the room. Through the deluge beyond the window I could see the shadow of the shutter as it flew wildly in the wind, twisting this way and that. I unlatched the window and leaned out into the tempest to grab at it. The wind flung rain at me, hitting me in the face with its sharp claws.

Drenched, and struggling to see with the rain and wind buffeting me, I wrestled with the shutter. But the wind was too strong and swept it out of my hands. I'd need a rope to secure it, but I'd tidied away all the ropes and other odds and ends from the house into the garden shed, and there was no way I was going out in this storm to fetch any of it.

Another flash of lightning struck closer by, and I jumped back. Then another gust of wind grabbed at the shutter, and the matter was taken out of my hands completely as the rusted hinges gave way, and the shutter took wings and careened out into the darkness. I hoped it didn't inflict any more damage along the way.

Sopping now from the rain blowing in through the open window, I battled with the window to get it closed and latched again, then sank back in relief.

Another crack of thunder had me bolting for the stairs and my bed. I had to change into dry clothes first, and the only other pyjamas I had was the red lace-and-silk negligee Cleo had laughingly packed in for me all those many weeks ago. Not the warmest clothing I had, so once dressed I dived back into the bed and dug myself deep under the duvet, pulling it up over my ears. It wasn't thick enough, though, to drown out the howl of the wind or the hammering of the rain. Wind whistled down the chimney, the sound eerie in the big, empty house. The storm was so loud, so furious, that sleep was impossible.

I pressed my eyes closed and tried to think happy thoughts. I tried to imagine my office in London, the bustle and thrill of being a part of such a vibrant company. The high of big deals and champagne celebrations, the lure of partnership.

But the pictures didn't work the way they used to. The image in my head seemed blurry and distorted, and didn't give me the feelings of calm and joy it used to.

Maybe it was the howling wind making it difficult to focus. Would the roof tiles hold against the wind? I knew some of them were loose. Perhaps I should have asked Ettore to start up there, rather than with the walls?

An ominous creaking rose above the sound of the wind, a noise that sounded like the screech of the warped front door but magnified a hundred times over. My eyes flew open, just in time to hear the most awful rumbling, thundering sound

I'd ever heard, followed by a crash which shook the house. And then I watched as the beamed ceiling above me parted, and a monster crashed in.

I screamed.

Rain streamed in, and not just water, but a rain of leaves and bits of roof tile. I covered my face with my arms, too terrified now even to scream.

After an eternal, heart-stopping moment, the creaking seemed to settle, and I opened my eyes to stare straight up into a massive tree branch. No, not just a branch. An entire umbrella pine had crashed through the roof and come to rest, still quivering, mere feet from my face.

I sucked in a breath to still the panic. I was alive. I was unhurt. That was all that mattered.

I was also trapped beneath the splaying branches. A hysterical giggle of relief bubbled up.

The wind still howled, the rain still fell, but I didn't care. I laughed.

'Sarah?' Footsteps sounded on the parquet of the hall outside, and then my bedroom door was flung open. 'Sarah? Are you okay?'

Tommaso skidded to a stop, panic in his voice. My laughter ended on a hiccough. 'I'm fine. I just don't know how I'm going to get out of here.' I had to shout to be heard over the caterwauling of the wind.

'The power's out,' he shouted back. 'The tree must have brought the cables down. Wait there!'

As if I had any other choice.

I had no idea how long I lay in the dark, listening to the

wind, and the creak of the branches, pinned in the bed beneath an increasingly sodden duvet, scratchy leaves brushing at my face and bare arms, before Tommaso returned with a hacksaw.

'This house seems determined to collapse on us.' My voice sounded wobbly.

'Well, it was your turn to have something collapse on you.'

The giggle started to bubble up again and I only just managed to suppress it. I didn't want Tommaso to think I was hysterical. 'I think the house is trying to tell me that it wants me to leave.'

'Or maybe it's trying to keep you here.'

Now that it had made its point, the wind and rain eased. The dark clouds, only just visible through the branches above my head, blew off to the east at a rapid rate, and wan starlight flickered above the canopy of branches.

I closed my eyes and listened to the sound of the hacksaw as Tommaso tunnelled a path through the dense foliage to reach me. The room smelled overwhelmingly of pine resin.

'How can I stay when I don't even have a roof over my head?' The giggle was back. It took more effort this time to suppress it. I was shivering, too.

'Let's worry about that once you're out of there.' His voice was closer now.

It was at least another twenty minutes before I could see Tommaso through the gap he'd managed to saw through the tangle of broken branches. He kept talking as he worked, keeping me calm with innocuous chatter about television shows, and spin-offs, but I have to admit I didn't pay much attention. He was bare-chested. The waxing moonlight gave me just enough glimpses of bare male torso to keep me entranced and prevent me from turning hysterical again.

Tommaso was breathing heavily now with the strain, and I hiccoughed back another laugh. If I'd ever pictured a man in this bedroom, half-naked and panting hard, this was most certainly not how I'd have imagined it.

When the gap was big enough for me to crawl through, I rolled over onto my hands and knees. The massive branch overhead scratching at my back and shoulders, I crawled commando-style across the bed towards Tommaso. He helped me out the last bit of the way, his big, strong hands hooking beneath my armpits to drag me out in the most undignified manner imaginable. Not that I could have maintained my dignity anyway, not with my hair plastered to my face, and the silk negligee plastered to my body.

'Nice togs,' he commented.

I was beyond blushing.

Once free of the branches, I scrambled to my feet and looked around. Only about half the ceiling had caved in. The dresser and armoire were mercifully undamaged and protected from the rain by the remaining shelf of ceiling.

'You're shivering.' Tommaso pulled me in close against his chest and wrapped his arms around me. He wore nothing but boxers, and his hair was a mess, with leaves and twigs sticking out of it. His chest was warm, his arms safe, and I didn't want to move.

'We need to get you warmed up.' He rubbed my back.

But I wasn't cold. In shock, maybe, but I'd never felt warmer and safer. 'My dressing gown is in the armoire.'

'That thing? I've seen it. It wouldn't protect you from a mosquito, let alone a storm. Let's get you back to my place, and you can have a warm bath. You can sleep in Nonna's room the rest of the night.'

I retrieved the gown anyway. I needed it for more than the cold. I hadn't missed the heated look he'd cast over the wet negligee, or the way his gaze lingered on my chest, which under different circumstances would have had a good shot at winning a wet T-shirt contest, and I certainly hadn't missed the odd answering tug I felt low in my own stomach.

On our way through the house, we checked on the other rooms, using Tommaso's big torch to light the way. The only bedroom that hadn't sustained any damage was my father's. The bulk of the tree had fallen into my room, but on its path down it had damaged the ceilings of the four other bedrooms too. Gaps showed through between the tiles, where the rain sneaked in.

I was going to have one hell of a mess to clean up in the morning. If it wasn't morning already.

With Tommaso's arm still wrapped around me, we followed the bobbing torchlight down the stairs, through the kitchen and across the yard. I could have walked perfectly well on my own, but somehow that encircling arm gave me a support I hadn't known I needed. Maybe being a damsel in distress wasn't quite so bad after all.

The cottage, mercifully, still had power, so while I showered in the compact bathroom, surrounded by all the masculine reminders that this was very much a man's home, Tommaso boiled us a pot of tea. When I was warmed, and my fingers and toes were tingling as they returned to life, I wrapped myself in the enormous fluffy bathrobe I found behind the bathroom door, and headed downstairs.

We sat together at the kitchen table, and the tea warmed me from the inside out, reaching places even the hot shower hadn't managed to warm.

'Better now?' he asked.

I nodded. He'd made the tea exactly the way I liked it: strong, with just a dash of milk. When I looked up, he was staring at me, expression thoughtful.

'What?' I asked defensively.

'You sleep with your hair tied up. Don't you ever let it down?' A ghost of a smile lifted his full mouth. 'Literally as well as figuratively?'

I absently stroked my freshly re-braided hair. 'My hair gets tangled so easily, it's just easier to keep it up.'

He shrugged, changing the subject to talk about getting in electricians and needing roof tiles, and my thoughts began to drift.

Once the tea had settled my nerves, Tommaso fetched a pile of fresh bedding, and helped me make up the bed in what had once been Nonna's room. The bedding was grey and masculine, just like the set in my own room in the *castello*, confirming what I'd long suspected: it was he who had made up the bed for my arrival, and provided the milk.

By the time I settled into the freshly made bed, and lay looking up at the beamed ceiling, I was too tired to sleep. With the adrenalin rush fading, my body ached but my mind was still alert. And the image it kept replaying, over and over, wasn't my life flashing before my eyes, or the sustaining vision of my corner office. It was Tommaso, bare-chested, hair tousled, sopping wet, bedraggled, his heart racing against my cheek as he'd pulled me in for that relieved hug.

Chapter 20

Non vendere la pelle dell' orso prima di averlo ucciso

(Don't sell the bearskin before you've caught the bear)

In the light of day, with the last of the rain falling drip, drip, drip through the gaping ceiling, the damage looked even worse than it had in pitch darkness. Broken tiles were strewn everywhere, and the bedrooms I'd cleared and cleaned were now littered with leaves, branches and puddles. I could only pray that the furniture hadn't sustained irreparable damage. I sighed. I'd have to bring Bernardo in to work his restoration magic.

'Today we stop plastering,' Ettore said, his deep voice a rumble. 'And we fix.'

I eyed the hole above my head. Even I knew that roof repairs weren't going to be quick or cheap. Two weeks of Ettore in my space had just turned into a month. At least. Thank heavens I was developing a liking for opera.

'Have you ever re-tiled a roof before?' I asked.

Ettore nodded.

'It's going to take a while to clear your bedroom enough so you can sleep in it,' Tommaso said. 'Will you move into your father's room, or do you want to stay in my spare room a while longer?'

It was childish, but I felt a dizzying sense of relief at not having to sleep in John's room. And I definitely didn't fancy sleeping alone in this house until the power was back. 'Thank you. I'll take your offer of the spare room.'

He nodded, a brisk movement, completely devoid of emotion. 'It's yours as long as you need it.'

The rain cleared away the summer dust, and the air smelled fresh and clean, rich with the dark scent of wet earth. The colours in the garden seemed more vibrant after the storm, and the dry creek at the bottom of the garden, which I'd never before seen with anything but a trickle of water, now gushed with a steady flow, making music as it bubbled over stones and tree roots. Ettore and I drank coffee and ate flaky cornetti in the warm sunshine on the terrace, to provision ourselves for the day ahead.

Then, while Ettore headed into town for supplies, I baked for the *trattoria*. I hoped no one would mind that I only made breads and scones, but they were the quickest and easiest, and I could whip them together with my eyes closed.

When Ettore returned, he'd not only brought a chainsaw, tarpaulins, roof tiles and other materials, but he'd also brought me a coverall to work in. It fit perfectly.

'How did you know my size?' I asked, but he just shrugged and set to work.

Together we cleared what debris we could from the upstairs rooms, and Ettore helped carry my possessions across to Tommaso's cottage. There was no opera music today, only the shrill whine of the chainsaw as Ettore hacked away at the branches so that I could carry them down to the composter, to join the wisteria that was already there.

The sounds were so deafening that I didn't even hear when a great big truck rolled into the yard, until the sound of men's voices floated up the stairs from the hall.

Tommaso had sent us backup: a truck with a high-reaching grapple to remove the immense tree trunk. From the back yard, Ettore and I watched in fascination – and just a little breathless trepidation on my part – as the grapple hook was secured, and the tree slowly winched off the roof.

'That's a beauty!' the truck operator shouted gleefully. 'That pine must be at least two hundred years old! So old that all it needed was a little blow to bring it down.'

If that was his idea of a 'little blow' then I didn't want to stick around to see what winter would bring.

When Tommaso returned, in much better spirits now that he'd ascertained the vines hadn't been hit too hard by the storm, the three of us clambered up onto the roof to secure tarpaulins over the gaping holes. Not that we need have bothered. Naturally, the skies stayed clear and sunny for days afterwards.

'I learned to lay roof tiles today,' I told Cleo when we finally managed to catch up.

'You go, girl! Perhaps you should consider a career flipping houses when you get home.'

I laughed. 'I don't think anyone could pay me enough money to go through this again. Tell me instead how things are going with the Delta Corporation.'

'All resolved and back to business as usual.' But she sounded remote, as if there was something she wasn't saying.

'What about The Arse? You didn't fall in love with him, I hope?'

I was joking, because surely she'd tell me if she had, but she didn't answer. Instead, she said: 'Tell me about your new housemate.'

I had to think for a moment. I wasn't sure what words to use to describe Tommaso. He was contradictory: withdrawn and brusque one moment, then engaging and laughing and so incredibly solicitous of my needs the next. And always so devastatingly sexy. When I thought of the perfect male torso now I didn't think of Luca or even of Chris Hemsworth.

I sighed, and Cleo gasped. 'Oh my God! He's hot, isn't he?'

I should deny it, stop Cleo getting any uncomfortable ideas, but before I could stop myself, I'd closed my eyes and was once again picturing that bare, tanned and very fit torso. I could immediately picture his lean abs, and the way they made a V-shape down towards the boxers resting on his hips. 'It's an Italian thing. Everything here just seems better than back home. When you're on holiday, things always do seem bigger and brighter and heightened, don't they? But none of it's real.'

Cleo sighed. 'Who cares about real? Sometimes a girl deserves a little fantasy in her life. I could sure do with some fantasy. Tell me all about him!'

'I can't talk now,' I whispered. 'He's in the other room, and these walls are paper thin.'

'Then email me! You need to dish. Better yet, send pictures!'

I said goodbye and hung up. On the other side of the wall, the shower had started. I pressed my eyes closed again and listened to the water falling. Listened to the slight stutter in its flow as Tommaso stepped beneath the spray.

My breath hitched. On the other side of this bedroom wall, Tommaso was naked. And hard as I tried to will the image away, I pictured him there. His strong, golden body, muscles bunching and flexing as he moved, rivulets of water cascading down over his pecs, down across his abs, lower...

Down, girl!

I rolled over and pulled a pillow over my head.

The electrician arrived the following day, and I discovered one of the miracles of Italy: despite the laidback approach to work, some things could be accomplished at the speed of light.

Ettore brought in some extra hands, a couple of men who looked even bigger and more bruising than he did, though I wouldn't have believed it possible to find anyone more intimidating. But they worked quickly and without fuss, and freed me up to return to the kitchen.

When I offered them my first attempt at rabbit stew – Beatrice having sent a brace of freshly skinned rabbits with the farm's driver – they applauded. I looked around the big kitchen table, packed with workmen dressed in dirty overalls and great big smiles, and felt like an Olympic champion receiving a gold medal. It wasn't quite the kind of big, raucous family meal I'd envisioned for this room, but it was close enough.

Tommaso only got the leftovers that night, and there wasn't much left.

'Wine?' he offered, hovering the bottle over my wine glass.

I nodded, but half an hour later I regretted it. The wine only seemed to heighten my awareness of him, rather than dulling it. Maybe moving in with him hadn't been a particularly bright idea.

This is stupid. It's just the holiday effect. It doesn't mean anything.

I'd seen enough of my friends and colleagues succumb to holiday romances to know how being relaxed and away from home could make people behave completely out of character. Men they wouldn't give the time of day to in a pub in East London suddenly became romantic heroes under the Mediterranean sun.

More than once, Geraldine had sworn some guy she'd met on her travels was the great love of her life. It had never lasted more than a few months, and every time she'd been heartbroken.

But I was stronger than that. I wasn't going to give in to this stupid crush. Because that's all this was. In my right mind, there was no way I'd find Tommaso di Biasi even remotely attractive. No way.

Bernardo dropped by early one morning to inspect the bedroom furniture. 'You did well, getting it out to dry as quickly as you did.' He nodded his approval. 'But your bed!

It's lucky it didn't collapse. They made furniture tough in the old days!'

We had to raise our voices over the soaring aria playing on Ettore's boom box, and the mix of baritone and tenor voices rising above it. There'd never been a more unlikely barbershop trio than my tattooed, ex-con handymen.

His inspection complete, Bernardo lingered in the kitchen. I was getting used to the unhurried Italian custom of turning every business call into a social event, so I offered him coffee and fresh *zeppole* balls, stuffed this time with sweet custard cream, and settled in for a chat.

'Beatrice tells me you want to sell this house?' Bernardo reached for the last *zeppole* on the plate.

'Oh yes!'

'I know someone who might be interested.'

I sat up straighter. 'But it's only the house that's for sale, not the vineyard.'

'*Nessun problema*. They are customers of mine, a couple from Köln who visit every summer, and they are looking for a holiday house here. Can I give them your number?'

I was so grateful, I gave him an entire bag of fresh *zeppole* to take home.

The phone call arrived that night, just after Tommaso had called to let me know he was leaving the cellar and on his way home. I set the table, the phone crooked between my ear and shoulder.

'This is Florian,' the man said. 'Bernardo tells me you have a *castello* for sale near Montalcino?'

'Well, it's really more of a big villa than a *castello*. But it has decorative towers and crenellations.'

'It's in good structural condition?'

I crossed my fingers, which was hard to do while carrying cutlery. 'Yes.'

'My partner Yusuf is a landscape gardener, and his only requirement for the property is a garden. Does the *castello* have a big garden?'

There at least, I could be completely honest. 'The garden's very big. It's a bit of a jungle at the moment, but it has a swimming pool, a fountain, and a gazebo we never really use.' Because it was still completely overgrown.

Tommaso's Alfa ground to a halt outside.

'That sounds perfect. Will you send me pictures, and we can talk price?'

'You don't want to see it in person?' Not that I was even vaguely ready to walk potential buyers through the house. I thought of the sections of roof that were still untiled, the neglected scaffolding where Ettore had been working on the stucco, the terrace that was no longer shaded but baked in the too-hot sun, and the pile of weathered shutters lying beside the woodpile.

'We only just got home and have a lot of work to catch up on, so we can't get back to Italy again any time soon.' It sounded as if he was rifling through the pages of a diary. I held my breath.

Tommaso stepped into the kitchen, stomping his feet on the welcome mat to clear the dried mud off his boots. I held up a finger to my lips, and he stilled.

'We're realists,' Florian continued. 'We know any older house in Italy is going to take some work to maintain. But as long as it's not falling down, we are ready to make our dream of a house in Tuscany come true.'

Could I really be this lucky that they'd buy the house just like that, sight unseen? 'It's in a very good location,' I said, and I wasn't sure if I was trying to reassure him or me.

'Would the last weekend in September be too late for you? Can you wait that long?' Florian asked. 'We can visit then to sign any papers that need to be signed.'

I let out my breath on a gush of air. Tommaso's brow quirked upwards in a question.

'Yes, I think we can wait that long.' While I kept my voice cool and professional, I did an excited fist pump. I'd need to delay my flight back to London by a week, but after four months of leave, would one more week really make a difference? That gave us seven weeks to get the house fixed and ready. We could do this.

Tommaso watched me, both his brows now high and expectant.

I jotted Florian's details on the back of an envelope, and when I hung up, I was beaming. 'We have a buyer! And they only want the *castello*. It's their dream to have a holiday home close to Montalcino. Isn't that great? It's the perfect compromise: we get the cash, you can buy me out without waiting for the next bottling, and you can keep the vineyard without losing a single vine.'

'And you can leave.'

'Yes, exactly.' I practically danced over to the stove to dish up our dinner. 'And I can go back to my life.'

When I brought the bowls of creamy zucchini risotto to the table, Tommaso still hadn't moved. His expression was stony. I really would have thought he'd be happier about this. He'd been wanting me to leave since I arrived.

I forced my smile to stay bright. 'Just think: you'll own the vineyard outright, without having me as a partner.'

He shrugged and turned away, moving to the sink to wash his hands. By the time he sat down at the table to eat, his frown was gone, his face expressionless.

With a hopeless shrug, I sat across from him and concentrated on my dinner. The man was so infuriating – did nothing ever please him?

Chapter 21

Non è tutto oro quel che luccica

(Not all that glitters is gold)

August dawned hot and stifling. Every time I stepped out of the cool *castello*, the wave of heat hit me like a wall. In town, tourists thronged the streets, even though many of the restaurants and guest houses closed as the locals took their annual summer vacation.

At Castel Sant'Angelo, we were busier than ever. While Ettore and his friends re-built the damaged roof, I became a pro at laying stucco. And I never thought I'd ever utter *those* words!

Aside from the work on the house, and the clock ticking down towards the Germans' arrival, there were more tour groups than ever passing through the vineyard. I'd gotten to be quite good as a sidekick on these tours, and when it was just a small family group, Tommaso even let me lead the tour myself. For bigger groups, like the visit of a group of British sommeliers, we arranged wine pairings, presenting a selection of foods that brought out the flavours of the wines, and offering little gift bags containing my trademark ricotta *zeppole* as a farewell gift. At least two Michelin-starred restaurants would now be serving the Sant'Angelo Brunello and Sangiovese blends on their wine lists.

In the two weeks since I'd signed the loan agreement, I hadn't heard from Luca. Not even a response to my texts. *Maybe he's just busy*, said the defensive little voice in my head. *He is a lawyer after all. Or maybe he's just giving you space. You should be glad he's not one of those clingy types.*

Somehow none of the excuses helped unclench the anxious knot in my stomach. He'd never been too busy for me before. But what if I'd had it all wrong? What if it wasn't sex he'd been after all these weeks, but a hold over Castel Sant'Angelo? And now that he had it, our friendship was over.

At last I screwed up my courage and called him. I planned to be all business, and not to sound desperate or too interested, but when he heard my voice, his warmth and enthusiasm swept me along on its usual tide, and all was forgiven.

'*Now* you are phoning to finally accept my invitation for *pici*?'

My stomach unclenched, and I couldn't help but laugh at his boyish enthusiasm. 'Only if you teach me how to make it.'

'Tonight? I will pick you up.'

'*Non preoccuparti*. I will borrow the truck.'

'You are sounding just like an Italian now! Six o'clock and we will turn you into a *real* Italian.'

He gave me his address, and just as the town's bell tower

chimed for the sixth time, I navigated the narrow street not far from the Piazza Garibaldi, holding my breath and praying that no other car tried to come from the opposite direction. I parked outside Luca's house, hugging the winery's truck up against the wall. His home was a traditional, narrow three-storey building of local stone, squashed into a row of similar houses. Unbelievably, his house had a garage downstairs. I had to admire the skill that would be required to contort his tiny sports car in there. Even by London standards, the space felt tight.

Above the garage, the forest green shutters were closed against the early evening sun. I rang the modern door buzzer and a moment later a latch clicked and the arched wooden door swung open.

Luca wore a black suit and a crisp white shirt, and my heart did that familiar flutter at seeing such perfection. Then he ushered me inside, and up a flight of stairs to the first floor living rooms. His apartment was unexpected, surprisingly modern and bright, not at all the chic bachelor pad I'd pictured. Black and white art prints decorated the walls, and the sleek lines of the Swedish-style furniture were softened by bright-coloured rugs and potted plants. The windows on the opposite side of the house had been thrown open, and light flowed in through tall windows which opened onto a balcony over-flowing with potted geraniums and overhung by a vibrant purple bougainvillea. Only in Italy would a bachelor's house be so filled with plants and colour. The only greenery in Kevin's apartment had been a cactus. And I'd given it to him.

'My home,' he said, both proud and pleased to have

surprised me. He led me into the compact kitchen, where he'd already laid out the ingredients for our dinner. 'You can wash your hands in there, and then we will get started on making dinner.'

'In there' was a cloakroom that was more high-tech and elegant than anything I'd seen since my arrival in Tuscany. I washed my hands, glanced at my reflection to ensure my make-up was still holding, and hadn't yet melted off my face in the summer heat, then returned to the kitchen. Luca had removed his jacket and tie, and rolled up his shirt sleeves, but he still looked as if he was posing for a photo shoot, rather than about to cook dinner.

The *pici* were surprising easy to make. We started with a well of flour, ordinary flour mixed with semolina, into which we fed eggs, olive oil, and a little water to moisten the dough.

I delighted in the familiar feel of squishing my fingers into the gooey mix. When it reached the right consistency, pliable, strong, and not too sticky, we set the big ball of dough aside to rest, and Luca poured me a glass of crisp white wine. Not a Fioravanti wine, I noticed. Clearly it was good enough for them to sell, but not good enough to drink.

'Haven't you learned yet that I don't get drunk easily?' I teased.

I watched as he tossed together a sauce with shavings of white truffle, sipping my wine slowly. Very slowly. While I no longer felt the urge to repeat my old mantra of *no holiday romance* in the same way, I still wasn't taking any risks.

'*Pici* is a strongly flavoured pasta.' He offered me a spoonful of sauce to taste. 'So it needs a strong sauce.'

I'd never tried truffles before. The taste was complex and earthy, and I licked my lips to savour every drop of the sauce.

When he removed the finished sauce from the heat, we cut the dough ball into sections, then rolled each section on a floured board using a long thin rolling pin, into long round strips a couple of feet long. This was the complicated part, getting the thickness of each string of pasta just right. Luca moved behind me, his arms on either side of me, his chest pressed against my back as he showed me how to roll the dough to get the right thickness. Too thin, and the string would break. Too thick, and the *pici* would remain doughy.

Having his body pressed up against mine should have done all sorts of strange things to my insides. But all I could think of was the time Tommaso showed me how to trim the vines. We'd stood in this same position, and my heart had thumped a good deal harder than it was doing right now. But I didn't want to think about Tommaso today.

Luca's hands were deft and slender, a complete contrast to Tommaso's less refined, more workmanlike hands. I brushed that thought away too.

Go away! I don't want to think about you! And I most certainly did not want to think about his hands, the way they seemed capable of anything, or of his strong arms.

I felt like Goldilocks again, with Baby Bear's temptingly perfect porridge right in front of me – or rather pressed up against my back. And all I could think of was Papa Bear's porridge. Too hot, too lumpy, and not right for me at all.

When Luca shifted away to reach for more flour, I drank a very deep sip of the wine, and forcefully banished these thoughts. I was here with Luca. It was Luca who made me feel warm and special and beautiful, Luca who had shown an interest in me, and who was never too busy when I called. Not a certain grumpy, grey-eyed man who'd barely spoken to me since Florian's phone call.

So I threw myself into rolling out the pasta with my bare hands, concentrating on the feel of the dough between my fingers, on making my strings even and consistent.

'Unlike other pastas, you don't want too much flour,' Luca said. 'It should still be a little moist, a little sticky, to make it roll easier, and the surface of the *pici* should be rough, to make it stick better to the sauce.'

When we were done, we were both covered in flour, and laughing.

'It's so unfair that you can be covered in flour and still look so good,' I giggled, all too aware that I'd managed to get flour in my hair and on my silk blouse.

In fact, Luca managed to look even sexier than usual, with his thick dark hair tousled, and his eyes alight with laughter. He brushed his floury fingers across my cheek. 'You should look in a mirror.'

I expected a shiver, at least. But nothing came. No flutter in my stomach, no expectant thrill at where this evening might be headed. I was enjoying myself, sure, but I wasn't turned on. What the hell was wrong with me? Maybe Kevin was right, and I was frigid. But then I remembered the feel of Tommaso's arms as he'd carried me out of the smoke-filled *castello* kitchen, and frigid was absolutely the last word that could be used to describe how I'd felt.

We boiled the finished *pici* in salted water, then Luca drained the pasta, mixed it with fine gratings of pecorino cheese, and poured in the sauce.

We ate at a little wooden table on the terrace, watching the comings and goings on the next street down the slope. The pasta was thicker than spaghetti, substantial and chewy, and just perfect.

'I heard you had vandals at the cellar?' Luca said, after he'd cleared away our plates, and we sat with our wine glasses, watching the town's lights come up and the darkness settle. My wine had warmed in my glass, and the afternotes turned bitter, but I was in no hurry to empty the glass.

'Did you lose very much wine?'

'Tommaso estimates we lost around eight thousand bottles of the next Angelica.'

Luca whistled. '*Porca miseria*! It seems that nowhere is safe anymore.' He seemed genuinely concerned, banishing any lingering fears I'd had that somehow the vandalism had been linked to the loan agreement I'd signed with his father.

'It won't affect your ability to make the loan repayments?' he asked.

I shrugged. I was learning to shrug like an Italian. This one said 'what's the use in complaining?' With the sale of the *castello* imminent, the winery's cash flow worries would soon be a thing of the past, but... 'Short of flood, fire, or act of God, Tommaso will make the repayments.'.

I don't know why I didn't want to tell Luca about Florian's offer. *I'll tell him when the offer to purchase has been signed, sealed and delivered*, I rationalised.

'Well, perhaps my estate agent friend will be able to sell the *castello* for you, and that will offset the damage done by the vandals,' Luca suggested. 'Have you heard from her again?'

I nodded. 'She came to have another look at the property a few weeks ago and take some pictures, but she doesn't yet feel enough improvements have been made to attract a decent price.'

And that had been before the big storm. But Florian's offer, emailed through this morning, was more than decent. Hopefully, I would never even need to list the house with an agent.

Luca twirled his empty wine glass so that it caught the light. 'Perhaps I can help you with that too,' he said. 'I have a friend from university who restores frescoes. I could ask her to come up here one weekend to work on your frescoes. Maybe she will offer you a good price.'

'Thank you. That would be wonderful.' Florian and Yusuf sounded like the kind of people who would appreciate a beautifully restored piece of art in their new home.

'Fiorella lives in Rome, though, so she will need a place to stay.'

'We have plenty of rooms.' And soon they might even be roofed again.

'I will call her tomorrow, then.' Luca smiled, reaching out to re-fill my glass.

I held my hand across the top of my glass. 'I have to drive home!'

'Or you could stay the night?' His voice was husky. On a scale of one to sexy, it was at least a twelve. But the temptation to stay was no longer as strong as it had been in Porto Ercole. Without the fresh sea air, the romantic piano music, and the intoxicating Syrah, the chemistry no longer buzzed in my veins, making it easier to say 'no, thank you.' Proof positive that chemistry couldn't be relied upon.

I shook my head. 'I really need to get going. I need to be up early to bake for the *trattoria*.' I'd left Tommaso a note, and the leftover risotto to heat up in the microwave, but I didn't fancy sneaking into his house in the early hours like a naughty teenager. Not that I'd *ever* sneaked home in the early hours as a teenager. That had been Geraldine's MO.

Luca sighed dramatically. 'You break my heart, *bella*. But for you, I will wait a thousand years.'

Yeah, right.

He walked me to the truck, and held the door open, but before I could slide into the driver's seat, he pulled me into his arms and kissed me.

He was a really good kisser, and my body responded. But my mind didn't follow where my body led. Instead, it went some place I really didn't want it to go. I pulled away. '*Buona notte*, Luca.'

Chapter 22

Il cioccolato è sempre la risposta non importa quale sia la domanda

(Chocolate is the answer, no matter what the question)

Returning from our market day jaunt one Friday afternoon, Beatrice and I discovered a party taking place on the terrace. The final roof tiles had been replaced, and Ettore, his friends, and Tommaso had cracked open a bottle of prosecco from Veneto. Though the repaired roof only meant we were back at the starting point, I took the glass Tommaso handed me and raised it in salute to my assembled team. '*Grazie mille*! And here's to getting all the rest of the work done before the Germans arrive!'

The others raised their glasses and joined the toast. Mozart's *Magic Flute* played in the background as we settled around the new patio table to share a feast of crisps with olives and melanzane dip.

'Could you imagine doing this back in England?' Tommaso asked in an undertone, as he opened a second bottle of bubbly.

I *had* done this dozens of times in the office in London. I couldn't count how many times we'd celebrated a completed project or a new client with champagne – expensive French champagne rather than prosecco, admittedly. But Tommaso was right. A bunch of people in grey suits assembled in the glassed-in breakroom, all in a hurry to be somewhere else, had nothing on this moment.

I looked around the terrace, at my tattooed, bald-headed handyman, at Beatrice laughing at a joke from one of his equally heavily tattooed friends, and I laughed.

'Admit it,' Tommaso said, his voice soft. 'You're going to miss this.'

What did he want me to say? That I wanted to stay? There was nothing for me here. No future, not even a home once Florian and Yusuf arrived to take possession of the *castello*. Everything I had was waiting for me in London – my house, my job, my office, my friends, people who wanted me, unlike Tommaso who'd made it clear from day one he wished I'd never come.

But I just shrugged and smiled. 'There's a lot I'm going to miss.'

I would miss the sunshine, my new friends, the garden, the fabulous food ... even the *castello*, though I certainly wasn't going to miss the cobwebs, the slow-filling bath, or the back-aching labour.

'*C'è nessuno?*' a woman's voice called suddenly through the house. *Anyone home?*

I started. I'd been so absorbed in my thoughts I hadn't even noticed a car approach up the drive. Tommaso and I exchanged a look, then we both rose and headed for the front door.

The woman hovering in the open doorway was dressed like a tourist, in jeans, a peach-pink T-shirt, and sneakers. But the car parked outside the front doors was no casual tourist vehicle. It was a sporty midnight-blue BMW.

'I am Fiorella,' she said, looking between us. 'Luca said you would be expecting me?'

I hurried forward. 'Oh, of course! You're the fresco restoration expert. Please come in.'

With a small, serious smile and a nod, she turned away. 'I must fetch my tools from the car.'

Tommaso picked his jaw up off the floor. 'Let me help you.'

The young woman turned another smile on him. '*Grazie*.'

She was the kind of woman I'd have loved to hate on sight. She had that innate Italian chicness, a trim figure with perfect curves, heart-shaped face, and a tumble of stylishly ombred curls, honey-blonde above and rose gold below. But she was younger than I'd expected, with big doe eyes and a tentative smile that screamed 'girl next door'. So when Tommaso hurried after her to her car, like a kid after candy, all I could do was roll my eyes.

He removed Fiorella's toolbox and bag from the back seat of her car and chatted to her as he carried them into the house, winning another shy smile.

I led the way to the dining room, where Fiorella unpacked a selection of tools onto a cloth on the dining table, before turning to inspect the mural. The fresco filled half the wall, from the panelled wainscoting up to the ceiling. The scene was an idyllic landscape, showing an eighteenth-century view of Castel Sant'Angelo bathed in sunlight. On all sides, the *castello* was surrounded by vineyard, where workers industriously harvested the grapes from the last of the summer vines.

'Magnificent!' Fiorella said. 'A very festive painting.'

To my eyes it seemed sad, so faded in places that the images were hard to make out, but maybe Fiorella's training enabled her to see potential I couldn't.

She inspected the painting through a specialised magnifying glass, bending and stretching for a better view. Tommaso's gaze was glued to her denim-clad butt. My jaw clenched. What was it with him and younger women?

'How old are you?' I couldn't help asking.

Fiorella smiled, amused. 'I get that a lot. I'm older than I look, and I know what I'm doing.' And studying the painting, she did look more confident and assured, losing a little of that youthful, shy look.

Having noticed our absence, the rest of the party now clustered into the dining room, and I made the round of introductions. Fiorella's appeal clearly wasn't limited to Tommaso. The other men's gazes took on the same slightly dazzled look.

Maybe it was the 'damsel in distress' thing she had going for her?

Who was I kidding? She was simply gorgeous.

'We were having a small celebration on the terrace,' Tommaso said. 'Would you care to join us?'

'No, thank you.' Without even taking her eyes off the painting, Fiorella shook her head. The movement set her curls dancing.

Okay, now I really wanted to be jealous of her. If I let my hair loose, it hung straight and flat. Back in my vainer years, I'd spent hours with a curling brush to get that kind of bounce. Usually it had lasted only until I left the building, and the fine mizzling London rain turned it all flat again.

'Could I offer you a glass of prosecco then?' Tommaso offered.

Fiorella shook her head again. 'No, thanks. Just a glass of water.'

Way more eager to please than I'd ever seen him, Tommaso dashed off to the kitchen. Beatrice rolled her eyes, where only I could see, and we shared a bemused smile.

Ettore and his friends, realising our impromptu party was at an end, said farewell, and soon after I heard their Vespas head out down the drive. Fiorella, meanwhile, swept the frescoed wall with an infrared tool, examining the layers of paint, so absorbed in the painting that she seemed to have forgotten she had an audience. Beatrice and I watched in respectful silence until Tommaso returned with a pitcher of water and a glass.

She turned to him. 'There isn't much structural damage, thankfully. There is no damp or mould, and no cracking or physical degradation. I think a little surface re-touching is all that is required to repair the discolouration of the pigments. Are there any other frescoes?'

My chest tightened, and it took me a moment to recognise the sensation. It was stress, that same anxiety I'd felt on a daily basis until I arrived here in Tuscany. It took me another moment before I understood why – Fiorella had turned to

Tommaso first, in the same way countless clients had turned to the man in the room, assuming he was the boss.

I rolled out my shoulders and forced a smile. 'Only this one, as far as we know.'

She nodded, as if apologizing for her assumption, and turned back to her scrutiny of the wall. 'And this room has always been a dining room?'

'As far back as I can remember. Is that important?'

'Not really, but it is an unusual positioning. Most villas have frescoes on display in the drawing rooms, where they will be seen and admired by the greatest number of guests. This one's position, in a room where only the inhabitants and their dinner guests would see it, suggests it was intended more as a good luck charm, to bring in a prosperous harvest, thereby ensuring that food remains on the table, rather than as a display of wealth. Is this a working vineyard?'

I nodded.

'Yes, that would make sense then.' Fiorella's gaze stroked lovingly over the wall. There was both admiration and tenderness in that look. This was clearly a woman who loved her job.

Did I have that same look when I presented my proposals to a client? Or when I sat at my desk late at night, comparing figures and doing calculations? I suspected not. But when I baked...? Yes, that was certainly how baking made me feel – absorbed, as if the rest of the world receded, and my focus narrowed to this one simple act of creation.

After another few moments of rapt inspection, Fiorella stepped back from the wall, her gaze sweeping first over

Tommaso, with the same appreciation she'd viewed the painting with, as if properly seeing him for the first time, before settling on me and Beatrice. 'I can do the work for you this weekend, but first you need to decide if this is something you really want done.'

'Why wouldn't I?' Surely restoring the artwork was a no-brainer?

She looked very serious. 'The trick to retouching a painting is to make it as indiscernible as possible, but even the subtlest alteration detracts from the material authenticity of the artwork. However, since this is a very personalised art piece, and integral to the building, its integrity lies more in its appeal to the inhabitants than it does on its merits as a work of art. So I think we need have no qualms about undertaking a restoration.'

'Glad to hear it,' I muttered drily, more to myself than to anyone else. At a confused quirk of Fiorella's eyebrow, I amended: 'I wouldn't want to get in trouble with any authorities for messing with a piece of art.'

She smiled, as if I'd given the right answer. 'I would like to begin now. I need quiet and space to work. Luca said you would have a room for me to stay in?'

'I'll take your bags up to one of the guest bedrooms,' Tommaso said.

With another shy smile, Fiorella turned away to tie back her hair, don a white coat and latex gloves, and without another word to us, she set to work.

Leaving her to it, Beatrice and I retreated to the safety of the kitchen. Without thinking, I set the kettle on the stove to boil.

Beatrice gazed thoughtfully in the direction of the dining room, as if she could see through the walls. 'Now that is surprising.'

'What is?' I busied myself with the teapot and cups, though I really had no appetite for tea. Something stronger, though...

Beatrice smiled. 'It's high time Tommaso showed an interest in a woman.'

I banged the teapot down on the tray a little harder than necessary. 'What is it with men being attracted to soft and helpless women anyway?' Or maybe just one man?

Beatrice laughed. 'It's caveman instincts – that urge to protect.'

'Then I don't stand a chance.' Because heaven only knew I was never going to be soft, helpless and doe-eyed – and I didn't want to be.

I felt an inexplicable need for sugar. I cut two slices from the braided peach strudel I had in the pantry. 'I thought Tommaso usually went for a different type of woman?'

From Beatrice's description, I'd imagined him with worldly-wise, pleasure-loving, looking-for-casual-sex holidaymakers – women like Geraldine – and Fiorella certainly didn't fit that picture.

Beatrice made a disparaging sound. 'Picking up women for sex isn't the same as real interest. And Fiorella is just perfect for him. She's the complete opposite of Gwen.'

The knife I'd been using slipped through my fingers. It clattered on the kitchen table, and I frowned at my own clumsiness. 'Who's Gwen?'

'Tommaso's ex-wife. You didn't know her?'

I shook my head and poured out the tea. 'I didn't even know he was married.' Chalk that up to yet another thing my dear old Dad hadn't thought important enough to mention.

'Well, not anymore, obviously. They married years ago, when they worked together in some fancy hotel chain in Edinburgh. They had big plans to open a guest house here together, but she never came. She was very independent and career-focused and didn't want to give up city life to live in the middle of nowhere, so they divorced.'

Career-focused and independent. Just like me.

Which explained a lot. But I wasn't going to let him off the hook that easily. Just like my father, given the choice between sharing his life with someone and his precious vines, Tommaso had chosen the vines. And any woman who wasn't willing to give up everything to support that dream was pushed aside. I don't know why that made me angry, but it did.

After Beatrice left, I made up the bed in the spare bedroom for my guest. Fiorella's overnight bag was already there, but there was no sign of Tommaso. No doubt he'd returned to the winery.

I toyed briefly with the idea of moving my things out of his cottage and back into my own room, now that the roof was repaired, but then I had a vision of Tommaso inviting Fiorella back there after dinner, to the place where we'd watched *Buffy* marathons and played Rummikub.

Since Fiorella didn't seem the type of woman Tommaso should seduce and walk away from, I left my things where they were. In the interests of protecting the sweet young woman from his wiles, of course. It had absolutely nothing to do with the extremely irrational jealousy that had started to bubble inside me.

For the first time ever, I set the table in the dining room – which also gave me a chance to peek at what Fiorella was doing. She had daubed solvent across a section of the fresco, and the results of the chemicals reacting with the pigments, and the simple effect of a little additional brushwork, were magical to witness. Beneath her brush, the colours seemed to spring to life.

Tommaso returned from the cellar earlier than usual, and he showered and changed before he joined us for dinner. He brought wine. 'This is our most exclusive vintage of the Angelica,' he said, filling Fiorella's glass.

For now, I added. With eight thousand litres of wine lost, the next bottling of the Angelica was going to be way more exclusive.

Fiorella had worked until dark and hadn't changed her clothes, only removing her white coat and gloves for dinner, but she still managed to look effortlessly elegant. Hot from the kitchen, with my hair plastered to my neck and my cheeks flushed, I was acutely aware that I did not appear to my best advantage beside her – even though I'd changed into the teal-coloured dress I'd worn to Porto Ercole. The same dress which had made Luca look at me as if I were edible.

Tommaso barely even seemed to notice I was there.

After an appetiser course of olives, marinated artichoke hearts, and parcels of soft goat's cheese wrapped in salami, I served a first course of ravioli stuffed with pecorino and smoked prosciutto, followed by the hearty *ribollita* stew over little cakes of polenta, and finished off with slices of the peach strudel.

If only Cleo could see me now, a domestic goddess, and a world away from instant frozen meals and takeaway vindaloos. The nearest Indian restaurant was over an hour's drive away, in Arezzo. I'd looked it up on Google.

'You are an excellent cook,' Fiorella said politely.

'I definitely won't be eating this well after you leave,' Tommaso added.

'You're leaving?' Fiorella's eyes widened. 'But aren't you two...?' Her question trailed off as she looked between us.

'No, we are definitely not.' Tommaso's denial was unequivocal, and I felt as if a bucket of ice had been thrown over my head. Did his denial have to be quite so emphatic? There'd been a time he'd flirted with me the way he flirted now with Fiorella. *He* might have forgotten, but I hadn't.

That last summer, when I'd just turned seventeen, I'd felt so grown up, so ready to take on the world. A place at a prestigious university in the bag, and an end in sight to being passed from parent to parent like a hot potato. And all those new emotions and sensations coursing through me...

Since he'd gone away to university, Tommaso had started working out, and he was no longer the bookish boy I'd grown up with, but a man. Years at an all-girls boarding school made me keenly aware of that. Three years older and worldly-wise, and yet he'd still treated me as an equal. I'd felt so mature. For the first time in my life, I'd felt desire, and desirable.

My father hadn't seen the changes, but Nonna had. 'Your mother wasn't much older than you when she came to Tuscany and met your father,' she'd said, and the warning had rung as clear as a bell. *Don't lose your head. Don't do anything you might regret for years after.*

And I so nearly had.

There was that one night we'd walked alone through the vineyard. It was late summer, and the harvest was nearly over. Only the last fruit still hung on the vines, and the air had a ripeness about it, that last blush of summer heat before the nights started to draw in. The moon had been high, and Tommaso had taken my hand as we strolled between the vines. It had no longer been the casual touch of childhood friends, but a super-charged touch...

'Sarah? Are you okay?'

I blinked, and I was no longer walking through the vineyard holding his hand, but looking at him across the gleaming dining table.

'Shall I put the moka pot on for coffee?' Tommaso asked, as if repeating himself.

I pushed away from the table. 'No, I'll do it.'

I couldn't get away to the kitchen fast enough. As soon as I had the coffee brewing, I opened the freezer. But Tommaso and I had finished the last of the ice cream during a recent marathon of *Lucifer*, having already run through all seven seasons of *Buffy*. So I hid in the pantry and dug out the rich dark chocolate I usually kept for baking. The chocolate melted on my tongue, making everything seem right again.

What had gotten into me? I hadn't allowed myself to revisit

that memory in years. And certainly not since I'd been back in Tuscany. I'd believed it safely buried where it belonged.

After stuffing my face with another few blocks from the chocolate slab, I returned to the dining room far more composed. I served the coffee with a platter of cheeses and fruits, then as soon as I could politely do so, excused myself. I stacked the dirty dishes in the sink, but didn't bother to wash them, and hurried to Tommaso's cottage, showering and getting into bed as quickly as I could. Then I lay in the dark, unable to sleep, listening for his footsteps in the yard beneath the window. He followed not too long after, and I breathed a sigh of relief.

I lay awake, listening to the soft sounds of his movements through the paper-thin walls. As I had too many other nights, I listened as he showered, then heard the gentle snick as his bedroom door closed. I let out a breath I hadn't even known I was holding.

The small rustling movements faded into silence. Still unable to sleep, I pulled on my dressing gown, and snuck down to the kitchen. Maybe it was the after-dinner coffee keeping me awake. Maybe a glass of warm milk would help. Geraldine had always given me warmed milk when I couldn't sleep.

The microwave pinged, and I took the steaming mug out and headed back up the stairs. I'd nearly reached the top when the bathroom door opened, spilling out hot steam and light.

Tommaso emerged from the tiny bathroom, towelling his head dry. Another towel wrapped snugly around his hips. Everything else was bare. His torso, his muscled arms, his legs with their dusting of dark hair.

I swallowed, and inadvertently spilled scalding milk all over my fingers, though I scarcely noticed the burn.

'Can't sleep?' he asked, his voice low and rumbly. I'd have called it his sex voice, if I had any idea what he sounded like when he whispered sweet nothings into a woman's ear.

I nodded. 'It's hot tonight.' It was August, so that might even be true. Though right at that moment, I could have stood at the Arctic and still have been burning up.

Since Tommaso didn't seem in any hurry to move, I averted my gaze, climbed the last few steps, and brushed past him, my arm grazing a firm bicep in the narrow hall.

'*Sogni d'oro*,' he whispered. Sweet dreams.

I kept putting one foot in front of the other until I was safely in Nonna's old bedroom, with the door firmly shut. I sagged against it. I had to be falling ill. I hadn't felt this hot and bothered and stupid since I was a girl.

Pull yourself together. You're not a girl anymore. You know exactly what this is. It's that holiday thing. This is nothing more than the chemistry that happens when you're away in an exotic place and in close proximity to a member of the opposite sex. It's not real, and you'll get over it, just the way you got over Luca. Just the way you got over Tommaso the last time.

Chapter 23

Amore e gelosia nacquero insieme

(Love and jealousy go hand in hand)

We didn't have our usual intimate breakfast in the cottage kitchen next morning. Instead, I laid out a buffet of eggs, bacon, toast, tomatoes and mushrooms in the dining room. I was only half-pleased that the formality and bigger space of the dining room meant I didn't have to look directly at Tommaso.

Usually, he didn't linger over breakfast, eager to get to the cellar, but it was only when Fiorella insisted she needed to start work, that he took himself off to the winery.

'I can't do another night like that,' I complained to the bathroom mirror, examining the bags under my eyes.

The problem wasn't that I was jealous of Fiorella. Okay, well maybe I was just a little jealous. The problem also wasn't that I disliked her. As much as I wanted to, it was impossible. Once she relaxed a little, Fiorella made the perfect guest. She'd complimented the food, and chatted happily, giving equal attention to both me and Tommaso – though the same could certainly not have been said of him.

No, the problem was that she was so right for Tommaso, in ways I never would be.

She'd grown up in Rome but would just as happily live in Tuscany (it housed Florence, after all, and she loved Florence). Her family was obscenely wealthy (hence the sporty BMW) so marriage with her might put an end to the winery's financial worries. Her career was a hobby rather than a necessity, and she'd told me quite unconscientiously over the ravioli that she wanted marriage and children.

She was the kind of woman who wouldn't mind giving up her career for her future husband's passion.

Listening to their animated conversation about the importance of doing what you loved, of following your heart, it would have been obvious to anyone how much they had in common.

While I was the outsider, the practical one who'd chased security and financial stability rather than my passions. Because if there was one thing I'd discovered on this 'garden leave' it was that I wasn't passionate about my job. Dedicated, determined, disciplined? Sure. But I had certainly not followed my heart when I'd chosen a career in finance. I didn't even know what my heart wanted. And if I did, I still wouldn't trust it, fickle things that hearts were.

I stared now at the mirror. Maybe financial security and a mortgage were my passions. Those counted, right?

And just because I was thirty-five and still single didn't mean there wasn't a Mr Right out there for me. When I got back to London, I'd pay more attention to my work–life balance. I'd even go speed dating with Cleo.

But I still had six weeks left in Tuscany, and I did not plan to spend even one day of those six weeks being a spare wheel to Tommaso and Fiorella. They say that misery loves company – so I called for backup. 'I think the occasion of the *castello*'s first guest in decades deserves a dinner party,' I said to Beatrice. 'Will you join us?'

While Ettore took over re-stuccoing the house's façade – to my immense relief – I cooked. And baked. And cooked some more. And in between cooking, I moved all my things out of Tommaso's cottage and back into my own room in the *castello*.

The best way to avoid temptation was to stay as far away from it as possible – not a lesson I'd put into practice much since I'd arrived in Tuscany. And I didn't think my fickle heart would cope with another late night, barely-dressed encounter.

When we gathered on the terrace for a pre-dinner drink that evening – me, Beatrice, Fiorella, Beatrice's older brother Aurelio and his wife Silvia, Daniele and Ettore, now dressed in smart trousers and a crisp white shirt that concealed his tattooed arms – I was more than ready for a drink.

'We have something wonderful to celebrate today,' Beatrice said, raising her glass of apéritif, a negroni cocktail I'd prepared. 'Today the *trattoria* got two new Google reviews; the first praised the perfection of the bruschetta we served with the *zuppa*, and the other said ours was the best *zeppole* he had tasted in his entire tour through Italy. That is all thanks to you, Sarah.'

The others raised their glasses in salute, and I basked in

the glow of their praise. Financial advisers never got much praise. We certainly didn't get Google reviews.

'You can't be persuaded to stay?' Beatrice asked hopefully.

I laughed as I shook my head. 'In six weeks the German buyers will be here, and I'll be back in the office.' My chest tightened in a way I hadn't felt in months. But that couldn't be stress at the mere thought of work, surely. I was looking forward to going back to the office. To the bustle of London streets, and the after-work drinks with Cleo in the trendy little bars around Cheapside, to the packed pub on Wanstead High Street on Friday nights, and strolling through the park on Sunday mornings...

Yet somehow all I could picture was rain and cold.

'You are selling the *castello*?' Fiorella asked, her big dark eyes rounding in surprise.

I nodded. 'To a German couple who've made a very generous offer. They want to take occupation in October already.' Florian and Yusuf had cooed over the photos I'd sent them so far – though I'd had to get a little creative with the angles to show the *castello* in the best light. 'They're even taking it fully furnished.'

Fiorella frowned, then looked around. 'Tommaso is late.'

'Tommaso is often late. When he's working in the winery, he loses track of time.'

But he *wasn't* working late tonight.

When he finally joined us on the terrace, a collective gasp whispered through the assembled guests.

Daniele was the first to find his voice. 'You clean up good.'

Everyone laughed, Fiorella smiled like a cat that had just

discovered a great big bag of catnip, and I threw the entire contents of my cocktail down my throat.

'I'll serve dinner, then,' I said.

By the time I joined my guests in the dining room, carrying a platter of appetizers that included phyllo-wrapped asparagus and rolls of bresaola beef stuffed with soft mozzarella, I was better prepared for the sight of a clean-shaven Tommaso.

He did indeed clean up good, and I wasn't the only one who'd noticed. Fiorella sat as close to Tommaso as she could at a twelve-seater table that was set for only eight. Her shyness was gone tonight, and her eyes sparkled. When she addressed Tommaso, she unconsciously reached out to touch his arm. He didn't move away.

My first – and only – dinner party at the *castello* was a failure before it had even begun. Sure, the crystal and silverware glittered in the romantic candlelight, reflecting the sparkling chandelier overhead. The heavy scent of lilies filled the air, and the antique ivory tablecloth and napkins added sophistication. The dining room looked as I'd always imagined it would – magnificent. Wine flowed, and food was passed around, and my guests laughed and chatted, relaxed and happy.

But I couldn't wait for it to be over.

I didn't need him to shave off his beard and trim his hair to see how attractive he is, I thought. And promptly knocked over my wine glass, spilling wine like blood across the antique linen and into the asparagus.

'Are you okay?' Tommaso asked from the far end of the long table, as I scrambled to my feet. 'Do you need help?'

'I'm fine. Just fine. I don't need any help.' I hurried to the kitchen for dish cloths, though I knew it was futile. No dish cloth was going to clean up the mess I'd made.

I was such a fool. No holiday romance, indeed! I'd been so busy resisting a repetition of Geraldine's biggest mistake, of being seduced into unprotected sex, pregnancy and single parenthood, that I hadn't realised there was an even greater danger: the danger of falling in love.

Angrily, I slammed the door shut on the oven's warming drawer. Why couldn't I have fallen in love with Luca, who was easy-going and fun, and who actually wanted me around? No, I had to go and fall for Tommaso – complicated, difficult Tommaso who couldn't wait for me to leave.

I hadn't been able to walk away from him unscathed the last time, and I doubted I'd be able to walk away unscathed this time.

But walk away I must.

We had no future together. We were on such different paths. If I really loved him, I'd want him to be happy, wouldn't I? I'd want him to find a woman he could share his life with. Instead, I wanted to scratch her eyes out.

I carved the roasted lamb with aggressive slices. And didn't I deserve the same – someone to share my future? Someone who would put *me* first, for a change?

I'd only just brushed away the suspicious leakage from my eyes when Beatrice stepped into the kitchen.

'Oh good.' I forced a smile. 'You can help me carry in the next course.'

In true Italian style, dinner lasted hours and hours, as my guests laughed and chatted through course after course made from the finest local ingredients; *pappa al pomodoro* soup, a thick tomato soup served with my now Google-famous bruschetta, followed by a simple porcini pasta, and then the grand *chef-d'oeuvre*, a main course of lamb, slow-cooked in herbs from my own herb garden, with chickpea salad, beans in a lemon and thyme sauce, and potatoes chopped and lightly sautéed in olive oil and rosemary until perfectly crisp.

I tried my best to laugh and chat along with my guests, but it seemed as if the minutes ticked by as slowly as if I were re-sitting a uni exam, praying for the ordeal to be over. My face ached from forcing a smile all evening, and my chest ached with a feeling I'd only ever felt once in my life before, and it hadn't been the afternoon of Kevin's birthday when I'd left work early to surprise him with the cake I'd baked – lemon drizzle, his favourite – and found he'd already started celebrating with someone else.

'If you ever decide to give up banking, you could work as a chef,' Aurelio joked, dragging me back into the present. I smiled at him, grateful for the distraction. Those weren't memories I wanted to revisit tonight either.

Dessert was a chocolate torte, served with fresh cream from the Rossi farm. Now that my tastes had adapted to the less sugary diet of Tuscany, I found the chocolate too sickly sweet for anything but the smallest portion. The fruit and cheese platter which followed was almost a relief.

Tommaso insisted on helping me clear away the empty plates and making coffee.

'You're very quiet tonight,' he said, when we were alone in the kitchen.

'Am I?' I didn't need to make an effort to sound distracted. I was. My gaze kept wandering back to his face, to this new Tommaso who was both a stranger, and a memory that refused to be suppressed. 'It's probably just the heat.'

There was that excuse again. And he wasn't buying it now any more than he had last night. He frowned, as if wanting to contradict me, but then the coffee was ready, and he turned away to attend to the pot.

When at last the interminable meal ended, and Fiorella excused herself, saying she needed an early start the next day to finish her work on the fresco before the weekend was over, Tommaso and I walked my guests to their cars and waved goodbye until the last headlights had disappeared from view.

'*Now* are you ready to tell me what's eating you?' he asked.

'Nothing.' I wrapped my arms around myself, as if to keep warm, though the hot August night couldn't have been any more stifling.

'Why did you move out?'

'There's no longer any need for me to stay at the cottage now that the roof has been fixed. I thought you might like your space to yourself again.'

'Still always running away, Sarah?' His eyes were dark and guarded, and for a fleeting moment I wondered if he was remembering the time when I *had* run away.

But it's not running away. It's a strategic withdrawal. And with that thought, I withdrew, all the way back to my bedroom in the *castello* where I lay awake for yet another sleepless night, staring at the new ceiling and re-living the past.

*

On Sunday, while Fiorella worked in the dining room, I allowed Ettore to distract me with the task of re-painting the wooden shutters a bright forest green. Some were too rotted to be of any use, and had to be replaced entirely, but there were enough to keep me busy all day while Ettore continued his job of re-plastering to the sound of Verdi's 'Rigoletto'.

At the end of the day, when Fiorella's work was done, the frescoed wall had never looked so vibrant, as full of life and colour as it must have been when it was first painted.

'It's gorgeous,' I said. Now the painting truly did look festive.

Fiorella smiled, pleased. 'There's something else I'd like you to see.'

She led the way into the drawing room, where she peeled back a corner of the hideous burgundy-coloured wallpaper to reveal a layer of pale daffodil-yellow paint beneath. She dabbed a cloth with solvent, then carefully rubbed the cloth in tight circles across a small section of wall. The solvent melted away the paint, and soon other colours emerged through the yellow. Bright colours, forming an indistinguishable pattern.

'I won't be able to get another weekend away from Rome for a while,' she said. 'But I would really like to return and see what is under this wallpaper. Look at those colours! I am almost sorry I must leave.'

Fresco or no fresco, I wasn't sorry to say goodbye, though I had to admit Fiorella had been nothing but friendly and professional. I was the one with the irrational jealousy eating a hole inside me, and I prayed it would go away as soon as Tommaso returned to work at the cellar and stopped hanging around the house.

Chapter 24

L'uva cattiva non fa buon vino

(Bad grapes can't make good wine)

But of course life never runs that smoothly, does it?

I'd thought by moving back into the big house I'd see less of Tommaso. Instead, he seemed to be around more than ever. When the stucco work was finished, he helped Ettore re-hang the shutters. I would have been grateful for the help, because at least on the outside the house looked ready for its new owners, but since I suspected he was only helping to get the house done and me gone quicker, my gratitude was not exactly effusive.

When the shutters were done, and Ettore began the task of stripping the peeling wallpaper inside, Tommaso mowed the lawn, repaired the pump for the fountain, and refilled the cistern from the old garden well, so that the fountain splashed its musical melody once again.

And having him around, in my space every day, was not helping me resist temptation very well. I hid myself in the kitchen, blending new flavours, finding innovative ways to present the seasonal produce, rolling out delicate flaky pastry, stewing summer fruits, and icing an elaborate birthday cake for Beatrice. At least those were things I could control.

'Don't you have work to be doing at the vineyard?' I asked grumpily one day, when Tommaso came into the kitchen to re-fill his pitcher of lemonade.

He only shrugged, which made his shirt pull tight across his shoulders. My fingers itched to reach out and touch, and I had to stick them away in the back pockets of my jeans to keep them from straying.

The next Sunday, Tommaso offered to rebuild the trellis over the terrace, and I accepted gratefully. Since I'd chopped away the wisteria and relegated it to the composter, no further progress had been made, as Ettore had had far more pressing tasks, and my carpentry skills were non-existent. Yes, I'll admit it: sometimes I can't do everything on my own.

Though Yusuf had assured me he would take the garden in hand once they took ownership, I found an excuse to work in the front garden so I could watch Tommaso work. The garden was still a mess of tangled beds separated by paved paths, yet it had its own wild beauty, a lush green backdrop splashed with bold colours. Along the brick wall that hid the swimming pool from the rest of the garden, a bank of sunflowers bowed their heads in the midday heat, and there were silvery-green sage bushes, climbing roses, wild jasmine and irises.

Kneeling on the paving to pull the nettles that had pushed up between the slabs, I was able to steal glances at Tommaso from behind my sunglasses. Each time, my pulse raced and my mouth turned dry.

I sighed. I had it so bad. As bad as any hormonal teenager, though thankfully without the skin breakouts and insecurities.

Tommaso wore low-slung jeans that hung on his lean hips, and a wife-beater vest. I'd always hated those vests – the uniform of plumbers and other men with hairy butt cracks. But now the sight made my mouth water. His muscled biceps flexed and rippled as he moved, the pecs outlined through the tight white fabric ... yup, my hormones were having a field day.

When I could no longer hide that I was staring, I moved away, to the furthest end of the garden, where the slope dropped away to an endless view of the countryside. Here, in my youth, the view had been framed by a neat box hedge of lavender, maintained by a young man who'd come in once a week from Montalcino. Tired of having me and Tommy constantly beneath his feet, he'd often given us work to do, taught us which seedlings were flowers and which were weeds, which were edible, and which weren't. Fleetingly, as I removed my thick gardening gloves and set to work trimming back the riot of bushy lavender, I wondered where that gardener was now.

The air was rich with the scents of summer, lavender and roses and earth baking in the sun. Birds hummed and bees sang. I closed my eyes to breathe it all in, to save up the memories for autumn, when I'd be back in London with the smell of petrol fumes and blocked drains.

But as happened too frequently these days, the moment I

stopped moving, the moment my mind stilled for even a second, the replays started. Only I was no longer sure if it was a memory, or wishful thinking, as I temporarily lost myself in the vision of Tommaso's strong hands splayed on my waist, his sun-warmed lips against mine, the scratch of his cheek beneath my mouth.

'Hey, Sarah!' I spun as the unexpected voice broke through my daydream, raising the gardening shears defensively as I turned.

'Ooph!' Tommaso doubled over, holding his ribs.

'Oh my gosh! I am so sorry! Are you okay? Are you bleeding?'

He straightened up, still clutching his side. 'Nothing to worry about,' he wheezed. 'Probably just a broken rib. You are determined to kill me, aren't you?'

'Well, it's your fault for sneaking up on me,' I bit back.

'I thought you might want to take a break for some lemonade. You're going to get sunburned if you stay out here too long.'

He'd fetched a jug of lemonade from the kitchen, complete with ice and a sprig of mint. I joined him on the terrace and he poured the ice-cold drink into two glasses, and held one out to me.

'Are you sure you're okay?' I asked again.

'*Certo*! I'll live.'

He stood so close I could smell the warm, male smell of sweat and sun on him. I watched in fascination as he emptied his glass, the taut muscles of his throat working. Without the facial hair, he looked younger and leaner, and the five o'clock stubble starting to appear was just about the sexiest thing I'd ever seen. I shifted my gaze, staring up instead at the finished trellis. 'You've done a great job. Thank you.'

He shrugged. 'Without the wisteria, though, it's not going to provide much shade. We should plant something new, something that won't grow so heavy. A vine, maybe?'

I shook my head, trying not to let the way he said *we* go to my head. 'I was thinking of a bougainvillea, like the one with bright orange blossoms you have growing in the courtyard at the cellar. And morning glories winding up the posts for contrasting colour.'

He grinned. 'I'll take care of the bougainvillea, if you take care of the morning glories, whatever they are.'

I rolled my eyes, but I laughed. It felt good to laugh again. I hadn't laughed much all week.

'Have dinner with me tonight.'

My laughter died. 'What?'

'Have dinner with me tonight. I'll make one of Nonna's special stews, and perhaps I can teach you to play *briscola*.'

Heat flooded my cheeks, and I looked away. 'I can't...'

'You have other plans?'

I nodded. I did now, even if I didn't yet know what they were.

I drove into town with no real plan for the evening, but when I arrived and parked in the usual spot where Beatrice parked on market days, I discovered the parking lot almost full. Streams of people were heading to the *fortezza*, so I trailed after them. A jazz concert was in progress within the high, ruined walls of the fortress. I wasn't a big jazz fan, but in the warm twilight, as the stars started to come out overhead, I thought I might become a convert.

Wandering through the crowds, I stopped here and there to chat with people I knew. I was no longer 'John Langdon's daughter' but Sarah Wells, neighbour and member of the community.

What I loved most about Wanstead was its village-y, community feeling. When I first moved there, I'd loved sitting in the little park that edged the high street, listening to the church bells and the children's shrieks from the playground. But this was even better. Here in Montalcino I not only saw that community feeling, but I was a part of it.

Bernardo and his wife invited me to sit on the picnic blanket they had spread out, and I joined them for a glass of *vino rosato*.

'Where is Tommaso this evening?' Bernardo asked.

I shrugged, pleased that I was learning to speak with my shoulders like a true Italian. It saved me from having to give a real answer.

When my glass was empty, I said farewell to Bernardo and his family, and resumed my ramble through the crowd. On the far side of the *fortezza*'s open air space, a bar had been set up. I made my way towards it, still pausing to greet acquaintances, including one of Ettore's friends who looked more intimidating than ever in his biker leathers.

Around the edges of the gathering, a little apart from the families, there were couples, some holding hands, some with heads bent close together, one in a very intimate embrace, the woman straddled across the man's lap as they kissed. The woman looked very much like the Monica Bellucci lookalike estate agent. I recognised the fire engine red dress. And...

'*Luca?*'

Both heads turned my way, and then Luca unceremoniously dumped the woman out of his lap and jumped up. 'Sarah! I did not expect to see you here tonight!' He managed to sound as delighted and cheerful to see me as he always did, as if I hadn't just seen him with his tongue down another woman's throat, and his hand caressing her breast.

It was not unlike watching Kevin dump Geraldine out of his lap all those long, long months ago. Except that Luca and the estate agent were clothed.

'Clearly not,' I said drily.

He spread his hands. 'Ah, Sarah,' his voice was soft and coaxing now. 'We never made any promises to each other. You understand...'

'Yes, I understand completely. We never discussed being exclusive.'

'Exactly!' Pleased that I understood, he reached out and took both my hands in his. 'I am so glad you are here!' His smile was the same warm, seductive, dimpling grin that had always made me feel so special. Now, it made my stomach turn, and not in a good way. 'Because now I can invite you to join me for a little party at my parents' winery on the weekend. Will you come?'

'As a neighbour, or as your date?'

'My date, of course.' He cast a glance towards the estate agent, as if belatedly remembering her. 'She won't mind. She understands too.'

'I'm sure she does.'

His thumb brushed my palm, an intimate promise of pleasure he'd used on me before, and his smile turned to a seductive pout. 'You never told me you had a buyer for the *castello*.'

'Fiorella told you?'

'Of course.'

I had to resist a snort. Did Fiorella *understand* as well? I hoped not. She deserved far better than Luca. She deserved someone like Tommaso.

Gently, I extricated my hands from Luca's. 'We might never have talked about exclusivity, but if any man is trying to get me into his bed, I'm afraid I sort of expect it of him. Because I deserve nothing less than a man who'll stay faithful to me; a man who'll put my happiness before everything else.' I smiled sweetly. 'And that man clearly isn't you.' And how had I ever thought it might be?

I'd have liked to think I made a grand exit, leaving Luca looking after me open-mouthed and full of regret for what he'd lost, but when I finally risked looking back he had already re-joined the estate agent on their picnic blanket, and she was melting into his grin in the same way I used to do.

'She's the one with the spring?' I heard the woman ask.

I had no idea what she meant, and I didn't care to know. I felt ill. Not because of Luca, but because of that very old sense of betrayal, duller now, but still there, like a sore tooth that was tender to the touch.

'I need a drink,' I said to the bartender when I reached the bar.

'Brunello, Sangiovese, or *vino rosato*?' the bartender asked.

'She'll have a Malfy.' I looked up into the tanned face and laughing eyes of Daniele Rossi. 'It's an Italian gin; they call it the grown-up cousin to *limoncello*. It'll help you put him behind you very quickly.'

'You saw that?' Thankfully, the low lighting of the bar hid my blush.

'*Sì*. It's men like Luciano Fioravanti who give all Italian men a bad name. I hope you know we're not all like that?'

I nodded, though I wasn't entirely sure if I *did* know. It wasn't only Italian men who were cheating, self-serving pricks after a good time.

Daniele's brows drew down in concern. 'You aren't in love with him?'

'Good heavens, no!'

'Good. I am surprised Tommaso didn't warn you about Luca.'

'He did. I didn't believe him.' I'd thought he was just jealous, but he'd been right, damn him.

Luca had only been using me. Whether for a fun time or for the vineyard, it didn't matter. Like everyone else, he hadn't wanted *me* enough. And maybe that was why I felt like I either wanted to throw up or hit someone. Why couldn't I ever be enough?

The barman slid the ice-cold glass, misted with condensation, across the bar towards me, and I raised it to Daniele. '*Salute*!' Then I downed the gin.

Chapter 25

Non c'è amore come il primo amore

(There is no love like the first love)

Beatrice's thirtieth birthday fell on the Feast of the Assumption in mid-August, giving the Rossis an excuse to throw a great big party. Beatrice and I went shopping at the big outlet mall on the way to Arezzo for new dresses for the occasion.

'I don't care how classic a Little Black Dress is, you are not wearing black to my party!' Beatrice insisted, when I chose a sedate black number from the rack.

'Then let me wear my teal sun dress.'

But that wouldn't do either for Beatrice. 'You've worn that dress before. It's pretty, but you need something that will make you shine.'

I laughed. 'I don't need to shine. *You're* the birthday girl.'

She ignored me. 'How about this one? It brings out the colour of your eyes.'

'It's the colour of mud?' I asked, turning to look.

'Your eyes are not like mud! They have beautiful green sparks in them.'

The dress Beatrice picked from the rail was a Fifties-style cocktail A-line dress with a full skirt and round neckline in a shade of hunter green that made me think of the *castello* garden at twilight. The cut was simple, but the bodice had an overlay of lace in the same colour of the dress that added subtle texture. I glanced at the label, and my heart stuttered. 'This is a major fashion brand!' I hadn't earned commission in months, and even when I had, I couldn't have afforded this brand. My eyes narrowed. 'This isn't a knock-off shop, is it?'

Beatrice laughed. 'It's the real thing. But this is like a factory shop. It's where we get last season's prêt-à-porter clothing at really good prices.'

A definite perk of living in Italy.

I tried on the dress and twirled before the mirror, and had to admit it did make my eyes look greener and less like brackish water. 'And what about you, birthday girl?'

It took Beatrice three more shops and at least ten more dresses before she found the perfect one, a figure-hugging dress in rich claret red. I sighed when I saw her in it. 'Perfect!'

And now, at last, we could go for gelato.

On the day of the party, Daniele fetched me early, so I could help with the party preparations. We hid the multi-tiered birthday cake in the *trattoria*'s larder, where Beatrice wouldn't see it since Matteo had banned her from the kitchen for the entire day.

We laid out long tables and benches on the grassy lawn between the *trattoria* and the farmhouse, and strung bright-coloured lanterns from tree to tree. The tables were decorated with green tablecloths, bowls of white roses from the garden, and scattered with white petals. Even in broad daylight, it looked magical.

As the sun dropped, Beatrice, her sister-in-law Silvia, and I, hurried inside to get ready. It was like one of those prom night scenes from a Hollywood movie, with clothes strewn everywhere, and shoes and hair curlers and make-up, except that the protagonists were no longer starry-eyed teens, but starry-eyed women.

I stood before Beatrice's full-length mirror, and scarcely recognised myself. With all the unaccustomed exercise, I looked leaner and a little less soft around the edges than I used to. There was, naturally, more colour in my face than when I'd arrived in Tuscany. I still needed mascara for my barely-there lashes but I no longer needed make-up to cover my vampire pallor. I looked healthier, and I felt healthier.

My hair had grown out too this summer, the straight chestnut length, streaked now by the sun, falling passed my shoulders. I brushed it into a sleek ponytail, then twisted it up into a classic chignon and secured it with bobby pins.

Beatrice moved to stand beside me. 'You look nothing like that serious, pale woman who arrived here a few months ago.'

I laughed. 'Must be all the exercise I've been getting. Fixing an old house is hard work!' And the fact that I hadn't eaten junk food in months, only preservative-free whole foods.

By the time we returned to the terrace, the lanterns had

been lit, and there was music, played by a live band. Guests mingled, sipping prosecco, talking and laughing.

We hovered in the farmhouse door, taking in the sight, and Beatrice looped her arm through mine. Then Daniele brought us glasses of bubbly, and we began to weave through the crowd, exchanging greetings with the guests. All the Rossis' family, friends and neighbours were present, dressed in their finest. Many I recognised, and those I didn't Beatrice introduced me to. I was immensely relieved that the Rossis and Fioravantis were not good friends, so there was no risk of running into Luca here tonight, but no matter how much I craned to look for him through the big crowd, I didn't see Tommaso either.

'You don't need to babysit me all night,' I whispered to Beatrice. 'This is *your* party.'

'Everyone else will still be here for my next birthday, and the next, but you'll be gone in a few weeks.'

My throat felt clogged. I was going to miss her. I was going to miss them all. I smiled to cover the sudden emotion and let her lead me through the crowd.

In the few months I'd been here, my Italian had vastly improved, and conversation had grown a great deal easier, and less like a bad mime show.

When our glasses were empty, I volunteered to re-fill them, and headed across the lawn to the table Alberto had set up as a bar.

Through the blue twilight, children in swimsuits ran between the trees, playing catch and hide-and-seek, or kicking a soccer ball, or shrieking with laughter as they catapulted into the swimming pool beside the farmhouse. Smiling, feeling more than a little wistful, I dodged them as I crossed the lawn.

'Are you enjoying yourself?' Alberto asked.

'Immensely. It's a wonderful party.'

His gaze roved over the guests. 'It is the people who make a party wonderful.' He sighed happily.

'There's so much laughter! In England, people don't seem to smile or laugh as much as you do here.' At least, not in the circles I moved in, with the possible exception of Cleo.

Alberto tapped the side of his nose, as if to say he knew a secret. 'That is because here we work to live. We don't live to work. How can anyone be happy when you are a slave to what you do? Would you like a re-fill of prosecco, or would you prefer wine?'

I studied the labels carefully, then selected a Brunello I hadn't yet tried, and turned the bottle to read the label on the back. Alberto laughed, a deep, vibrant sound. 'That is exactly how your father would have chosen too.'

He filled a glass with the rich, velvety-red Brunello, and handed it to me, waiting as I tasted it. 'He was so proud of you, your father. Always talking about his daughter, the important banker in London, and about your achievements.'

How could he, when he barely knew anything about me? My eyes glazed over again, and I blinked. I wasn't twenty-one anymore and hoping my father would make the effort of a few hours' travel to see me graduate.

Alberto's smile turned from regretful to a grin of welcome as his gaze slid over my shoulder. I turned to see who had occasioned such a warm welcome, and my breath stuck in my throat, making me momentarily light-headed.

Tommaso, dressed in a tailored navy suit, with a crisp white shirt open at the neck, strolled towards us across the gently sloping grass.

Sure, Luca was sexy in that boyish, photographic model way (the way that said 'I'm sexy and I know it') but he couldn't hold a candle to Tommaso. Even clean-shaven and without the long hair, Tommaso exuded rugged masculinity. I swallowed an appreciative sigh.

'I heard a rumour you'd shaved off the beard,' Alberto boomed. 'What, or rather who, inspired that, I wonder?' Then he turned to me. 'About time too, don't you think?'

I mumbled an indistinct response into my glass.

Tommaso smiled. 'I was tired of being mistaken for a thug and beaten over the head, so I thought I needed to look more respectable. Not that it helped much.' His eyes twinkled as our gazes connected.

'The pruning shears were an accident.' I tried to keep a straight face, but my mouth quirked against my will. Tommaso really had a lovely smile when he wasn't scowling, and it was hard not to smile back.

Without offering Tommaso a choice, Alberto poured red wine (not the Brunello I was drinking) into a glass and held it out. 'Tell me what you think.'

Tommaso breathed in the wine. 'A delicate floral bouquet.' He took a sip, swirled it around his mouth. 'Cherry fruit, with a subtle peppery after-taste. Barolo?'

'Of course. But can you guess the year?'

'Is this an Italian man thing?' I interjected. 'You know, like other men arm wrestle to prove who's stronger?'

Tommaso laughed. 'It's something your father started when he was teaching me about wine.'

'It worked.' Alberto clapped him on the back. 'For someone who came to winemaking late in life, you're one of the most knowledgeable winemakers I know. You'd hardly know you weren't born to it.'

'Oh, I was born to it, though it's been a few generations since my forebears worked the fields.' Tommaso dropped his voice and leaned towards me, as if sharing an intimate secret. 'Though my ancestors were the ones *working* the Sant'Angelo land rather than owning it.'

He'd certainly turned that around.

A bell summoned our attention, and together with the other guests we moved towards the long tables to start the feast. And a feast it was. I'd never seen so much food. A full size wild boar presided over the lavish buffet. The tables groaned under the weight of antipasti, tube-shaped rigatoni pasta in a cheese and sausage sauce, vegetable side dishes, summer salads, fruits, cheeses, and a range of my own breads.

I found myself seated next to Adriano, one of Beatrice's cousins, who worked with the local police force. He was friendly and engaging, and spoke very good English, and it was no fault of his that my attention kept straying down the length of the table to where Tommaso seemed to be permanently mobbed by a group of young women. Clearly, the shorter hair and lack of beard had made him a whole lot more attractive to the opposite sex. I was probably the only one who missed his wilder look.

As with any good Italian meal, time stood still. Around us,

twilight faded into darkness and the moon rose, bathing the gardens in silvery light. There was no sense of hurry or of urgency. Only more laughter, more wine, more food, more friendship.

Adriano invited me to dance, and I let him whirl me around among the dancers on the *trattoria*'s terrace, with the scent of dying honeysuckle wafting through the air. I laughed, feeling light as air. I wasn't a particularly good dancer, but with a partner as confident as Adriano all I had to do was let him sweep me along.

I glimpsed Tommaso at the edge of the dance floor, watching us, and then Adriano spun me away and I lost sight of him. When I'd finished, laughing, breathless and a little giddy, he was gone.

Later, Alberto and Matteo wheeled out the birthday cake, and the *ooohs* and *aaahs* of appreciation bubbled inside me like prosecco bubbles. The cake consisted of three tiers of dense orange cake, covered in fondant icing, and decorated with delicate green vine leaves, yellow climbing roses and tiny oranges in royal icing. I'd spent the better part of the last week learning how to make them courtesy of YouTube.

Beatrice blew out her candles and cut the cake, and soon slices were being handed out to the crowd. In England, I'd have looked at a cake like this and thought it too good to eat. But here in Italy, nothing was too good to eat. Here, life was for grabbing with both hands, not for admiring from a distance.

I had no idea what time it was. Certainly past midnight. A few of the older partygoers had started to leave, but it looked as if the music and dancing would go on for hours yet.

I glanced at the crowd clustered around the remains of the cake, at the dancefloor where young couples moved to the lively beat, and then towards the bar where Daniele was serving glasses of grappa. There was no sign of Tommaso.

Since I wasn't driving tonight, and since I didn't feel in the least tipsy yet, unless being drunk on the atmosphere counted, I headed to the bar and let Daniele pour me a glass of grappa.

With the amber, barrel-aged liqueur in hand, I wandered back towards the tables beneath the trees, where groups of people still lingered over plates of food and glasses of wine. And that was where, at last, I found Tommaso.

For the first time all evening, he was alone. He sat with his chin propped on his steepled hands and watched my approach. As our gazes met, his mouth curved in a rakish grin. Then he nodded towards the dancefloor and arched an eyebrow in a silent question.

I downed the contents of my glass, feeling the strong liquor burn courage into my veins, and crossed the remaining bit of lawn. I was ready to grab life with both hands.

Without a word, he smiled and rose, waiting for me, and took my hand when I reached his side. Then he led me towards the dancefloor. But he didn't simply start gyrating like the other couples. He pulled me into his arms, hard up against his body, my hips pressed against his. I forgot how to breathe.

The party faded, moving out of focus and far away, as we danced together. The music changed, as if to fit our slower pace, and I was dimly aware of couples leaving the dance floor, and of others arriving.

Tommaso's arm cradled my waist, his fingers splayed against my back, just as they'd done dozens of times in my fantasies, pulsing heat and awareness through the thin silk and lace of my dress. My hand rested in his, pressed between our chests, and his cheek brushed against my hair.

Breathe, Sarah. Damn it, breathe.

But when I drew in air, his scent intoxicated me; subtle aftershave and the rich, earthy aromas of sun and soil and heat. I was lost. There was no going back. Or maybe I *was* back. Seventeen again, and falling in love for the first time.

'Do you remember?' he whispered against my hair.

Of course I remembered. There'd been a wedding. I couldn't remember whose it was; someone who worked on the farm at Castel Sant'Angelo. It was the first time I'd drunk grappa, and I'd felt brave then too, and wild and free and capable of anything.

Tommaso and I had danced that night too, just as we did now, and I'd known then too that there would be no going back.

He could no longer be Tommy, my friend, because I was utterly and hopelessly in love with him, as one could only be at seventeen.

We'd walked home from the party through the vineyard. It was September, and the nights were growing cooler, but I'd been burning up from the inside out. Though the leaves hadn't yet started to turn, there was change in the air.

We'd walked hand in hand through the vines, with

moonlight washing a silvery path before us, and we'd talked, and laughed, and touched. And we'd kissed.

I looked up now into those same serious grey eyes, saw the same spark of desire I'd seen then.

And he said the same thing now that he'd said all those years ago: '*Ti voglio*'. *I want you*.

Chapter 26

Amore e pianto, vivono accanto

(Love and tears are intertwined)

We drove home in silence, the kind of delicious, anticipatory silence that says more than words ever could. His hand rested on my thigh, and I placed mine over it, twining my fingers through his, and resenting every moment he had to remove his hand to shift gears. From the provincial road, Tommaso turned off onto a smaller side road. It wasn't a road we took often; not the main route into town, but a rough dirt road that was a shortcut home.

Other farm houses flashed by in the darkness as the classic Alfa churned up the miles, then there was nothing but vines, and even in the darkness I recognised the fold of the land. We were on our own property now, and soon we'd be home. My body tightened with desire.

'What's that?' I pointed ahead to a band of grey cloud on the horizon, and Tommaso slowed the car. The cloud hung ominous, light against the dark sky, strangely illuminated a sickly shade of orange by the moonlight.

Tommaso frowned, peering through the front windscreen, gearing down as he slowed further. The cloud grew, seeming to swallow the sky, and then we saw the tell-tale pulse of a red flame at its heart.

'The vineyard is on fire.' Tommaso's voice was low and tense. He pressed his foot to the pedal, the car skidding a little on the loose stones as he swung onto an even rougher farm track between the vines. We jolted over the bumpy track, and I clung to my seat.

Then we could see the flames themselves, a long line of fire ahead of us that grew bigger, clearer, more frightening, as we approached. And now we could not only see the fire, but hear its crackle and roar, and smell the burning vegetation through the car's open windows. Even as we approached, the fire seemed to flare up and grow. Smoke thickened on all sides of us, eerily reflecting the beams of the car's headlights.

Tommaso skidded the car to a halt, dug his mobile out of the cubbyhole, and thrust it at me. 'Phone Alberto. He'll know who to call.' Then he was out of the car and running.

I had to walk down the track a way, back towards the main road, to get signal. The smoke was thick enough around me that I coughed as it hit my throat.

Surprisingly, Alberto answered on the third ring. 'You left early,' he said, sounding not just jovial but a tad slurry.

'Our vineyard is on fire. Tommaso said you'd know who to call.'

'I do. We'll be there as soon as we can.' In an instant, Alberto sounded stone cold sober.

I stowed the mobile back in the car. With nothing better to do, and no sign of Tommaso, I ransacked the boot of the car and found an empty picnic basket containing a plaid blanket. I rolled the blanket under my arm and headed in the direction Tommaso had taken.

I found him at the edge of a field of vines, beating at a line of low, licking flames with his jacket. As fast as he beat at the flames, others sprang up. The heat was intense, and though the warm summer breeze came from behind me, fanning the flames away from us, it whipped up tiny sparks that seared my skin. I moved to join him, a few feet away, where another lick of flame was snaking towards a vine trunk. Unfurling the blanket, I began to beat at the flames as Tommaso was doing, but it seemed so hopeless. Beyond this front line of fire, we could see the flames spreading away from us, the tinder-dry vines cracking as they ignited.

A pick-up truck loaded with the *castello*'s workers was the first to reach us, its engine audible over the roar of the fire before it bumped into sight.

'Daniele called us,' Marco called, hopping down from the cab and reaching into the bed of the truck to haul out buckets of sand.

'Didn't you bring extinguishers?' I asked, barely pausing in my frantic attempt to keep the smaller flames at bay.

Marco shook his head. 'The chemicals will harm the grapes. We cannot afford to lose any more than what the fire has already taken.'

We stretched out in a long semi-circle around the edges of the fire, attempting to keep the flames from advancing, but weren't able to do more than keep it contained and to prevent the sparks from jumping the farm road to reach the vines on the other side. The heat grew more intense, the smoke almost impenetrable, obscuring our vision of just how far the fire now extended. Fine ash blew up, stinging the skin on my bare arms and my face.

I choked on the thick air, feeling heat scorch down my throat. My eyes streamed, blurring my vision, and I was coughing, struggling to breathe.

And then there was the relief of sirens and more cars, and in the smoke and confusion there wasn't just one but two fire engines. Alberto was there, and Daniele, and Adriano the policeman, and many other men armed with buckets of sand and water and fire blankets.

The firemen had their hoses out, and soon a high-pressure spray of water arced over our heads, into the heart of the fire where we had been unable to penetrate. A light drizzle splattered down over the firefighters, and I lifted my face to it, the sudden cool blissful against my over-heated, singed skin. My arms ached with strain and exhaustion. How long had we been at this? It might have been half an hour. It might have been all night.

The blanket in my hands was useless now, charred and full of smoking holes. I tossed it aside, stamping on the tiny embers clinging to it, and turned to look for Tommaso.

He was at the very edge of the fire, as close to the flames as he could get. He'd long ago discarded the tattered remains of his jacket, and now he held one of the fire-retardant blankets, using it to smother the embers that threatened still to ignite one of the untouched splayed vines. His body was taut, his expression one of pure focus and concentration, as if he was on fire himself.

The uniformed firefighters advanced on the blaze, and at last there seemed to be more smoke than flame.

There was so much ash. It coated everything, settling on our hair, falling thick on the ground, turning the vines ghostly.

That was when Tommaso stopped fighting. He stood, arms at his sides, his face a mask as he looked out across the vines, growing slowly more visible as the breeze wafted away the smoke. I moved to stand beside him.

I wanted to reach out and wrap my arms around him, but he seemed so remote, so far away, so instead I took his hand. Did he even want to remember that a few hours ago we'd been caught up in giddy, grappa-fuelled desire, and headed home to make love?

'At least five or six hectares,' he said quietly, and squeezed my hand.

I squeezed back, offering what little comfort I could. 'Which grapes are these?'

'Mostly the Malvasia Nera.'

The secret ingredient in his Angelica.

Saying nothing, I stood beside him and watched as the smoke slowly cleared, and the grey light of dawn revealed the extent of the damage. As far as we could see, the vines were blackened and charred. Hissing trails of smoke still spiralled up from the vines, and from the ground where the water and heat had merged. It seemed to take forever for the firefighters to douse every last ember, to prevent the fire from re-igniting.

We were the last to leave, after the workers and the party-goers had departed, after the fire engines had disappeared back towards the provincial road. We thanked everyone, nodded when the fire chief said his investigators would come by later in the day, and then we stood alone beside Tommaso's car.

'I am so sorry,' I whispered.

He still held my hand. He lifted it to his mouth, and kissed my palm, his stubble scratching the soft skin. 'Thank you.'

I managed a painful laugh. My throat burned, and my mouth tasted like ashes. 'For what?'

'For being here. For helping fight the fire.'

'Of course I helped. This is my vineyard too.'

This time, the statement didn't cause his eyes to narrow as it usually did. Instead he pulled me close, buried his face in my hair. 'If I hadn't been in such a hurry to get you home, I would never have taken this road. And this section of the vineyard can't be seen from either the *castello* or the cellar.'

If we hadn't taken this road, at this time, we might not have seen the flames for hours yet. The damage would have been much, much worse. I shivered, and he let me go, sliding his hands into my hair.

Looking up into his face, I could only imagine how I looked. His hair was wild and unruly, and scorched in places. Black streaks smeared his cheeks, and the ash in his hair, and on his face and his clothes, had mingled with the water to create a grey, gungey mess. My beautiful party dress was no doubt as ruined as his suit, and we both reeked of sweat, charred cloth and smoke. It wasn't a sexy look by any means, yet I'd never felt more desirable than I did right then, with his big, rough hands turning my face up to his, and his gaze trapping mine.

And I'd never desired anyone more than I wanted Tommaso right now.

Only once before had I burned this way for someone. And it had been Tommaso then too.

To hell with holiday romances. This wasn't chemistry, and it wasn't fleeting. I'd been in love with this man since I was seventeen.

I smiled as he bent his head and touched his lips to mine. His kiss tasted of ashes and adrenalin and desire, and I kissed him back, wrapping my arms around his waist. This kiss was even better than the memory of that first kiss so long ago. This was no fumbling, nervous encounter fuelled by a first taste of grappa. Even stone cold sober, this kiss was sweeter and more intoxicating and more passionate.

When we broke apart, breathless and eager as teenagers, he lifted me off my feet so he could look me in the eyes. 'Are you having second thoughts, or can we pick up where we were so rudely interrupted?'

'No second thoughts. But I could really use a shower first.'

He grinned. 'Excellent idea.'

Chapter 27

Casa sporca, gente aspetta

(A messy house invites unexpected guests)

It was hard to believe, after a night filled with smoke and ashes, that the day could dawn so beautiful. As we approached the *castello*, the sky was streaked with pink and gold. A bank of soft cloud hung low on the horizon, casting a rosy glow over the house.

Whatever the estate agent said, the *castello* looked ready to sell. That thought should have given me a thrill, but this morning I didn't want to think about selling. Or of leaving.

Our hands still entwined, we pulled around the building to park in the back yard. There was another car already there.

We exchanged a glance. I think I may have given an audible sigh.

Since both the house and cottage were locked, a precaution we'd taken since the vandalism at the cellar, we found our unexpected guests waiting on the terrace.

Or rather *my* unexpected – and unwanted – guests.

'Hello, Sarah darling!'

It couldn't be. Anger burned through me, sending my libido to an instant death. Ice flowed through my veins now where there had been heat a moment before.

'What the hell are you doing here?'

Geraldine, and a fair-haired man who looked not much older than Tommaso and I, sat at the patio table beneath the new bougainvillea-covered trellis. A number of battered wheeled suitcases, covered in airline stickers, sat between them.

Their eyes widened at the state we were in. 'Hello, darling! I called your home, and your lovely flatmate told me about John's passing and that you were here.'

I was going to kill Cleo. She knew better than anyone I would quite happily never lay eyes on my mother again.

Geraldine grinned, seemingly oblivious to my hostility. Tommaso, beside me, wasn't. He eyed me as if I'd suddenly grown another head. I ignored him and crossed my arms over my chest. 'If you're here in the hope of getting a share of the vineyard, you can take a number.'

Geraldine shook her head, setting her long tinkly earrings bobbing. 'Don't be ridiculous, darling. I know you must be really cut up about your father's death, so I thought I should be here for you in your hour of need.'

That was certainly a first. I wasn't buying the devoted mum act. Even if the concern was genuine, I always took second place to Geraldine's own needs and desires. 'You could have called and saved yourself the hassle.'

'I tried, but I kept getting your voicemail, and you know how I hate leaving messages.'

The man who was with her had risen. He stepped forward now and for the first time I took a good look at him. With his blond shaggy hair and baggy shorts, he looked like a surfer who'd lost his way to the beach. He grinned. 'You must be the daughter!'

I rolled my eyes. Of course she'd brought a boyfriend. There was always a boyfriend. I supposed I should be grateful. When there wasn't a boyfriend in tow, she helped herself to mine. And I didn't plan on sharing Tommaso with anyone.

Geraldine rose too, fluttering her eyelashes at Tommaso. 'And who are you? You've been a dark horse, Sarah, love.' She winked meaningfully, and held out her hand to Tommaso. He shook it politely.

I drew up my shoulders. 'This is Tommaso, John's business partner.'

He caught my eye. He looked bewildered, and I didn't blame him. But I wasn't about to introduce him as my ... what was he, anyway?

'This is Geraldine Wells,' I said to him.

Tommaso's eyebrow arched, but he said only: 'It's a pleasure to meet you, Ms Wells.'

'Oh, don't be silly – call me Geraldine. Everyone does! And this is Per Gunnarsson. We were just leaving Thailand for Sweden when we heard the terrible news that John had died, and Per so kindly agreed that we detour here to check on my Sarah.'

Tommaso nodded a greeting at Per. 'Well, Geraldine. You've caught us at rather an awkward time, as you can see.' He smiled at her, and I frowned. 'We've been up all night fighting a fire in the vineyard, and we're not exactly prepared for guests.'

Geraldine's gaze swept over me from top to toe. 'I hardly recognise you without your office "uniform", darling. Who would have thought you'd be adventurous enough to go firefighting?' Then she turned back to Tommaso and laughed, another light, tinkly sound. 'Don't mind us – we won't be any bother! I remember my way around. We'll just get settled in, and…'

I shook my head furiously. No way was my mother going to make herself comfortable here at the *castello*. 'There are plenty of hotels in town, Geraldine.'

Both Tommaso and Geraldine's eyes rounded at the sharpness of my tone, Tommaso's in surprise, Geraldine's with a really good imitation of hurt. Only the blond surfer seemed unperturbed.

'You can't let your mother stay in a hotel,' Tommaso protested. 'The *castello* has plenty of rooms.'

'Thank you, Tommaso. It's nice to know that *someone* here has some manners.' Geraldine tossed back her tumble of honey-blonde hair. The ends were coloured mauve. Last time I'd seen her she'd had cobalt blue streaks. On another woman it might have looked like a vain attempt to look like a teenager. Annoyingly, on Geraldine it looked good.

I glared at them both. 'Fine, but this isn't a hotel. I won't be cooking and cleaning for you, and while you're here you help out. Understood?'

'But of course, darling.'

Without another word, I spun on my heel and headed back to the yard to unlock the door into the kitchen. I needed a shower and I needed coffee – in that order. And alone.

*

'You call your mother Geraldine?' Tommaso asked when we were finally alone in the office at the winery. I'd showered, and downed two cups of coffee, but my throat still burned, and the hairs on my arms still looked singed. I couldn't get the smell of smoke and burning out of my nose, even though I'd washed my hair twice.

Tommaso sat behind his desk, looking far more alert than he had reason to be, while I paced the office like a caged tiger.

'Trust me, she prefers it. She doesn't like to be reminded that she's old enough to be my mother.'

'She certainly doesn't *look* old enough to be your mother.'

I glared at him. 'That's what happens when you fall pregnant at seventeen. Everyone always assumed she was my *au pair* rather than my mother, and Geraldine was more than happy to let them think it.' And she'd loved it when my friends treated her more like a big sister than a mum. While I'd just wanted a mother like everyone else, someone with rules and a steady job. Someone who could cook dinner and whose head wasn't always in the clouds.

I rolled out my shoulders. I didn't want to discuss my mother's age, and I certainly didn't want to admit that at 53, Geraldine could pass for nearly two decades younger. She'd always kept herself fit, dressed well, and she avoided sugars and fats of any sort. My biggest act of rebellion had been stocking the kitchen with the most sugary pastries I could create.

I glanced down at the insurance policy in my hands, needing a diversion. 'This policy is straightforward enough. As soon as we get the investigator's report, we send it with the claim forms to the insurance company, and then wait for the assessor to contact us. The most complicated part is going to be calculating the value of what was lost so you can claim compensation. Whatever amount you claim, the assessors will be looking for weak spots to bring the payout amount down.'

'So *we* can claim compensation,' Tommaso corrected gently, moving around the desk to stop me in mid-pace. 'And I didn't ask you to come here to talk insurance, as much as I appreciate your expertise. I asked you to come here so we could be alone.' He circled an arm around my waist.

'I don't think this is a good idea.' I stepped out of his embrace and around him, resuming my pacing.

He frowned, looking very much like the grumpy Papa Bear I'd once taken him for. 'I thought you weren't having second thoughts?'

'I wasn't then, but I am now. This is a *really* bad idea.'

'Because your mother's here? She seems like she's quite capable of handling the fact that you're a woman and old enough to have sex. You don't really think she and Per will be sleeping in separate rooms, do you?'

'No. But it's not because my mother's here. Okay, well maybe just a bit. It's just...' But I couldn't put it into words. How could I tell him that I was having second thoughts because I didn't want to be like my mother?

At seventeen, I'd walked away from him because I hadn't wanted to screw up my life the way my mother screwed up hers. But now, at thirty-five, I was going to walk away because I didn't want to be the slut who'd fall into any man's bed, whether the relationship had a future or not. Tommaso had a history of only bedding women who were leaving. I was leaving. Was that the only reason he wanted me – because I wasn't going to stick around long enough for this to get complicated?

But for me it was already complicated. Grappa and adrenalin-fuelled desire aside, I wasn't the kind of woman who could be happy with a little bit of fun and an easy goodbye. I needed a man to make at least some sort of commitment before I gave my body to him, and Tommaso wasn't making me any promises. He hadn't even said he *liked* me. Just that he wanted me, and in the cold, bright light of day, that wasn't enough.

With my lower lip between my teeth, I faced him. 'This is all moving too fast. You, my mother, the fire ... I need some time.'

His eyebrows pulled together in a frown. 'So we just pretend last night didn't happen?'

'Nothing *did* happen last night.' One mind-blowing kiss aside.

Tommaso's eyes narrowed, then he sighed and reached up to brush my cheek with his fingers. 'For you, I'll wait as long as it takes,' he said softly.

I heard the echo of Luca's promise, '*for you, I will wait a thousand years*' and sighed. I'd heard it all before. When I'd told Kevin I wanted a long engagement, that I didn't want to rush things, he'd told me he'd wait as long as it took too.

I shook my head. I'd told Luca I deserved nothing less than a man who'd put my happiness before everything else. Tommaso wasn't that man either. Like my father, he always put the vineyard first. Seduced by wine and moonlight, I'd very nearly forgotten that.

I spun on my heel and headed for the door. 'I have to get back to the *castello*.' With a bit of luck, Geraldine would have decided there wasn't enough adventure for her here in Tuscany, and she and Per would continue on to Sweden, and I'd have the place to myself.

I walked out, leaving Tommaso behind with a very familiar scowl on his face.

I strolled back through the vineyard, breathing in the fresh scents of earth and growth, and the not-so-fresh stench of burning that permeated even here. Sadly, when I returned to the *castello*, Geraldine hadn't left, but Ettore had arrived for work and set the visitors to peeling off the horrid floral wallpaper in the upstairs bedrooms. Hugely grateful, I invited Ettore to the kitchen for some of the lemon meringue pie I had in the pantry, and as we sat together at the kitchen table, I filled him in on the night's drama.

That afternoon, investigators swarmed over the burned fields. Tommaso and I walked with them through the eerie vineyard, a black, charred dystopian landscape that stretched out of sight, explaining our version of the night's events. The cloudless blue sky mocked us with its cheerfulness.

Once they'd interrogated us with questions about the timeline of the fire, and every detail we could remember, they shooed us away, so Tommaso headed to the winery to greet an Australian tour group, and I returned to the *castello*. There was nothing for me to do at the cellar but pace, and pacing was just giving me a headache.

Assembling ingredients, I began to roll out pastry dough.

I didn't need to bake, since the *trattoria* was closed today, but I needed something to take my mind off the strange sense of foreboding that seemed to be hanging over me.

Knowing that Geraldine didn't like shortbread as well as sugar, I made *torta della nonna*, grandmother's cake, the first cake I'd ever learnt to bake right here in this kitchen – a shortbread base slathered in fluffy custard cream, with subtle hints of lemon, vanilla, and pine nuts.

I was just pulling it out the oven when Tommaso's car pulled up outside. He looked as tired as I felt, so I cut him a slice of the still warm pie, made us both coffee, then sat across the table from him.

'Where's your mother?' he asked.

'Ettore's making her work. She's terrified of him. When I checked in on them earlier she made these big puppy eyes at me to get her out of there.'

'She obviously hasn't heard him sing "O Sole Mio" yet – because then she'd know he's just a softie.'

'Good point. I'll ask him to stick to more martial music while they're here.'

Tommaso laughed again, that lovely deep rich sound I enjoyed so much, and I was pleased he wasn't still mad at me. 'What is it with you and your mother?'

I shrugged and changed the subject. 'You're back early.'

'The fire chief's coming here shortly to present his findings.'

'Is that usual? Couldn't they simply email the report through?'

'We've never had more than a small bush fire here before.' Tommaso shrugged. 'But it's been a hot, dry summer, and fires can happen, so I suppose this must be routine for them.'

'I know losing most of the malvasia nera grape is going to affect the production of the Angelica, but we can turn this to our advantage. With a big insurance payout we can pay back a lot of the winery's debts. Next year will be a better year.'

He grinned. 'You're not planning anything dodgy, are you?'

'I've never done anything illegal in my life!' I protested. 'But I've spent enough years playing with numbers to know how to make this work for us. But about that loan...'

'Yes, I know. It's likely now that we won't be able to keep up with the payments, with the loss of so many litres of the next bottling, and now the loss of the malvasia grapes. We may lose the fifteen hectares we offered as collateral.' He laid his hand on my arm. 'But I'm so grateful to you for negotiating that deal. I'm well aware that the stake we put up was far less than the value of the loan. We'd have lost a great deal more land if you hadn't re-negotiated such a good deal.'

He wasn't going to be grateful for long. But I didn't have an opportunity to tell him more, as the others all piled into the kitchen just then looking for coffee, and the fire chief arrived soon after. He wasn't alone. Adriano, Beatrice's policeman cousin, was with him.

I served coffees and pie, and once the niceties were done, Adriano cleared his throat, looking uncomfortable. 'The investigators believe the fire was started deliberately, soon after dark last night. They found a cigarette butt at the place where the fire originated.'

Tommaso shook his head. 'Carelessness, maybe, but a cigarette butt doesn't make it a deliberate act.'

Adriano crossed his arms over his chest. 'The preliminary investigation revealed the use of an accelerant too.' Our faces must have looked equally bewildered, because he huffed out a breath and leaned forward, resting his arms on the kitchen table. 'A trail of ignitable liquid was laid to ensure the fire would spread quickly.'

My stomach clenched. That sense of foreboding had just escalated into full blown alarm bells. 'Who would do that?'

Adriano looked down at his pie, and it was left to the fire chief to deliver the final blow. 'Maybe one of you, hoping to make some money from the insurance. According to our sources, the winery has a lot of debt, and you filed another insurance claim recently.'

Tommaso and I exchanged a look. He seemed perplexed, but I wasn't. I had a pretty good idea who their 'source' about the loan was. This was bad. Very bad.

'Tell me one winery that doesn't have debt.' Tommaso's frown was firmly back in place.

'And we were both at Beatrice's party,' I added. 'You saw us there, Adriano. You know neither one of us could have started the fire.'

'You could have paid someone to do it.' Adriano shrugged helplessly. 'We might never be able to prove who started it, or why. Any evidence might have been destroyed in the fire. But we have called in a specialist arson investigator from Rome.'

Arson. I'd read the fine print of the insurance policy. Unless

Castel Sant'Angelo could be cleared of any involvement with the fire, the claim would be denied. And without an insurance payout there'd be no silver lining to this mess.

On top of the vandalism and the loss of the malvasia nera grapes, we would be unable to repay our loan. And Tommaso would lose a quarter of his land to Giovanni Fioravanti.

Chapter 28

La famiglia è la patria del cuore

(Family is the heart's homeland)

'It wasn't me who told Geraldine where to find you,' Cleo protested. 'It must have been Moira. Why don't you just send her packing?'

'I tried, but Tommaso invited her to stay. He seems to think it's rude of me to throw my own mother out on the street.'

'You could tell him about her and Kevin.'

I laughed. 'Yeah right. "*I haven't seen my mother in a year because the last time I saw her she was naked and had her legs wrapped around my equally naked fiancé's hips*" is not a great conversation starter.' And I didn't want Tommaso's pity.

'It's the truth, though.'

'He has enough on his plate. He doesn't need to be burdened with my parental issues too.'

'Since when do you care so much what Tommaso feels? Isn't this the same man you hit over the head with an iron – the man who stole your birthright?'

'The iron thing was an accident, and it's hardly my birthright. We're partners, not rivals.'

There was a moment's silence on the other end of the phone. I traced the pattern of the crocheted blanket with my finger.

'You're starting to sound as if you're having second thoughts,' Cleo said.

What?

'Are you sure you want to leave Tuscany?' Cleo asked, and my heart stopped its racing. *Whew*. For a moment there I'd thought she'd guessed what had happened between me and Tommaso. She'd probably tell me I was being foolish, and that I should have my wicked way with him and get laid, the way she'd wanted me to do from the very beginning of this adventure. And I wanted that advice even less now than I did then, because now I might just be tempted to give in.

'Of course I want to leave Tuscany. Why wouldn't I want to return to London? Or is there something you're not telling me – has Kevin replaced me?'

'Don't be silly. Kevin would have had you back at your desk weeks ago if HR had let him. Not having you here has made him finally realise what you're worth. No, I meant that it sounds as if you care about the vineyard and the *castello*.'

'Of course I care, but what reason would I have to stay?'

'What reason do you have to come back?'

'A home, a job, a future...' But for once my heart wasn't in the words. Lack of sleep had robbed me of enthusiasm. Or maybe it was Geraldine's arrival that had sucked away my enthusiasm. Or maybe the spectre of arson hanging over the property. I rubbed the throb in my temple.

'You're so set on this plan you have for your life, that you could be missing something really wonderful right under your nose.' Cleo sounded exasperated. 'Why does home have to be a terrace house in London? Why does your job have to be behind a desk? You've sounded happier these last few months than I've ever heard you.'

'Even if I wanted to, staying isn't an option. I have a signed offer to purchase from Florian and Yusuf, and I need their money to pay off the winery's debts.'

'Don't you mean *your* share of the winery's debts?'

I picked at a loose thread in the blanket's pattern. 'No. I plan to pay it all off.'

Silence. Then: 'Have you gone insane? If you pay off the entire debt with what you earn from the sale of the *castello*, you'll have nothing left. You'll have to stay on as a partner in the business until Tommaso can buy you out. I thought you wanted to be shot of the place?'

I let out a long breath. 'I can't let Tommaso default on the loan. It's my fault the vineyard is endangered. I've lost my edge. Arranging a consolidated loan should have been the easiest thing in the world, something I could have done in my sleep. And instead I got suckered.'

Cleo sighed. 'You haven't lost your edge. You just didn't have all the facts. You and I are numbers people. We understand assets and liabilities, not motives and emotions. How can you tell from a balance sheet whether a client is ethical or not?'

Because if something looks too good to be true, it probably is. 'I should have done due diligence. I should have dug deeper and asked more questions.' I pulled my shoulders straight. 'Look, I have to go. I need sleep if I'm going to face Geraldine again in the morning. I'll let you know what happens.'

'Just promise me you won't kill her.'

'I promise. At least not where there are any witnesses.'

The kitchen was at its best in the mornings, before Ettore arrived for work and while my house guests still slept. Alone, with the dawn chorus floating in through the open windows, and the scent of warm bread filling the air, I felt able to face anything without committing murder. Well, almost anything.

There was just one thing I wasn't able to face, and that was Tommaso if he found out who I'd signed the consolidated loan agreement with. Yes, it was cowardly. But after tossing and turning all night, I'd decided I'd rather be a coward than lose Tommaso's respect and his friendship. Because if he ever found out, then he'd know as certainly as I did that Giovanni Fioravanti was responsible for both the vandalism and the fire.

Without proof, there was no point in even opening that can of worms.

I'd just pulled a second tray of bread rolls out of the oven when Geraldine swanned into the kitchen, dressed in a gauzy black negligee, with her blonde-and-mauve curls sleep-tumbled.

'Doesn't this place have an electric kettle?' she grumbled.

I'd long since stashed the electric kettle in the pantry. It was a waste of electricity when the stove was already hot. 'There's fresh coffee in the moka pot,' I said.

I set the baking tray on the table-top, the scent of the fresh-baked bread filling the kitchen with homely warmth.

Geraldine sniffed. 'That smells divine, but oh my word! Just the sight of so much gluten makes my tummy ache.'

'Then just as well it's not for you.'

Geraldine hadn't been gluten intolerant until it became fashionable.

She poured a mug of black coffee then sat at the kitchen table, her chin in her palm. 'Look at you, all chained to the stove like a real domestic goddess. Who would have thought my hotshot corporate daughter would turn out to be so domesticated?'

I had to be. Someone had to be the grown up and cook the meals and do the laundry. I drew in a steadying breath and concentrated on moving the star-patterned *semelle* rolls from the baking tray to the wooden box with the Rossi *trattoria* logo. Then I returned to the apples I'd been peeling before the timer pinged. It was the season for apples, so this month there were apples in everything I made. Next month would be blackberries, which were still hard and pink and inedible now.

'Though maybe domesticated isn't really the right word either.' Geraldine surveyed me while she sipped her coffee. 'You never do anything halfway, do you? Instead of enjoying your vacation like a normal person, you have to turn it into a cottage industry.'

If something is worth doing, it's worth doing well. John always used to tell me that. I focused my gaze on my hands. 'Maybe because, unlike you, I don't just want to drift through life. I like having a purpose.'

Geraldine barked a laugh. 'We all have a purpose. But you've always been so *driven*. You must have gotten that from your father, because you sure as hell never got it from me.'

I couldn't help myself. 'No, no one would ever accuse you of being driven. You just float from one self-indulgent impulse to the next. Thailand one month, Sweden the next. Haven't you ever wanted a home?' *Or a family? Or me?*

Geraldine didn't rise to the bait. She smiled, almost sadly. 'And haven't you ever just wanted to be happy? All those things you've chased – top marks in school, the high paying job, the fancy flat, the man in a suit – did any of them make you happy, or did they just bring you stress? Are they what you really want, or are those the things the world says you should want?'

Here we went again with the hippie anti-commercialism rant. I'd heard it often enough over the years. I started chopping the peeled apples, more viciously than usual. 'There's more to life than the pursuit of pleasure. We all have responsibilities.'

Weren't mothers supposed to encourage their daughters to get good marks in school and sensible jobs? Mine had to be the only mother who encouraged her daughter to be reckless. 'Security makes me happy. Knowing where I'll be tomorrow makes me happy. Knowing I can pay my own way without relying on anyone else makes me happy.'

'And so you tie yourself down and become a slave to a desk or an oven?' Geraldine shook her head.

'I am not a slave! I've never been more free than I am right now. And I *am* happy!' I sucked in a deep breath, staggered by the sudden revelation.

Cleo was right: I was happy here. Happier than I'd been in years.

Wiping my hands on my apron, I moved to the pantry to buy myself a moment alone to process the thought. Here, I lived according to my own timetable, not chasing the next train, the next meeting, the next client. Like a true Italian, I'd got that work-life thing down to an art.

But it was more than that. I was happy here because I'd done it all for me. Not to impress anyone. Not to win accolades, or to earn my father's love, or to make myself good enough for people to want me. Perhaps for the first time in my life, I hadn't been trying to please anyone but myself. I'd done what Geraldine usually did.

I leaned my forehead against the shelf where the heavy antique iron now sat. Carmelo the antique dealer had offered me a really good price for that old iron, but I hadn't been able to part with it.

Did I want to stay? Sure. Who wouldn't want a low-pressure job doing what they loved? Who wouldn't want their own *castello* in Tuscany? And a gorgeous man with laughing grey eyes?

But I couldn't have any of those things. By signing that loan agreement with Tommaso's greatest rival, I'd given up any chance at my own happiness. I had to sell the *castello* and go back to my job in London, because if I didn't, Tommaso would lose everything he loved most. And I was not going to let that happen.

No, I wasn't like my mother at all. I wasn't going to follow my impulses or do whatever I liked, no matter who it hurt. As always, I was going to be responsible and practical, and get on with what needed to be done.

'Are you okay in there?' Geraldine called.

'Fine. Just fine.' I grabbed the box of bran I sometimes used as a substitute for bread crumbs, and returned to the kitchen, plonking the box down in front of Geraldine. 'It's not gluten free, but that's about the least fattening thing you'll find to eat in this house.'

And then I set about cooking the biggest fry up I'd ever made, with olive oil, bacon, fat Italian sausages, eggs from the Rossi farm, tomatoes and zucchini I'd grown myself, and porcini I'd foraged in the forest between the *castello* and the winery. I even fried slices of the bread I'd made that morning.

'I've died and gone to heaven,' Per said, rolling into the kitchen half an hour later, still rubbing sleep from his eyes.

I offered him coffee, and a plate loaded with as much fat and gluten and cholesterol as any one person could manage. And when we were joined by Ettore and Tommaso soon after, I gave them each a heaped plate too. Silence fell over the kitchen as they all tucked in. All except Geraldine, whose bowl of milky bran had been abandoned still half-full. I smirked. It was the little pleasures that made life bearable.

It was Ettore who discovered that Per had been a plumber before he was a dive instructor and set him to work installing the marble sink I'd bought in Grosseto. Then, leaving Geraldine to continue removing wallpaper and scrubbing down walls, he volunteered to drive into town to buy paints. When I offered to go with him, he waved away the offer.

'But shouldn't I be there to choose the colours?'

For a moment, he looked exactly like the terrifying ex-con I'd first met. '*I* choose the colours.'

I didn't dare argue.

Since I had no desire to work anywhere near my mother, I instead tackled the next chore on my list: bottling tomatoes. Birds had already begun to attack the tomato patch, and I needed to harvest the fruit before I lost any more.

Once I'd brought in my little harvest, I washed the store of jars Nonna had kept for preserves, packed the tomatoes into the jars, and crowned them with basil leaves. Then I capped and sealed the jars and set them in boiling water.

There was no feeling more satisfying than setting jars of preserves to cool in the pantry. I'd take them back to England, so I'd have the flavours of Italy to get me through the winter months. To help me hang onto what I'd found this summer.

'Did you know that tomatoes aren't indigenous to Italy?'

I spun at the voice, my hand over my thumping heart. 'You need to stop sneaking up on me like that!'

'I'm not sneaking. I came to offer my help, if you need it.'

'Don't you have work to do at the winery?'

Tommaso shrugged. 'It's just a waiting game now, until the grapes are ready for harvest. Until then, I'm all yours.'

My heart thumped in a completely different way, as if it had skipped a beat. 'So where are tomatoes from?'

He grinned. 'South America. They were introduced to Europe by the Spanish conquistadors.'

When Ettore returned with the paints, I had to admit he'd made a surprisingly good selection: a soft pistachio-green for the kitchen, reflecting the green of the porcelain tiles on the wood stove, a cheerful sunny yellow for the drawing room, to match the colour Fiorella had revealed beneath the hideous wallpaper, eggshell blue, soft buttery yellow and pale lavender for the bedrooms. White was only for the ceilings.

'It's rather more colourful than I'd have chosen,' I said tentatively.

Geraldine peered over my shoulder. 'If you'd chosen the colours, *everything* would be white.'

I didn't deny it. 'But we have no idea what colours Florian and Yusuf might prefer,' I protested.

'They will like,' Ettore said simply, as if they had no other choice.

'Your bodyguard has hidden depths,' Geraldine whispered.

I had to admit it was rather fun painting with company. With Ettore's rollicking baritone as accompaniment, we all set to work. Since Tommaso had been assigned the job of sanding and sealing the ceiling beams, I made sure I painted in whichever room he was working in. It gave me plenty of opportunity to ogle his rear as he balanced on the ladder. It also gave me plenty of time to wonder if I hadn't been a fool turning him down. Maybe I should have taken Cleo's advice and gotten laid. Followed my heart rather than my head just once. Not that it was my heart demanding to be heard. The feeling came from a great deal lower down than my heart.

After sunset, when it grew too dark to carry on painting, we assembled in the dining room, beneath the bright colours of

Fiorella's restored fresco, for a meal I'd thrown together – *pici* with a sauce of fresh fava beans and pecorino cheese.

Tommaso opened a bottle of Sant'Angelo Sangiovese, and Ettore, who'd been invited to stay for dinner, made the toast: 'To family!'

'*Salute*!' we all replied – even me, since I'd grown rather more charitable with Geraldine after she'd spent most of the day working with unfailing enthusiasm. She had even carried on working when Ettore wasn't watching.

After supper, I served apple crostata, then, once we'd waved Ettore off on his little Vespa, we took our drinks out to the terrace to enjoy the warm evening.

Geraldine sat in Per's lap, and they cuddled like teenagers, while I did my best to ignore them, and *not* to imagine myself in the same position in Tommaso's lap.

I heard the noise first, a snuffling, grunting, wild animal sound. I peered into the darkness and listened.

'What is that?' Geraldine asked, sitting up straight in Per's lap. She sounded scared.

Tommaso and I exchanged a look, then, '*Cinghiale*!' we said together.

We leapt to our feet, and Tommaso grinned as we ran towards the sound, waving our arms and whooping. Like excited children, we chased through the garden to scare away the boars rooting in the flower beds. We chased them all the way out through the mesh fence that circled the garden, and then Tommaso patched together the hole where they'd broken in.

When we returned to the terrace, we were still breathless and laughing.

'What were those things?' Geraldine asked. She stood now on the edge of the terrace, waiting for us, her arms wrapped around her waist.

'Pigs?' Per asked, moving to join her.

Tommaso shook his head. 'Wild boar. At this time of year, they're in a feeding frenzy, stocking up for winter. And there's been a population explosion in recent years, so they're venturing further and further afield for food.'

In the cold hard light of the next day, we examined the damage the boars had done. They'd dug holes in the lawn, rooted up the iris bulbs, and left a path of destruction across the garden. Tommaso spent the morning checking the mesh fencing, but it did no good.

When I returned from the weekly trip to the market, I heard Geraldine screaming. At a run, I followed the screams around the house and down the slope to the swimming pool, arriving at the same time as the men. Geraldine was in the water, surrounded by wild boar who'd come to the pool to drink. They'd broken through the fence again, uprooting the posts and tunnelling beneath the wire.

'Tomorrow, I'll put in an electric fence,' Per offered, once we'd chased them out again.

'You know how to do that?' I asked.

He nodded. 'Before I was a plumber, I put up electric fences.'

I laughed. I might wish my mother gone, but Per was a most welcome house guest.

One afternoon, we stopped work to forage in the forest behind the winery for hazelnuts, before the wild boar ate them all, and that evening, we sat around the big kitchen table, wrapping the toasted nuts in hot, damp cloths to steam the skins loose so they could be peeled.

With the bounty, I made chocolate hazelnut biscotti and heavy fig and hazelnut panforte, which I stored ready for the harvest feast. For the *trattoria*, I made hazelnut meringues, and chocolate calzone filled with hazelnut cream.

'I'll be happy never to see another hazelnut as long as I live,' Geraldine moaned, when we'd finally peeled the last nut. 'I desperately need a manicure now!'

Since my bedroom smelled overwhelmingly of wet paint, I slept in one of the spare rooms for a couple of nights. When I finally returned to my own room, at the end of another long day of scrubbing walls and painting, I discovered that Ettore had left me an unexpected gift – a trail of painted yellow roses climbed the pale blue wall and twisted around the window. The flowers were delicate, and so incredibly realistic. I climbed into the big wooden bed and lay for a long time looking at the whimsical design as the familiar song of the cicadas lulled me to sleep.

The next day, I found Ettore in John's room. I perched on the bed, which he'd pushed into the centre of the room and covered with dust cloths, and watched as he painted a twining branch of vine leaves, heavy with clusters of purple grapes, as a border where the ceiling met the wall. His big beefy hands wielded the tiny paintbrush with surprising care and delicacy.

'You never told me you're an artist!' I said.

He shrugged. 'I didn't know I was. I never had the chance to try before.'

With a few delicate brush strokes, he created a green, writhing tendril of vine, his tongue stuck between his teeth.

'My father would have liked that. He would have liked to go to sleep looking at the vines.'

Ettore nodded.

'Did you know him?'

'I worked the harvest here sometimes, before...' His voice trailed off.

I knew him well enough now to feel only the slightest trepidation at asking the next question. 'Before you went to jail?'

He didn't answer. I cleared my throat. 'Ettore, what were you in jail for?'

For a moment, I didn't think he'd answer. Then he set down his paintbrush and turned to face me, wiping his hands on his overalls: 'I beat up a man. Badly enough to put him in hospital.'

Though I'd thought very differently when I first met him, I couldn't imagine Ettore hurting a fly. Not once had I heard him even raise his voice, unless it was in song.

'Why?' I asked softly.

'He wasn't nice to his date. She said "no", and he didn't listen. She needed someone to help her.' He said it simply, as if that was all there was to it. And perhaps it really was that simple. If I had a date who wouldn't take 'no' for an answer, I supposed I'd want Ettore in my corner too. He turned away, to add a hint of shadow and texture to a cluster of grapes, and I slipped away.

*

In two weeks, I'd barely managed a single moment alone with Tommaso. There was always someone around, always something to be done. It was as if fate were conspiring to keep us apart these last weeks of my stay in Tuscany. *It's probably better this way*, I thought. But my body didn't agree.

At night, as I lay in bed and looked at the yellow painted roses, I still fantasised about Tommaso's hands on me, and replayed our kiss amid the scorched and smoking vines.

The first week of September arrived with showers that cooped us up indoors. When the rain stopped, the air was pungent with the scent of ripening grapes and I could almost taste them on my tongue when I breathed in. The fruit hung heavy on the vines, and the rolling hills took on that magical golden glow that made for such enticing travel shop posters.

Each day, Tommaso prowled the vineyard, watching and waiting for the grapes to reach the perfect balance between sweetness and acidity. Each evening, he anxiously scanned the weather reports, watching for more rain, which might cause the grapes to rot. 'The grapes must be dry when they're picked, so there's no excess water in the fermentation process,' he told me. 'The *veraison* was early this year, so the harvest should be too, but the cooler air is delaying it.'

I, though, was grateful for the cooler temperatures that came in the wake of the rain. The heat was more bearable now as we madly worked to put the finishing touches on the *castello*. I could scarcely believe this was the same house I'd arrived at four months ago.

And I only had three weeks left to enjoy it.

I sent Florian pictures of the re-painted rooms, of the terrace lined with pots of white hydrangeas, of the restored frescoes in the dining room. I even sent him pictures of the bathrooms, though, apart from the plumbing issues Per had fixed, we'd made no changes to them.

'I always knew we'd have to do some renovation work if we bought an old villa,' Florian texted back in reply to the pictures of the out-dated Seventies' bathroom suites.

You have no idea!

Then one night at the end of the first week in September, Tommaso was late for dinner. He burst into the dining room like a firecracker. 'It's time! Tomorrow we start the harvest!'

Chapter 29

Col tempo e con la paglia si maturano le nespole

(With time, everything comes to fruition)

Tommaso woke us early by the simple expedient of shouting up the stairs, his voice echoing through the sleeping house. It was early even for me.

'Do you have any idea what time it is?' Geraldine grumbled, popping her head out the door of the bedroom she and Per shared. She rubbed her bleary eyes.

'Yes, it's 2 a.m.,' Tommaso answered brightly, then he bounced away back down the stairs to stoke up the stove. Once we were dressed in comfortable clothes and shoes, and fuelled with coffee, we bundled a grumpy Geraldine into the back of Tommaso's little Alfa and headed to the winery. A light mist filled the valley, eerily reflecting the pale moonlight.

'Do we really have to do this in the dark?' Geraldine asked. She'd still managed to find the time to put on make-up, I noticed.

'Picking when the air is cool is better for the grapes.'

Tommaso's gaze remained steady on the pool of light cast by the car's headlights. 'It ensures the sugar levels remain stable. And trust me, you'll soon appreciate not doing this in the worst heat of the day.'

There were already cars parked outside the cellar, and a fleet of Vespas. Tommaso unlocked the tasting room, and we all piled in, farm workers and friends and neighbours, and the crowd swelled and grew louder as Geraldine and I poured out coffee from flasks, and distributed the sage shortbread biscuits I'd kept in reserve for the occasion. We were joined by student volunteers and migrant farm workers, and even a handful of curious tourists.

Almost everyone I knew seemed to be there: Ettore and his friends, Carlotta and Marco, Alberto and most of his family. Even Adriano, the policeman.

Marco carefully signed them all in.

'That's a lot of people to pay,' I commented.

Marco shook his head. 'Not everyone gets paid. Many are volunteers. But we have to keep records for insurance.'

Alberto had brought a mountain of focaccia bread for all the workers, a quick breakfast before the start of the day. 'Beatrice will bring lunch later,' he said, giving me a quick hug.

I looked around at the throng. 'She's going to need a very big truck!'

There was a lot of laughter and chatter as we set off down the dusty road through the vines, everyone in a good mood despite the early hour. Some of the workers rode on the back of the tractors that were loaded up with crates and baskets, and some of us walked. When we reached the fields where the picking would start, lights mounted on the tractors were switched on to illuminate the dark rows of vines.

Tommaso climbed up on the back of one tractor and waved his arms for everyone's attention.

'Most of you know how this works,' he said, first in Italian then repeating it in English for the visitors. 'Those of you who are new, find yourselves a partner to work with until you know what you are doing.' He unstoppered a bottle of Sangiovese, and poured some on the dry ground. 'Since there's no time to waste, let's go!'

As the crowd broke apart, he jumped down from the truck and took my hand. 'You're with me.'

I pointed to the bottle in his hand. 'What was that for?'

'It's something your father used to do.' He smiled. 'Did you know that the name "Sangiovese" comes from the Latin *sanguis Jovis*, the blood of Jove, the father of the gods? John always said it was wise to start the picking with a libation to the gods to ensure a successful harvest.'

I hadn't thought my father had such a romantic streak. I smiled back. 'Did you know that it was also the Spanish explorers who introduced grapes to Europe from the Americas?'

Tommaso nodded. 'And did you know that grapes consist of about eighty per cent water, making them one of the lowest calorie foods?' He squeezed my hand. 'I can go on with random facts about grapes all day.'

'Okay, you win. But one of these days I'm going to find something you *don't* know.'

'You can *try*.'

I stuck my tongue out, and he laughed.

Still holding my hand, he led me to an aisle of vines where Marco was already showing Geraldine and Per how to pick the grapes with small pruning scissors.

'Hold the cluster in one hand and snip the whole bunch off the vine,' Marco said. 'Breaking the cluster with your hands is difficult and will damage the plant, so you must use a sharp cutting tool. Then, place the grapes in your basket, taking care not to break the skins.'

'Don't you have fancy machines to do the picking these days?' Geraldine asked.

Tommaso laughed. 'Machines would bruise the skins and start the fermentation too soon.' He took her hand and flipped it over, stroking the soft skin of her palm. 'It needs a gentle caress to keep the fruit undamaged, and to keep the flavours trapped inside the skin.'

'You are such a charmer! Isn't he, Sarah?' Geraldine was all smiles now. I rolled my eyes. My mother really was the most incorrigible flirt.

We worked through the dawn, as the sky first took on a grey tinge then turned to murky blue. The light slid slowly down the slopes and into the valley, stealing between the vines, gradually lightening the air around us. Then the sun came up, picking out the green-gold of the leaves, the browns of wood and soil, the violet of the grapes. The big tractor-mounted lamps were switched off, and our sense of urgency increased as the day grew warmer.

The recent rains had left the ground muddy in places, and the grapes were sticky, the juices running down my fingers as

I picked and picked and picked. Soon, my jeans and shirt were spattered, and with all the bending and stooping, muscles I didn't even know I had began to ache.

The sun rose higher, beating down on us with a ferocity that felt more like July than September. Tommaso stripped off his shirt and gave me all the eye candy I needed to motivate me to keep going. I wouldn't have minded being able to strip mine off too. Sweat trickled down my back, between my shoulder blades, under my arms, until I was dripping and dirty and hot, and no longer felt in any way loving and gentle towards the grapes.

Heavy as they hung on the splayed branches, the clusters did not simply fall off the vines into my hands, but had to be cut off, and though I wore gloves Tommaso had found for me, the cutter was already scoring blisters into the soft skin between my thumb and forefinger, and my arms were scratched from reaching through the gnarled vine branches to reach the grapes.

Tommaso, walking between the vines to check our progress, paused to rub my arms. 'Want me to kiss it better?' His eyes twinkled dangerously, making me forget every reason why I'd said 'no' to him.

'Sod off,' I replied instead, my tone a mix of frustration and amusement.

I wasn't entirely gratified when he *did* sod off, heading back to his own spot to continue picking. I'd rather enjoyed the up close and personal view of his bare chest and shoulders. No wonder he had such a good tan.

But it wasn't all hard work and sweat. As we moved from

vine to vine, we chatted, laughed and shared gossip. Some of our fellow workers even sang. I watched, amused, as Ettore flirted with one of the students who had come up from Rome by bus with her friends to pick grapes. I learned that Aurelio and Silvia were expecting their first child, that Carlotta's baby sister, who was studying to be a teacher, had taken the day off school to help with the harvest, and that Marco had a wider repertoire of dirty jokes than anyone I'd ever met.

From mid-morning, Marco and a team of drivers shuttled the filled baskets and grapes to the winery, stowing them in the cool, climate-controlled processing room.

When the sun peaked, we stopped for lunch, sitting in what little shade we could find to eat the foods Beatrice and Matteo had brought from the *trattoria* – cold cuts, and bread with cheese: crostini with prosciutto and olives, bruschetta with salami and succulent tomato, all washed down with wine. And as many of the round, sweet grapes we'd picked as our heart's desired.

'Who's cooking at the *trattoria* if you're both here?' I asked Matteo.

'No one. It's *La Vendemmia*, the harvest. We close the kitchen and hang out a sign until all the grapes are in.'

After lunch, with the sun high overhead, we headed back to the cellar, all piled on the tails of the trucks between the crates and plastic bins filled to overflowing with juicy grapes.

'Same time, same place tomorrow,' Tommaso said cheerfully, as everyone headed home for well-earned showers and rest.

I couldn't wait for my own shower, but 'aren't you coming with us?' I asked Tommaso, when he handed me his car keys.

He shook his head. 'Now we start sorting the grapes.'

'I'll stay too. Equal partners, remember?'

He caught my hand and pressed it to his mouth, the rough stubble scratching teasingly against my skin.

Unlike the picking, sorting was no longer done by hand. A high-tech optical sorter separated the mouldy and flawed grapes from the best ones, which were then placed on a conveyor. With a grimace, I watched as the discarded berries were ejected. *Ker-ching*. Yet more wastage. Though it didn't bother me as much as it once had. Only the best grapes could make the best wine, and Castel Sant'Angelo had a reputation to maintain.

When Tommaso and I finally returned to the *castello*, I was both surprised and relieved to find that Geraldine had prepared dinner, even if it was a strange concoction of eggs and vegetables that may or may not have been intended as an omelette. The dining table had been set, and there was chilled Malfy gin awaiting us.

'John loved his gin,' Geraldine said reminiscently.

I showered and changed, and though I felt less sticky and sweaty, it made little difference to my smell. My hair and clothes still smelled of grape must, and the aroma seemed to have permeated the whole house. We ate in near-silence in the dining room, too tired in both body and mind to talk. It was still light outside when I fell into bed and snuggled down to sleep.

It was the same again the next day. I lost track of how many vines I'd worked, how many rows, how many fields. Tommaso no longer harvested alongside us. Instead, he supervised the sorting and pressing of the grapes that now streamed into the cellar, tractor load after tractor load.

Geraldine found herself a new job too, collecting the filled crates and baskets, carrying them to the waiting tractors, and returning to place the emptied crates ready for the pickers. And so Per and I worked as a team, in friendly competition against other teams of pickers to see who could pick the most. Working side by side with him, I discovered that the taciturn Swede had a wry sense of humour. And I finally discovered why Geraldine was really here in Tuscany, why she'd thrown herself so whole-heartedly into the harvest.

'I asked her to marry me,' Per said.

I dropped my pruning scissors.

Per didn't seem to notice my shock, or if he did, he took it in his stride as he did everything else. 'We are on our way to Sweden so she can meet my family. My children are so excited to meet her.'

No wonder Geraldine was delaying. She'd never been good at playing at big, happy families. I averted my gaze. 'I didn't know you had children.'

'Two sons from my first marriage. They're in their late teens now.'

Hopefully then he wouldn't want more children. I tried to picture my mother as stepmum to two boisterous teenage boys and smiled. As long as they were adventurous, and willing to ski or surf or dive, like their father, she'd probably get along with them way better than she ever had with me. And since she wouldn't have to be responsible for everyday things like getting them to school on time, or ensuring they had a packed lunch, or a regular routine, or identifiable food, they'd probably like her just fine too.

That evening we ate in the kitchen, a quick supper of re-heated soup and *semelle* rolls.

'I'm so glad we came here,' Geraldine said, smiling at Tommaso. 'This has been so much fun! Do you know that I met John right here on this farm at harvest time? My friends and I spent the summer travelling around Europe, and in September we came here to pick grapes. We hit it off straight away, and I remember how we talked late into the night and drank gin, at this very table.'

They'd done a whole lot more than talk and drink gin. I was the proof of that. But Geraldine only sighed and fluttered her eyelashes at Tommaso. 'The eye candy is as good now as it was then. Do you always work shirtless?'

I choked on my soup.

Tommaso only laughed.

When supper was over, I caught up with Geraldine on the stairs. 'Is one man not enough for you?' I hissed, keeping my voice low so it wouldn't reach the kitchen below.

'Don't be silly, darling. A little harmless flirting never killed anyone. You're in Italy. Surely you've learned that by now?' Geraldine tossed her abundant hair. 'No, you haven't, have you? If you had, you and Tommaso wouldn't still be dancing around each other when anyone with eyes can see you're crazy about each other.'

My hands fisted. 'It isn't that simple, and this isn't about Tommaso. What about Per? Don't you think your *fiancé* deserves a little respect? You don't think he deserves not to have his future wife throw herself at other men in front of him?'

She went still. 'He told you?'

'Yes, he told me. Though it would have been nice to hear from my own mother that she's getting married. For the first time in her life.'

'I'm not entirely sure I want to get married.'

'You're not scared, are you?'

She pulled her shoulders straight. 'Of course I'm scared. I'm fifty-three, love, and it takes an effort to stay fit enough to keep a man half my age interested. One day I'm going to lose that battle, and he's going to wake up and realise he's married to an old woman.'

I was grateful the dim lighting on the stairway hid my smile. 'He's not half your age. He's only twelve years younger than you.'

'Your father was twelve years older than me, and that felt like a lifetime of difference.'

'Only because you were so young. But you're not seventeen anymore. Don't let what happened with John affect every decision you make.' I took her hand, the first contact I'd initiated with her in I couldn't remember how long. 'Per is good for you.' Certainly better than most of the men she'd dated. 'Just don't keep him waiting too long or you might lose him.'

She wiped her eyes and laughed. 'Now if that isn't a case of the pot calling the kettle black! Don't keep Tommaso waiting too long either.'

I shook my head. She didn't understand. Even I could see that what she and Per had went beyond chemistry. But

Tommaso and I ... there was too much at stake for this to ever be more than chemistry.

For another couple of days we worked at the same punishing pace, from the early hours into the heat of the day. The number of workers dropped with each passing day, as the tourists and volunteers returned to less strenuous activities. But the Rossis came every day, and the *trattoria* remained closed so that Beatrice could feed us all. Even Silvia insisted on coming every day, scoffing at the idea that her pregnancy made her any less efficient, and she was right – though after I'd whispered in Tommaso's ear, he allocated her a less physical job out of the sun, helping to keep track of the loads arriving at the cellar.

At last the harvest was in. Only one field remained unpicked, the white Trebbiano grapes Tommaso had kept back to make Vin Santo. That last afternoon, all the workers gathered in the courtyard of the winery for a feast of epic proportions. A whole lamb had been grilled on a spit, and there was the ubiquitous wild boar, marinated to remove the raunchy flavours, both cooked to such perfection that the meat melted from the bone. There was eggplant parmigiana, gnocchi with lamb ragu, courgettes and canellini beans, chard served with pine nuts and garlic, and quiches made with goat's cheese and asparagus. I served the biscotti and the panforte I'd kept ready, and of course there was wine, poured straight from the barrel.

The party went on until long after dark, and though I'd been up since the early hours, I didn't feel tired at all. When the last of the guests finally departed, Geraldine and Per helped clear away the empty plates and glasses, then Tommaso handed them his car keys.

'We'll walk home once we've locked up the cellar,' he said.

I didn't argue. Though every muscle in my body ached, and I felt as if I hadn't slept in days, I'd have walked to the moon if he asked.

As the little Alfa disappeared around the curve in the road, Tommaso and I switched out the lights and secured the doors, but when we were done, he didn't lead me along the dirt track towards the *castello*, but away through the vines in the opposite direction.

The waning moon cast only a weak light over the valley. It was cooler now at night, and Tommaso offered me his denim jacket to pull over my work-stained clothes. We strolled down the long, gentle slope of the vineyard, across a narrow channel of water, and through a copse of juniper trees to the edge of the wasteland that had been left by the fire.

'We would still have had another day of harvest if these grapes had not burnt,' he said, when we paused at the edge of the blackened stumps of the vines.

I reached for his hand, twining my fingers through his, even though the touch made my pulse jump in a way that made resisting temptation very difficult indeed.

'I hired Ettore to protect you,' he said unexpectedly.

'I know.'

Tommaso turned to look at me, his eyebrow raised.

I shrugged. 'You hired an ex-con with a history of protecting vulnerable women the very next day after the cellar was sabotaged. It doesn't take a genius to work it out.'

He smiled, but his eyes were dark and serious. 'I had no idea who or what was behind the sabotage, and I wasn't willing to risk your safety. For all I knew, maybe you had a vengeful ex.'

He said it like a question, and I smiled back, glowing with the realisation that even then he'd cared so much for my safety. 'No exes that cared enough to follow me to Tuscany, let alone start a fire. And what about you – any vengeful exes I should know about?' I managed a teasing tone, trying not to sound as if I were fishing.

He raised my hand to kiss my palm, in a gesture that was growing comfortingly familiar. 'No one that matters.'

For a long while we stared out over the barren landscape without speaking.

'What will we do if the insurance doesn't cover the loss?' I asked.

'*Le preoccupazioni del domani appartengono al domani*. The problems of tomorrow belong to tomorrow.'

We turned back, cutting through the vineyard to reach the *castello*. We approached it from the front, a view I seldom saw of the house. In the pale moonlight, it looked like a picture postcard, with its fake façade of towers and crenellations.

I was going to miss this. The house, the smell of grape must, Tommaso ... I blinked against a sudden blur in my eyes. I didn't want to spoil these last weeks by torturing myself with things I couldn't have. I wanted to make the most of what I did have.

He walked me to the door, not the back kitchen door as

he'd done so many times before, but to the newly painted front door which opened now without protest.

I slid the old antique key into the lock and turned it, but when I moved to push the solid iron door handle, he placed his hand over mine, pulling me gently to face him.

And then he kissed me.

I opened my mouth to his tongue, inviting him in; savoured the taste and the feel of his mouth, as earthy and decadent and intense as any Brunello. His hands slid around my waist, hauling me close, and my hands were in his hair, and on his back, wanting desperately to feel all of him, his strength and his solidity. I pressed myself against him, felt the telltale sign of his desire against my stomach, and my own body ached with want and need. It was every fantasy I'd ever had come true.

When he broke the kiss and moved to step away, I clung to him. 'Don't go.'

His eyebrows lifted. 'I thought you wanted more time?'

Time was the one thing I no longer had. I shook my head.

Grinning, he lifted me off my feet to kiss me again, even more hungrily. With only one hand, he swung open the door, its low creak overloud in the still night. I giggled, burying my face in his neck to stifle the sound. When he set me down again, I took his hand and led him across the threshold. He took more care to ease the door shut quietly, then we tiptoed up the stairs, hand-in-hand, like a pair of naughty teens. Up to my bedroom, where the big wooden bed with its fresh white linen made a pool of light in the darkness. Kicking off our shoes, we fell on the bed, breathless with silent laughter.

My hands were everywhere, sliding under his shirt to finally, finally feel those hard abs, which felt every bit as good as they looked. He stroked my face, kissed my collarbone and my neck, and I sighed and closed my eyes, smiling at the sensation of his mouth on my jaw, his breath on my cheek.

And then he yawned.

I laughed softly. 'You really know how to make a woman feel desirable.'

'I'm sorry,' he muttered against my neck.

I stroked the hair back from his forehead. 'Sleep now. We have time.' Two more weeks until the Germans were due to arrive. Not nearly enough, but I planned to make the most of every moment.

Chapter 30

Si canta sempre di cuore – quando si è pieni d'amore

(One sings from the heart when one is full of love)

I woke the next morning to an unfamiliar weight across my hip. My eyes fluttered open. Last night I'd been too tired to draw the curtains, and now blinding morning light flooded the room. I twisted in Tommaso's arms to watch him sleep, his chest rising and falling in a gentle rhythm, his face relaxed, his mouth curled up in a small smile. I kissed the edge of his mouth, but he didn't wake.

We were both still fully clothed, and my jeans had left an uncomfortable imprint against my skin. We must have been truly exhausted to fall asleep as we were. I eased out of his embrace and tiptoed to the windows to pull the curtains closed. Tommaso shifted and sighed but didn't wake. Then I found fresh clothes – the summery sage-green shift dress I'd brought from England – and headed to the bathroom to shower.

Geraldine and Per were already in the kitchen when I joined

them. Geraldine had found the electric kettle and made a pot of tea, and even buttered some of the bread rolls she'd found in the pantry. I was grateful not to have to make breakfast. My entire body ached from the workout of the last few days.

'Someone called Carmelo phoned for you,' Geraldine said.

I sipped the scalding hot tea she passed me. 'He's the antiques appraiser.'

She sat down across from me. 'I didn't want to wake you, but he said you should call. He sounded very excited.' Then she frowned. 'I see you haven't cleared out John's things yet. Don't you think your buyers might want to use that room as their own?'

I shrugged. Packing up John's personal things felt too final, an acknowledgement that he really was gone. 'I wonder what Carmelo wants?' I said instead.

He wanted nothing, it turned out, but he had news: 'There is a shop in Siena that has a whole pile of eighteenth-century hand-painted Neapolitan tiles. For the house you are restoring, they will be perfect. But you must be quick – they will sell soon!'

I thanked him profusely for the tip and was still sitting beside the old rotary dial phone when it rang again. I picked it up, cradling the receiver to my ear. 'Hello?'

I expected Cleo to call, since we hadn't spoken in days, but I wasn't ready yet to tell her about me and Tommaso so I was guiltily relieved when a man's voice, heavily accented, came down the phone. 'Signora Wells?'

'*Sì*.'

'I am phoning in response to the insurance claim you

submitted for the fire damage to your farm. The claim has been denied.'

My voice came out a whisper. 'All of it?' I'd spent hours and hours preparing the claim, calculating not only the loss to our profits over the next few years, but also the costs of re-planting.

'Yes. In light of the special investigator's finding of arson, this company will not pay out in terms of section eight of your policy, unless it can be proved beyond doubt that the arsonist was in no way connected with Castel Sant'Angelo. Do you understand?'

'I understand.' My heart was in my throat, making it hard to speak. 'And was there any evidence of who the arsonist might be?'

'The evidence is inconclusive.' He sounded reproving, as if he suspected I might be guilty. I could hardly blame him. I blamed myself enough already.

I swallowed down the disappointment and fear. Disappointment because I'd hoped the investigators would find evidence that would link Giovanni Fioravanti to the fire. Without proof, it would just be my word against his. The visiting foreign girl against a well-respected and influential winemaker whose family's history in the local area went back hundreds of years.

And fear, because we were still vulnerable, always watching over our shoulders. It hadn't skipped my notice that there were always at least two workers on security duty at the cellar these days, even last night when everyone else was feasting.

I rolled out the tension from my shoulders. Without

evidence, it wasn't enough for the vineyard to keep up with loan repayments. Because this sure as hell had never been about restoring an old gambling debt.

The sabotage would continue until Tommaso finally defaulted, and Giovanni Fioravanti got the land he wanted. Not just those fifteen hectares, but all of it. And more than anything in the world, I did not want the Fioravantis to get their hands on even one hectare of our land.

There was only one solution. Everything now relied on Florian and Yusuf signing on the dotted line. I needed to sell the *castello* and repay the loan in full, as I'd told Cleo. Only then would we get Giovanni Fioravanti off our backs.

I rubbed my eyes tiredly and looked around John's room. Aside from the re-paint, I'd done nothing with this room. His clothes still hung in the big wardrobe, his books and papers still filled the desk beneath the window, his bedding still covered the bed, and his toiletries still cluttered the bathroom shelves. Geraldine was right. This was the main suite, and Florian and Yusuf would no doubt want to use it as their own.

For the substantial sum they'd agreed for the *castello*, the buyers deserved this master suite to be renovated. If I could get those period tiles, and find a decent-sized hip bath, and a new toilet and basin, we could still finish this bathroom before they arrived.

And if I was using the bathroom as an excuse to avoid the inevitable task of packing up John's belongings, that was understandable, right?

*

By the time Tommaso emerged, blinking sleepily and looking for coffee, I'd already plotted out my route. I'd take the winery's pick-up. I waited until he'd finished his first cup of coffee and sufficiently woken up before I told him my plan for the day. 'Siena is only an hour's drive each way. I'll be back this afternoon.' And hopefully we could pick up where we'd left off last night ... my stomach fluttered with a mix of anxiety and anticipation.

'I'll go with you,' he offered, depositing his empty coffee mug in the newly installed sink.

'You don't have to. You must have a ton of stuff to do at the cellar.'

He took both my hands in his, and raised them to that full and generous mouth, the mouth that had been all over my skin last night. I shivered at the memory.

'*Tesoro mio*, it's a beautiful day. Let's do a little sight-seeing, maybe have lunch somewhere nice.'

I smiled, feeling again like that seventeen-year-old girl who'd first fallen head over heels in love with him.

Because it *was* such a lovely day, Tommaso drove a meandering route through the rolling hills of vineyards and silvery olive groves and wild forests as we headed first east, then north. We drove with the windows open, and the heady scent of late summer wafted through the car. I breathed it in, trying to preserve it in my memory.

In the large valley below the Rossis' *trattoria*, lay the Romanesque Abbey of Sant' Antimo, one of the most photographed scenes of southern Tuscany, its warm travertine stone glowing in the sunlight.

'The church was built in the twelfth century,' Tommaso

said. 'But did you know that there has been an abbey here since Charlemagne's days?'

I laughed. 'Actually, I did. You told me that when we were kids.'

'Was I really that boring when I was young?'

'You were many things, but boring wasn't one of them.' I laid my hand on his denim-clad knee, and he wove the fingers of his free hand through mine. 'Do you remember when Nonna took us to mass there, and we heard the Gregorian chants? I've always dreamed of going back there to hear the mass again.'

'You're a few years too late.'

Dismayed, I swivelled to look at him. 'They don't do the chanting any more? But I read a blog post about it just a few months ago!'

'The last monks moved out in 2015, after more than a thousand years of service.' His eyes took on that devilish glint again. 'The abbey is still worth a visit, but if it's chanting you want, I can do better than that.'

Since he refused to explain what he meant, I sat back and enjoyed the flow of the landscape around us. We passed Montalcino, basking on its hill in the midday sun, then falling behind us. Barely fifteen minutes further, Tommaso swung the car right, off the provincial road and onto a side road.

'Where are we going? Siena's that way.' I pointed back the way we'd been headed.

'Just a little detour to make your dream come true.'

I rolled my eyes. It had to be in the genes, the way Italian men could turn anything into a grand statement.

Our new destination turned out to be another abbey, an even larger one of charming red brick perched on top of a cliff and surrounded by dark forest. Tommaso parked, and we held hands as we walked the rest of the way, entering the abbey across a drawbridge watched over by a bright-painted statue of the Madonna and child.

'This abbey is relatively new, since much of it was built only in the fifteenth century,' Tommaso said. 'But it's still a working monastery, and their Gregorian chants are legendary.'

We'd missed the morning mass after all, and the church was closed in the middle of the day, so we ate lunch at the abbey's little café, killing time until the church re-opened and we could wander through the quiet cloister surrounding a courtyard of lemon trees to admire the frescoes that adorned the walls. Unlike Luca, Tommaso did not hurry me past, but let me take my time to admire the series of bright paintings showing the life of Saint Benedict. Now that the high tourist season was over, we had the place to ourselves, and we lingered, enjoying the air scented with lemons, and the serenity of the place. The library too was a revelation, cool and calm and filled with treasures.

'I'm sorry we didn't fulfil your dream today,' Tommaso said as we returned to the car, 'but perhaps we can stop in for vespers on our way home from Siena.'

Once we reached Siena and had found parking and located the little antique shop Carmelo had directed me to, it was barely half an hour to closing time.

'You are too late,' the little man behind the counter said, spreading his hands wide. 'The tiles went this afternoon to a shop in San Gimignano.'

We stood outside on the cobbled street, and Tommaso glanced at his watch and cursed. 'We won't make it to San Gimignano before closing time. We'll have to return home and try again tomorrow.'

I smiled, an odd impulse nudging me. It was the kind of impulse that Geraldine followed all the time, but just this once I didn't mind following its prompting. 'We don't have to go home. Geraldine and Per are old enough to take care of themselves for one night.'

He arched a brow, and my smile widened. 'We could be spontaneous and stay here in Siena overnight.'

'*You* want to do something impulsive?'

I laughed. 'I've been living an adventure for nearly four months. I don't think one more day of being impulsive and crazy will hurt. Italy must be rubbing off on me.'

'We can only hope.' He took my hand. 'But as long as we're being spontaneous, let's go on to San Gimignano. It's a beautiful town, and if we arrive at sunset, you will see it at its best.'

We stopped for gelato, sitting on the sun-warmed tiles of the Piazza del Campo to eat them. The piazza throbbed with the energy of tourists and locals, with laughter and talk and music. I sent a cowardly text to my mother, explaining that we would only be home in the morning, not wanting to hear her gloat that for once I was doing something even remotely adventurous. Then we started on the journey north again, and we timed it just right, approaching the fairy tale hilltop town as the late afternoon light caught the many towers of its skyline, turning them to gold against the darkening blue sky.

The buildings of the town were the colour of sienna, ochre and peach, aged by the endless passage of years and sun and ongoing lives. It felt as if I'd entered an alternate universe, a magical world separate from the one I'd always known. It was almost impossible to believe that people lived their everyday lives in this perfectly preserved medieval town, that they had jobs, that their children went to school and battled with homework, and that they stressed about bills and rent payments, just like my colleagues and neighbours in London.

It was as if time stood still here. I wished I could make my own time stand still. I wanted to hold onto this moment forever – just me and Tommaso, holding hands as we joined the *passeggiata*, that evening hour when couples strolled, and neighbours visited, and children played in the streets.

I pressed my eyes closed against the emotions welling up, against my grief for everything I would soon be leaving behind: this place where people took time to savour life instead of following a relentless need to be constantly on the move, where whole foods reigned, and where success was measured not by material wealth but by friendships and laughter.

Despite the fact that tourist season was mostly over, we struggled to find a hotel with rooms available. Just as I was beginning to regret my impulsivity, we found a small, contemporary-styled hotel within the town's medieval heart, not far from the Piazza della Cisterna, that wasn't fully booked.

'It's a busy night,' the clerk at the front desk said. 'There is an art history convention in town, and every hotel is full, but you are in luck – we had some cancellations.' She looked down her long Roman nose at us, noting the absence of luggage. 'Will that be one room or two?'

Heat flooded my cheeks, but Tommaso's expression remained cool. 'One room is fine.'

Though minimalist and very white, the room was generously proportioned, dominated by the huge wrought iron bed dressed in clean white linen and scattered with pink rose petals. We stood awkwardly on either side of the big bed. My stomach pulled tight, a mix of anticipation and anxiety.

The last time we'd faced each other across a bed like this, with the same desire weaving tight around us, I'd been so scared. It had been more than the fear of losing my virginity. It had felt so much bigger than that. It had felt life-changing. And I'd run.

It still felt life-changing, and it still felt scary, but I wasn't seventeen any more, and this time I wasn't going to run.

'Shall we go for a walk and see a little of the town before dinner?' Tommaso suggested, not seeming to notice my hesitation. I glanced again at the rose-strewn bed and nodded.

We strolled to the second of the town's three encircling thirteenth century walls, and wandered along the path as the sun set, looking out over the scenic landscape.

When we paused to admire the view, I let out my breath on a long sigh. 'Italy seems truly eternal. England is old, but there it feels as if the past is just that – past. Gone, leaving only ghostly remains behind. But here, the past is a living, breathing thing. We stand here, under the same sky, looking at the same hills the Etruscans looked at, and the Romans, and the Benedictine monks, and the Medicis. And now here *we* are, a part of that endless cycle.'

I spread my arms wide, as if I could take it all in, as if I could hold on to it. I wanted to bottle this moment, this feeling of peace and timelessness. Of rightness with the world.

Tommaso stood close behind me. I leaned back, closing the distance between us, and his arm snaked around my waist. His chest was warm and solid at my back, his arms a safe haven. I breathed him in, his rugged, masculine scent, the enduring aroma of grape must.

Then he pressed his lips against my temple, and my eyes fluttered open. It had grown dark while we stood there, and the sun was now little more than a glow over the western hills.

'Let's find somewhere to eat,' he said. 'Lunch feels like hours ago, and I'm starving. And the local white wine is worth trying.'

I groaned. 'If I never taste another grape again, it'll be too soon.'

He laughed. 'Not if you're your father's daughter.'

He was right. There must have been more of my father in me than I realised. I tried the local wine, a light, lively white made from Vernaccia grapes, unoaked, and it was refreshing and pleasant after the heavier reds I'd grown used to drinking.

We dined at an *osteria* with red brick walls and crisp white tablecloths. Candles decorated the tables, setting a romantic mood – though the mood didn't last long. A large group of academics arrived, pushing together several tables and taking over the restaurant. They were nothing like the serious, tweed-and-khaki set I remembered from my own uni days. These academics oozed confidence and were as well dressed as the fashionistas on the streets of Rome. They also grew increasingly lively as the wine flowed, and the arguments on the merits of one Renaissance artist over another grew more heated.

To the horror of our waiter, we hurried through our meal, and skipped coffee and dessert. Instead, we queued for yet more gelato in the odd triangle-shaped Piazza della Cisterna with its big public well, then wandered back to our hotel, licking the dripping ice cream from our fingers. But the hotel was equally overrun with noisy and half-drunk academics. They filled the bar and the lounge and the outdoor terrace.

'I'm still far too sober to be able to handle all this intense intellectual debate,' Tommaso whispered in my ear. When I nodded, he ordered a bottle of chianti and two glasses from the bar, and we headed out into the garden, which was mercifully quiet.

We stretched out on the grass to watch the stars, as we had so many nights through the summer. The moon was nothing more than a sliver against the velvet night, and the stars seemed hard and bright and crystal clear. At last, the chianti loosened the knot of tension that had gripped my stomach from the moment we'd stood beside the big hotel bed, and I'd realised the enormity of what I wanted.

Now, with my head cradled against his chest, and the drifting scents of fresh cut lawn and the pine trees that surrounded the garden, it no longer felt as if I was about to take a life-changing gamble. It just felt right.

I turned to face him, and Tommaso kissed me, a light,

tender kiss that sparked and caught fire. Then I was in his arms, and my hands were under his shirt, exploring the planes of his lean abs, and his taste was on my tongue.

He moaned, his hands sliding down over my back to cup my bottom and pull me against him. We rolled together on the grass, and my body was alight with need and desire.

'*Voglio sentirti sulla mia pelle*,' I whispered, repeating his words from that other night so long ago. *I want to feel you on my skin.*

Chapter 31

Il bacio sta all'amore come il lampo al tuono

(The kiss is to love as lightning is to thunder)

Tommaso rolled off me and onto his feet in one smooth movement, and helped me up. Without letting go of my hand, he pulled me in for another kiss, then together we hurried up the stone stairs to the terrace. The academics seemed oblivious as we rushed past.

We took the stairs to our room two at a time and were laughing and breathless by the time we reached our door. Twice Tommaso had to slide the key card through the lock, and I was glad I wasn't the only one as nervous as if this was our first time.

I shook my head. It *was* our first time.

Then we were inside the darkened room, both breathing heavily, and Tommaso pressed me up against the door, his hand sliding up beneath my dress, setting my body on fire. We kissed, and, barely breaking contact, frantically stripped off our clothes and stumbled towards the big bed, falling together in a mess of naked limbs onto the petal-strewn covers.

His body slid over mine, his mouth on my collarbone, on my neck, on my jaw, the head of his cock rubbing against my desperate core.

'Tell me what you want.' His voice was a growl against my cheek.

'You.'

He shifted away, lifting himself off me to rest on one arm and look down at me. 'Tell me what you want me to do to you.'

I'd never been good at this, at expressing my desires or asking for what I wanted, but with Tommaso it seemed so easy. I held his gaze. 'I want you inside me.'

I arched against him, and his lips crushed mine again. His cock brushed once more against my entrance, and then he slid into me. The slow glide of skin against skin was exquisite. He paused, giving us both a moment to adjust, to enjoy the sensation of fullness. Then he moved, and I placed my hands on his waist, and gently but firmly held him still.

'We can't get carried away,' I said with regret. 'Not like this, no matter how much we want to.'

Buried deep inside me, his cock trembled. Then with a sigh, he pulled back out, and rolled across the bed to reach for the wallet he'd lain on the bedside table. I hoped that wallet was a lot bigger than it looked. I hoped he'd had the forethought to bring more than one condom.

By the time he rolled back to me, he'd opened the packet, removed the condom, and slid it over that breathtakingly beautiful cock. I was sad to see it sheathed, but there was no way we were going further without protection. At least I'd have the memory of that one golden moment, of his bare cock sliding into me, filling me, and stretching me, to treasure.

I closed my eyes, opening them again only when he leaned back over me, bracing himself on one arm, his big, rough hand gently cupping my naked breast.

'I don't think I can go slow,' he said, his voice low and hoarse. 'After that taste, I want you, and I can't wait.'

I nodded, and held his gaze as he plunged, thrusting deep and hard, but I was ready for him, and lifted my hips, matching his thrust with one of my own. He groaned and pulled back, driving into me again, setting a rhythm I was more than happy to follow.

I lost myself in the movement, in the primal dance of thrust and glide, every part of my being focused on that point where our bodies met and merged. My pulse thundered in my ears. Even if he'd wanted to wait, I couldn't have. My muscles began to bunch and contract, my moans grew loud, and then his body turned rigid. He shuddered, and for a wild, insane moment I wanted to feel him release without the barrier. Then my own climax wrapped me in its grip, and my head went back, my body taking over, spasming around him, dragging out his release.

When the wave of my orgasm passed, he stopped moving and collapsed beside me, turning me towards him. I sighed, gently expelling my breath, and buried my head in the curve of his neck. He wrapped an arm around me, holding me close, as safe and strong and secure as I'd imagined those arms to be. And lying like that, with our chests rising and falling together, with our bodies still joined, I closed my eyes and let sleep pull me under.

The campanile bells woke me with their echoing chorus, and through the gap in the white curtains I caught a tantalising glimpse of the town's famed towers. I stretched luxuriously and rolled over. Tommaso was already awake and watching me. The sheet barely covered his waist, leaving his gorgeous tanned chest bare and tempting. I smiled and reached out to run my palm over all that solid muscle.

He stroked the tangled hair back from my face, his fingers gentle against my skin, and I groaned, burying my face in his chest. 'I must look such a mess!'

In our first frantic tumble into bed last night, my hair had come loose and I'd been too preoccupied and too tired afterwards to braid it before falling asleep. I reached up now to pull it back, and he stopped my hands, encircling my wrists. 'Don't! I like it loose.'

Then, still holding my wrists above my head, he straddled me, and kissed down the line of my throat. 'I need a shower!' I managed, though my voice came out rough and needy.

He laughed against my neck. 'Only if you promise me you'll leave your hair loose when you're done?'

I grinned back. 'Promise.'

I showered quickly, washing my hair in an attempt to disentangle it, more than a little disappointed that Tommaso didn't join me. But when I re-emerged, wrapped in the fluffy hotel towel, he'd made coffee.

'It's only instant,' he apologised as he brought the two

steaming mugs to the bed. 'But I've brought you more than coffee.'

I glanced down his naked body and grinned appreciatively. He was all golden planes and edges, covered in a smattering of hair. And he was already hard, his erection standing tall.

He set the mugs down, and expression intense, eyes burning, crawled onto the bed. I spread my legs, and a slow, heated smile curved his mouth. Then he bent to kiss me, his mouth warm against the exposed skin of my throat. He untied my robe and it fell open, and his hands stroked down over my skin, running sensuously over every inch, raising tingles and goosebumps, even though I wasn't cold.

He slid all the way down my body, placed his mouth at my core, and I shuddered at the sensitive touch, at the sudden flick of his tongue. He took his time, in no hurry to rush this, and if I hadn't already been in love with him, I most certainly was now.

When I'd come, he shifted up the bed, the weight of his body heavy against my sated limbs. I arched against him, my body still hungry for him. His laughter was a soft rumble against the tender skin of my throat, then he shifted away, reaching for the bedside table again and I sent up a silent prayer of thanks that he kept his wallet well-stocked.

Long after, we lay in a tangle of limbs, sated and breathless. My cheek rested on his chest, where the thud of his heart slowly resumed its normal pace. As he stroked my damp hair, I closed my eyes and let my thoughts drift. Despite the stubble burn on my face, and the gentle ache between my legs – or maybe because of them – I'd never been happier.

Unbidden, a vision of my future unrolled before me, blindingly clear. Not a vision of my house in Wanstead with its tidy, modern kitchen and pocket handkerchief garden. Not my corner office with its floor to ceiling glass windows, and the hustle of people on the street below. Not a man dressed in a sharp suit and charming smile, like Kevin or Luca.

No, the image was of the high-ceilinged *castello* kitchen, with its porcelain-fronted vintage stove, and the stone hearth decorated with copper pots. Of Tommaso, in jeans and an open-necked shirt, dusty from a day on the farm, his eyes alight and smiling.

The vision was so real I could taste it, taste the rich, red wine on my tongue, and hear his throaty voice rumble 'guess the vintage.'

I wanted to do what Geraldine had always done: grab what I wanted with both hands. And what I wanted was a man who was moody and grumpy, and passionate and thoughtful, and who looked sexy even with long hair and a shaggy beard. A man who was happy spending his evenings doing nothing but looking at the stars or watching supernatural TV shows, and who made love as if we had all the time in the world.

I wanted this life, the timelessness, the flow of the seasons, of *veraison* and *la vendemmia*, the slow lull of mornings spent naked in bed. More than anything, I wanted *time*: to watch things I'd created grow and take root. Like the bougainvillea clippings we'd planted on the terrace, and the grape must now fermenting in the cellar.

I shifted to look at Tommaso. His eyes were closed, but he

opened them again, smiling lazily, and I lost myself in the depths of those extraordinary grey eyes.

And just like that, the vision shattered.

Because I wasn't Geraldine, and I wasn't going to make a fool of myself over a man who saw me as just another woman passing through his life.

I was Sarah Wells, responsible, practical, sensible. And the sensible thing to do was to sell the *castello*, pay the vineyard's debts, and move forward with my life, even if that meant leaving my heart behind in Italy a second time.

I rose, swinging my feet off the bed onto the cold, tiled floor, moved to collect my discarded clothing from across the room, then headed to the bathroom.

Dressed, and with my hair once again tied up, I felt in command of myself enough that I could smile and laugh and chat as if I hadn't just experienced the most life-changing night ever, as if I wasn't completely in love with this man, and as if my heart wasn't already breaking.

Two weeks was all I had, and I was not going to spoil one moment with what ifs and maybes and regrets.

The hotel's terrace was quiet, and we ate breakfast alone, with no company but the unobtrusive hotel staff. Either the art historians had moved their arguments into the town's conference rooms, or they were still sleeping off almighty hangovers.

'When do you plan to return to London?' Tommaso's voice sounded almost absent as he focused on pouring honey onto his toast.

I sipped my espresso, scalding my tongue, and had to take

a moment before I could answer. 'As soon as the Germans sign the purchase papers, I guess. Two weeks at the most.'

He set his knife down carefully on the edge of his plate, then looked up at me. 'Do you have to leave?'

Oh.

It took me a moment to unscramble my brain and remember to breathe. 'I thought...' I trailed off, unable to finish that sentence out loud. How could I say I'd thought that this meant nothing to him? That I thought he'd only made love to me because I was leaving.

He wanted me to stay?

'But what about the *castello*? What about Florian and Yusuf?'

Tommaso shrugged. 'Don't sign the papers. With all the work you've done on the house, we could open the *castello* as an *agriturismo* in the spring. We might still have to forfeit those fifteen acres to the company that gave us the loan, but with income from a guest house we could make it through.'

We. I stared down into the dark depths of my cup, unable to meet his gaze. He wanted me to stay. He was handing me everything I wanted on a platter. And yet ... what was he really offering – a business partnership, friendship with benefits, or something more?

He hadn't said he loved me.

Besides, I had a job in London, a mortgage, responsibilities I had to return to. I couldn't just give that all up, could I?

'Could I have a little time to think about it?' I managed.

He nodded, and resumed spreading the honey across his toast, imperturbable as ever, as if he hadn't just dropped a bombshell into my life. Now I knew how he must have felt when I'd blindsided him with the antique iron.

Could I do this? Swap my old life for this new one? But making a life here would be very different from being on holiday. And without knowing what he wanted from me, how he felt...

My breath felt like sludge, choking me.

And then my mobile rang. I fumbled it out of my bag, and answered without even checking caller ID.

'They're here.' Geraldine sounded breathless.

'Who's there?'

'Florian and Yusuf.'

My heart started an instant, staccato beat. On top of the sludgy feeling, it made me feel almost light-headed. 'But they're not due for another two weeks!'

'They arrived early. They flew in yesterday and booked into a bed and breakfast in Montalcino. They'll be here in a couple of hours.'

'A couple of hours? We'll be home as soon as we can.'

Tommaso's eyes widened in alarm, but I shook my head to reassure him. 'The Germans arrived early. We need to get home.'

We checked out of the hotel and walked to the antique store. The tiles lay in a crate, packaged between layers of soft tissue paper, and they were beautiful: white ceramic with a painted pattern of twisting vines and great big sunflower heads, in forest green and canary yellow and lapis blue.

With great care, we carried the treasure to the car park, and stowed the crate in the boot of Tommaso's little Alfa.

'How fast can this car go?' I asked.

Tommaso grinned. But the smile didn't reach his eyes.

Not wanting to think about what Tommaso had asked over breakfast, I filled the journey home with mindless conversation. He let me get away with it, though he didn't hold my hand as he drove this time, and his fingers beat a rhythm on the steering wheel that wasn't quite in time with the indie rock playing on the car's sound system.

We passed the turn off to the Abbazia di Monte Oliveto Maggiore, the Benedictine monastery we'd visited the day before. Would I still have a chance to hear the monks singing the Gregorian mass?

'What are your plans for the rest of the day?' I asked.

Tommaso shrugged. 'I need to check in at the cellar, see how things are going there, and I also need to arrange for the spring to be checked and cleaned. There may be a blockage somewhere, or a leak, as I noticed the water level in the stream wasn't as high as it should be.'

'The spring?' I repeated, hearing a distant echo to my words.

He glanced across at me. 'Yes, we have our own natural spring. It's the source of the stream that runs through the *castello*'s gardens and feeds the garden well. Mostly we use the water for irrigation on the farm.'

He turned his attention back to the road, not noticing my sudden stillness. I remembered now why the words seemed to be an echo. The estate agent had asked Luca if I was the one with the spring. Goosebumps rose on my arms, and this time not in a good way. 'Do most vineyards have their own springs?'

He must have heard something in my tone because he looked sideways at me, frowning. 'Not really. And with the increasing water shortages, having our own water source is becoming increasingly important.'

I had to clear my throat to speak again. 'Is this spring on the land Giovanni Fioravanti wants to get his hands on?'

'Not on that land, but very close. Why?'

'Near enough that he could divert the water's course?'

Tommaso's frown deepened, etching lines into his forehead. 'It's possible, I suppose, but not likely now. First he'd have to get past the company we took the loan from. I never thought there'd be a silver lining to losing that piece of land, but I guess there is: now we have a buffer along the border between us and the Fioravantis. I hardly think that company would let him divert the water away from our vineyard. If they did, one dry season and we might be put in a position where we couldn't repay the rest of the loan.'

Oh shit.

How had I ever thought I'd be able to get away without telling Tommaso the truth?

My breathing seemed to have become shallow. But maybe I still could get away with it – as long as I sold the *castello* and paid off Giovanni Fioravanti's loan.

But if there was no *castello*, and no *agriturismo* business, would Tommaso's invitation from this morning still hold?

Chapter 32

A ogni uccello il suo nido è bello

(To every bird his nest is beautiful)

There was a hire car in the yard when we got back. Tommaso parked beside it, and I opened the door almost before he'd parked. He laid a hand on my arm to stop me. 'What are you going to tell them?'

'I'm not going to tell them anything. We need their money.'

His hand fell away. When I hurried towards the house, he didn't follow. From the kitchen, I heard the Alfa pull out the yard and head towards the cellar.

Florian and Yusuf waited on the terrace where Geraldine had offered them coffee and some of my sage shortbread. They were younger than I expected, in their early forties. Yusuf was the darker and leaner of the two, while Florian, with his salt-and-pepper hair and warm chocolate eyes, reminded me of my father. They were an attractive couple, well-dressed, polite, and in raptures over the house. I'd be leaving the *castello* in good hands.

Too anxious to drink more coffee, I led them on a tour,

and they *ooh*ed and *aah*ed with satisfying appreciation at the renovations we'd done. The house and gardens had never looked more idyllic. The sun shone, not too hot, but bright enough to fill the rooms with cheerful sunlight, and to pick out the vibrant colours of the garden. The only time their enthusiasm dimmed was when we reached John's suite.

'I planned to have this finished before you arrived,' I apologised. 'I have the most gorgeous hand-painted tiles in the car. We brought them from San Gimignano this morning.'

I was babbling, but since that moment when I'd realised Giovanni Fioravanti's true intentions, my stomach had been twisted in knots. I couldn't afford to let this sale slip through my fingers. Who knew when we'd get another offer to purchase, especially one as generous as this, and especially with the local estate agent working for the Fioravantis. Because I had no doubt now that Luca had briefed her to deliberately stall me from putting this house on the market. He had never wanted me to sell, because he needed leverage over our vineyard. My hands clenched into fists.

Yusuf nodded and turned away from the bathroom. 'We had unexpected time off and were so excited to see the house. Of course we're happy to give you another two weeks to finish the renovations. I can't tell you how happy we are that you've done this work for us! It's saved us a lot of time and effort. This way, we can already invite our first guests to stay before the weather gets too bad.'

I coughed to release the lump in my throat. It didn't work. 'So you'll take it?'

'Of course!'

We sat on the terrace to sign the purchase agreement. Bees buzzed around the pots of white hydrangeas, their low musical hum interrupted only by the scratching of my pen as I initialled each page.

This was the right thing to do. Selling the *castello* would save the vineyard. But a leaden weight settled in my stomach.

I signed the last page and pushed the document toward Florian who beamed. 'I'll get my lawyers to arrange the transfer. Unless you have a local lawyer you'd prefer to use?'

I shook my head then managed a smile, since it was what was expected of me. 'You'll be very happy here. I have been.'

When they had gone, I stood alone in the *castello* kitchen and looked around. The room was so different from that first day when Luca had sat me down at the table and told me I wasn't my father's heir.

It was no longer just an oasis in a derelict house. It was the heart of a home. I sat down at the kitchen table, my legs no longer able to support me.

Here was the home I'd believed I'd never had. The place where Nonna had taught me to bake, where Tommaso and I had first met, as shy kids skirting around one another. It was as if the *castello* had always been here, waiting for me to claim it. And now I'd sold it to strangers. Lovely people, admittedly, but still strangers.

John would be so disappointed. I'd nearly cost him his vineyard. And because of me, the vineyard and *castello* would be forever separated.

'Sarah, love?' I looked up. Geraldine hovered in the doorway, looking unusually tentative. 'Per and I are getting married.'

My heart lifted. 'That's great! I'm so happy for you. What changed your mind?'

She crossed the threshold and came to sit beside me at the table. She looked more at peace than I could ever remember her being. 'We were in John's bathroom, removing the old tiles, and I just looked at him, and it hit me. This isn't a summer fling with him. Summer is over, and he's still here. Oh, I'll admit, that's the way it started. I mean, look at us: he's young and hot, and he could have any woman he wanted. I was flattered, and I figured "what the hell? Why not make the most of it while I still can?" But then he surprised me. It's like he really sees me. There's only ever been one other man who made me feel that way, and that was your father.'

I swallowed. 'So why couldn't you and John make it work?'

'We tried. Not that first time, when we fell pregnant, of course. That was just a holiday romance, and it was romantic and passionate, and stupid. But later. You probably don't remember that first time I brought you here? You were only about five, and John invited us to spend the summer, and it was magical. For a while, I really thought we could make it work. But life isn't just one long summer, is it? Eventually reality set in. I was only 23, and I didn't want to spend the rest of my life in this kitchen, being a housewife and a mother while he followed his passion. I wanted to find my own passion, chase my own dreams, and I couldn't do it here.'

If the lump in my throat got any bigger, I'd choke on it. 'I remember.'

Maybe not that my parents had been happy together, but I remembered that *I*'d been happy that first summer here. And the next year, Geraldine had left me here alone, and John had been distant and awkward, and I hadn't understood why.

She smiled sadly. 'Maybe it was selfish of me, but I'm not sorry for any of it. We had you, after all.'

I blinked.

She leaned forward, her arms crossed in front of her on the table. 'We haven't talked about Kevin.'

Oh no. Not now. This conversation had already dredged up more than I could handle. 'It's okay. You really don't have to say anything. I'll admit I was hurt, but you know, Kevin's a grown man. He knew what he was doing.'

'Yes, but that doesn't excuse what *I* did. I'm your mother. Your feelings should have come first for me, and I'm sorry they didn't.' Geraldine sucked in a breath. 'I told myself over and over again that I was having a mid-life crisis, that I was weak and vulnerable, but the truth is, those are just excuses. I've been very selfish and I am sorry. I know I can't make it up to you, and I'll understand if you can't forgive me, but I'm asking you to try.'

I exhaled a long, slow breath. 'It's okay, Mum. Let's put it behind us.'

'That's the first time in twenty years you've called me "Mum".'

'I'm sorry. It just slipped out.'

'No, I like it.' She reached across the table and laid her hand over mine. 'I know I was a lousy mother, but since I'm the only one you've got, will you be my bridesmaid, or maid of honour, or whatever they call it these days?'

I laughed. 'Sure, I'd like that. Just tell me when and where.'

'Tomorrow, in the town hall.'

'Tomorrow! Then what are we doing just sitting here?'

I called a taxi and took Geraldine and Per into town. They would happily have married in jeans, but I wouldn't hear of it. 'Since you're only doing this once in your life, you need to do it right.'

I sent Per off to be fitted for a suit, and Geraldine and I went dress shopping. I called Ettore in to help sort flowers and a photographer, and as soon as I returned home, I got busy in the kitchen. Since Per didn't like fruit cake, and Geraldine didn't like chocolate, I made a lemon drizzle cake. I figured I'd earned the right to a little irony.

There wasn't time to make elaborate decorations, so I wrapped the cake in fondant icing, and decorated it with a wide lilac-coloured ribbon and a sprig of lavender from the garden. Its simplicity suited Geraldine and Per better anyway.

From town, I'd texted Tommaso with the news but heard no reply back. Perhaps he was out on the farm somewhere, out of signal range.

He didn't come home for dinner either. Worried, I called the cellar, but it wasn't Tommaso who answered the phone. It was Marco. 'He's in the laboratory,' he said. 'I'll let him know you called.'

Cleo shrieked down the phone at the news. 'God, I wish I could be there! I can't believe this!' Then she calmed down. 'And how are things with you and her? Did you talk?'

'Yes, we've talked. We're good.'

'Then what's wrong? You sound off.'

'It's nothing. I'm fine.' I paced towards the window of John's dark bedroom, as far as the phone cord would reach. The cottage was still dark. Tommaso hadn't yet come home, and he hadn't returned my call.

'Liar, liar, pants on fire. If you're fine, why do I get the feeling you're a million miles away?'

I managed a weak smile. 'Only about a thousand miles.'

'You know what I mean. There's something you're not telling me.'

I paced back to the bed, not knowing what to say. Cleo would probably think it was great that I'd let my inner wild child loose and finally indulged in a fling. But it didn't feel great. It felt shitty.

'I think I'm in love.' It came out on a sob.

'Not with that bastard lawyer?' Cleo sounded horrified.

'No, of course not. This is worse.' I sniffed. 'At first, I thought it was nothing more than a stupid old teenage infatuation ... but then ... and now I don't know what to do—'

'What do you mean a teenage infatuation – this is someone you knew when you were a teenager?' A pause. '*Tommaso*?!'

When I said nothing, Cleo hissed out a breath. 'Well, goodbye frying pan and hello fire!' I could practically hear her frowning down the phone at me. 'I've known you for fifteen years, and not once have you breathed a word about you and him. Why the big secret?'

'He was my first kiss. It wasn't a big deal.'

'Of course a first kiss is a big deal.' Another moment's pause. Another revelation. 'He was your first love!'

'I didn't even know what love was. I was only seventeen. I was only a year younger than my mother was when she had me.'

'You are not your mother, and you're not seventeen anymore.' Cleo sighed, exasperated. 'Sarah, you know I'm only saying this because I love you, but you really need to get your head out of your arse and stop letting your parents' mistakes rule you. You need to make a few of your own.'

'I have. Kevin was a mistake, wasn't he?'

'Yes, but only because you seem to think that a man with an English mortgage is the only man for you. Sleep with Tommaso. Didn't I tell you that you needed a holiday fling? This is it!'

When I didn't answer, Cleo gasped. 'You *have* slept with him! Way to go, girl!'

See, Cleo thought this was a good thing. But I'd slept with Tommaso, and it had been amazing and life-shattering, and now he'd disappeared on me, returned to his one true love, his vines, just as my father had.

I sniffed again, willing the threatening tears not to fall. '*This* is why I don't believe in holiday romances. Because I'm not the kind of girl who can walk away with my heart intact. It's always destined to end in heartbreak.'

Not that I'd been exactly heartbroken over Kevin. But then I hadn't loved Kevin. Not really, and certainly not for eighteen years.

'Then don't walk away.'

Easy for her to say, but she didn't understand. 'I can't stay. I sold the *castello* today. And now Tommaso probably thinks

I did it because I want to leave, and I can't tell him the truth without making him hate me. If I don't pay off this wretched loan, he'll lose everything he cares about. I can't let that happen, and I can't think of any other way to fix this.'

'There's always another way to fix things. If in doubt, follow the money – isn't that what you always tell me? So that's what you should do.'

Chapter 33

Una buona moglie fa un buon marito

(A good wife makes a good husband)

Tommaso didn't come home until very late. I was already in bed, staring at the pale shaft of moonlight slipping through between the shutters, when I heard the car. He didn't come into the *castello*, even though I'd left the kitchen door unlocked. The cottage door slammed shut with a resoundingly angry *thunk*.

Nor did I see him the next morning. I'd barely slept all night, and when I did it felt as if only ten minutes had passed before my alarm rang. And even though I'd set the alarm, I still missed him.

If I'd had any doubts that he was avoiding me, I didn't now. And now I also had my answer: it was never me he'd wanted. Sure, he'd had his fun, just as he had with all the other women who'd passed through his life, but that invitation for me to stay hadn't been made because he loved me, but because he wanted to prevent me from selling the *castello*.

I wasn't even sure if he would come to the wedding, until we were all already standing before the mayor in the high-ceilinged Palazzo Comunale, in an elegant room with tall windows and painting-adorned walls. Tommaso dashed into the hall at the last possible moment to stand beside Ettore, hair unruly as if he'd run his hands through it, and two-day-old stubble making him look wild and sexy.

The mayor spoke the words of the civil ceremony in Italian, and waited patiently as the official translator translated, and it couldn't have been more romantic.

The bride wore an ivory knee-length dress, classic, elegant, and clinging to her gorgeous curves. In his dark suit, Per stood beside his new wife, looking radiant.

But it was Tommaso I couldn't take my eyes off. He wore a black suit, and a white shirt open at the neck. I averted my eyes. He had no right to come in here looking so damned breathtaking and devil-may-care, when I hadn't slept all night.

When the ceremony was over and the paperwork signed, we stepped out of the shadows of the fourteenth-century palazzo into the sunlight flooding the piazza.

Tommaso gave Geraldine a quick kiss on the cheek and shook Per's hand. 'I wish you both well,' he said.

'You're not coming with us to lunch?' Geraldine asked, disappointed.

He shook his head. Then without a glance at me, he turned and walked away. I ran after him. 'Tommaso, wait!'

The expression he turned on me was the same scowl he'd worn the night I hit him over the head with the iron.

'We need to talk.' I hadn't meant to blurt it out like that, and certainly not here, in a busy piazza with shoppers and tourists strolling past, but he'd left me no choice.

His eyes were stormy, like terrifying dark clouds shot through with lightning. 'There is no "*we*". You're free now. You can go back to England, just as you always wanted.'

'I *had* to sell. I didn't have a choice.' It took all my courage to face him and not to run. 'There's something I need to tell you about that loan I arranged.'

He paused to listen, but anger still radiated off him in waves.

'The thing is...' I had to clear my throat to continue. 'The creditor is Giovanni Fioravanti.'

His eyes narrowed, but he said nothing. The silence drew out, so painful it was as if I was breathing in glass shards.

'That wasn't the name on the loan agreement you showed me,' he said at last.

'It's a holding company owned by Giovanni.'

He pressed his lips into a thin line. 'So, even after I told you that the Fioravantis couldn't be trusted, you went behind my back and did a deal with them?'

'It was a really good deal,' I said defensively, even as I heard John's words of warning repeat in my head.

'Well, at least we know now who was behind the vandalism and the fire.' His eyes narrowed. 'Or did you know all along?'

I put up both my hands, as if to say '*whoa*!' 'Are you accusing me of being involved in this? Why would you even think that?'

'So you could force me to sell. So you could get your money and run, which you've made abundantly clear was all you wanted from the day you arrived.'

Anger and fear and hurt churned in my stomach. 'You're a

good one to talk! You've made it abundantly clear from that first day that you wanted me gone.'

'I should have been so lucky! I'm just glad your father isn't alive to see how you've destroyed his life's work. Well, you can now take your big fat cheque for the *castello* and go back where you belong.'

I'd had a lot worse said to my face in boardrooms and offices, but Tommaso's words cut deep. He didn't want me here, any more than my father had wanted me here. I should never have come. I should certainly never have stayed.

But if I hadn't stayed, I'd never have rediscovered myself. I'd never have made peace with Geraldine.

I spoke slowly and clearly to hide the tremor in my voice. 'I had nothing to do with the sabotage or the fire. If I'd known Giovanni would stoop so low, I'd never have signed that agreement.'

He simply shrugged, as if shaking me off, and turned and walked away. For a long moment I watched him walk away from me, while my heart splintered into a million pieces.

When I returned to the others, Geraldine gave me a sharp look.

'What?' I asked, squaring my shoulders so I wouldn't give away how broken I felt.

'Don't "what?" me, young lady! What's up with you two? What happened in San Gimignano that you two can barely look at each other?'

'Search me. Let's go celebrate. Beatrice has prosecco on ice for us.' And I seriously needed a drink.

*

Beatrice had gone all out for the wedding lunch. She'd hung swathes of white cloth around the *trattoria*'s terrace, and there were bunches of lavender and white roses in small vases on the table.

'Where is Tommaso?' Beatrice asked when we were seated.

Everyone looked at me. I shrugged. I seriously hoped this shrug said 'please don't look at me because I'm only just holding it together, and if you all keep looking at me I might just cry.'

'They had a tiff,' Geraldine said.

I glared at her. Which helped. At least I no longer felt the urge to cry.

'A lovers' tiff?' Beatrice asked, trying and failing to hide a smile.

'No, a business partners' tiff,' I said, now glaring at them both. 'He reminded me that he's never wanted me here and he can't wait for me to leave.' And there was that burn in my eyes again. I blinked the tears back.

Beatrice laid her hand on my arm. I had to blink even harder.

'Of course he doesn't want you to leave. In all the years I've known Tommaso, I've never seen him as happy as he's been these last few months. Even when Gwen was still here.'

I stopped blinking. 'I thought she stayed behind in Scotland?'

'No, she moved here with Tommaso when he came to look after Nonna. But she didn't stay long. She didn't fit in and she hated it here.' She leaned closer, dropping her voice so only I could hear. 'I'll admit, the first time I saw you, you reminded me so much of her. I was sure you would get bored and want to leave too. But then that first time we went to the market, you looked so at home...'

Because I *had* felt at home. I swallowed. Had I reminded Tommaso of Gwen too? Was that why he'd always been so grumpy with me?

The lunch Matteo served us was the usual Tuscan fare, simple and hearty, and oh so good: my bruschetta with basil pesto and sun-ripened tomatoes, *pappa al pomodoro* tomato soup, and a main course of roasted veal in a rich truffle sauce, with baby potatoes and spinach and other vegetables fresh from their garden.

We emptied several bottles of prosecco toasting the bride and groom, and I may have had a little more than was strictly necessary. Okay, a *lot* more. But the light, bubbly sensation of the prosecco wasn't enough to ease the aching numbness in my chest.

The cake was just perfect too, and it looked almost too good to eat. Almost. This was Italy, after all.

Together, laughing, Geraldine and Per cut the cake and fed each other slices, though Geraldine did send me a rather arch look when she realised what flavour cake I'd baked. Everyone tucked in, Ettore, Beatrice and Matteo, and Alberto who'd driven up on his tractor to join us – even the tourists at the other tables on the terrace.

But the bride and groom didn't have time to linger. They were booked on a flight from Rome to Stockholm that evening, and their car would soon be arriving to whisk them away.

'I'm scared,' Geraldine admitted when we finally had a moment alone as we waited outside the *trattoria* for the taxi, while Alberto and Per fetched their suitcases.

I managed a laugh, quite a convincing one, I thought, since my heart wasn't in it. 'It's not as if you haven't slept together before.'

'I'm not talking about the wedding night. I'm talking about Per's family. What if his kids don't like me?'

'Of course they'll like you. Everyone does.'

She rolled her eyes. 'And what are you going to do about Tommaso?'

'I'm not going to do anything. He's just like John. He cares for the vineyard more than he cares for me.'

Geraldine shook her head. 'Your father wasn't always like that. He didn't know any other way to deal with hurt, except to close himself off from everyone. He became a virtual recluse, and that was my fault. I did that to him. Don't repeat my mistakes. Talk to Tommaso. Fix this. You really don't want to wait another thirty years like I did to find another man who'll love you like that.'

I frowned at her. 'You're assuming that Tommaso loves me. He doesn't. Because if he did—'

'But if he didn't love you, he wouldn't be so hurt that you sold the *castello*.'

'Exactly! He's upset because I sold a building he had plans for. He hasn't even said he loves me. I deserve to be loved more than several hectares of vineyard or an old building!'

She gripped my hands and forced me to look at her. 'Yes, you do. John and I were selfish, and so wrapped up in our own feelings, that we didn't put you first the way we should have. And you absolutely deserve that. But Tommaso isn't anything like us. Give him a chance.'

'You don't understand. There's the sale, and the loan, and—'

Geraldine huffed out an exasperated breath. 'You are way over-complicating this. You work for a fancy finance company, so don't tell me you can't take care of a little loan. But whatever you do, promise me you won't repeat my mistakes. Promise me you'll tell Tommaso you love him and give him a chance to answer before you run away.'

For once she looked at me like a mum rather than just Geraldine. I squirmed, but I didn't answer.

Then the taxi was there, and Per and Alberto arrived. They loaded the suitcases into the boot, and there were hugs and goodbyes.

Geraldine held onto me. 'You know I love you, don't you?' she whispered. 'You're the best thing I've ever done with my life.'

Her eyes looked suspiciously shiny, and I felt my own well up too.

'Don't cry!' I said sternly. 'You'll mess up your make-up, and you don't want to meet Per's family with mascara trails down your face.'

That made her laugh. She gripped my hands tightly. 'Promise me,' she insisted.

I heaved out a sigh. 'Okay, I promise.'

Then she climbed into the car and leaned out the window. 'Take this. I can't take it on the plane with me.' She threw her lavender bouquet, and I caught it.

The car pulled away, but Geraldine leaned out even further. 'Call me! I want to know what happens!'

*

Ettore took me home on the back of his Vespa. I clung to his leather jacket as we bumped over the broken dirt road, way too fast for comfort. At the crossroads, the familiar shrine came into sight, and I tugged at his jacket. 'You can drop me here,' I shouted over the noise of the wind and the scooter's little engine.

He slowed to a stop on the grassy verge. I hopped off, my legs a little shaky from the hair-raising ride. 'I'll walk from here,' I said as I held out his helmet. He smiled and pulled me in for a hug. 'Your father would be so proud if he could see you today.' Then he hopped back on his bike and was gone with a wave and '*A domani*!'

I watched him leave without really seeing him, as my eyes were too full of tears. John wouldn't have been proud. Tommaso was right. I'd destroyed everything my father loved. And maybe a part of me had wanted to destroy it. For so many years I'd blamed the vineyard for making me feel unloved and unwanted. But it hadn't been the vineyard at all. It was just two flawed and hurt people who hadn't known how to love each other.

I breathed out a shaky sigh and turned to the little shrine. If I was going to fix this mess I'd made and honour my promise to Geraldine, I was definitely going to need a little divine intervention.

I knelt down in front of the shrine. Unbelievably, I'd never visited it before, though I'd driven past more times than I could count. The painted angel sat within a marble arch. The paint was old, faded, and flaking a little in places, but the image was still clear. It showed an angel with outspread wings beside a pool of water. The faded water sprang out of a rocky hillside and collected in a pool surrounded on all sides by rows of vines.

A little bronze plaque had been screwed into the stone below the painting. Its inscription read *Arcangelo Raffaele alla piscina di Bethesda*. Archangel Raphael at the pool of Bethesda.

My knowledge of archangels was about what you'd expect for someone who'd devoted her life to working with numbers, but I had heard of the pool of Bethesda in Jerusalem, which was supposed to have healing powers. Though I somehow doubted there was a vineyard around the pool in Jerusalem.

If this was the angel who'd given his name to Castel Sant'Angelo, then maybe, just maybe, he'd be inclined to helping me save the vineyard. Besides, I was his namesake in a way. My middle name was Raphaela.

I closed my eyes. It had been many years since I'd prayed for anything, and I felt more than a little daft kneeling at a crossroads, surrounded by nothing but vines as far as the eye could see.

'I need a fresh start,' I said to the angel. 'Because things can't ever go back to the way they were. I'm not the same person I was four months ago, and even if I go back to London, my life will be very different.' But that wasn't really what I wanted, was it?

I'd never been good at asking for what I wanted. It felt incredibly selfish to say the words out loud, but I said them anyway. 'I want to stay here, at the *castello*. I want to make a life with Tommaso. I want him to feel about me the way I feel about him.' Oh, and while I was asking for miracles... 'I want my father to have loved and wanted me.' As much as he'd clearly liked and respected and wanted Tommaso.

I blew out my breath. There it was. I couldn't ask for any more than that. Well, maybe one thing. 'I want Geraldine and Per to be very happy together.'

Since I didn't have a votive candle, or any other kind of offering, I left Geraldine's bouquet propped up at the base of the arch. I didn't think she'd mind.

Chapter 34

Chi non fa, non falla

(He who does nothing, makes no mistakes)

I was relieved to see Luca's car parked outside his office. Considering how little time he seemed to spend working, I'd been worried I wouldn't catch him in.

His assistant was a motherly grey-haired woman who ushered me straight in without announcing me. Luca looked up from his desk, startled at first, but then he grinned, his eyes lighting up.

'You have forgiven me?' he announced, rising to meet me, his arms outstretched.

It was still impossibly hard to resist that melting smile, those dimples, and his contagious enthusiasm. But I managed.

'This isn't a social call, it's business.' The door closed gently behind his assistant and I faced him, hands on my hips. 'We can do this the hard way, or ... well, actually, there's only the hard way.'

That dimmed his enthusiasm. He even looked a little

confused. Maybe there was still hope for him after all.

'Would you like to sit?' he asked, offering me the armchair beside his desk.

'No thanks. I don't intend to be here long. I only came to bring you this.' I removed the cheque from my bag and placed it on his desk. It was a prop more than anything, since I hadn't used a chequebook in years, and certainly not for this kind of money. But it was far more dramatic than offering an electronic transfer. All those zeroes looked a whole lot more impressive in black and white.

'Payment in full for the loan. Not only will we retain full control of the land we put up as collateral, but if I remember correctly, there was a considerable settlement discount should we settle the debt before the due date.'

Of course there was. I was the one who'd insisted on it.

'You sold the *castello*. But what about your share of the property? Surely you're not giving it all up now to settle Tommaso's debt?'

'*Our* debt. Thanks to that partnership agreement you drew up between me and Tommaso, we're equal partners until such time as Tommaso is able to buy me out, and thanks to a number of "misadventures" we've experienced, he won't be able to buy me out for at least another year. So it seems he's stuck with me as his partner until then.'

I didn't know how well Tommaso was going to take that news. Hopefully not as badly as Luca, whose face had turned a strange sort of grey.

Then he rallied. Even managed a smile. 'I am very happy you have managed to clear the debt. I know you will not believe me, but I had no idea what my father intended, or how far he would go. But he is my father...'

'I don't believe you were involved in the vandalism or the fire.' Luca was too transparent for that. 'But you must have suspected after the fire. It was far too coincidental that the vandalism took place immediately after we signed the contract, and the fire was set soon after you discovered I had a buyer for the *castello*. Your father had to find another way to force us to default on the loan after that, didn't he? And I was kind enough to even give you the idea, wasn't I? Nothing short of flood, fire or act of God, if I remember correctly.'

He paled, spreading his hands, as if pleading for my understanding. And I did understand. No one could understand as well as I did how it felt to spend a lifetime trying to win your parent's approval. It didn't take a psychology degree to realise we had that much in common.

He frowned. 'But what did you mean about doing this the hard way?'

I resisted the urge to be petty and smile as I delivered my coup-de-grâce. 'You were right about your father being a bad gambler.'

Luca's brow furrowed in confusion.

'You are aware that I work for an investment bank?' Though not for much longer. I'd sent Kevin my resignation letter this morning. I had no idea what I was going to do, but whatever it was, it wasn't going to involve a sixth-floor corner office or a long commute. Maybe I'd open a bakery in Wanstead...

'If you raise the money to finance a big acquisition – or to make a rather substantial loan – by selling shares, you're gambling with a great deal more than a piece of land.'

He still looked confused, and I took pity on him. 'Your father didn't have cash readily available to offer us a loan, so he raised the money through offering portfolio stock. That stock is now owned by my investment bank.'

I gave him a moment to let that sink in.

'My bank now owns a controlling share of the Fioravanti vineyard.' Who'd have guessed there'd be an upside to having a boss who still felt guilty about cheating on me? And I owed Cleo a lifetime supply of wine. Not cheap box wine, but the real deal. After all, she was the one who'd reminded me to follow the money.

Luca sat down heavily on the closest thing at hand, the same armchair he'd offered me not so long ago. 'I cannot blame you for being angry,' he said. 'My father deserves this.'

'I'm not angry. But I'll admit, I was more than a little hurt to discover that you were only using me to get your hands on my vineyard.'

He shook his head, and I was both surprised and relieved to see the indignant spark in his eyes. 'I will admit to being many things, but I am not a liar. You are a beautiful woman, and I spent time with you because I like you, not because my father asked me to. I do not want you to think that I am not attracted to you, because I am.' He shrugged. 'It is just that I am attracted to many women…'

As always, Luca was good for my self-esteem, but I couldn't help myself. I laughed. 'One day, Luca Fioravanti, that is going to come back to bite you. I hope you meet a woman you *do* want more than any other, and I hope she gives you a really hard time.'

I opened the door but hovered on the threshold. 'One last thing: you can tell your father that fire doesn't destroy DNA. It's surprisingly easy these days for arson investigators to get DNA off a burned cigarette stub. And if whoever he hired has any kind of record, their DNA will be in the system.'

It was a long shot, and I had nothing to back up my guess but a hunch and what I'd learned from Google, but Luca nodded, his expression serious for the first time in all the months I'd known him. 'I'll tell him.'

Following the money trail and facing Luca was the easy part of what I still had to do. Making good on my promise to Geraldine was another matter entirely. But first, there was something else I'd put off for far too long.

I started with John's bathroom, throwing out his shaving cream and shampoo, and the body wash bottle that was nearly empty. Tomorrow Ettore would be stripping this room, ready to install the new fittings.

Next was the big wardrobe. John's clothes no longer smelled of him. Instead, the closet simply smelled musty. I boxed up the clothes and shoes for goodwill, then wiped down the shelves.

The desk was next, and really – why had I made such a big deal out of clearing out this room? The desk drawers contained nothing more than the usual detritus that people accumulate in desks: bits of stationery, a letter opener, unopened packs of batteries, a few old bills. The bottom drawer contained paperwork which I saved for later – John's expired passport, bank documents and identity papers, all the official documents that proved that a life had been lived.

I stripped the bedding off the bed, and immediately the room looked bare and unlived in, all personality stripped from it. I was about to bundle up the bedding to take it downstairs to the laundry, when I realised there was still a box under the bed. Kneeling down, I pulled the box out. It was a large wooden keepsake box, with a smooth lid and carved side panels. I flicked the latch, lifted the lid, and my heart lodged in my throat.

Brushing impatiently at my eyes, I lifted out the contents: the Mont Blanc pen I'd given John as a Christmas gift one year, the gold cuff links engraved with his initials which I'd sent him as a 50th birthday gift, the Piaget dress watch I'd sent him for his 60th, which I now realised was far too impractical to wear on a farm. And the photograph frame containing my graduation picture.

I sat for a long time staring at these items, but I couldn't tell if they'd been packed away out of sight or kept as treasures.

There was a sheaf of handwritten letters underneath, neatly tied up with an old Fortnum & Mason chocolate box ribbon. I had no right to read those letters, but with my emotions already rubbed raw, I eased the ribbon off the pile and opened the first letter.

It was addressed to me.

And it was dated the day of my Master's degree ceremony.

My father's scrawling handwriting filled the page, and it took me a moment to blink away the blur in my eyes so I could read.

Dear Sarah,

I wish I could be with you today as you receive your Master's degree. I know your mother is there to support you as always, and I will be there with you in spirit. I am so very proud of what you have achieved.

Today we start bottling a new blend I have created. In honour of your special occasion, I have named this wine Angelica, my little angel.

For you are my own angel Raphaela.

Why had he never sent these letters?

The next was dated a few years later.

Dear Sarah,

Nonna is ill, and will not be with us much longer. Tommaso has come home to look after her. He is married now, and his wife reminds me in so many ways of you. She has your smile, your energy, and your drive. But Tommaso does not look at her as he used to look at you. Or maybe I am being fanciful. There was a time long ago, when I hoped you and he would fall in love and be happy together.

Another was dated the day after I told him I'd called off my engagement. I'd told John that Kevin had cheated on me, but I hadn't shared the details, and I most certainly hadn't told him *who* Kevin had cheated on me with. Instead, I told him I was all right, that it was better this way, and then I'd changed the subject and talked about work. I'd been so proud of myself for how calm and together I'd been.

Dear Sarah,
I know how it feels when your heart breaks, and the temptation you feel to hide from the pain by burying yourself in work. You are too much like me, and you use numbers as a refuge. But I beg of you that you do not do as I did, and let work become your whole life. Because one day you will look around and realise you have lost everything of value.

There is a difference between being content and being happy. Happiness requires that you take a risk. When your mother left, I should have asked her to stay. I should have gone after her. But I was too afraid, and I did not take that risk, and I lost both her and you. Do not let fear rule you as I have done. Take that risk. Do not settle for content. You deserve happiness.

I set the letter down. I wasn't really able to read much more anyway. My eyes were too blurred. He was right. Numbers had always been my refuge. They were predictable, they could be controlled, unlike emotions. I wiped my eyes on my sleeve. We'd been more alike than I ever imagined. Or maybe I'd spent so many years trying so hard not to be my mother, that I'd turned into my father instead.

The last letter in the pile was dated Christmas Day – the last time I spoke to my father.

Dear Sarah,
If you are reading this letter, it is because I am gone. By now you will know that I have left my estate to Tommaso.

I hope that you will not be angry with me, but this is the only way I can think to bring you home. If I split the vineyard between you, it will be too easy for you to wrap up the estate and go on with your lives. This is Italy, and you will not be left without your share, but this way you must come here and work with Tommaso to settle the estate.

I love you both, and it hurts me to see you both so alone. Maybe you believe you are happy, but you don't remember the way it was when you were young, when you loved each other, when you both laughed. My one wish for you both is that you find your way back to that, that you remember what it is to be happy.

I am not good with words or with feelings. But I want you to know that I have always loved you. You will always be my little angel.

Thank you Archangel Raphael. Two out of three was really good odds. But if I was going to go for broke and see if the third thing I'd prayed for could also come true, I was going to have to take my father's advice, take a risk, and put my heart on the line. Even if it meant finding out that Tommaso didn't love me.

Chapter 35

Chi non risica non rosica

(Those who don't try can't win)

A sixty-hectare vineyard is a very big place when you're searching for one person.

Tommaso wasn't at the cellar, and Marco didn't know where on the farm he might be. So, with no real destination in mind, I struck out through the vineyard, heading south, towards the border with the Fioravanti property.

This was the area that hadn't yet been harvested, where big, green grapes still hung on the last of the summer vines, their sweet scent heavy in the September sunshine. The vines reached only to chest height, enabling me to see in all directions, so it was a surprise when I heard the sound of a waterfall. Then, around a gentle spur of land, the vines suddenly parted to reveal a mound of rocks from which water gurgled, falling into a pool before running away down the hillside between the vines. The small waterfall flung up a fine mist, spattering cool droplets against my skin.

It was the same pool that was painted on the shrine at the crossroads. Not the pool of Bethesda after all, but our very own spring. This pool had no angel beside it, only Tommaso, knee deep in the water as he bent over, straining to move a rock that had been lodged in the channel. It seemed the course of the water had indeed been diverted, in such a primitive way that it could almost have been an accident.

I paused to watch; to appreciate the sun tangling in his thick hair, and the bulge of his muscles beneath the fabric of his shirt as he heaved at the rock. Then suddenly the rock shifted, rolling sideways, and Tommaso was knocked off his feet, falling backwards into the water.

I laughed. He looked up at me and scowled.

The stream, re-directed, began to flow again down the dry channel bed.

Tommaso picked himself up, and waded to the water's edge, looking terrifyingly like a vengeful angel. 'What are you doing here?'

His wet shirt clung to his torso. I think I may have licked my lips.

'Looking for you. I have good news and I have bad news.'

When he didn't take the bait, I carried on regardless. 'The good news first: I've paid off the loan from Giovanni Fioravanti. In full.'

Tommaso's eyes narrowed. 'I suppose you'd like me to say thank you?'

'That would be a good start.'

'You want more?'

'I always want more. I'm an over-achiever, remember?'

He didn't respond. But he did take off his wet shirt, pulling it up over his head and giving me an even better view. My mouth was suddenly dry.

'So what's the bad news?' he asked.

'The bad news is that I took out another loan.'

He rolled his eyes. 'Why did you do that?'

'Well, strictly speaking, I raised a private equity investment to pay off Giovanni's loan. It turns out quite a few investors see a future in the wine business. There's just one little problem...'

He balled up the shirt and tossed it up on the grassy bank. 'Why am I not surprised?'

'You see, now that Castel Sant'Angelo has a big debt to pay off, you won't be able to buy me out any time soon, which means you're going to be stuck with me as a partner for a while longer.'

'I agree. That is bad news.' Tommaso set his hands on his hips, and though he still stood ankle deep in water, shirtless, with his jeans covered in mud, and I looked down at him, he still managed to look like he was the one in command of this situation. 'What sort of partnership did you have in mind? The in-my-face, pain-in-the-neck kind, or the kind who's already packed her bags and booked a flight back to London?'

Be brave. Take a risk. Channel Buffy Summers. 'That very much depends on you.'

He raised an eyebrow but said nothing.

'You asked me to stay. Was that as a business partner, as someone to run your *agriturismo* business, or...'

He eyed me for a long moment, his gaze inscrutable. My

heart beat a horrible panicked rhythm in my chest. What if he only wanted me as a business partner? What if he didn't want me at all?

Then he leapt up the low grassy bank to stand in front of me, and God help me, but my heartbeat got even wilder.

'Definitely *or*.'

With great difficulty, I kept my face straight. 'I'm going to need you to be a bit more specific than that.'

His mouth quirked. '*Or* you could stay as my wife.'

I hadn't expected he'd say those words, but I'd hoped. Though in my head it had sounded more like, 'stay as my lover.' I hadn't really expected the W word. I bit back a smile. 'Shouldn't you be on your knees when you ask me that?'

Dutifully, he knelt on the grass. 'Will you marry me, Sarah Wells?'

'On one condition.'

'*Al diavolo*! A simple yes or no will suffice.'

There was that scowl again, making lines in his forehead and drawing his brows down – oh, how I loved that scowl!

I held up my hands. 'One condition!'

He huffed out an impatient breath.

'I need to know if it's me you want, or the vineyard.'

The emotion flashing in his eyes was part annoyance and part amusement. 'Don't you know that the vineyard was always the consolation prize for me? There was only one thing I ever really wanted, and I'm still waiting for your answer to see whether or not I'm going to be able to get it.'

Golden warmth flowed through me. 'Yes.' I replied. 'Yes, I will marry you, Tommy di Biasi.'

I half-expected him to rise to his feet, but instead he grabbed my waist, and pulled me down onto the wet and slippery grass with him. We overbalanced and lay sprawled on the bank, and then he laughed and kissed me.

'You're not going to leave me for the bright lights of the big city?' he asked, when we finally disentangled ourselves.

'I don't have anything to go back for. I quit my job, and Cleo is buying my house.'

He grinned, as if I'd just told him he'd won the lottery.

'I don't have a big fancy *castello* for you to live in,' he warned. 'The best I can offer you is a two-bedroom cottage, and that's only if your German buyers let me stay on.'

I smiled. 'Then isn't it lucky that I do have a big fancy *castello* for us to live in? Though in the interests of full disclosure, it's really just an over-sized farmhouse with pretensions.'

He frowned. 'What are you talking about?'

'I couldn't sell the *castello*. The new investors wanted to see a business plan that outlined the vineyard's future revenue streams, and I sort of included a guest house as part of that plan.'

'But what about the money?'

I smacked his arm. 'Weren't you listening to a word I said?'

'Well, you were standing there, looking a bit like Buffy about to kick ass, and the sun was shining through your skirt. It's tough for a man to think under those conditions.'

'When you say such nice things, how can I resist?' I giggled like a giddy teenager, though that might have been because I was prone on my back on a grassy bank, with Tommaso leaning over me, and I *felt* very much like a giddy teenager again.

'How did Florian and Yusuf take the news?' he asked.

'They weren't very happy, but as it happens, there's a rather nice villa for sale on the outskirts of town, and since they plan to entertain a lot of guests at their new holiday home, I suggested they might be happier being closer to bars and restaurants. They've agreed to take a look at it. It even has fully functioning bathrooms.'

Tommaso's face turned thoughtful. 'So we're the proud owners of a vineyard, a quarter of which looks like a dystopian wasteland, a crumbling *castello*, and a massive debt?'

'Yup. That about sums it up. You're not having any second thoughts about asking me to marry you? You don't want to find yourself a sweet Italian heiress, perhaps one who restores frescoes for a living?'

'I have no idea who you're talking about. There's only ever been one woman for me. I've loved her since the day I met her.'

'You're lying,' I clouted his arm again. 'You liked Fiorella enough to shave your beard for her.'

He huffed out an impatient breath. 'I shaved my beard for *you*. Since trying to make you jealous hadn't worked, I hoped *that* might gain your attention.'

'Oh, it did.' I swallowed the sudden lump in my throat. 'But I still say you're lying. You can't possibly remember the day we first met. That was nearly thirty years ago.'

He twisted his fingers into my hair, pulling loose the chignon I'd had it tied up in. 'I remember that you were seven, and I was ten. I was sitting at the kitchen table in the *castello*, licking the batter from the bowl of cake mix Nonna had just made, when your father brought you home from the airport. You were wearing a pink dress, and I remember thinking "Oh no! She's a girl!" And then Nonna said—'

'She said "take your fingers out of that bowl and fetch two spoons, because from now on you're going to have to share".'

I looked up into those twinkling grey eyes, ran my hand through his thick hair, which was already growing shaggy again, then stroked his cheek where his beard was growing out, and my heart swelled, so full of love and happiness that I thought I might burst.

Tommaso grinned. 'And then you smiled, and I thought, "If I'm going to have to share, there's no one else I'd rather share it with". Now are we done talking, because I'd really like to kiss you again?'

Epilogue

Chi si volta e chi si gira, sempre a casa va a finire

(No matter which way you turn, you will always end up at home)

Though it was barely five o'clock, it was already dark outside the windows, that early dark of winter which comes suddenly, with none of the lingering twilight of summer. Snow had started to patter against the windows, but inside the drawing room was deliciously toasty and bright. We'd spent the day putting up decorations, and in the corner of the vast room stood the tree Alberto and Daniele had cut for us on their farm.

A fire burned in the big stone hearth, casting flickering patterns over the recently restored frescoes on the drawing room wall, a painting of Archangel Raphael blessing the vines at Castel Sant'Angelo. In the distance lay Montalcino, barely changed from the town we knew today. The fairy lights on the Christmas tree added a richness to the colours of the painting; burnt orange, wine red, burnished gold, dusty green, bright coral pink and indigo blue.

Tommaso leaned towards the hearth to turn the chestnuts roasting beside the fire. In her basket beside the hearth, Buffy, our gangly Labrador, snuffled in her sleep.

This was the calm in the heart of the storm. For the last few days we'd had DOCG inspectors swarming all over the winery, certifying us as worthy of the highest quality endorsement available in Italy, and tomorrow our guests would arrive, Geraldine and Per, Cleo, Tommaso's father and his girlfriend. On Christmas Day we were hosting the biggest party this house had seen in at least half a century. The entire Rossi clan would be joining us, together with Florian and Yusuf, and Ettore was bringing his girlfriend, the lovely student from Rome who'd joined us for the harvest.

I was using this Christmas party as a test run for our spring wedding. And after that, the *castello* would open for business with our first paying guests.

I closed my eyes and breathed in the fragrant scent of the burning olive wood. Tommaso snuggled back down beside me in our bed of blankets on the floor.

'Guess the varietal,' he said, handing me a glass. I held it up to the firelight, and watched the lights dancing in the dark amber liquid. Then I breathed it in, savouring the sweet bouquet. 'It's a Vin Santo.' I took a sip. 'Mostly Trebbiano grapes.'.

'*Brava*! Did you know that Trebbiano grapes are also used to make balsamic vinegar?'

'I did. But did you know that balsamic vinegar was once so prized it was included in the dowries of the nobility?'

He didn't answer and I gloated. It wasn't often I caught him out.

He reached behind him and pulled out a small squashed parcel in plain brown wrapping. 'I have a Christmas gift for you.'

'But Christmas is still days away!'

'I wanted to give it to you now, while it's still just the two of us.'

He handed me the parcel, and I ripped open the paper, then laughed as I held up the brand new Sunnydale High School Slayers T-shirt.

'Your old one was getting a little ratty,' he said. The firelight caught his eyes, turning them darker than usual. He looked happy.

'I can't believe you're the same grumpy man I met all those months ago when I first arrived,' I said with a smile.

'Can you blame me for being grumpy? You hit me over the head with an iron and didn't even recognise me!'

'Are you ever going to let me live that down?'

'No.' He rolled me over onto my back, crushing my favourite new T-shirt between us. 'I plan on telling that story to our children and our grandchildren.'

Over Tommaso's shoulder I glimpsed the mantel above the hearth, where I'd put up a display of family photographs. A black and white photo of John had pride of place. I smiled up at the picture.

Thank you, John, for bringing me back to Tuscany. Thank you for bringing us back together, and for encouraging me to take the risk and put my heart on the line. It was worth the wait.

What is the fatal charm of Italy? What do we find there that can be found nowhere else? I believe it's a certain permission to be human, which other places, other countries, lost long ago.

– *Erica Jong*

Acknowledgements

This book would not exist without my editor, Charlotte Ledger. I really lucked out the day my first manuscript landed on your desk, and five years later I still feel so incredibly lucky to be working with you. Thank you for inspiring me to write this book, and I hope I've done your vision of Tommaso and Sarah justice.

Thank you to Claudia Dallabona and Manuela Steffenini for their help with the Italian language. Any errors are all mine and no reflection on them!